Seven Turns

Kim Beall

This is a work of fiction. All characters, places, and events
described within are products of the author's imagination or are
used fictitiously.

Except Doctor Boojums. He is absolutely real, and will fight
anyone who says otherwise.

ISBN 978-1-7339964-8-8
Published in the United States of America
2nd Edition December 2020
Illustrations by Kim Beall

Vale House Floor Plan

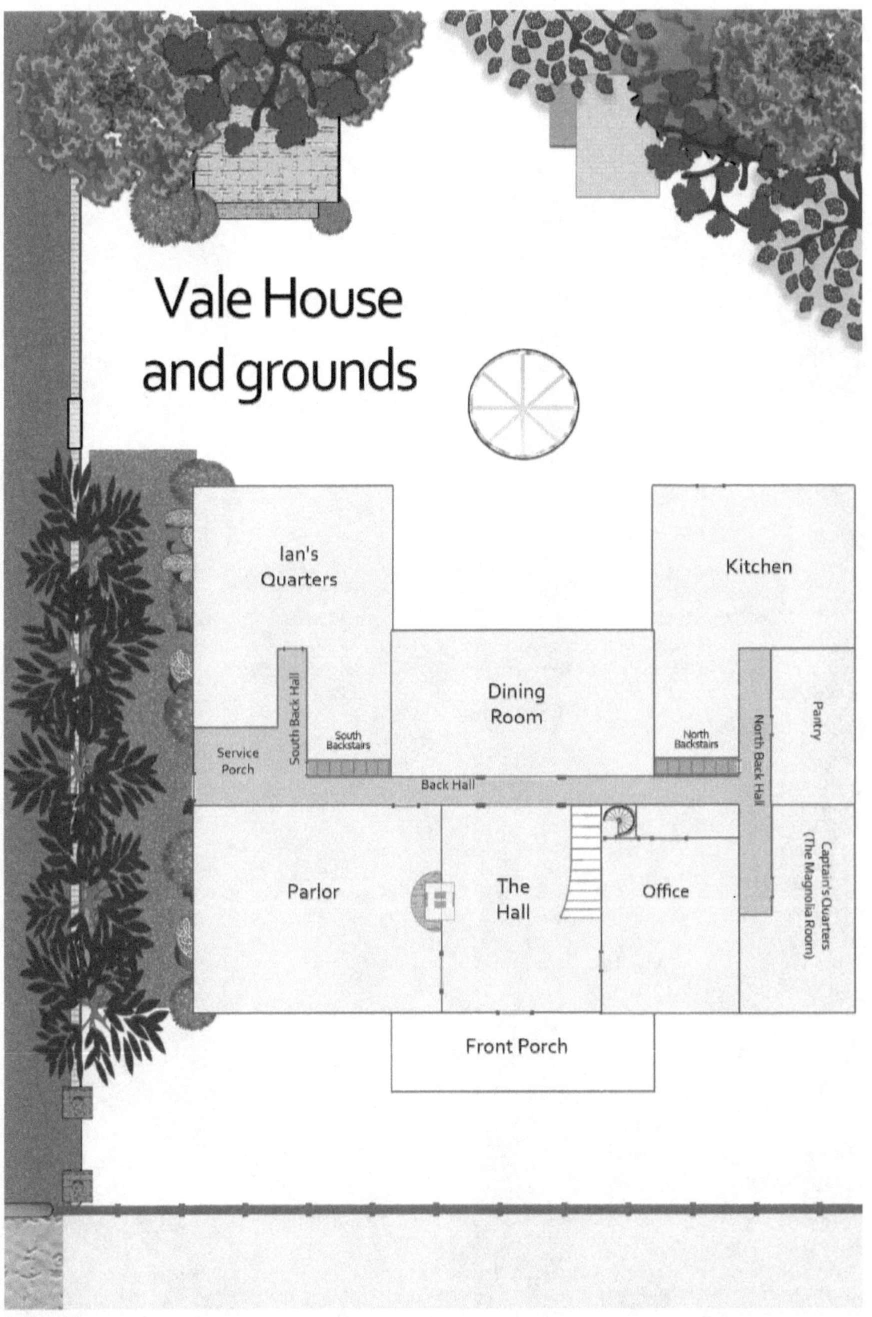

Map of Woodley

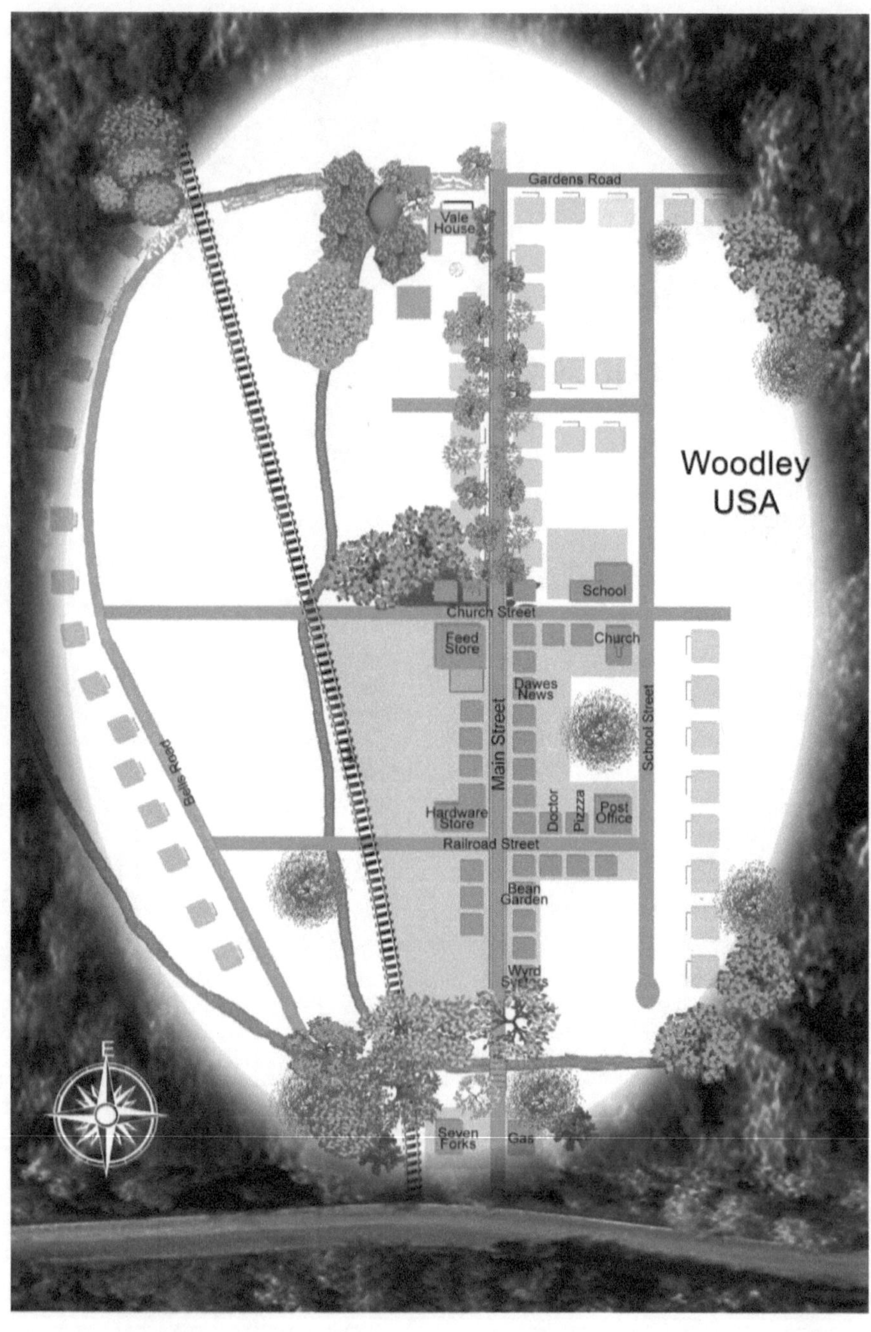

To all my friends and family who never rolled their eyes at me
when all I could talk about was my fictional world (and to some of
you who did!)

Also to Greg Allman and his hauntingly beautiful descant at the
end of the eponymous song.

Somebody's calling your name.

Contents

In Which a Ghost is Pleased to Introduce the Story

Dear Friends:

It is a great honor for me to be able to introduce this book to you. I have lived in this world for a very long time and have made many friends, but few have been as dear to me as Miss Cally eventually became. After all, it was she who made it possible for me to be able to read books at all! I owe her a great debt of gratitude, and so do all of us.

Arranging her arrival took many years and the combined efforts of many. It was I who first discovered her, by way of the television set in the parlor. Modern technology holds so many new advantages for people like me! The task of convincing her to join us, however, was made quite difficult by the fact that she did not actually believe we existed. She had been adept at seeing things all her life, of course, which is why we thought she would be well-suited to the job. On the other hand, she was equally adept at convincing herself she had not seen things that were right in front of her face. Still, she had a bright spirit and a high heart, and we needed her. Working together, we all contrived to convince her to come to Vale House.

Then came the task of gently introducing her not only to ourselves, but to her new work here. This task, due to my temperament and also to the various skills I have acquired over the years, fell mainly to me. Without the help and talents of others, however, I know I could never have succeeded.

I realize many of you who helped me are not able to read books, but one day I will read this one to you, and then you will understand!

Anyway (as they say) this is the story of how Ms. Callaghan McCarthy came to Vale House, and the beginning of how she eventually saved not just this house but the town in which it stands, and that which it guards, and thereby quite possibly all of us. Who knows?

Though, unfortunately, there was one person she could not save.

2

Dear friends, until the end of this world, when all things
will be understood,
I remain
Your faithful servant,
Guacanagarix

1 -   Fly By Night

"Your destination is on the left," whispered the soft voice. "You will be safe here."

Cally's eyes flew open. "Shit shit shit!" She grabbed the steering wheel hard and pulled herself up in the seat. Her heart pounding in her ears blotted out the whine of tires on concrete, the rattle of boxes in the back seat. The highway still lay straight in front of her, unrolling dark and endless in her headlight beam. No lights, no signs, no exits broke the unending monotony of tall, dark pines marching along both sides of the highway. The only sign other humans ever used this road at all had been the occasional tractor trailer roaring up out of the night to pass by her, usually going in the other direction.

As her heartbeat gradually returned to normal, fatigue of body and spirit threatened to overtake her again. She opened the window and gulped in deep breaths of cool night air. It didn't help. She hit the "skip" button on her MP3 player until she came to an old southern rock anthem (*Green Grass and High Tides,* for what must have been the tenth time that night) and sang along loudly, drumming on the steering wheel through the guitar solos to stop herself yawning – or was it to stop herself panicking?

A glance at the GPS on her phone, lying useless in the passenger seat, showed only the words "NO SIGNAL" astride a straight blue line between a town named Coppersmith, at the top of the screen, and Blackthorn at the bottom. So it could not have been the mechanical voice of the GPS that had awakened her, she realized. Maybe it had been a dream, or some tiny inner part of her that did not actually want her to die alone on the road in the middle of the night in the middle of nowhere. She wasn't sure whether or not to be grateful. In any case, there was certainly no destination on the left, or on the right, or anywhere that she could see.

According to the equally useless printed directions she had received from Emerald, the exit to Woodley should be on the left, four miles south of Coppersmith, and "if you get to Blackthorn, you've gone too far."

But Cally had already got to Blackthorn. She'd been there twice that night, had turned around and gone back to Coppersmith, and turned around again. She had pulled over and tried to text Emerald to explain her dilemma, but had been unable to get a signal. Sighing, she turned her red Corolla around in the median and headed back, again, toward Coppersmith, this time watching to the right for an exit, an opening, anything. Maybe, she thought, if she got out of the car and held her phone above her head, she could get a GPS signal. Maybe reception would be better at the crest of the rise just ahead. Maybe her car would sprout wings and fly.

Her breath caught in her throat when something ran through the headlight beam. She stepped on the brake and braced herself for the impact, but the white figure reached the other side of the road safely, then paused and turned to look at her, its eyes glowing blue in her headlights. Cally thought it might be a deer, but it was white and a little too large – a horse, maybe? She continued to slow down until she was abreast of it.

Then it was gone but, to her relief, she did see a dark gap in the trees where it had stood, and a glimpse of a blacktop road stretching away through a tunnel of overhanging branches. She pulled off the highway and stepped out of the car, staring down the dark road. She could hear hoofbeats on asphalt, fading away into the night. Could this be the elusive exit to Woodley? There was no sign, but the road did have yellow lines painted down the middle, which was reassuring somehow, and in the distance she could see lights glowing softly through the trees.

An eighteen-wheeler rushed past behind her, heading north, blowing her hair forward into her eyes. She shook it back and decided to take the little blacktop road, wherever it went. She didn't dare hope she'd find anyone awake to ask for directions at this hour, but at least she might find someplace safe to take a quick nap.

She switched off the MP3 player and steered onto the dark

asphalt. The sound of crickets floated in on the damp night air. In her headlight beam, the road sloped down a gentle grade to a narrow bridge over a creek, and then back up again. Cally thought she could see something white just this side of the bridge – that horse, probably. She slowed down in case it tried to play chicken with her car again. As she drew near, though, she realized it was not the horse at all, but a person standing next to the bridge, waving at her with one hand and clutching a white jacket closed with the other. Cally paused, and a young woman bent down to peer through the open window. She couldn't have been more than fifteen.

"Hi!" she said.

"Are you OK?" Cally asked. "Was that your horse?"

The girl looked across the bridge and waved dismissively into the distance. "She has a mind of her own. I wish she would stay away from the highway!"

Cally wanted to ask where the road led, but was more concerned, at the moment, that a young woman was walking alone so late at night. "Are you OK?" she asked again. "Do you need a lift or something? I don't think you're going to catch that horse now."

"There's not a fence made that can hold her," the girl said, peering into the interior of Cally's car. Her mass of curls, bright red even in the dim light from the dashboard, nearly filled the entire window. Her large green eyes widened as they took stock of all the boxes and suitcases in the back seat.

After an awkward moment, Cally asked, "Can you tell me where I am and how to get to Woodley?"

The girl seemed to make up her mind, then, and walked around the car to the passenger door. Cally reached across the seat and unlocked the door, and the girl got in, accompanied by the smell of wet leaves and moss. "I'm Errin," she said, dropping Cally's phone into the cup holder. "With a double 'r'. That way," she added, pointing forward through the windshield.

"Pleased to meet you, Errin. I'm Cally. So, is that Woodley up ahead? I'm afraid I'm completely lost."

"It's a nice little town," Errin said, which was really not the answer Cally was looking for. But the girl smiled and gazed intently down the road, so Cally drove across the bridge and up the hill on the other side. The lights she had seen ahead came into view. They were street lights, standing outside a diner ("The Seven Forks") and a gas station ("Gas.") Both were closed for the night.

Errin continued smiling and gazing forward, so Cally passed these buildings and followed the road into another dark stand of trees. The girl glanced from side to side into the trees – looking for her stray horse, Cally assumed.

"Hopefully she'll just go back to the barn on her own," Cally suggested. "I understand horses tend to do that." Errin laughed at this, and Cally didn't bother asking her to explain why.

The road leveled out and exited the trees; here it became a quiet street with sidewalks on either side. None of the brick buildings was more than two stories high; most of them appeared to be small shops, all currently closed, some lit softly from inside. No other cars could be seen on the street.

"You can stop here," Errin said as they came abreast of a storefront where a light over the door cast a soft half-moon on the sidewalk. A wooden sign reading "Dawes News" hung above the door. Cally pulled over to the curb.

"Are you sure you're going to be OK from here?" she asked, pulling the parking brake and shutting off the engine. A "Closed" sign hung in the news store window and Cally despaired of finding anyone to give her some directions. She wished her passenger would be more helpful. "Dawes – is that the name of this town?"

She turned to see if Errin might be forthcoming with any useful information, but saw only an empty passenger seat. She had not heard the car door open or shut. She looked up and down the sidewalk, but did not see the girl walking away.

"Damn!" Something in the back of her mind tried to tell her she should feel alarmed, but this was overridden by the dismay of realizing she really wasn't going to find out where she was, now.

Then she laughed. "It's just like one of those stupid ghost stories!" she said to the empty car. She picked up her phone to see if there might be cell reception here. "Damn!" she said again.

Her phone's GPS app was working again at last. It showed a little red car-shaped icon on a map indicating she was two miles east of Interstate 85, halfway between Blackthorn and Coppersmith. The map did not show anything around her car, though, not this little town, and not even the street on which she was currently parked. It was as if she had driven into the middle of an empty field.

That was not what had caused Cally to swear, however. Her dismay was due to the fact that while she had been out of cell phone range, she'd missed five incoming calls, all from the same number. "Oh, Gods, I'm in for it now," she said, and resignedly called the number back.

"Mom!" Her daughter answered on the first ring. "Where are you? Gordon and I went by today and found your apartment completely cleaned out. We've been worried sick!"

"I'm fine, Kelleigh, " Cally said. "I did text you."

"I know, but..." An exasperated sigh sounded like loud static in Cally's ear." I didn't think you'd actually *do* it! I've been going out of my mind! I haven't been able to get any sleep. I haven't even told Brandon yet. He would totally freak!"

"Well, now you know what you kids always used to put me through when you were teenagers," Cally responded.

A long silence followed, during which Cally could picture her daughter mustering her "patient expression." At length, Kelleigh said, "Okay, I get it. You're a runner. It's what you do. But... Dammit, Mom. You're too old to go running off into the middle of nowhere, on the advice of someone you've never even met!"

"I've known Emerald for years," Cally reminded her.

"Over the internet! You've never met her face to face. For all you know, she's actually an old pervert living in his mother's basement!" Kelleigh's voice was uncomfortably loud in Cally's ear and she had to hold the phone a few inches away from her head. "This is nuts!" Kelleigh was saying. "And completely unnecessary. I keep telling you, Gordon and I would love to have you come and stay with us. And Gordon knows several people who could set you up with a real job, and..."

"Look, sweetie, I solemnly promise you I will not just let myself die of exposure on a park bench somewhere. If this doesn't work out, I will take you up on your offer." She loved her daughter tand son-in-law, but she had tried a thousand different ways to explain to them that dying of exposure on a park bench still seemed better, to her, than depending on someone else's good graces, in someone else's home, pursuing someone else's career, living someone else's life just to stay alive. She had broken out of that trap once. She would never go back into it willingly. "I promise I'll call you when I get there."

"You aren't even *there* yet? Where are you?"

Cally looked through the windshield at the quiet street. "It's a nice little town," she said, taking a page from the girl Errin's book of evasive answers. "I'm going to get some rest now. Get some sleep and stop worrying. I'm fine."

2 -   News and Coffee

When Cally woke, the sun was just coming over the tops of the trees at the far end of the street. Her seat belt was digging into her cheek where her head had fallen against it. She rubbed her face with both hands and looked into the rear-view mirror. The seat belt had left a long crease in her cheek, and her hair, long and unruly at the best of times, stood out around her head like a cloud of windblown straw.

Digging in her purse for a comb, she took stock of her surroundings in the morning light. Her own car was one of only three she could see parked on the entire street. The street itself was no more than four or five blocks long. She could see from where she sat that it disappeared into a tunnel of trees at both ends. A wide storefront on the opposite side of the street displayed hand-lettered signs in its windows, advertising fertilizer and chicken feed and "Free Firewood!" which was stacked unclaimed on the loading dock. On her own side of the street, many of the storefronts appeared to be completely vacant, but the sign in the news store window had been flipped to "Open." Cally hoped this meant she would finally be able to find someone to give her some information.

Stepping out of the car and pausing to arch her aching back, she could see movement inside the news store. Most important, she could smell coffee. She walked to the door and tugged on the wooden handle. It didn't budge; she tried pushing. She looked again to make sure the sign really did say "Open." It did. She gave another tug and stepped back, peering inside. There she saw a man with a broom in the back of the store, holding up one hand in a "wait a minute" gesture as he ran toward her. He gave the bottom of the door a solid kick, and it shuddered open. Smiling broadly, he leaned out and held the door open for her. "It sticks!" he apologized.

"Thank you," Cally said, squeezing in past him. He had a generous, warm smile behind a graying brown mustache and beard, and his eyes were a most unusual shade of china blue.

"I really need to get around to fixing it," he said in a soft-edged southern accent.

Cally turned her eyes from his blue gaze and looked around the dim interior. "That coffee smells good. Is it for sale?"

"Help yourself," barked an older woman from behind the counter on the far side of the shop. She jerked her head toward the coffee maker on the counter, but didn't lift her eyes from the newspaper she was reading. Cally walked toward the counter, scanning the racks of snacks and candy, looking for something semi-healthy to press into service as breakfast.

Her footsteps echoed in the quiet interior, which was lit only by the sunlight coming in through the windows. She felt as though she had stepped backward in time about fifty years. The floor was made of wood. Cally hadn't seen that in a long time. Almost everything in the store – the shelves, the sales counter, even the register – was old-fashioned and made mainly of wood. And really could stand a good dusting, too, she noted. The man who had let her in returned to the back of the store and resumed sweeping, stirring up more dust.

She selected a granola bar that was probably ninety percent sugar but looked to at least contain real oats, and set it on the counter while she poured coffee into a white foam cup. A revolving wire rack of paperback books stood next to the counter. Cally turned it slowly, looking for the same thing she always looked for when she saw a display of books. She found it, too: a thick volume with a picture on the cover of a tall gothic revival house which someone had apparently thought would look good painted in shades of dark gray and black, backlit against a moonrise sky. Only one window in a top story was lit. An attractive young woman, one pale hand clutching a cloak to her otherwise mostly exposed bosom, was fleeing from the house toward the viewer, her voluminous hair and equally voluminous skirts flying as ragged clouds scudded across a gibbous moon. *Escape the Haunted Heart* was the title, printed across the stormy sky in a loud font, with the byline, "Callaghan McCarthy," in smaller letters beneath it.

Her fingers left smudges in the dust on the cover when she took it from the rack and regarded it. A second copy lay behind it. For all that the paperback had collected plenty of dust, it appeared to have been read, possibly more than once. The cover was bent back, and the edges of the pages were foxed. As Cally put the book back, she noticed most of the books in the rack were in the same condition.

"It's good. I've read it," said the man who had opened the door. "Take it if you want it." He smiled beautifully at her.

"No thanks," she said. "I wrote it." She put the book back in its slot and turned to pay for her improvised breakfast.

"I've read all of them," he was saying. "People just read them and put them back. But this really is one of the best. I'm not just saying that to flatter you.

"I'm Ben Dawes," he added. "Pleased to meet you, Callaghan McCarthy."

Cally turned to the counter and opened her wallet, hoping he wasn't "her biggest fan" despite his lovely blue-eyed smile. She didn't feel awake enough to deal with the Inevitable Question which always followed declarations of Biggest Fanhood.

"No charge for the coffee," said the old woman as she moved from her paper to the register without looking up. Her accent was thick and edgy, and Cally had to concentrate to understand her.

"I have a stupid question, " she said, pulling out bills to pay for the granola bar.

"Well, I might charge you for that."

Cally hesitated. The woman sounded serious. She looked serious, with her black-framed glasses and black-streaked white hair pulled back into a tight bun. Behind her, Cally heard Ben clear his throat, and the old woman gave a perfunctory little chuckle to assure them she'd only been kidding. Cally continued. "Where, exactly, am I?"

The woman's fingers were cool and bony as she pressed change into Cally's hand. "You're exactly where you were trying to go," she said. "The name of this town is Woodley, at the moment. It has had other names. And this is Main Street, in case you can't tell. If you turn around and head back the way you came, you'll get back to I-85 in about two miles."

"Oh!" Cally breathed a sigh of relief, her shoulders unclenching for the first time in at least twenty four hours. "Then I actually am exactly where I was trying to go.”

"That's what I said." The old woman finally raised her eyes and looked at Cally. Cally did not find this new attention at all reassuring. The woman's gaze was sharp and critical, though her eyes were the same shade of blue as Ben's. She looked like she was trying to think of some biting remark to make about people who are "not from around here." Then suddenly she smiled. Actually, she laughed. "So," she said gleefully, "Do you believe in ghosts?"

3 -   The Inevitable Question

The Inevitable Question, Cally had come to call it. Every talk-show host and magazine interviewer had asked it, and all of them seemed to think they were the first person ever to have thought of it. Every Biggest Fan had asked it, with hopeful sincerity and their own "I saw a ghost once" story ready on their lips. And every critic had asked it, with the intention of exposing her as a charlatan, or at least a fool. "So, do you really believe in ghosts?"

There had been a time when she had tried to answer truthfully, telling them she had really only written the book as a catharsis, to help exorcise her own personal ghosts which were a metaphor for the bitter, betrayed feelings she'd had, then, about her failed marriage. But nobody wanted to hear that answer. They wanted her to be a True Believer. She had learned to skirt the question coquettishly, letting people draw their own conclusions. But she was tired, and frankly tired of the whole thing, and she didn't owe the book anything anymore since it had stopped making her any money, to speak of, a long time ago.

She closed her fingers around her change and stuffed it into her purse, letting it fall to the bottom in a jumble. "I'm too tired to believe in anything anymore," she answered. The old woman seemed to think that was a perfectly acceptable answer. At least, she released Cally from her gaze and nodded, shutting the old register drawer with a bang. "Well, you're here to write another book, anyway."

Ben leaned his broom against the counter. "Bree," he said, "Be nice."

"I'm always nice," said the old woman, and smirked at him. Cally guessed she must be his mother, based on their matching eye color and the gentle way he looked at her. Bree looked back at Cally. "Don't worry, I'm not psychic, which is fine since you don't believe in that kind of stuff anyway. But this is a small town and news of your arrival precedes you. Everyone is excited about it. They think you're going to save this town by writing a book about it."

Cally really just wanted to get back to her car and maybe, hopefully, find the bed and breakfast in which she had booked a room, somewhere in this town. She juggled her coffee, granola, and car keys and said, "Well, I'm just hoping to get a little inspiration here. I don't intend to write a book about the town per se."

"Oh, you'll get plenty of inspiration at Vale House, alright!" Bree said. "Maybe not the kind you're looking for. Do you see that?" She pointed past Cally to the wide window looking out into the street.

Cally turned and saw only a large dog with long, gray fur standing on the opposite sidewalk and staring in through the store window. A car passed by and when it had gone, the dog was no longer there.

"See what?" Cally asked, not sure if that was what the woman had meant.

Bree gave her a long, skeptical look, as if Cally had been trying to sell her magazine subscriptions. "It seems you see a lot of things you don't believe in. Anyway, Vale House is just about half a mile more that way." She jerked her thumb over her shoulder at the wall behind her. "Just get back in your car and drive to the east end of town, and then keep driving. You won't be able to go too far. The road ends at the meadow and the house will be on your left. Give Ian my regards." She snapped her newspaper open again and returned her attention to it.

"I'll get that for you," Ben said, hurrying to open the stubborn door for Cally.

"Thank you," she said, treating herself to one more glance at his smile. "Thank you for the coffee," she also called to Bree, who waved vaguely at her without looking up.

4 -   Vale House

The old woman had been right. It really was a short distance to the end of town. Just past the feed store and a few more storefronts, what served as the business district of Woodley ended and the residential district began.

Three or four blocks of gracious old homes with wide porches stood at comfortable distances from one another along the oak-shaded street, here. Past these, where the trees stood back and gave way to the early morning sunshine, the road simply ended at a wide, sagging metal gate. Beyond the gate, a rutted dirt road faded off into a grassy field. To Cally's right, another road ("Gardens Road" said the battered old street sign) ran past more old homes, but no trees lined this road. The houses here faced across Gardens Road directly into the sunny field.

To her left, as Bree Dawes had promised, Cally could see through over-arching branches of two ancient crape myrtles to the broad white gable wall of a house. A gravel drive, flanked by a pair of masonry columns with pineapple-shaped lanterns at their tops, curved between the trees into a parking area mostly overgrown with lawn grass. Several cars and an old, red pickup truck were parked there under the massive oak tree shading the barn. Cally turned her car through the pineapple-flanked gate to join them.

Three horses ran to the fence separating the parking lot from the meadow, tossing their heads as if to greet Cally when she got out of her car. One of them was white, and she wondered if it was the elusive creature Errin had been chasing the night before. She left her car door unlocked, leaving two suitcases lying on top of the boxes for later, and took only a small bag and her computer case out of the car.

She made a point of taking a long look at Vale House as she approached it along the flagstone walk. If she really was going to write a book about a haunted bed and breakfast, she thought, it would be a good idea to remember her first impression of this one. The grand white house did not look very haunted, though, despite the internet stories she had read about it, and it certainly did not at all resemble the fictional house on the cover of her book.

Vale House did not face the street, but faced east into the meadow like the houses on Gardens Road. White clapboard siding gleamed in the sun, and a freshly painted green tin roof stretched over all. The wide, covered porch looked nothing but cheerful and welcoming, with its deeply cushioned wicker chairs and two drowsy cats sitting on the railing. It was certainly a much bigger house than any of the others in the town, but it didn't even look pretentious, let alone atmospheric. Though, for what it was worth, Cally did glimpse a single pale figure regarding her from one of the windows above the second-floor belvedere. That was something, anyway.

Before she reached the bottom step, a woman came running out onto the porch, letting the wooden screen door bang shut behind her. One of the cats, a skinny, wide-eyed calico, jumped off the railing and ran down the steps into the shrubbery. The old gray tom slept on. The woman was about ten years older than Cally, her good-natured round face framed with dark silver curls hanging halfway to her shoulders. She was drying her hands on the apron she wore over a flower-print dress. "You must be Ms. McCarthy!" she called down the steps. "We were expecting you last night. We were worried about you. This town is hard to find!"

"You can certainly say that again," Cally agreed, ascending the wooden steps. "I should have called, but I was so tired, and I couldn't get a signal."

The woman met her halfway up the stairs and took her bag from her hand. "Let me get that for you. I'll get Ignacio to bring in your other things..." She looked at Cally's car and her mouth fell open when she saw the stacked boxes visible through the rear windows.

"All I need is this one, for now," Cally said.

The woman carried Cally's small bag to the top of the porch steps, then turned and extended her hand. "I'm Bethany Chase," she said. "I take care of things around here. Mr. May is down at the pond and I've reminded him he promised to meet with you today." She pushed the door open for Cally. Inside the entry hall, an antique kneehole desk had been set up across a wide fieldstone fireplace. A man dressed in a dark suit stood quietly in front of the desk, and Bethany walked around him to set Cally's case down beside the fireplace fender.

"I'm afraid breakfast is already over," she said, and Cally wasn't sure whether she was speaking to her or to the other customer waiting there. "But there's some Danish left if you're hungry."

"It's OK," Cally assured her, "I just had a granola bar." The man in the suit said nothing.

Bethany laughed. "Well, if you change your mind... Here you are." She flipped open a large registry book and ran her finger down the page. "You'll be staying two weeks, is that right?"

"To start," Cally said, glancing back at her heavily packed car. "I might be staying longer, if I start writing. I mentioned this on the phone. That will be OK, won't it?"

"Oh, yes, of course, it will be more than OK." She turned the book around on the desk and handed Cally a pen. "We're all very excited about having you staying with us! Just sign here." Cally signed next to her name, where small print stated she would pay for her stay with her credit card on record. She hoped she was telling the truth.

The man standing at the desk beside her continued to wait patiently, gazing silently at two large pictures in massive frames above the fireplace mantle. Cally followed his gaze: the naïve-style portraits depicted a serious-faced woman and a smiling older gentleman in antebellum dress. Bethany nodded and explained. "Those are Ian May's grandparents, Lionel and Isbel May," she said, affecting a tour-guide demeanor with hands folded across her stomach. "Some people believe the White Lady who is sometimes seen haunting the upstairs hallway might be Isbel."

Cally wondered why there must always be a Lady in White. Why didn't ghost ladies ever wear red? Or yellow, or navy pinstripes? Even Isbel May, in her faded portrait, wore purple. Maybe, she thought, when someone died, their fashion sense died with them.

She took a quick look around the entry hall of this reputedly authentic haunted house. Morning light spilled into the room through the screen door and the leaded glass sidelights flanking it. A magnificent stairway with a white, hand-carved railing, dominated the room. Its lower steps widened as they reached the polished floor, as if to embrace all who entered. If conventional wisdom were to be trusted, Cally knew, stairways in old houses were all but fated to have a ghost or two running up and down them. This one, however, gleamed in the sunlight and did not appear to be at all conducive to a good haunting.

Beyond the staircase, a doorway almost as wide as the entry hall itself opened into a dining room with a linen-covered table. The far wall of this room was composed almost entirely of tall windows whose antique lace curtains blew gently in a breeze that admitted bird song and the scent of jasmine. That room, also, could not possibly harbor any self-respecting spectre. Perhaps the house's dark spirits all lurked behind the heavy, carved oak door at the right of the Hall?

"We currently have only two other guests," Bethany was saying as she closed the book and opened a small drawer on the side of the desk. "A nice couple from Tennessee who are on their way to the outer banks, and also Ian May's daughter and her husband, who are staying with us this week while Foster gets some business done in Blackthorn. We've given you the Rose Room. It's not haunted, that I am aware of, but it has a nice, big writing desk we thought you'd find useful." She took a key from the drawer and showed Cally the picture of a rose on the fob. "I'll show you the way."

"Please," Cally said, "feel free to wait on your other customer first. I can wait." She smiled and stepped back to let the man in the suit have Bethany's full attention, but was startled to see he was no longer standing there.

Bethany stood with the key in her hand for a moment, giving Cally a long, considering look. Then, as she opened her mouth to speak, the oak door across the hall from the desk opened and a woman emerged. Her heels clomped sharply on the polished floor as she strode across the hall, extending a well-manicured hand, festooned with rings and bracelets, to Cally.

"Welcome to Vale House!" she said. She seemed to be about the same age as Bethany, but was much taller with a smart, short-clipped hairstyle colored a brassy ash blond. She wore tan slacks at least a size too small for her, and an equally ill-fitting beige blouse. "I'm Joan," she said. "I'm the marketing manager here. So you're the famous author?"

"I wouldn't say I'm famous, really." Cally reached out to accept the woman's hand, but was only able to brush her fingertips before Joan withdrew her hand and turned to look at Cally's small bag beside the desk.

"Is that all you brought?" she asked. "Where's your luggage?" She turned toward the front door and shouted "Pedro! Get the customer's luggage!"

Even as she was in mid-shout, a slender man with brown eyes and bronze skin came running up the porch stairs and into the room, being careful not to let the screen door bang shut behind him. "Just making sure," he said, smiling at Cally. "The two large suitcases in the back seat, right? But not the boxes?"

Cally started to tell him that was right and to please lock her car afterward, but Joan interrupted, shouting at him "Rose Room! Un-da-lay! Chop chop!"

He crossed the Hall to pick up Cally's small bag from beside the fender. "Thank you!" Cally called after him as he disappeared up the stairs with it.

"Some people have no concept of customer service," Joan muttered at Cally. "I don't know why Ian keeps him around. If it wasn't for me, the staff here would walk all over him." She cast a disapproving gaze all around the sunny hall, letting it come to rest on Bethany. "And turn some lights on! This Hall looks like a funeral parlor!" She turned on her heel and went back to the room from which she had come. "I have to get back to my *own* work," she added, slamming the oak door shut behind her.

Bethany did not turn on any lights to compete with the sunshine in the room. "Joan takes her job very seriously," she said as if apologizing to Cally. "Well, then, let's get you to your room so you can get some rest!" She put the key in her apron pocket and headed toward the stairs.

"Is Joan Mrs. May?" Cally asked, following.

Bethany started to laugh, but quickly covered her mouth and glanced at the closed door. She grinned at Cally over her hand. "No! Oh, no. Though she would like to be, I am sure. Ian May is a widower." Her expression changed back to a gentle smile. "His wife passed away many years ago now. It was a real tragedy. He never really got over her. Their love was like some kind of tale from a story book."

"That's sweet," Cally said perfunctorily, though she didn't, personally, believe in that kind of fairy tale, any more than she believed in any other kind. Not anymore.

5 -   The Rose Room

"Well!" Bethany explained as they ascended the grand stair. "I have had the most fun decorating the rooms! Mr. May gave me carte blanche to use my own judgment, so I chose a southern botanical theme. Each room is devoted to a specific flower. It's taken me years!"

The stairs rose to the middle of an upper hallway extending both left and right. Directly across the landing, a railing matching the stairs opened to a view of the dining room below. "We call this the gallery," Bethany said, gesturing for Cally to look down. The white-clad table below was sprinkled with rainbows cast by sunlight striking the crystal goblets on the sideboard.

"This looks like a perfect place for a ghost to hang out," Cally mused aloud. "To taunt the living while they're trying to have a quiet breakfast."

"Many people think so," said Bethany. "This is where people most often claim to see the White Lady, and some say they get a strange chill when they stand here."

"Have you ever seen her?" Cally asked.

"Not I," said Bethany. "But Katarina, our cook, could tell you some stories. You'll meet her soon. She's very excited about you staying here."

She turned her back to the Gallery railing and spread her arms to indicate closed doors all along both sides of the upstairs hall. Instead of room numbers, each door was labeled with a small botanical print in an oval frame. The dark ends of the hall were illuminated by small green-shaded lamps on more-or-less matching butler's desks. Leading Cally to a door bearing a plaque depicting a pink tea rose, she said proudly, "This is the Rose Room."

As she fitted the key into the lock she added, "I apologize. I had hoped to give you the Wisteria Room, which is our most famously haunted room." She gestured toward a door diagonally across the hall. "But the Iversons booked the room months ago. They always stay in that room when they come every summer. They love to tell everyone they're sleeping in a haunted room."

Wisteria, thought Cally, or hysteria? But aloud she said "Aren't they afraid?"

Bethany laughed. "Not Mrs. Iverson! She says she would love to see a real ghost. Though I think her husband just humors her. She says she hears footsteps in the night, and feels strange chills, and sometimes her things get moved around. She says it's thrilling to think there might be more to this world than we know.

"If you want," she added, "I would be happy to help you move across the hall into the Wisteria room after the Iversons check out."

"That won't be necessary," Cally said. Bethany turned the doorknob and found the door already unlocked. "There you are: Ignacio has already brought your small bag in. He's probably fetching your other ones from your car right now."

"Is his name Ignacio, or Pedro?" Cally asked. "Only I thought I heard Joan call him Pedro."

"Joan says she can't pronounce Ignacio's name," Bethany explained, "so she just makes something up." She didn't say what she thought of this as she opened the door. She stood just inside with her hands clasped in front of her, watching Cally enter.

Cally looked around the room and struggled to find the words she knew Bethany was waiting to hear. Her small black bag looked completely out of place lying amid several rose-shaped throw pillows on the floral bedspread. Chintz-upholstered furniture had been shoehorned into the wide but shallow space, so the foot of the bed nearly touched the back of the desk chair, but the desk was wide, and Cally did appreciate that. Tall casement windows opened behind the desk onto the belvedere she had seen from the parking lot below, and through the rose-patterned curtains she could see a magnificent view of the meadow bordering the property. The room's walls were covered in vintage rose wallpaper, and rose-shaped rugs were placed in strategic places over the pink carpet. Framed oil paintings of rose-covered garden gates hung on the walls. Cally swallowed and said

"You have been very thorough."

Bethany beamed with pleasure and handed Cally the key. "There is your closet," she said, gesturing, "and this room has a private bath, which is just through there." The bathroom door looked like it had also once led to a closet. "I hope you'll be comfortable."

"I'm sure I will." She was surprised to realize, in spite of the busy abundance of details, she was telling the truth. The gentle slant of sunlight in the room was already beginning to make her feel calmer than she had in a long time, and she especially liked the view of the meadow. She hung her purse on the rose-shaped closet doorknob, a habit she had got into during her years of touring for her book, and this made the room feel like it was officially hers, for now, anyway.

"If you need anything at all," said Bethany, "just press zero on the phone. It rings straight to my desk." She gestured toward the phone on the night stand. The phone was pink. "I can still have Katarina re-heat some breakfast for you if you're hungry."

"No, really, I'm fine," Cally assured her. "What I think I need most right now is some rest. I really didn't sleep very well last night."

Bethany clasped her hands and backed toward the door. "You rest, then. I'll just tell Ignacio to leave your bags outside the door and not disturb you. We hope you'll find your stay very inspiring!" She pulled the door shut behind her.

Cally sat down on the bed and let herself sink into the rose-covered pillows. "I hope so, too," she said. "You just wouldn't believe how much I hope so." It was pretty much the only hope she had left.

6 -   A Talk With George

When she woke, the sun had already moved across the peak of Vale House and the light in the Rose Room had grown soft and shady. Cally rolled onto her side and hugged a pillow hard to calm the knots in her stomach, not because she didn't know where she was, but because she did, and she remembered what she was doing was crazy.

A little alarm clock on the night stand (with roses painted on its dial) assured her it was only one thirty in the afternoon. Her meeting with Ian May was not until three. She got out of bed and crossed the room, looking out the window to the sunny meadow. One of the horses – a chestnut so bright it could almost qualify as scarlet – was visible grazing far off in knee-high grass.

Beside a vase of silk roses, a small printed sign on the desk informed her of this week's WiFi password. Cally sighed resignedly and decided the responsible thing to do would be to use the time, before her meeting with the proprietor, to check her email. She sat down and, moving aside a rose-colored notepaper cube with matching pen and a small plush bear clasping a tiny bunch of silk roses, she opened her laptop on the pink desk blotter.

To her surprise – or was it dismay? – the internet connection went through right away, and several weeks' worth of unread email began to arrive in her long-unchecked inbox. She scanned through the titles as they stacked up. Most of them were offers for cheap but astounding methods of enhancing her "performance," and these she deleted as soon as they appeared. Two messages from her agent she filed, without opening them, into a folder labeled "Later." A new message from Emerald, dated that day, hoped she had arrived safely, and asked that Cally let her know how things were going as soon as she got a chance. There was also a string of messages from Kelleigh, each headline a reminder in increasingly assertive tones of her promise to call.

The cell signal in the Rose Room was feeble at best, and Cally found the reception better if she stepped through the casement window onto the belvedere. Kelleigh answered on the first ring, but her tone was much calmer today.

"Seriously, Mom," Kelleigh reiterated in her Patient Voice, "you don't have to spend all the savings you have left. You are completely welcome to come and live with Gordon and I until..."

"Gordon and me," said Cally.

"Mom!"

"See? We would drive each other crazy."

She heard her daughter take a deep breath, doing her best to change the subject. "So," she said at length. "How is the place?" she asked. "Nice and haunted?"

"I haven't met any ghosts yet, myself," Cally told her. "But according to the staff there are lots of mysterious footsteps, and strange chills."

Kelleigh laughed, and Cally breathed a sigh of relief to hear it. She, along with her daughter and son who had just been teenagers at the time, had lived through years of people eagerly sharing their Mysterious Footsteps and Chills stories with them, and Cally had to admit she really was thankful both her children had turned out to be normal, responsible adults in spite of it all.

"Anyway," Cally said, "it really is a charming old place." She glanced back through the window and began to describe the house and the Rose Room with its garish rose-covered bedspread...

...and noticed her purse hanging on the coat hook on the back of the door. She distinctly remembered having hung it on the closet doorknob.

"Mom? Are you still there?"

"Yes..." Cally stepped back through the window into the room, causing the phone's signal to become crackly. She ducked her head back outside and said hurriedly, "I'm sorry, the signal really is terrible here. I'll email you, ok? Love you! Bye!"

She threw the phone on the bed and spun on her heel, looking around the room. She rattled the door knob and assured herself the door was still locked. She looked carefully into the closet, which was empty but for a row of hangers padded with chintz, and into the little bathroom. Nothing else seemed amiss. Maybe she was misremembering. "Or," she said, laughing just a little too sharply, "maybe it's the White Lady trying to be helpful!"

She went into the little bathroom to wash the sleep from her face before her meeting with Ian May. It was obvious the bathroom had indeed once been a closet, but it had been charmingly, if snugly, fitted with an old-fashioned claw-footed tub, a small window, and a mauve vanity and commode. "I wonder where Bethany found those!" Cally thought, unwrapping one of the rose-scented soaps on the vanity. Running a comb through her tangles, she saw in the mirror that her slept-in t-shirt was wrinkled beyond hope, and wondered if Ignacio had brought her luggage as promised.

She opened the door and was gratified to find her two suitcases in front of the door. A tall young man stood next to them with his hands in his pockets, smiling broadly at her. "Oh!" she said. "I was expecting Ignacio. Thank you for bringing up my things." The old gray tom cat she had seen on the porch was also there, sitting with its back to them as it gazed through the Gallery railing at something in the dining room below.

"Oh, Miss," the young man said, "That was none of me. Mr. Ignacio brought them an hour ago. I just came to see if you need anything." He spoke with a musical accent. Cally thought it sounded Jamaican – some kind of Caribbean, anyway – and she found herself wishing he would keep on talking. "I am George," he said.

"Ah, yes, George." Emerald had told her to expect to meet someone named Georgie at Vale House; she hadn't mentioned he looked like an angel. He was a beautiful young man, with dark mahogany skin and broad cheekbones sloping back under luminous eyes. His hands were pushed deep into his pockets, his posture easy and lithe, like a cat that could spring from repose to action at a moment's notice. He couldn't have been twenty, if that. "Very nice to meet you," Cally said, extending a hand.

He did not take his hand out of his pocket to shake hers, and he did not say anything else, but continued smiling at her. If he was expecting her to tip him for Ignacio's work in bringing up her bags, Cally thought, he had another thing coming. "Well," she said after an awkward pause, "I don't need anything right now, that I can think of. I have a meeting with Mr. May in a few minutes. But my friend Emerald suggested you might be able to tell me some good stories about the ghosts that are supposed to haunt this house. Or maybe you can give me a tour of the house and show me where all the ghosts are supposed to be lurking. That would be nice, later, maybe." For that, she thought, she would certainly tip him.

He nodded, straightening up. "Emerald is right. You can't swing a dead cat around here without hitting a spirit of some kind!"

"A *dead cat*?" Cally bristled at the expression. Even the old gray tom cat swiveled its head around to look at George.

"Sorry," he said quickly. "Sorry, it was something my old boss used to say."

"He must have been a charming man."

"Oh, no, he wasn't really very nice at all," George said, and Cally realized sarcasm was lost on him. Maybe it was a language difference thing.

She bent down to pick up her bags, expecting George to protest and insist on doing it for her, but he didn't move from where he stood. She dragged her bags into the Rose Room and George said behind her, "I think Mr. May is ready for you."

"Thank you, yes. I'll be right down."

"Good, good," said George. "We just want you to be happy here."

She turned to close the door, an apology for cutting short their conversation ready on her lips, but the young man had already gone. Cally wondered what Joan would have to say about that kind of "customer service." She shrugged and closed the door, then opened one of the bags on the bed and rifled through it until she found a blouse that wasn't too wrinkled. The rosy-faced clock on the desk now read a quarter to three; she would have to worry about putting a few things away later. For now, she quickly changed into the fresh blouse, shoved her notepad and pen into her purse, and locked the door behind her as she hurried down the stairs.

7 -   Two Cold Beers

Bethany was seated behind the desk, talking with a white haired older gentleman standing in front of it. They broke off as Cally ran down the last couple of steps, and Bethany stood to introduce her. "Mr. May," she said, "This is our guest Callaghan McCarthy. Ms. McCarthy, this is Ian May, the owner of Vale House."

"Please call me Ian," the old gentleman said in a beautiful southern accent that was almost an old-time brogue. He reached out his hand to Cally, palm upward. "It's a pleasure to meet you," he said graciously, smiling and bowing slightly as she put her hand in his. He was a handsome man for his age, clean shaven, with a thick mane of white hair combed softly back. He was dressed in a crisp windowpane-check shirt tucked into gray slacks. Thick calluses on his hands, however, belied his genteel image. "What an honor to have a famous author as our guest," he said. "And so lovely, too!" He straightened and gazed into Cally's eyes, and his own eyes sparkled with genuine pleasure.

"I'm not really famous," Cally said. "*Or lovely,*" she also thought but did not say aloud. "I'm very grateful to you for letting me come and stay in your home for a while."

"We hope you'll find it inspiring," Ian said. "We get those paranormal investigators in here sometimes, you see, but never a famous author before."

"Ghost investigators!" Joan's voice came from the dining room behind Cally. She clomped into the Hall, a large mug clutched in one hand. "Bunch of quacks, if you ask me. And always trying to get their room and board for free, in exchange for the 'exposure'!" She made air-quotes with her free hand. Then she smiled and strode over to Ian's side, positioning herself between him and Bethany.

Kissing him on the cheek, she said sweetly, "I hope you're charging Ms. Callaghan the full rate."

Ian's charming smile never dimmed. "Ms. McCarthy is a paying customer," he said evenly. "I know you'll treat her with the courtesy for which we are so well known."

Joan had no reply to this. She marched with her mug to her office door and turned as she went in. "Excuse me, I must get back to work. I have all this paperwork to get through." She shut the door behind her, but much more softly than she had earlier.

Bethany was frowning and shaking her head, but her smile returned as soon as Ian spoke again. "Now," he said to Cally, "we don't normally serve dinner at this bed and breakfast, but my daughter and her husband are in town and so we're all having a nice family meal this evening. We would all be honored if you would join us."

"Oh, no, I couldn't impose," Cally said. "I thought I would just get something in town."

"It's no trouble," Bethany assured her. "Katarina is already expecting you. And the Seven Forks is closed on Sundays – your only other choice would be pizza."

Ian added, "Besides, my daughter Nell is your biggest fan. She would be disappointed if you didn't join us tonight."

Cally winced inwardly at the thought of meeting a Biggest Fan, but the thought of one less meal against her bank balance carried considerably more weight at the moment, so she forced a smile and said, "Alright, then. I mustn't disappoint a fan, after all."

"Well, we have plenty of time before dinner," Ian said. "I was thinking we could have our talk out on the Pirate Ship." He turned toward the door and offered her his arm. Nodding to Bethany, he said, "Please send Ignacio to find us if we don't return in time for dinner."

Bethany smiled like a schoolgirl at him and promised she would.

They stepped out onto the porch, where the scent of freshly mown grass rose on the warm afternoon breeze. "Pirate Ship?" Cally had to ask.

Ian gave a little chuckle as he worked his way down the stairs. He groaned softly with every step and Cally had the feeling she should be supporting him, instead of hanging onto his arm like the lady he seemed to have the impression she was. "It's a little project of mine," he explained. "Down by the pond." At the bottom of the stairs, he lingered a moment with his hand on the railing, steadying himself, and Cally was unable to stop herself moving her hand up his arm to support him. He grinned sheepishly at her. "It's my knees," he explained. "They always do this when there's a storm on the way." He glanced up at what Cally thought was a perfectly mild summer sky, with just a few large white clouds shining bright white as they climbed higher into the blue.

Ian turned around to face the house, clearing his throat and making a wide gesture toward its columned porch and the belvedere above. "Vale House," he said, "is a classic example of antebellum architecture. The original structure..." He launched into a thorough explanation of architectural styles in the south, and the various fires and remodelings Vale House had endured over the years. It seemed to be a well-rehearsed speech he had made often, and it was clear he enjoyed making it.

"How did the house get its name?" Cally asked him, fishing in her purse for her notebook. "Was the original builder named Vale?"

"No, no," he said, turning to lead her across the lawn to the hill sloping down behind the barn. Willow trees at the bottom revealed glimpses of a shady green pond. "This entire place was called The Vale, once upon a time." He swept his arm to indicate everything around them: the house and grounds, fields and woods on the far side of the pond, the meadow, even the town beyond the house.

"My family's relationship with this land goes back many generations. This house was once the only building around. They grew cotton here, for a long time, and after the war it was a tobacco farm. When my great, great grandfather inherited the place, he sold a lot of the land for what eventually became the town of Wood Leigh, until..."

Cally tried – mostly in vain – to write in her notebook as they walked. Ian continued to talk about the history of the area until they reached the bottom of the hill. There they rounded a group of three large willows, and Cally saw what must be the Pirate Ship. It was really more of a derelict fishing trawler, half grounded on the bank of the pond, with trees grown up around and probably through its stern.

"It's not really a Pirate Ship," Ian admitted, grinning as if apologizing for having made a bad joke. "My guests just started calling it that, and made up legends about why it's haunted."

"It's haunted?" Cally asked, trying to wrangle her pen and notebook.

Ian laughed. "Well," he said, "not that I'm aware of. But some of my guests want it to be, so I let them think what they like. It's really just an old fishing boat I had brought here in pieces from my uncle's place on the outer banks. My wife..." His eyes went misty, and he gazed across the pond to the fields beyond it. "Well, I wanted to move out to the coast, and she said all I really ever did, whenever I was there, was sit on Uncle Jim's boat and fish, so all I really needed was the boat. She was right, of course." He looked back and smiled at Cally. "She was very wise, then, in her own way."

Cally smiled awkwardly and said, "I'm so sorry she's not with you anymore."

"Oh, she is," he said softly. "She is. In her own way, of course." He stepped onto a wooden walkway connecting the bank to the half of the boat protruding over the water. "Would you like a beer?"

Cally stammered a little. She had pegged Ian May as the kind of southern gentleman who would sip mint juleps on a veranda, but he disappeared into the boat's cabin and she could hear the clank of bottles in ice. When he emerged again, he was holding two dripping brown bottles, which he carried to a pair of folding chairs on the boat's narrow deck. Cally sat down carefully in one of the chairs; the deck was far from level, and the chairs leaned backward against the bulkhead. Ian sat down next to her and used a yellow plastic cigarette lighter as a bottle-opener. He handed her one of the frosty bottles, and clinked his own against hers. "To your next bestseller!" he said.

Cally took a big swallow to that. The cold beer did feel good going down. She thought she would have liked to sit there all afternoon and watch dragonflies landing on cattails at the pond's edge, and the family of ducks paddling among them. She suspected this was exactly how Ian spent most of his afternoons. With an effort, she reminded herself she was there to get work done.

Balancing her notepad on her knee, she poised her pen above it and began. "Mr. May," she said, "I can't tell whether you actually believe in ghosts, yourself, or not. Have you ever seen any of the spirits they say live at Vale House?"

"Call me Ian," he reminded her. He was gazing dreamily across the pond to the trees on the other bank. "Well," he said. "I certainly don't see any reason why ghosts shouldn't exist. But I've never met one, myself.

"I have, however, met my neighbor, Rum. Can you see him?"

He made a gesture like a salute with his bottle toward the other shore of the pond. There Cally thought at first she could see only the broken-off stump of a tree sticking up from the muddy bank. As she continued to look, however, the stump blinked, and smiled, and then Cally could make out a grizzled brown face above a long, white beard tucked behind the bib of greasy denim overalls. The little man waved a crooked walking stick at them before turning to walk away, up the hill she and Ian had just come down, until he was out of sight beyond the barn.

"Rum?" Cally asked. "That's an odd name."

"He's lived around here a long time," Ian said. "He passes through my property often on his way to his other job."

"Other job?" Cally thought Rum had looked like he should have retired from any job ages ago. "Well, good for him, I guess."

Ian regarded her quietly for a long while. At length he said, "But that's not what you came here to hear about. Over the years people have told me many stories, about ghosts they say they've seen in my house. Would you like to hear those stories?"

"I've read a few of them," Cally said. "Mostly on the internet. I was hoping to get some personal, first-hand accounts."

"In that case, you might want to bring the subject up at the dinner table tonight," he said. "They all have stories they love to tell. I'll invite Bethany to join us; she's had a few interesting experiences. She doesn't really like to talk about them, but I have a feeling she won't mind telling you.

"And tell me, Miss Callaghan McCarthy, author of *Escape the Haunted Heart*: what about you? Do you believe in ghosts?"

Maybe it was the beer, or maybe it was his gentle and genuinely interested demeanor, but whatever it was, the Inevitable Question didn't put Cally on the defensive the way it usually did. She didn't give him the canned, non-committal answer she had developed over the years to fend off talk-show hosts and Biggest Fans. She told him the truth.

"No," she said. "I don't believe in ghosts at all. The whole idea is preposterous. When I wrote my book, I meant it as a metaphor. It was sort of biographical, you know? The ghost was symbolic for the elephant in the room of which everyone is aware but about which nobody wants to talk. The spirits, which my main character didn't want to believe existed, were a metaphor for all the things I was seeing, in my own life, which I conveniently explained away, the affairs my husband was having, and other things to which I deliberately blinded myself. The ghosts that wouldn't let the heroine leave the house were my own self-doubts and recriminations, things I had to work so hard for years to exorcise. The heroine's escape was my own escape from my denial of what a mess my life had become. I wrote the book to heal my heart. I never meant to have it published. But my daughter found it and said it was very good and encouraged me to send it to a friend of a friend of hers who was a literary agent and... well, I figured why not. I thought maybe it would help someone else as it had helped me, to let go of old ghosts. But that's not how it turned out. People don't want to let go of old ghosts. They want to believe in things that aren't real."

"And why do you suppose that is?" Ian asked her.

The afternoon flew away. Cally's notebook sat unused on her knee, and somehow she had become the interviewee rather than the interviewer. She found herself telling Ian May her whole life story.

She told him about the nerdy girl who had been swept off her feet by a handsome jock who had turned into a jerk as soon as he'd married her and got her away from her friends and family. She told him about giving up her own dreams without having quite figured out first what they were, and raising her children and taking care of her household like a good girl should, until finally leaving her train-wreck of a marriage and assuming a career writing product manuals and advertising copy. She told him about the windfall of an unexpected best-selling novel, and using the money from it to put her children through college, about running out of money and having her agent breathing down her neck for a sequel, until finally she loaded everything she owned into her car and struck out across the country to a place that had been recommended to her by a friend she had only ever met on the internet, in one final bid to find out what she wanted to be when she grew up. She sensed she should stop talking and give Ian a chance to speak, but his patient gaze encouraged her to go on until the dregs of the beer had grown warm and bitter in the bottom of the bottle.

"Mr. May! Ian, sir!" A voice was calling from the top of the hill near the barn. Ignacio stood there, waving. "Kat says to tell you, dinner is almost ready!"

Ian grasped the railing and pulled himself up out of his chair. "Best not to keep the cook waiting, " he advised, offering Cally a hand to help her up. "I've been most charmed by our conversation."

They returned slowly to the house, with Ian explaining to Cally the history of every outbuilding and ancient willow-oak they passed. The clouds above them were definitely building higher into the sky now, joining hands overhead as the sun moved westward, throwing the long shadow of Vale House across the front yard and on into the meadow. It occurred to Cally this sort of thing would make for some very good, atmospheric description with which to build tension in a ghost story, but then she dismissed the idea as just a bit too trite.

8 -   CreepyPasta: It's What's For Dinner

The Hall was filled with the aroma of good country cooking. Ian took his leave of Cally here, passing through the dining room and turning left into a narrow back hall. He asked her, as he went, to please tell everyone he would see them at dinner.

Cally took the opportunity to return to the Rose Room to drop off her purse. Hanging it on the closet door knob, she hesitated briefly before deciding to also leave her notepad behind. She could ask people to tell their ghost stories during the dinner conversation, but it would be rude, she imagined, to actually take notes next to her plate.

As she turned to leave the room, she saw her open suitcase had been moved from the bed to the luggage rack beside the desk. The other stood neatly beside it. Cally appreciated the customer service, but decided to power off her computer and tuck it into the desk drawer before she left, even though it did not yet contain her potential "next bestseller."

Two other guests were also exiting their room at the end of the hall as she locked her door behind her. A man and a woman who looked to be in their late thirties joined her at the Gallery railing, making appreciative remarks about the aromas rising from below. Nobody could yet be seen seated at the dining room table. "At least we aren't late," Cally remarked to the couple.

The young woman smiled but looked at the floor as she extended a hand to Cally. "You must be Callaghan McCarthy," she said. "I'm Nell."

"Oh, you're Ian's daughter," Cally said, grasping the proffered hand, which was thin and cool and lay limp in Cally's hand until she released it.

Large brown eyes peeped out from behind auburn curls as Nell giggled softly. "I really loved your book," she said. "I can't wait until your next one comes out! I love to read. I see you have the Rose Room! I..."

"Don't pester the poor lady, Nell," said the man accompanying her. He reached for Cally's hand. "I'm Foster Brentwood, Ian May's son-in-law. Pleased to meet you." He smiled down at her from his six and a half foot frame and pumped her hand up and down enthusiastically. Dark, straight hair flopped over his forehead, and his black-framed glasses slid down to the end of his nose. Pushing them up, he added "I'm also Ian's business partner. He's getting on in years, as you may have noticed, and he needs my help with things more and more often, these days."

Cally followed the couple downstairs. They went straight to what were apparently their accustomed seats near the head of the table. "You should probably take the Guest of Honor seat," Foster said to her, indicating the chair across from Nell. Nell giggled softly and fiddled with the silverware beside her plate. She seemed about to say something more to Cally, but a quick look from her husband silenced her, and she put her hands in her lap.

Cally did not sit down right away. She walked to the far side of the room where six tall windows framed with antique lace let in afternoon light and a jasmine-scented breeze. A formal garden lay outside the windows, nestled in the space between two wings extending back from either end of Vale House. Lush drifts of roses, hostas, and hydrangeas surrounded a neat strip of lawn, and a white gazebo adorned its center. Jasmine vines clambered over the gazebo, crowning it with clouds of yellow blossoms. At the very end of the lawn, an old stone building nestled in the shrubbery, surrounded by rust-red chickens clucking softly and scratching in the mulch. It was a picture-perfect scene well suited to a magazine cover but definitely not, Cally thought, the cover of a ghost story.

She turned at the sound of footsteps to see a very thin old man entering the dining room from the narrow hallway at the north end of the room. He leaned heavily on a polished wooden cane as he made his way to the foot of the table. Here he paused to hang his cane carefully on the back of a chair, and turned to the sideboard. "Anyone want a little aperitif?" he offered cheerfully, picking up one of the brandy glasses next to the crystal decanter there.

"Let me get that for you, Captain!" Foster called, jumping up from his seat to pull the old man's chair out for him so he could sit down without spilling his drink. Then he dashed around the table and pulled out Cally's chair for her, as well. As Cally took her seat, Bethany came into the room from the same narrow hallway from which the old man had come. She wore a fresh white apron and was carrying two covered bread baskets. A short woman with huge brown eyes followed her, carrying a large crystal bowl filled with colorful garden salad.

"Ms. McCarthy, this is Katarina, our cook," said Bethany. "Though she and I both also perform *other duties as assigned.*" She winked and tilted her head toward the Hall and Joan's office door.

Katarina put down the salad. Her black ponytail bobbed as she put out her hand and said "I'm so thrilled to meet you, Ms. McCarthy!"

"Please call me Cally."

"I will if you call me Kat!" She stood back and folded her hands over her apron, smiling proudly. "I just want everyone to know," she said, "this salad includes some of the first tomatoes of the season from Ignacio's garden!"

"Kat is married to Ignacio, whom you have already met," Bethany informed Cally.

Foster said, "It never ceases to amaze me how he gets so much to grow in such a small garden."

"It looks too pretty to eat," Cally remarked honestly.

"Where's Ian? It's half past six." Joan's voice came from the Hall. "Where's the food? Come on, let's show some efficiency around here!"

Katarina rolled her eyes and sighed. Bethany touched her arm and gestured toward the kitchen hallway, and both women left the room before Joan entered.

"Honestly!" Joan declared to the room in general as she swept through the doorway in a clatter of heels and bracelets. "Ian is too easy on these people." She clomped her way around the table to the windows and began banging them shut. "And who keeps opening these windows? No wonder my allergies are acting up. Outside air belongs outside!" With a final bang, she turned to the table. "Hello,

Foster, Nellie, and hello..." Stopping in mid-stride, she seemed about to say something else, but thought better of it and sat down quietly on Cally's right.

"I think you're in her seat," Nell said softly. Her husband nudged her with his elbow.

"Oh, I'm sorry!" Cally said, and started to get up.

"No, no, you're the Guest of Honor," Joan reminded them all just as Ian entered the room from the narrow hallway mirroring the one leading to the kitchen. She smiled sweetly up at him as he made his way to the head of the table.

"Are we all here?" Ian asked. "The Iversons won't be joining us, I'm afraid. They are spending the evening in Blackthorn, and will be back late tonight."

"They're bed and breakfast customers," Joan reminded him. "Not bed and three meals a day." She gave Cally a glance from the corner of her eye but quickly returned to smiling at Ian.

As Ian made his way to his seat, he opened each of the six windows as he passed them. "Ah, that's better," he said. "Such a beautiful evening! We should enjoy this good weather while it lasts." Joan said nothing as "outside air" filled the room once again. Foster helped Ian take his seat at the head of the table.

Bethany and Katarina returned with steaming platters which they distributed around the table. A beautifully braised brisket was set before Ian. "This smells wonderful!" he said, and gestured toward the empty seats around the table, indicating the women should be seated.

"Oh, I shouldn't stay," Bethany protested, glancing at Joan. "I've got some leftover soup at home that I really should..."

"Nonsense," Ian said gently. "Your leftovers aren't going anywhere. Please join us."

It was hard for Cally not to laugh out loud at the tension in the room as Bethany smiled sideways at Joan's careful silence. "Well, thank you, Ian," she said. She took off her apron and sat down at the Captain's left, and indicated the empty seats across from herself. "You and Ignacio can sit there," she suggested to Katarina.

Joan went red in the face and glared at Bethany, who looked studiously away, smirking. Katarina said, "Oh, thank you so very much, Mr. May, but Ignacio has already made his wonderful spaghetti for our supper tonight, with fresh tomatoes."

"Spaghetti?" Joan spat. "Seriously, Maria, shouldn't he have made tacos or something?"

"My husband is a very accomplished cook," Katarina assured her, nodding as she backed out of the room. "I'll be back later to help with the washing up," she told Bethany, and then was gone.

"Well, then!" said Ian, seemingly oblivious of the drama. "Introductions all around!"

"I think we all know each other's names," Joan pointed out. Ian ignored her and continued.

"First of all, our guest of honor is Ms. Callaghan McCarthy," he said, nodding toward Cally. "And this is my daughter and son-in-law, Nell and Foster Brentwood. Next we have my assistant and very dear friend, Ms. Joan Cromwell." Joan beamed at him possessively. He nodded toward Bethany. "The secretary here at our little bed and breakfast is Miss Bethany Chase. And, of course, we have my oldest and best friend, Doug Arkwright, otherwise known as the Captain."

The old man at the foot of the table nodded graciously to each of them in turn as Ian spoke, and raised his glass. "I am delighted to make your acquaintance," he said to the table in general. He drained the glass, and turned to refill it.

"You should know most of us very well by now," Joan reminded him. "You've only been living here for ten years." She muttered to Cally, "He's one of those freeloading hangers-on Ian doesn't have the heart to turn out. And he was never a captain, either. Everyone just calls him that. They say he's a war hero or something, but I have it on good authority he never rose above the rank of corporal."

"It's an honorary title," Ian said, smiling at Joan gently. He stood and began carving thick slices from the brisket. Nell took a roll from one of the baskets and passed the basket to her right. "Now," said Ian, by way of getting the dinner conversation started, "I must confess, I have never read Ms. McCarthy's book. But I know my daughter enjoyed it very much. Has anyone else here read it?"

"I haven't!" Joan proclaimed with a snort. She took two rolls from the basket Cally passed to her. "Books about ghosts and fairies and things. Nothing but a bunch of silly escapism, if you ask me, for people who can't deal with reality."

"I've read it at least six times!" Nell announced.

Bethany smiled indulgently at the quiet woman behind her curtain of auburn curls, and picked up the basket from in front of Joan to continue passing it around the table. "I've read it twice, myself," she said. "I'm looking forward to reading more of your work someday, Ms. McCarthy."

"Please, call me Cally," Cally reminded her.

"Is your next book going to be about Vale House?" the Captain asked.

"Well, not exactly," Cally tried to explain. She began to fear this might become the next Inevitable Question she would spend years deflecting. "I just hope to learn some interesting ghost stories here, and maybe get some ideas about creating haunted atmospheres, something I hope will give an authentic feel to a completely fictional story."

"You can ask me anything," the Captain said. "I have tons of stories."

"I do, too," said Nell. She snuck a quick glance at Cally between bites. Cally tried to smile at her before she looked away again, but missed the opportunity.

"I'd be happy to hear your stories," Cally said. "Maybe we could make an appointment to chat sometime tomorrow?"

Foster answered for Nell. "I'm afraid not, Ms. McCarthy. Nell and I have some business we have to attend to in Blackthorn tomorrow. Perhaps another time."

"Well, I have all day free tomorrow!" the Captain informed them happily. He swirled his brandy glass at Cally. "How about after lunch?"

His enthusiasm made Cally grin. "Alright," she said. "I'll make a note of it. Don't let me forget." She wondered if the old man himself would remember.

Bethany said, "I'll put it in the appointment book and remind you." She patted his blue-veined hand.

"And I can talk to you any time you want, after you get back," Cally said to Nell.

"We'll be gone until late afternoon," Foster said, more to Nell than to Cally. Nell looked down and picked at her food; Cally was starting to feel bad for the painfully shy young woman.

Foster went on, explaining as he pushed up his glasses, "I don't know if you've noticed, but this town's economy is crumbling. The few establishments still hanging on here barely get enough business to survive. And that doesn't help my father-in-law's business any, either, let me tell you. Since Ian retired from farming, this bed and breakfast business is his only significant source of incoming cash-flow. Now, I have a lot of ideas about how to turn this whole town into a thriving economy base again. And I'll be talking to a venture capital specialist in Blackthorn this week about some of them."

"I like this town the way it is," said Nell.

"But it won't survive if it doesn't make any money," Joan pointed out. "And that means neither will this house. I have some ideas of my own about how to turn it around," she said to Foster.

"I am sure you do," said Foster. His tone was conciliatory as he went on. "Joan and I actually have some ideas in common about how to turn Vale House into a going concern again. Though I'm not sure billing it as a Haunted Bed and Breakfast would actually be good for business."

"No, as I said, I don't plan to..." Cally tried to explain.

"There are at least six spirits in this house!" Nell declared. "And there are also..." She stopped as her husband gripped her forearm.

Joan curled a hand around her mouth and turned to Cally. "Don't mind her," she said in a whisper loud enough for everyone to hear. "She's what you call 'a little touched.' Foster has his hands full, taking care of that one."

Nell sat up and shook back her curls to look squarely at Cally. "I have been diagnosed with schizoaffective disorder and acute social anxiety," she explained quite cheerfully. "I'm taking medicine for it. I'm doing very well." She nodded. "The ghosts are just stories in my head. They aren't real."

"I don't know about that! " said the Captain. "The other day, I fell asleep in the parlor with the TV on, and when I woke up, it was turned off."

Cally smiled patiently and tried to enjoy her meal, while the Captain, Nell, and Bethany fell to telling her all the same tales everyone always told, all the creepypasta anyone could find anywhere on the internet: stories about flickering lights, cold feelings in hallways, missing cufflinks and falling knickknacks.

Doors opening and shutting. And, of course, the lady in the white dress who was believed, depending on the speaker, to be either one of Ian's ancestors or someone who had died in one of several fires Vale House had endured over the years. This house had everything.

"Yes, yes," Joan grumbled. "Shadowy figures and mysterious noises in the night and phantom footsteps. All these things probably have perfectly normal explanations. But that doesn't mean we can't take advantage of them to boost business."

"Not everyone thinks ghosts are exciting," Bethany pointed out, shaking her head. She told them how she often smelled smoke in the Hall, even though the fireplace there was rarely lit, and sometimes thought she saw a dark shape standing in front of the desk, which would disappear whenever she looked straight at it. "The shape, I mean, not the desk!" She laughed. "It used to really bother me. But I love my job and I love Vale House, and Ian is an old and dear friend of my family, so I just learned to shrug it off." She demonstrated by shrugging and cleaning her plate with the remnants of her roll.

Cally thought that was a more unique story than most she had heard, and said "I would love to hear your story in more detail, Bethany, if that's okay with you. Of course I would not use your name in anything I'd write about it."

Bethany stood and put her napkin in her plate. "I wouldn't mind helping you get inspired," she said, "but right now it looks like everyone is ready for dessert!"

She started to walk toward the kitchen, but a knock came at the front door just then and she made a detour into the Hall to answer it. A minute later, she returned with Ben Dawes, the blue-eyed man Cally recognized from the news store. He stood in the dining room doorway and smiled quickly at Cally before turning and nodding to Ian May.

"Young Bennet!" Ian called delightedly. "Come, sit. You're just in time for strawberry shortcake. Fresh strawberries from the garden! Ben, this is our honored guest, Callaghan McCarthy."

"We've met," he said, but he reached to take Cally's hand anyway, and shook it warmly and perhaps for a little too long. The Captain filled a brandy glass and offered it to Ben.

"Thank you," said Ben. "But I can't stay. I just stopped by to give you a message, Ian, from Merv Arkwright. He says there's a storm on the way. One of those big ones." His voice seemed heavy with portent, much more so than Cally thought talk of the weather should normally warrant. "Should arrive sometime in the next couple of hours. He says if you need any help with it, to please feel free to call him."

"There you are!" Joan said. She turned to Cally with genuine excitement in her face. "Now you're in for a *real* supernatural experience."

"Well, now, I think Ignacio and I have got it covered," Ian said to Ben. "You're welcome to come and watch it with us," he added.

Joan explained to Cally, "Sitting on the front porch watching summer storms is a big tradition in this house." She beamed at Ian with what Cally could almost swear was genuine affection. "It's almost like a party."

"It's kind of you to invite me," Ben was saying. "But I have things I'll need to attend to tonight. Thanks, Ian. Evening, all. " He bowed slightly, his gaze lingering on Cally as he backed out of the room. The Captain shrugged and drained the superfluous brandy glass.

9 -   Evening Storm

Katarina returned as promised to help Bethany clear the table. Ian excused himself from the table, promising to join everyone on the porch in just a few minutes. Covering his plate of dessert with a napkin, he headed down the hallway toward his quarters, and Katarina smiled at his retreating back. "He always does that," she told Cally, shaking her head as she whisked empty plates into the kitchen.

Joan went to her office "to make some important calls before that storm arrives!" and Foster stood and helped Nell up from her chair, "We'll just be spending the evening's festivities in our room," he said. "Nellie's terrified of thunder." Cally thought he looked like the terrified one, the way his hands twitched as he held onto Nell's arm, but she didn't say so.

While the Captain made his way slowly toward the Hall, Bethany switched off lights in the dining room until it was illuminated only by the light inside the china cabinet. "Now, feel free to help yourself to anything from the sideboard," she told Cally. "That's what it's there for. And if you're not interested in storm watching," she chuckled softly, "there's a television in the Front Parlor, just there through the doorway at the side of the Hall. It's not a very fancy set, but it should work. As long as the power stays on, anyway!"

"No, I'd love to join you all," Cally assured her. "I'll just run upstairs and grab a sweater, in case it gets chilly out there."

Nell and Foster had already closed the door of their room by the time Cally arrived at the Rose Room door, but she could hear their voices arguing about something. She tried not to listen, as she stood fumbling to find the keyhole in the dim light from the butler's desk, but she couldn't help but hear Nell shout, "That's not what the doctor said!"

"I think I know you much better than any of those doctors do, after all these years," was Foster's stern reply. "And anyway how would *you* know what anyone really said or not?"

Cally decided she didn't need her sweater after all. She turned quickly and headed back to the stairs, but hadn't reached the bottom before she heard Foster conclude firmly, "It's just to help you keep calm."

The bottom of the stairs and the Hall were dark, now, except for the porch lights shining in through the door, and a blue flicker coming from the open doorway opposite Joan's office. Cally peered into this room – the Front Parlor, Bethany had called it – and recognized the man she had seen when she was checking in, still wearing his dark suit, sitting on one of the sofas. He seemed to be deep in thought, with his hands pressed together almost as if in prayer. He was not watching the television, which showed nothing but static on its screen at the moment. Something about his drab clothing and serious demeanor made Cally think he must be a preacher of some sort. Maybe this was Mr. Iverson? She decided not to interrupt him, but turned away and stood a moment in front of the screen door, letting the rapidly cooling breeze blow her hair back from her face.

The Captain and Katarina were already outside; she could hear them chatting in the wicker seats beside the door. Bethany rushed into the Hall from the dining room, drying her hands on a dish towel, and paused to turn on a small lamp on the desk. "Has the show started yet?" she asked. "I used to make popcorn for these things, but the damp always ruined it." She laughed and pushed open the door, holding it for Cally and gesturing like a theater usher toward some of the empty wicker chairs.

Away to the south, a low rumbling could be heard above the Gardens Road housetops. The eastern sky was already quite dark; what light remained seemed to come from crimson sunset reflections along the top edges of the clouds above the meadow. The three horses were nowhere to be seen.

"I hope the rain waits until Ignacio gets back from locking up the chickens," Katarina said as Cally sat down next to her.

The breeze blowing in over the meadow grew cooler by the moment, and it took on a metallic smell. Cally was going to remark about this – she had always wondered how air could smell metallic when, as far as she knew, metal had no smell – but as she opened her mouth to speak, a terrific bolt of lightning split the sky, temporarily turning the porch to daylight. Katarina began to count slowly "One, two, three, four..."

A large, shapeless shadow leapt from the lawn to the porch stairs and Cally gasped, but it was just Ignacio, holding his jacket over his head to ward off the fat drops of rain beginning to fall. Katarina lost count as she stood to hug him, and took his jacket to hang over the back of a chair to drip. As the couple sat down, the thunder from the lightning bolt arrived, a deep, tearing *crrrrack!* If Katarina hadn't been trying to count the seconds since the flash, Cally would have thought it had come from directly overhead. "Well, three miles, at least," Katarina said.

"Still a long way off," Ian observed from the doorway. Ignacio brought two of the wicker chairs from the other end of the porch closer to the door and Ian sat in one of them, leaving the remaining chair for Joan, who arrived last, complaining about how the lightning was messing up all the telephone signals. She reached back inside the door as she came out, switching off the porch light and throwing the front of the house into deep, indigo twilight.

"You wanted to see something supernatural?" Joan said, sitting down and leaning across Ian to speak to Cally. "Well, you're in for a real treat now!" Cally couldn't imagine how a thunderstorm could be a "real treat," supernatural or otherwise, but it was refreshing to see Joan feeling jovial about something for a change.

As the crackling and flashing continued, the rain began in earnest, filling the lawn with the sound of hissing, and raising the fragrance of wet earth and grass.

"They have a name for that smell," Ian explained. "It's *petrichor*, and it translates from the Greek to something like 'rock blood'." Everyone smiled and thanked him for telling them this, though Cally could tell by their patient expressions they had already heard him say it many times before.

The breeze grew chilly, and Cally wished she had brought her sweater after all. The Captain passed a small silver flask down the row of people seated on the porch. Ignacio and Katarina each accepted a sip and Katarina passed the flask on to Cally. She feared it would seem rude not to also take a sip, and steeled herself to do so, telling herself the alcohol would kill any germs on the mouth of the flask. When she tasted how strong the whiskey inside was, she suspected it might kill her stomach as well. She swallowed carefully and passed the flask to Bethany. "I hope Nell is okay," she said, trying to cover up her choking.

"Oh, don't worry about her!" Joan said. "Foster'll have her drugged up nine ways from Sunday. She won't know a thing!"

Cally didn't think that was a very functional way to deal with one's fears, but she said nothing. It wasn't her place to judge and, as Foster had said, he had been dealing with Nell's illness for a long time and ought to know what was best for her by now.

Bethany plainly only pretended to drink from the flask before she passed it to Ian. He took such a deep swallow, Cally winced on his behalf, but he smiled as he handed it on to Joan. "Nell's mother used to love these storms," he said. His voice was husky and Cally couldn't tell whether it was due to the whiskey or emotion.

To Cally's surprise, Joan poured a few drops from the flask into her tea mug. She held the mug under her nose, inhaling with a deep, introspective expression on her face, saying nothing for once. At length she took a deep gulp from the mug, and that seemed to bring her back to herself. She handed the flask back to Ian and said, "Here comes another."

The words were barely out of her mouth before a wide network of lightning bolts arched over the meadow like a gigantic umbrella of light.

"One, two, three..." counted Katarina.

Cally looked over the meadow. The low hills stood out sharply against the fiercely lit eastern sky, like a black jianzhi cutout. After the light had gone, the reverse of the image floated before her eyes for many seconds.

"... four, five, six." Thunder boomed overhead, temporarily drowning out all talk and even the sound of the rain.

"Getting closer, Kat?" Joan asked as the thunder rolled away into the distance.

"Can't tell yet," Katarina answered. "But I think so. Maybe next time."

Cally looked at Joan, marveling at the way she was being so unusually civil, even to Katarina. Beyond Joan's silhouette, at the southeast corner of the porch, Cally could just make out the old gray tom cat sitting on the porch railing, curled up comfortably with its tail around its front feet, completely unperturbed by the storm. It was gazing out toward the crossroads, just outside the main gate, where the end of Main Street met Gardens Road.

"You would think the cat would hate the storm," she remarked.

"Oh, she does," Katarina laughed. "Little Cyndi came crying at the kitchen door two hours ago, and is hiding under the hoosier right now."

"No, I mean..."

Another great bolt interrupted her, and Kat began counting again. Over the sound of the rain, somewhere down Gardens Road, a dog began to bark, and then another. On the other side of Vale House, beyond the pond and the Pirate Ship, a third dog joined them with bell-like howls, before the clap of thunder drowned them all out.

"Four!" said Katarina. "It's almost overhead!"

"I just love storms," Joan murmured. "They always make me feel so peaceful."

Ian stood up stiffly and walked to the porch railing, wrapping an arm around the column next to the stairs to steady himself. He gazed out into the dark meadow and everyone followed his gaze, except Cally, who watched everyone else and wondered what they were looking at. The rumbling of the thunder rolled away until the dogs could be heard again, still barking, inciting others along Main Street to join their chorus.

The flashes of lightning that followed were not as impressive, but they were too frequent for Katarina to be able to count the seconds between the bolts and their respective booms. In the strobe-like light, Cally saw the cat on the railing at the end of the porch stand up and, to her surprise, jump down into the yard, running off through the rain toward the road. "Why would... ?" she started to wonder aloud, before being cut off by a series of thunderclaps all on top of one another.

"Now that's really close!" Joan remarked. She looked up to Ian and he nodded and smiled.

"Yes, I figure you're right," he said. Cally had to agree. It sounded as if boulders were landing on the porch roof and rolling down the tin sheeting, while gusts of wind began to blow the rain sideways onto the porch, dampening them all where they sat. Cally shivered and looked around her, beginning to feel a little worried the storm might be growing strong enough to damage the old house, but nobody else seemed concerned as they brushed raindrops off their cheeks.

Ian raised the arm he was not using to hang onto the porch column and reached out, palm up, as if to feel the rain sheeting down from the lip of the porch roof. No, Cally thought, it was more like the way he had reached out to take her hand when she had first met him. As if he were greeting a lady. Beyond him, in the brief flashes of illumination, Cally thought she could see someone standing at the metal gate where Main Street ended at the meadow. The person appeared to be wearing a hooded slicker, holding something out in their hand as they walked slowly toward Vale House.

"Who on earth would be out in this?" Cally wondered aloud.

"I'm pretty sure nobody would," Joan snorted. And then, between one flash and another, Cally could no longer see the dark figure. Ian lowered his hand. The breeze died down and the thunder and lightning grew softer and moved off toward the north.

"... six, seven, eight... Well, I guess it's over, then," said Katarina, and accepted another drink from the Captain's flask. The dogs stopped barking.

"See?" said Joan. "You see that? All Ian has to do is stand up, and the storm goes away." She beamed and nodded. "Seen it a hundred times. He's probably why this house is still standing."

"Well, that's Joan's little story," said Ian, peering at Cally as if trying to gauge her expression. "And now you have another tale for your book."

"I..." Cally couldn't think of what to say. She couldn't make sense of what she had just seen – or thought she had seen. Nobody else seemed to have seen it, and she was not about to ask them.

The flask had returned to her, but she passed it on to Ian without drinking. "I think I've had enough," she said.

10 - A Chat With Emerald

The upstairs hallway was dark and quiet, and George broke into a smile when he saw Cally reach the top of the stairs. "Are you happy here?" he asked her.

She stooped to squint at the lock on the Rose Room door. The lamp on the butler's desk was dim and flickering – she suspected the bulb needed to be replaced. "I like this place very much," she assured George. "I didn't see you at dinner or at the little... storm party."

"Oh, I'm not part of the family," he explained, nodding as if this was just fine with him.

"That doesn't seem to stop everyone else." Cally finally fit the key into the lock. She thought she knew the real reason George tended to make himself scarce. "I take it Joan is also her usual charming self toward African Americans," she guessed.

"Dear lady," he said, "I am neither African nor American."

Cally straightened up, turning awkwardly to face him. "I'm sorry! Sorry, George," she stammered, groping for a way to dig herself out of this faux pas. "That was presumptive of me. Where are you from, then, if you don't mind my asking?"

To her great relief, he did not seem at all offended. "I am from very far away from here," he said. "It's a fascinating story, full of action and adventure, and I would love to tell it to you. I think you might like to make it into one of those books you write."

"I would love to hear your story," she said, finally succeeding in getting the door unlocked. "But as to making it into a book, I think I ought to focus on ghost stories, for the present." She opened the Rose Room door and turned to apologize for this, in case it had been a further slight, but George wasn't there anymore.

"Great," Cally said, shutting the door behind her. "He probably thinks I'm a total jerk, now." Someone had switched on the little bedside lamp and she saw the bed had been turned down. The wrinkles she had made in the coverlet during her nap earlier had been smoothed, and all the little rose-shaped throw pillows had been stacked in the bedside chair, but otherwise Cally was gratified to see everything else was as she had left it.

She was an insomniac at the best of times, but after such an eventful evening, and because of her nap earlier, she knew it would be pointless to get into bed just yet. She sat down at the desk and took her laptop from the drawer, telling herself she might get started compiling some of the stories she'd heard that day, maybe make them into organized research notes. When she powered the computer up, though, she saw the chat icon was illuminated. She smiled at this, abandoning all thought of work, and clicked the icon to accept the chat.

The avatar Emerald always used, a cartoon image of a fairy dressed in purple, appeared on the screen with the first line of chat already beside it.

Emerald<< Having fun yet?

Cally>> Loads!

Emerald<< How do you like the place?

Cally>> It's beautiful. Everyone is great. Well, almost everyone.

Emerald<< Ah, so you've met Joan?

Cally>> LOL

Emerald<< And who else have you met?

Cally>> I've met Ian May. He gave me an interview this afternoon. He's lovely. Also met his daughter and son-in-law.

Emerald<< Is Bethany still there?

Cally>> She is. She's sweet. And Ignacio and Katarina, and the Captain.

> **Emerald<<** I remember the Captain. Listen to him - he has the best stories.
>
> **Cally>>** I have an appointment to interview him at lunchtime tomorrow.
>
> **Emerald<<** If he's awake. He should be getting on in years by now!
>
> **Cally>>** He is, but he still seems pretty spry. Oh, I also met your friend George.
>
> **Emerald<<** You've met Georgie! Excellent. Yes, very good!
>
> **Cally>>** All the ghost stories seem to be pretty standard fare so far, though.
>
> **Emerald<<** How about you? Heard any Mysterious Footsteps, yet?
>
> **Cally>>** Well, things have been moved around in my room. Does that count?
>
> **Emerald<<** ?!
>
> **Cally>>** Oh nothing has been taken, or anything like that. Only rearranged. I'm sure whoever it is thinks they're being helpful. Might be George.
>
> **Emerald<<** I don't think Georgie could do that. You should mention it to Bethany, if it bothers you.
>
> **Cally>>** I might.
>
> **Emerald<<** Maybe it's your first real ghost!
>
> **Cally>>** LOL yeah right ☺

They chatted for the better part of an hour about this most recent big change in Cally's life, even though Emerald already knew most of the details, as she had helped Cally plan them. Cally had "met" Emerald years ago by way of an internet listserv. The topic might have been Celtic Folklore or something similarly nerdy, but neither could really remember anymore. They had kept up their correspondence long after listservs had disappeared from the internet, and they still used outdated text chat applications to keep up their correspondence, partly because that was what they were used to, but mostly because neither of them had a computer new enough to support video chat. Emerald had been a source of strength and comfort when Cally was coping with her crumbling marriage, and it had been Emerald who had suggested Vale House to Cally when she had despaired of ever being able to break her writer's block.

The two of them had talked many times about finding a way to meet "in real life," but had not yet contrived to do so. They had each also talked about getting better computers so they could at least use modern video chat technology, but that would have to wait until Cally had an income again. For now it was enough, Cally thought, to just have someone she could let down her guard and be herself with, especially when the rest of life seemed so uncertain.

Emerald<< OK well it's going on 2:AM now where you are. You should get some sleep.

Cally>> I will try. Hope I'll be able to wake up in time for breakfast. I want to go back into town tomorrow and try to interview some of the locals.

Emerald<< The lady who runs the coffee shop knows a lot of good stories. I've chatted with her a few times. They say she serves very good coffee.

Cally>> Well that's important! Maybe I'll go back to that News Store, too.

Emerald<< Yes, Ben Dawes is a real hottie, isn't he? At least, he was last time I saw him.

Cally>> That's not what I meant! You know I am over men. Completely. Forever.

Emerald<< LOL sure, if you say so. ☺ Hey, while you're in town, you should also check out the bookstore.

Cally>> Oh, there's a bookstore! Great!

Emerald<< The two chicks running it are a hoot.
   You'll get a kick out of them.

Cally>> Really, Em, chicks?

Emerald<< You'll see what I mean! Goodnight.

Cally closed the laptop and turned off the lamp on the night stand, slipping under the rose-covered comforter. For the most part, she failed to follow Emerald's advice to get some sleep. This was completely normal for her, but the voices of people talking on the porch, and the sound of footsteps passing slowly by outside her door, didn't help.

"Well," she told herself, "you did want to stay in an authentic haunted house with authentic ghosts, didn't you?" She got up and opened her door. It was at this point in a good ghost story, she knew, she should see a lady in white wafting down the hall, gowns a-flowing, perhaps holding a candle, though what she really expected to see was the Iversons making their way at last to bed, or maybe Nell or Foster. When she peered out into the hallway, though, all she saw was the old gray cat sitting next to the lamp on the butler's desk.

She laughed and went back to bed and did her best to get some sleep. Eventually she dreamed a Lady In White was standing at the foot of her bed, gazing at her with a sorrow so deep it almost made her weep in her sleep.

When she awoke in the morning, she only saw the gray tom cat sitting on the rose-covered coverlet, glowering at her as if she had neglected to give it its breakfast.

11 - Walking in Woodley

The rose-faced clock told Cally she needed to hurry if she wanted to be in time for breakfast. She shooed the cat back out the window onto the belvedere. "However you got up here, you can just find your own way back down again," she told it. She pulled the casement window closed enough that the cat – probably – couldn't slip back in again.

The view outside the window now included two of the horses, the black and chestnut ones, running over the horizon in the morning sun. The sky was bright blue and utterly cloudless, and the previous night's rain had freshened the meadow to a brilliant green. Ignacio came into view, walking along the fence and whistling an old Beatles tune as he carried an armload of gardening tools toward the barn.

Cally threw her nightgown on the bed and dug through the suitcase still open on the luggage rack, pulling out a deeply creased sundress. She told herself she should put her clothes away in the dresser and closet, since she would be staying for a while, especially if she started writing soon. She wasn't sure why she was reluctant to get too comfortable here. Looking out the window, down into the yard at her little car packed with boxes, she felt as if Joan were standing right beside her, pointing a red-nailed finger and accusing her of being some kind of charlatan, one of Ian's "freeloaders and hangers-on" who were never going to leave because they had no place else to go.

Well, she would certainly be able to pay her bill for a few more weeks, at least, she thought, and hung up a couple of dresses in the closet.

Stuffing her notebook into her purse, she opened the door to see young George smiling there with his back to the Gallery railing. He was dressed smartly in a linen shirt and black trousers. His hair today was done in sleek corn-rows which swept back over his head and hung nearly to his collar. "Miss Bethany has served breakfast on the porch today," he informed Cally.

"Oh, that sounds lovely." She stepped past him into the hall. "Do you need me to leave the door unlocked for you?" she asked, assuming he was there to change the linens and towels.

"No, thank you." He shifted slightly as Cally shut and locked the door, but he continued smiling at her. "I am just making sure you're happy here."

"Everything's fine," Cally assured him. She went down the stairs and found Ian May standing in front of the desk. He was surveying a row of papers which had been spread out upon it, each with a sticky note attached reading "Ian please sign here."

He looked up as Cally reached the bottom step. "Ms. McCarthy, I trust you slept well?"

"Once I did get to sleep, yes, I did. The Rose Room is very comfortable. And please, call me Cally."

Bethany came into the Hall from the porch. She was carrying a pot of coffee in one hand and a platter of pastries in the other. "Good morning!" she greeted them. "Breakfast is on the porch this morning. I thought we'd take advantage of this lovely fresh air the storm has brought us. Come, let me introduce you to the Iversons." She started out the door, then turned back and looked at Ian. "Please remember to sign those things," she said to him. "They're due this week!"

"I promise, I will. But for now..." He picked a napkin off the tray Bethany was carrying and wrapped a Danish in it. "I think I'll just take this back to my rooms with me." Then, grinning, he also picked up a muffin. "I have some reading I need to catch up on," he said by way of explanation.

Bethany shook her head as he made his way toward the back hall. "God love him," she said. "He always does that."

Cally followed Bethany out to the porch, where small tables had been set up next to the wicker chairs. Katarina was taking up empty plates from in front of an older couple seated there. The Captain was also seated in one of the wicker chairs, but he held only a cup of coffee in his lap, and appeared to be dozing in the sunlight slanting in from the meadow.

Bethany refilled everyone's coffee cups, except the Captain's, while she introduced Cally to the Iversons. Mr. Iverson was an older gentleman with golden curls and a white beard, and was definitely not the preacher Cally had encountered the day before. Mrs. Iverson ("Please, call me Celeste!") was delighted to meet Cally, as she was her Biggest Fan. "How exciting it must have been to live in a house with so many ghosts!" she said. "Oh, I know most of them were not very nice ones, but just the thought that there is more to this life than science can explain, it gives you hope, doesn't it?"

Cally gave the very pleasant woman her usual ambiguous reply, and gave herself a mental pat on the back for successfully stopping herself from saying "Hope is overrated." She thanked Celeste Iverson for her kind compliments, and made herself a breakfast sandwich from the sausage and brown bread Katarina set on the little wicker table between them. "Please, no coffee," she said, putting her hand over her cup. "I thought I'd go in to town today and visit the coffee shop, and I don't want to be up all night again."

"Oh, you'll love the Bean Garden!" Katarina assured her. "Won't she?"

"You will!" agreed Mr. Iverson. "They have local artwork displayed on the walls. And the proprietor is a lovely woman."

"She is!" his wife agreed. "And while you're in town be sure to stop in at the Wyrd Systers book store. Those two young ladies have an amazing knowledge of the spiritual world. I'm sure they'll be thrilled to meet you. Raven might even give you a free reading!"

"I'll see if I have time..."

Nell came out onto the porch, then, but she didn't join them for breakfast. "Foster and I have business in Blackthorn today," she said, sitting down on the front steps instead. "We'll have to get fast food on our way."

Katarina gave her a sad look and went into the house. Nell waited patiently for Foster, extending a hand toward the cats sitting on the steps with her. The skittish little calico crept closer to Nell and allowed herself to be petted, but the gray tom, who had apparently found his way down from the belvedere, just gazed quietly at Nell as he dozed off in the sunshine.

The Iversons excused themselves and departed for their excursion to Coppersmith where, Mrs. Iverson explained, there was a railroad museum of interest to her husband, which she was willing to endure for his sake, even though it was not haunted, or was it? Bethany carried the rest of their things inside, and Cally picked up her plate and went to sit on the step beside Nell.

"I'm fine," Nell said, as if Cally had already asked how she was feeling this morning. "I slept right through the storm."

Cally hoped that was true, and the two women watched together as two horses ran back from where they had been cavorting in the meadow and dropped their heads near the fence to graze. As they did so, a third horse – the white member of the trio – came running from the field beyond the pond and, leaping in mid-stride, sailed straight over the fence to join them. Nell laughed and shook her head at this. "She's a mess!" she declared.

"Do the horses belong to you and your father?" Cally asked.

"I don't think they belong to anyone," Nell said. "But they sure do love that meadow. They come to it almost every day. It's not our meadow," she added, answering the next question on Cally's mind before she asked it. "It kind of belongs to everyone around here."

Cally cast a quick glance over her shoulder at the front door to make sure Nell's husband wasn't there before asking, "Do you think you'll have time later to tell me your ghost stories?"

"Oh," Nell didn't look at her. "Maybe I shouldn't. Foster says it's not good for me to keep on about those kinds of things. He says I don't want to end up in the hospital like my mother did."

"I'm so sorry..." Cally backpedaled quickly to get out of the murky waters into which she had inadvertently stumbled. "Sorry, Nell, I didn't mean to pressure you." She tried to think of a way to change the subject, and her eyes fell on the cats.

"This one is Cyndi Lauper," said Nell, also welcoming the change of subject. She scratched the little calico under the chin, and it purred and arched its back against her hand. "She's mine, but she lives here with Dad because Foster is allergic. That's Doctor Boojums." She nodded toward the gray cat. "He used to belong to Bethany, but he lives here now, too. You can call him Boo, for short."

The screen door opened behind them and Bethany came back

out onto the porch. Instead of a coffee pot, this time, she was carrying her purse and a thick brown envelope. "I have to make a quick run into town for Ian," she said to Cally. "Would you like a lift?"

"Oh, no, I really think it would be nice to walk, this morning," Cally said honestly. "But thank you just the same."

As they watched Bethany's car leave the parking lot, Nell told Cally, "I have a painting for sale in the coffee shop. It's a view of this meadow. I painted it while sitting right here on this step."

"I didn't know you painted," said Cally. "That's wonderful. Everyone should do what they love. I'll be sure to look for it while I'm there."

Foster burst out of the house, then. "Time to go!" he called briskly to Nell, letting the screen door bang shut and causing the cats to scatter into the shrubbery. "Would you like a lift into town?" he asked Cally, and she repeated her wish to walk instead. Nell smiled and waved at her and followed Foster to the car. Cally decided she should stop talking about walking, and start doing it.

Instead of going out through the parking lot and the main gate, she turned the corner around the south side of Vale House and followed a gravel path through the wild-looking shade garden between the house and the line of oaks along Main Street. Here, the thick canopy overhead rang with a joyful racket of songbirds. The path wound through plantings of ferns and vinca and led her past Vale House's small side porch, so overgrown with rhododendrons and Virginia creeper Cally might not have noticed it at all but for the bright red cardinal in the middle of its stained glass window. Beyond it, the south wing of the house extended into the little green lawn with its gazebo, which Cally had glimpsed from the dining room the evening before. She could see a dozen chickens scratching busily for early worms around the doorstep of the little stone cottage.

The shade garden ended at a low gate through the hedge. It was made of the same white-painted wood as the gazebo, and Cally had only to pass through this to find herself standing on the sidewalk in the shaded residential portion of Woodley's Main Street.

It seemed that, as she walked toward downtown, people in almost every house were just then coming out onto their porches to take their dogs for walks or to let their cats come out to sit on the railings. Each one of them waved to Cally, and she began to realize they were all curious about the newcomer, the so-called celebrity in their midst. Nobody attempted to speak to her beyond "Good Morning," though, so she relaxed and waved back with a smile each time. She looked at all the cats getting comfortable on their porch railings, and thought she would like to someday have a porch with a railing and a cat to sit on it. Her former husband had never been willing to consider having a pet.

The sun was already growing hot, shimmering on the concrete by the time she stepped out from under the trees and entered the town proper. The storm the night before had swept away some of the humidity, but Cally could already feel it beginning to return – an unavoidable fact of life in the south, she had been warned by her daughter when she'd first spoken of coming here. As she passed the feed store, its proprietor came out onto his loading dock and touched the brim of his baseball cap to her, saying "Morning, Ms. McCarthy. Gonna be a hot one."

Cally recognized the little Dawes News Store across the street, and decided she should buy a newspaper to take with her to the coffee shop. She crossed the street and tugged on the stubborn door until it opened.

Ben was nowhere to be seen at the moment. Cally convinced herself she was not at all disappointed about this as she selected a local newspaper and a magazine. The old woman at the register, however, was not fooled.

"He won't be here today," she said without looking up as Cally handed her purchases to her.

Cally ignored this. "How good is the coffee at the coffee shop?" she asked.

"Wouldn't know. Overpriced gimmick, if you ask me. Folks seem to buy a lot of it, though. You can have some of this boring old ordinary coffee if you want."

"Thanks," said Cally, pocketing her change. "But I thought it would be nice to get to know the local businesses, while I'm here. How do I get there?"

"It's on this same side of the street," Bree said. "Just keep going. You can't miss it. You can't miss much of anything in this town." Then she gave Cally an impish grin. "While you're at it, you should check out the Wacky Sisters book shop, too. Might get some real inspiration there. Apparently they Know All!" She waggled her fingers in the air and made "woo woo" sounds as Cally kicked the bottom of the door to leave.

The owner of the feed store was sitting in a lawn chair on his loading dock, reading a newspaper of his own, when Cally emerged back onto the street. The proprietor of the hardware store next door to him came out of his store at the same time. "Morning Merv. Morning Ms. McCarthy. Looks like it's gonna be a hot one." He flipped the sign on his door to read "open" and went back inside without waiting for a reply. Cally wondered if all the stereotypes about small towns were true, after all, but she was surprised to realize that she was smiling even as she shook her head.

12 - Coffee and Books

She kept on, as Bree had instructed, walking down the street past an appliance repair shop that did not appear to be open, and a storefront advertising custom wallpaper and carpet installation. Every third or fourth storefront appeared to be vacant.

Railroad Street intersected Main Street a few doors down from the news store, and as she crossed it Cally spotted Bethany's car parked in front of a door labeled "Johnston and Reid, Law Offices - Faxes and Photocopies $1 each." A few more shops faced Main Street on the other side of this intersection, and Cally caught the rich fragrance of good coffee wafting from an open doorway. Above this door hung a wooden sign carved in the shape of a coffee cup, painted steam above it spelling out "The Bean Garden."

The inside of The Bean Garden reminded Cally of the news store, all wooden counters and floors, except that the floors here gleamed with a dark polish. Paintings of varying genres and skill levels, as well as painted t-shirts and other art objects, hung on the walls with prices written on index cards taped next to them. Cally spotted the painting that had to be Nell's. It was a somewhat impressionistic rendering of the meadow in front of Vale House, showing the three horses standing peacefully knee-deep in wildflowers, only in Nell's interpretation, the horses all bore spiral horns on their foreheads. "Our Nell certainly has some talent," Cally thought.

A couple was seated at one of the small, square tables, both of them bent over and thoroughly engaged in whatever was on the screens of their phones. Three young people stood at the counter, giggling and poking straws into brightly colored drinks in plastic cups. Cally recognized one of them as the girl she had met on the road when she had been so desperately trying to find Woodley in the darkness.

"Hello, Errin," she said. "I'm glad to see you made it home alright the other night." She refrained from mentioning the girl's sudden departure or lack of a proper thank-you for the lift. "Did you ever catch your horse?"

Errin took a quick sip of her bright pink drink. "Oh, yes, she's fine!" she said. Errin and the other girl (a blonde with incredibly large, blue eyes) looked at one another and giggled at some private joke. Their companion was a dark-eyed boy with an enviable head of long, black curls. He muttered something and looked impatiently at them.

"These are my friends, Mima and Zenbe," Errin said. "We have to go. Thanks again for all your help. Really! Bye!" The trio collected their drinks and went out the door, the girls giggling and the boy telling them to stop being rude.

"Shouldn't those three be in school?" Cally wondered aloud as a black woman about her age approached her from the other side of the counter.

"They say they're home-schooled," said the woman, "though I'm not sure what they're learning by buying fruit smoothies. It's just nice to see young people who think this town is worth hanging out in, I guess."

She reached around the espresso machine and shook Cally's hand. "I'm Andi," she said. "And if I'm not mistaken, you're our celebrity visitor, Callaghan McCarthy." The woman's accent was more familiar to Cally than the soft southern one she had been hearing since arriving in Woodley. She guessed Andi was also "not from around here," and felt a reassuring sort of kinship with her because of this.

She grinned and looked around behind herself. "Where?" she asked. "Where is this celebrity everyone keeps talking about?"

Andi laughed. "What can I get for you, Ms. McCarthy?"

"You can start by calling me Cally." She looked at the chalkboard menu above the back bar. "It smells wonderful in here – I can already tell the coffee is good."

Andi rattled off a list of the organic, free-trade artisanal coffee suppliers she used exclusively, and offered to make Cally the best latte she'd ever had in her life (with organic milk from local pasture-raised cows.)

"You know, I think maybe just a regular coffee, please," Cally said.

"Any flavorings? Whipped cream?"

"Let's just go with coffee-flavored coffee, for now." Cally set her purse down next to the register beside a small sign that proclaimed "Free WiFi!". "If I had known you had WiFi, I would have brought my laptop," she said.

"Well, bring your lappy next time," Andi said, filling a deep white mug from a huge, gleaming coffee machine that had more buttons and gauges than the dashboard of Cally's car. "You can write your next bestseller in here, and I can brag about it. Here..." She handed Cally a small card with a hole punched in it. "Buy ten get one free."

Cally put her change in the tip jar and the card in her purse. She sat down at one of the tables facing the open door and gazed out at the view it afforded. The wide windows allowed her to see across Main Street to the north end of Railroad Street, which ran gently downhill to where it crossed the railroad track for which it was named. Cally turned to Andi, who was polishing the already gleaming espresso machine. "Is that the famous haunted railroad crossing?" she asked.

"You've heard that story?" Andi asked.

"Well, no. But every town needs a haunted railroad crossing. Generally they have a light that moves along the track as the engineer searches for his missing head, or ghost children who push stalled cars out of the way."

"Well then ours is even better," said Andi. "It has disembodied screams in the night. Only on Tuesdays, though."

"Oh, that *is* unique." Cally opened her notepad and pulled her pen out of the spring binding to scribble a brief description of this version of the story.

Andi resumed polishing the espresso machine. "On the other side of the railroad tracks, Railroad Street becomes Bells Road. People who live along that road tell a story, too, about hearing wild laughter in the trees on summer nights."

"That's interesting," said Cally. "I haven't seen that one yet on the internet."

"People who've grown up here don't really seem to realize there's anything unusual about these things." Andi laughed. "But, I'm Not From Around Here, as you can probably tell!"

When Cally laughed and nodded at this, Andi continued. "When I first got here, this town kind of weirded me out. But I got used to it. Well, okay, I can't say I ever actually got used to it, but I have grown to love it, over the years. And I've heard a lot of stories, if you want to hear them."

Cally said she did want to hear them, so Andi told her the one about mysterious lights seen over the fields every several years, and another about a banshee said to haunt certain crossroads, even though most of the roads involved had reverted back to woods and fields many years ago. Cally was impressed – the stories were not the usual hackneyed creepypasta often repeated on the internet, and the way Andi told them in her friendly, laughing voice put Cally at ease.

Best of all, she did not seem to expect Cally to believe any of it. "There are a lot of things about Woodley I will probably never understand," Andi said, "but fortunately that doesn't seem to be a requirement for living here."

The couple at the other table got up and left the shop, never once looking up from their phones, and a young man in a pizza delivery hat came in and asked Andi to make him a strawberry chai.

"Here you go, Luke," Andi said as she got up to make it for him. "Tell this lady about the hitchhiker out by the highway. She's Callaghan McCarthy; she writes ghost stories. Cally, Jake Lucas – we just call him Luke – makes great pizza and keeps my WiFi working most of the time."

While he waited for his chai, Luke started to tell Cally about his own personal encounter with a phantom hitchhiker who disappeared as soon as he stopped the car. Cally said, "Oh, I think I met that one! Was it a red-haired girl in a white sweater?"

"It was a man," said Luke. "He wore an old-fashioned pantsuit, like they used to wear in the seventies. It was white, though."

"I wonder why they are always dressed in white?" Cally mused. "So they don't get run over in the dark, I suppose." She decided she was actually starting to enjoy this role-reversal, asking others about their belief in ghosts, instead of having her own beliefs dissected. She hoped she was being more courteous than those who had used to ask her.

Luke wished them both a good day and left, and before Andi could go back to polishing the espresso machine, Cally said, "What about you, though, Andi? Do you feel you have ever seen any of these spirits or things, yourself?"

Andi spread her cleaning rag out on the counter in front of her, smoothed it with her hands and folded it into a small, neat square. Then, seeming to make up her mind she shook it out and stuffed it into the pocket of her smock. She brought her own coffee mug around the counter and sat down at the table across from Cally.

"Well," she said, "this building does have its own history. It was once a dress shop, back when Woodley was a bustling young town. It was a big deal, back in the day. Anyway the upstairs of most of these shops was once also the living quarters of the proprietors. Sometimes I think the owner of the dress shop is still living up there." She pointed at the ceiling.

"And what makes you think that?"

Andi laughed. "Now you sound like a shrink!" Then she leaned across the table and spoke in hushed tones, as if there might still be other customers still in the shop, lingering over their phones and lattes. "OK, it was a couple of years ago. My youngest had just gone off to college. Kids in this town, you know, they don't stay around. It's so small, and at their age that's not charming, it's boring. And I was really proud of him, of course, but still, I was sad he was all grown and gone. You know what I mean?"

Cally did. "My youngest just graduated. I went through all the same things." She was going to add "plus a divorce," but she didn't want to try to out-martyr Andi, who hadn't said anything, herself, come to think of it, about a husband.

Andi nodded. "Well, one day I was just feeling so blue. I couldn't get anything done. Good thing it was a slow day. Anyway, I just sat down, right here at this very table, and stared out the door. I couldn't even cry." She sighed and looked over Cally's shoulder. "And, I don't know if it was real or not. There was this smell of flowers. Roses, like the kind of perfume our grandmothers used to wear, back when roses still had a smell. And I felt someone put their arms around me." She hugged herself gently and closed her eyes. "It was like they were just standing behind my chair with their arms around me, not saying anything, like a good friend would do. I broke down and cried my eyes out. And I felt much better after that."

Cally had a tear in her own eye, and found that she had reached across the table and laid her hands on Andi's. "That's a wonderful story," she said. "Thank you for sharing it." It occurred to her that if more ghost stories were like that, she might not be so inclined to roll her eyes at them.

Andi stood up. "If you put that in your book," she said, "please don't mention my shop. Don't want to scare business away!"

Cally drained her coffee mug. "I promise. Though Joan up at Vale House might advise you it would attract more business."

Andi scowled. "Oh, *that woman!*" She wiped vigorously at the spotless counter. "I think one thing that would attract more business to Ian's place would be to send her packing!"

Cally didn't agree out loud, but she grinned. "It was nice talking with you, Andi. I'll be back. Maybe I'll remember my computer next time. Thanks for everything."

She still had plenty of time left before her meeting with the Captain, so she decided to take Celeste and Bree's advice and look for the book store. She had learned, over the past few years, that it paid for authors to be on good terms with book store owners.

Turning left as she stepped out the door of the Bean Garden, she saw there was only one block left before Main Street ended and disappeared into the woods on its way back to the interstate. She imagined it would take a person on foot only a few minutes to make the entire circuit of Woodley's business district.

It certainly didn't take long to reach the book store, which was the last storefront on this side of the street before the sidewalk ended. It was just far enough away that the smell of coffee didn't conflict with the smell of incense coming from its own open door. The psychedelic hand-lettering on the glass door was backwards from Cally's viewpoint, but, squinting, she thought she could make out "Wyrd Systers Books and Gifts."

As she paused in front of the open doorway, she got the impression this was not at all the kind of book store she had been expecting. Instead of the latest bestsellers, the deep display windows beside the door showcased dream-catchers and boxes of tarot cards in many styles. Cally had a sinking feeling she knew exactly what was about to happen next, but it was too late to turn away; the woman behind the counter had spotted her.

"Oh, my Goddess!" called the tall blonde in a tie-dyed caftan. "Willow, it's what's her name, McCallahan, that author!"

Another woman, very short with a halo of curls dyed bluish black, stepped down from the chair she had been standing on to hang crystals above the cash register. "Well, blessed be," she said, crossing the store to shake Cally's hand. "Merry meet, Callaghan McCarthy. I'm Cindy Lucas, but everyone calls me Willow. And this is Jackie Forest," she said, indicating the tall blonde who had come around the counter to join them. Jackie Forest placed her fingertips together and touched the bridge of her nose. "Namaste," she said, bowing. "Call me Raven."

"Um, call me Cally," said Cally, certain she would not remember their names, especially since they each seemed to have the wrong one. They were both probably in their mid-twenties, but they spoke in high-pitched voices like school girls as they grinned at her, saying "Come in, come in!"

"Everyone is so excited that you're in town!" said the shorter woman. ("She calls herself Willow," Cally struggled to remember.) "We have a whole stack of your book for sale over by the summoning supplies. Maybe you could autograph them for us!"

"Cut her some slack," said the tall blonde called Raven. "I'm sure everyone has been all over her like a pack of puppies since she arrived."

"Everyone has been very nice." Cally said, but she smiled at the thought of a pack of puppies. She pretended to be interested in a sign that read "All hand-crafted greeting cards 20% off - Locally made!" Cally thought she could guess by whom.

"We try very hard to source local materials and talent," said Willow. "We discovered this little town a few years ago, and we fell in love with it. We both strongly believe America needs more places like this, and we really want to help Woodley achieve a stable economy. That's why we decided to set up our business here. Well, and it also sits on top of several very strong ley lines, so we know we've chosen the right place, if you know what I mean. Do you practice Wicca?"

"Uh, no," Cally floundered, trying to keep up. "I don't really practice anything..."

Raven rushed to explain. "It's alright – we support all paths. No one will ever find any judgment here. In the end, everything is love!"

Cally told them she had to agree with that. She looked around to see if there were any actual books in this book store, but amid displays of incense burners shaped like Egyptian gods, hand-held musical instruments, and "genuine" hand-embroidered silk scarves, she saw only a few books for sale. Most of them had to do with holistic healing or vegan recipes.

"We just thought that what with, you know, the subject matter of your writing, you would know a lot about the spirit world."

Cally smiled and focused on the crystals hanging above the register, trying to change the subject. "Those are interesting," she said. On closer inspection she could see they were actually necklaces, in myriad colors, each with beads and feathers complementing their central crystals.

The short woman Cally thought was named Willow selected one and took it down to show it more closely to her. "This one is crafted to enhance creativity," she explained. "The citrine opens the mind to new thoughts, and chalcedony facilitates communication. They are clustered around a smoky quartz crystal to help you access your subconscious energies. I think it's calling to you."

Cally thought it was a pretty piece of wearable art, but she said, "Oh, I have never been much for wearing jewelry."

"But you should!" Willow exclaimed. "You are so pretty!" She held the necklace against Cally's shirt. "And look, it matches your aura." She turned to get Raven's opinion and said, "I think we should give it to her for half off!"

"Actually," said Cally, "I am more in the market for something to send to my kids." She moved toward the rack of hand-made greeting cards, and the two women's faces fell.

"We also have a very nice deck of spirit communication cards," Raven offered. "They might help you connect with the spirits at Vale

House." She opened the box of cards and fanned them out for Cally, who had to admit that the artwork on the cards was truly extraordinary. One of them depicted a beautiful woman carrying two torches through a storm, with a pack of puppies at her feet. "Well, dogs, not puppies," Cally thought, but the image still made her smile.

"I understand there are quite a lot of spirits up at Vale House," Raven said.

"So I've been told."

"Have you interacted with any of them yet?"

"Not so far." Cally began maneuvering toward the door.

Raven cocked her head and looked at Cally through one eye. "I don't think that's true," she said. "I think you've met several of them already. In fact..." She went behind the counter and reached for something below it. "I think you've met many spirits throughout your lifetime, haven't you? Would you like a reading?" she concluded, drawing out a battered Tarot deck. "No charge!"

"Not today, thank you," Cally said. "I have an appointment to interview someone in a little while, and I shouldn't be late." Thankful to the Captain already for his promised tale, she backed toward the door. "It was very nice meeting you. I'll come again when I have more time."

13 - The Captain's Story

Cally got back to Vale House well before noon and stopped at her car to say hello to her belongings, promising them she hadn't forgotten them. She was concerned about her CD collection, currently in a plastic milk crate on the floor of the passenger side of the car; she feared the CDs would be ruined if she continued to keep them in a car in the hot sun. Her daughter had helped load most of her favorite songs (as well as quite a few of Kelleigh's own choosing) onto her MP3 player, but she still cherished the physical CDs. She had built her collection with the sudden flush of money from the publication of her book – it had been one of the first things she had ever done just for herself. She picked the crate up off the floor and tucked it under her arm before heading into the house.

She found Bethany and Katarina sitting on the porch steps, shelling peas into a colander. The fat gray cat sat next to them, basking in the sun and dozing with what was the closest thing a cat could have to a smile on its face. "Ms. McCarthy!" Bethany said cheerily, "I've left some cold cuts on the sideboard in case you want to make yourself a sandwich."

Cally didn't want a sandwich. She thought she'd use the time before her meeting with the Captain to unpack her suitcases and put a few things away. When she unlocked the Rose Room door, though, she found the suitcases were not where she'd left them. Setting the crate of CDs down on the desk, she let out a long, exasperated sigh and strode to the closet, flinging open the door. There her suitcases stood, side by side under her neatly hung clothes – all of them. Her shoes were lined up on the closet floor, and her slippers, she saw as she turned around, just peeked out from under the rose-patterned bed ruffle.

Yanking open the dresser drawers, she found her underthings folded and neatly arranged on the rose-scented drawer liners. Someone had even attempted to arrange all of her mismatched socks into matching pairs. "Now that is going just too far!" she said out loud. She switched the lingerie to the other side of the drawer, disarranging the neat stacks, and picked up all her socks in two hands, being sure to mix them well as she let them fall back in to the drawer in a pile. Then she slammed the drawer shut and stormed out of the room without locking it ("Why bother?" she thought.)

By the time she had got down the stairs and to the front door, she had calmed down a little. She took a deep breath and pushed the screen door open. "Bethany, may I speak to you for a minute?"

"Of course!" Bethany's warm smile did not change Cally's determination to be firm.

Bethany left Katarina to the peas and came back inside the Hall. "I appreciate how nice everyone is being to me here," Cally said as gently as she could. "But please can you ask that nobody touch my personal things when they go in to tend my room? In fact, I can make my own bed, if that would help. It's just that..."

"Oh, Ms. McCarthy!" Bethany looked truly upset. "I assure you, we have a strict policy here of never touching our guests' belongings! I made up your room myself today and I left everything as it was, well, except for your nightgown on the bed, which I tucked under your pillow when I straightened out the coverlet. I hope I didn't offend you?"

"Oh, no, no, of course not," Cally assured her. "Of course, that's fine. But... someone unpacked my suitcases and put everything away and – well that was thoughtful of them but – you understand. I could have had valuables in those suitcases... not that anyone here would, of course..." She faltered, seeing Bethany's face grow increasingly alarmed at what she was saying.

"I will certainly find out who did that!" Bethany said firmly, crossing her arms. She looked even more outraged than Cally felt. "That was completely unacceptable! I will see that it does not happen again." She glanced darkly at Joan's closed office door.

Cally followed her gaze, but somehow she couldn't picture Joan performing that kind of "customer service" with her own hands, though she may have ordered someone else on the staff to do it.

"Really, I didn't mean to get anyone into trouble," she said. "Everyone here is lovely, and I can't picture Katarina or George doing anything dishonest. Maybe I'm just too sensitive because my mother used to do that sort of thing when I was a kid, and it really drove me nuts."

Bethany's face softened and she laughed. Then she frowned. "George? I think... Oh, I see. Ms. McCarthy... I think you should know, Georgie isn't really there..."

She was interrupted by a rapping at the screen door. The Captain stood outside it, grinning and tapping the doorframe with the handle of his cane. "Hellooo," he called cheerily. "I believe there is a lovely young lady here who wants to chat with me?"

Both women smiled and turned to help him come inside, but he said, "Let's sit out here," and turned away, back toward the wicker chairs beside the door. Cally put a reassuring hand on Bethany's arm and said, "Thank you for understanding."

She went out to join the Captain. As they sat down, Katarina appeared as if by magic with a tray of cookies and two glasses of tea, which she placed on the small table between the chairs. "I hope you put a little whiskey in that," the Captain said, settling himself stiffly into one of the chairs. Cally hoped she hadn't.

She felt awkward, because she hadn't brought her notebook down with her in her haste, and she didn't want to make the Captain wait for her to go back and get it. Then she remembered her phone was still in her pocket, and decided to use it to record the old man's story. She set it on the arm of her chair and thanked the Captain for agreeing to be interviewed. He assured her that any day he could talk to a beautiful young lady was a good day, in his books.

There was no whiskey in the tea – anyway, there was none in Cally's. The Captain did not complain about his.

"Well!" he began. "This place is just *full* of spirits!" He spread his arms toward meadow and the grounds of Vale House.

"I've lived here all my life. Not here, in this house, mind. But in this town. I grew up right over there on Gardens Road, in the Yellow House, in full view of the meadow." He said "the Yellow House" as if that was its name, just as Vale House had a name. He pointed past the end of the porch and Cally could see, a few doors down Gardens Road on the other side of Main Street, a glimpse of yellow siding and the front porch of the house he meant. "That house had its own share of ghosts. My sisters and I..."

Katarina quietly excused herself, collected the colander of peas from the porch step, and went into the house. Across the parking lot, the horses came running in from a distant part of the meadow and stood near the fence, twitching their ears and jostling each other just like children trying to settle down to listen to a story.

"Back when my family owned the Yellow House, we always had at least three generations living there. I was part of the last generation of kids who slept in the attic. All us cousins shared the attic as our bedroom. Oh, it was hot up there in the summer, and cold in the winter, but it was wonderful! We could get away with anything. It was one big, open space, with the girls at one end and the boys at the other, and a big room down the middle with those great, round windows on either side. You could watch the moon set in the west window and then see the sun rise in the east window. And we often did! We would stay up late on summer nights and the grownups downstairs wouldn't hear us. We'd bring up puppies and goat kids from the barn..." He paused, eyes twinkling as he laughed silently at old memories. "But, it wasn't always fun and games," he said, growing serious. "Part of the reason we didn't sleep so soundly was because sometimes we were scared. Sometimes we'd see... things. Hanging from the rafters, from the big beam that ran down the middle of the attic from gable to gable.

"Yah I know what you're going to say. Every old house has at least one legend of someone who hanged themself in the attic. But we saw them – and it was always more than one of us who saw it, so it wasn't dreams. Long, white shapes swaying in the breeze, only there wasn't any breeze in that stuffy attic. And there was never just one shape hanging there. There would be three, or four. Or more. When I got older, I tried to find out if that house had maybe once been a courthouse. Because, you know, that's where they carried out hangings, in those days, right in the courthouses. But it's not likely. The architecture isn't right for a government building, and anyway the old courthouse is in the center of town. It's our post-office, now.

"But anyway that's not the strangest thing. Some other times, we saw... something else." He gazed out across the meadow, past the horses, to the horizon.

"We would be looking out the window, and this was always on a summer night, and we would see, far out across the field, we would see a fire. Like a camp fire someone had started out there for some reason. And we'd see other little lights around it, like people standing around the fire holding torches. The little lights would go up to the fire and then fly into it. Like someone was throwing them. I mean, we never saw any people holding torches or throwing them. It was too dark and far off. This is just what we were guessing based on what the lights were doing. So anyway these little burning brands would be added to the fire, and it would get bigger and bigger. And it would get closer. Or so it seemed to us. It was like we were looking through binoculars. It would get bigger and closer until we could see that it was actually a tree. A huge tree, gigantic, and burning like a torch, only not burning, you know what I mean? The branches and leaves had yellow and gold light running all along them, but it wasn't fire and it didn't burn up the leaves or branches.

"Once it got so close it was almost like daylight in the attic. My sisters and I and our cousin Merv ran downstairs to tell the grownups. They were all awake, for some reason, but they weren't out on the porch watching this spectacle, like you would think. They were all in the back parlor, sitting and talking quietly, like they were holding a Bible study or something. And when we ran in and tried to tell them to look outside, and all about what we were seeing, they all just gave us those patient looks you give to silly children and said, 'You're just having a bad dream. It's what comes of staying awake too late. Go back to bed and this time go to sleep.'

"We tried to protest but they just shooed us away. We went back upstairs and looked out the window but the tree and the fire was gone, like we knew it would be. That's how it always went.

"And next day the younger kids would run out to the meadow to look for scorch marks or a burned stump, but there was never anything. And anyway there has never been a tree in that field, not as far as the eye can see or as far as kids can walk in a day, and that's pretty far. So there's that."

Cally shut her mouth and looked down at her phone, which she was glad she'd been using instead of her notebook. The battery was running down. "That really was quite a story," she said sincerely. "Different from all the other things I've been hearing over and over.

Thank you for sharing it with me."

"It was my pleasure," he assured her, patting her hand. "For what it's worth, this house," he jerked his thumb over his shoulder toward the white clapboards of Vale House, "does have its ghosts, too. All those things that go bump in the night, and doors that won't stay shut, and things that get moved around."

Cally smiled. "Speaking of things that get moved," she said, "would you know who..."

She was interrupted by a scream and a loud clatter from inside the house.

14 - Just an Accident

When Cally ran into the hall, it appeared at first to be completely empty. Cally thought she saw someone running up the stairs, but then Katarina's voice behind the desk took her attention. She ran and looked over the desk to see Katarina frantically trying to move the toppled filing cabinet, calling "Bethany! Bethany! Miss Chase!"

Before the screen door could bang shut behind Cally, Ignacio came running through it. He vaulted over the desk and lifted the old wooden cabinet almost effortlessly, setting it upright again. There lay Bethany, bent in a very uncomfortable looking position on her back next to the toppled office chair. Katarina continued to call her name, and shook her when she didn't respond, until Ignacio warned, "No, don't move her."

Cally knelt behind the desk and put a comforting hand on Katarina's shoulder. Ignacio checked to make sure Bethany had a pulse, and assured Katarina she did. But Bethany was not responding, and there was a good deal of blood on the floor and the fender of the stone fireplace, where Bethany had apparently hit her head when she fell. Cally now regretted having let her cell phone battery run down, but Ignacio was already on his own phone talking to the 911 dispatcher.

Joan burst from her office door, shouting. "Oh, for Pete's sake! What's all this noise out here? I'm on a very important call with the paranorm..." She stopped when she saw the scene behind the desk. Then she muttered "Why must everything happen when I'm busy? Someone call 911!" She reached to where the desk phone should have been, but it, too, was tangled amongst the furniture and Bethany on the floor.

Then Ian May came in from the back hall, and his presence

seemed to quiet the commotion in the room. Ignacio said something in Spanish to Katarina, who left the room and returned quickly with a clean dish towel to hold against Bethany's bleeding head. Bethany groaned and opened her eyes, struggling to sit up.

"Don't try to move until the paramedics get here," Ian said to Bethany, and took the phone from Ignacio's hand to speak to the dispatcher. "It's kind of hard to find by GPS," he told them. "I'll send someone to stand by the highway to flag you down." He handed the phone back to Ignacio, who nodded and left. Soon the red pickup truck roared out of the yard and turned down the main street, heading out of town.

Bethany did not follow Ian's advice, and sat up on the floor, awkwardly trying to straighten her skirt around her knees. Katarina knelt behind her to give her some support, paying no attention to the blood soaking into her dress from Bethany's head. "This is so embarrassing..." Bethany groaned, and Ian smiled.

"If you're worried about that kind of thing," he said, "then you are going to be alright."

It seemed like hours to Cally, but was probably really only a few minutes, before Ignacio and the red pickup reappeared in the yard, followed closely by an ambulance with sirens wailing. "Oh, no, I wish they wouldn't use the sirens," Bethany groaned." Now everyone will be talking!" And then, "No, really, please. It's not necessary, I'll be fine," as two young paramedics rushed into the hall and set a stretcher down beside her. But she was clearly not fine – she shrieked and her face contorted in pain when they lifted her carefully and laid her on the stretcher. Ian patted her hand and assured her everything would be alright, and she smiled weakly. Then they wheeled her out the door, carried her down the steps, and were gone. Ignacio helped Ian into the passenger seat of the red truck and they followed the ambulance, promising to call as soon as they had anything to tell.

Joan flung her arms up and said, "I'm *never* going to get all this paperwork done this way!" She went back into her office and slammed the door sharply behind her.

Silence descended on the sunny Hall, except for the muffled sound of Joan's voice on the phone behind the door. Cally looked down at the vintage office chair, broken into two pieces between the seat and the wheeled base, and wondered what on earth had just happened.

Katarina kept folding and unfolding the bloody dish towel in her hands. "I don't know what happened," she said. "All she did was sit down in her chair. Then Boom! Crash!" She made a wide gesture with both arms, indicating all the wrecked furniture. "It's like the things just *attacked* her!" She nodded, wide-eyed, at the filing cabinet. "And." She turned her saucer-eyed gaze to Cally. "Just before, when I came in. I saw the White Lady. There, on the stairs!" She held the dish towel to her breast with one hand, and crossed herself with the other.

Cally glanced at the staircase. She recalled having seen a retreating figure, herself. She had assumed it had been Nell. "Well," she said, indicating the chaos on the floor, "I don't think a Lady would have done all that."

She felt numb and could think of nothing except that the Hall needed to be put back in order. Stepping behind the desk, she pushed at the filing cabinet. It was heavy, but it slid easily on its felt-covered feet back to where it had originally stood, at the end of the desk. Papers lay everywhere and Cally started scooping them up.

"Maybe you shouldn't touch all that," the Captain called, maneuvering himself, his cane, and his iced-tea glass through the screen door. "Interfering with a crime scene and all, you know."

"Crime scene?" Cally looked up at him. "This wasn't a crime. Just an accident," she said, but his words made her pause.

Katarina bent to help, righting the fallen base of the chair. Cally looked at it – it was the kind that screwed onto a threaded post rising up from the base, so it could be raised or lowered by turning the seat. "That's what must have happened," she said. "The old wooden post here must have broken off."

"Why would it break? It's better quality than modern furniture," Katarina said, clinging to her Attack Furniture hypothesis.

"How about we just call the sheriff's office and let them come take a look anyway?" the Captain suggested.

"You can't arrest ghosts," Katarina pointed out.

Cally wished Ian were there to decide what ought to be done. It was his home, after all, and she certainly wasn't going to advise consulting Joan on the matter. "Foster and Nell should be back soon," she remembered. "Why don't we let them decide whether or not to call the sheriff?" As she said this, she realized it really could not have been Nell she had seen on the stairs, but she refrained from mentioning this to Katarina. "We should at least get all these papers out of sight. They're all kinds of financial information that shouldn't be left out in public view."

The Captain agreed to that. "It always takes the sheriff hours to find his way here from Blackthorn anyway," he grumbled, and ambled off into the parlor.

Cally gathered the papers nearest her into one pile and opened the top drawer of the filing cabinet. Then she developed a new hypothesis, one that she suspected held more water than Katarina's. With the top drawer open, the cabinet was off-balance and started to topple forward toward her.

"Here you are, Kat," she said, shutting the top drawer quickly. "The filing cabinet was off balance because all the weight was in the top drawer. When Bethany opened the drawer, the cabinet fell over and took her down with it."

Katarina gave her a skeptical look, but said nothing. Cally opened the bottom drawer instead and stacked the papers inside it. "We can get them sorted out later," she said. But glancing at Joan's closed office door, she had a sinking feeling "we" would probably end up being Katarina.

She looked up at Katarina. "If Bethany takes care of all this stuff," she wondered, "then what, exactly, does Joan do in there all day long?"

"Oh, You know." Katarina rolled her eyes. "*All This Paperwork*!" she said in a very credible imitation of Joan's voice. Cally had to laugh, and she felt a little better then, but just a little.

15 - Other Duties As Assigned

Cally had meant to retreat to the Rose Room after her interview with the Captain, to get her notes in order and maybe even get started writing, but she was much too rattled to think about that now. Instead, she wandered out onto the porch. The sun had moved to the west side of the house, filling the front yard with cooling shade. It seemed far too lovely an afternoon for a nice person like Bethany to be having to spend in an emergency room.

She sighed and sat down on the step where she had so recently seen Bethany shelling peas and, though she had never really believed in such things, she said a prayer for her. The little Calico named Cyndi Lauper came out from under the shrubbery and joined Cally on the step, rubbing against Cally's hand to invite her to scratch her ears.

Presently Foster and Nell's car pulled into the parking lot. The red truck, carrying Ignacio and Ian May, followed before the couple had quite got out of their car. Cally met them all on the stone walkway while Ian was explaining to his daughter and son-in-law what had happened in their absence. "She's going to be fine," he assured everyone. "Two ribs in her back are cracked, and the muscles in her back have been badly bruised, but everything will heal up just fine with lots of rest. She needed a couple of stitches on her head but nothing is broken – maybe a mild concussion. They're going to keep her overnight for observation."

Nell's hands were shaking and tears were pooling in the corners of her eyes. "Oh, poor Bethany," she said over and over, biting her already well-bitten fingernails.

Foster pushed up his glasses. "She's definitely going to need pain medication and lots of bed rest when she gets back," he noted.

As if on cue, Joan appeared, coming down the porch steps to join them. "Well that just figures!" she lamented. "And with all this work to do, too!" She paused to kiss Ian on the cheek. "Ian, I have just booked the most wonderful opportunity for us! A paranormal investigation team is going to come and film a TV episode here!" she told him proudly, not letting Bethany's accident rain on her parade. "They'll be staying for free, of course, but the exposure will be great for business!"

Foster groaned, and Cally said, "I thought you said..."

"Someone should call the sheriff," Nell interjected, looking at the front door and nibbling her thumbnail.

"I'm sure this is not a police matter," Foster told her patiently. "It was just an accident."

"Absolutely!" Joan agreed. "We can't afford to have police crawling all over the place, talking about foul play, when we're just about to get so much publicity!"

All eyes looked to Ian for a decision on the matter, but his head was bowed. He looked tired and sad. "No, I suppose you're right," he said. "There's nothing to bother the sheriff over. Don't worry, sweetheart," he said, touching his daughter's arm. "Bethany will be alright."

Cally felt like putting her arm around his sagging shoulders. "Mr. May, is there anything I can do to help?"

"Well you can certainly help me!" Joan said. "I have a lot of work to do now to get ready for this investigation, and I won't have time to take over that woman's chores just because she decided to get herself put on R and R! Maybe you can do her job for a while. There's not much to it.

"If you're not too busy *writing*," she added, and something about the way she said it made Cally feel as if she had been slapped.

"No, no, of course I can help," Cally said. "I do have some secretarial experience..."

"Well, that settles that, then." Joan turned back to the house. "You can start by straightening up the mess in the Hall. I'd tell Maria to do it but I'm going to have lots of extra work for her to do, to get ready for this Investigation!"

"Her name is Katarina!" Cally said to Joan's retreating back. Joan waved a dismissive hand without turning around, and went inside.

Cally stood in the Hall feeling useless while Ignacio knelt beside the fender with a bucket and a sponge, cleaning blood from the floor. "That was very nice of you to volunteer," he told her. "You don't have to do it, though. Kat can take care of everything."

"No, I don't mind," Cally said. She couldn't imagine how Kat could possibly keep an eye on the phones and the door while doing all the other work she already had to do. "I'm sure it'll just be for a couple of days. Anyway I can at least get all those spilled papers sorted out and put away properly. That'll give Bethany one less thing to worry about when she gets back."

"Well" he said, dropping the blood-soaked sponge into the bucket and picking up the pieces of the broken chair. "You'll need a chair. I'll bring you a new one."

"Wait a second," Cally said as he started to carry the bucket and broken furniture away. "Look at this." She put a hand on the half of the chair that had been the base. The threaded wooden dowel that had screwed into the seat was smooth and neatly finished, and there was no broken-off remnant of it protruding from the seat. "This chair isn't broken. It's just been twisted all the way up, so far that the seat fell off."

"Why would Bethany do that?" Ignacio wondered. "She's almost as short as Kat."

"I don't know. Joan is tall. Maybe she was doing some work at Bethany's desk while she was away this morning..." But then their eyes met and they both shook their heads; Ignacio said, "Yeah, right!"

"Maybe we really should have called the sheriff," Cally said.

"No, I think it's just an old chair," Ignacio decided. "They design the new ones so they can't come apart like that. I have a modern one at my house. I'll bring it for you."

"I don't know..."

Ignacio smiled kindly. "Besides, who would want to hurt Bethany?"

Cally glanced at Joan's office door, then shook her head. It didn't make sense that Joan would do such a thing. She was grouchy and inappropriate, but she wasn't evil. And besides, why would she put a person out of commission on whom she depended to do all the work she didn't want to do?

After Ignacio left, Cally retrieved the jumbled bills and receipts from the bottom cabinet drawer and sat down on the floor to begin sorting them into piles, attempting to match them to the labels of the folders out of which they had fallen. Foster came down the stairs into the Hall and leaned over the desk to look down at her. "Had to give Nell a sedative," he said. "This sort of thing really puts her out of whack." He walked around to Cally's side of the desk and peered down at the papers on the floor, nudging some aside with the polished toe of his shoe. "We really appreciate you helping out," he said.

"It's fine," Cally said. "I used to do this for a living, before I discovered my true calling." She had her hands full, or she would have enclosed the words "true calling" in finger-quotes. "People with word skills always seem to get shunted into secretarial duties, for some reason."

"Well," said Foster, sitting on the edge of the desk, "I just wanted to tell you..." He looked around the Hall, toward the front door and the entry to the dining room. "You might want to watch out. That Ignacio and his wife, those foreigners, I don't quite trust them. They might stand to benefit from getting Bethany out of the way." He pushed up his glasses and cast nervous glances toward the parlor door and the stairs.

"Benefit how?" Cally asked, pausing with a lap full of papers. As far as she could tell, this accident could only have added to Katarina's workload.

"Well, my father-in-law, you see, he has a soft heart. He has already given them so much. They had nothing when they came here and he gave them a house. The old stone building that used to be the kitchen for Vale House, you see, back when kitchens were separate buildings." He nodded toward the dining room, where the tall windows faced out onto the lawn and its white gazebo and the little stone building nestled in the shrubbery. "He had it converted into a nice cottage for them, and he lets them live there rent-free. That made sense, back when this was a farm, and there was a lot of work for them both to do. But Ian is too old for farming now, and turning this house into a B&B a few years ago was sort of his way of retiring. There really isn't enough work, anymore, for as big a staff as Ian maintains around here. He's a charitable man, but unless business picks up quite a lot, he can't afford to keep everyone on. And, well... I don't know if you can tell, but he's really slowed down a lot lately. It may be time for him to consider a nursing home."

"I hardly think he's ready for that!" Cally said adamantly. "Not for a good while yet!"

"Maybe. Maybe. You don't know him as well as I do." He looked around the Hall again and pushed up his glasses. "Well, anyway, the thing is, the other day, I overheard Ian telling Bethany he was considering leaving the cottage to her in his will. Can you imagine if Ignacio and Katarina found that out? You don't see a will anywhere in that mess there, do you?" He toed the jumble of papers on the floor again.

Cally shook her head. If she had seen one, she would not have told him – someone else's will was none of his business. She had enough secretarial experience to understand that sort of thing, anyway.

"Well, what I mean is." Foster stood up and came closer to her, stepping on some utility bills as he did so. He leaned down and put a hand on her shoulder. "Just be careful," he breathed into her ear. "Like I said, they may seem nice, but just keep an eye on them. Especially him. There's something about him that just gets my hackles up. I don't know if we can really trust him."

He seemed to be looking a little too long at the papers in her lap, but Cally couldn't be sure what he was looking at. She put a hand across the top of her shirt. "I'll be careful," she promised him, though privately she thought he was barking up the wrong tree.

He patted her shoulder. "Good. It's probably nothing, but we can't be too careful." He stood and pushed up his glasses. "I'll be talking to Ian in his quarters, if you need me for anything." He gestured through the dining room toward the narrow hall that led to the south wing, and then went that way himself.

Ignacio returned a few minutes later with a modern-looking office chair. It was made of black steel with mauve upholstery and padded armrests, and it looked completely out of place in the antiques-furnished Hall. He rolled it around the desk and Cally sat in it resignedly, adjusting the seat height with the pneumatic lever. "Well, at least it's comfortable," she had to admit.

Ignacio smiled and nodded. "Now, listen," he said. "If you change your mind about this, just let me or Kat know. Nobody will hold it against you. This is not your *other duties as assigned*." He grinned and winked.

Cally laughed. "I'll just get everything filed away in some semblance of order, anyway," she said. As Ignacio went out the front door, she transferred the stacks of papers from the floor to the desk and felt like she had already accomplished quite a lot.

Looking around the sunny hall, she sighed. It was pleasant here, barring Joan's voice ranting about something on the other side of the oak door. She wouldn't mind helping out until Bethany recovered, since she was going to be living at Vale House for a while anyway. Perhaps she could bring her laptop downstairs and actually get some writing done during her stint as Bed and Breakfast Receptionist. It wasn't as if the phone was ringing constantly. Perhaps if she also brought her MP3 player and ear-buds, she could even block out Joan's voice...

Her hand landed on a thick envelope and she stopped sorting. It didn't look like a bill or an equipment warranty, and she wasn't sure which pile it belonged in. She opened the clasp and pulled the sheaf of papers out far enough to see what they were about. The first page read, in bold-face centered type, "Last Will and Testament of Ian Lionel May" and bore today's date. Cally shoved it back into the envelope quickly. She realized this must have been what Ian had sent Bethany to the lawyer for, just that morning – it seemed ages ago, now.

Joan burst out of her office and Cally set the envelope down quickly. "I suppose you'll have to join us for dinner tonight," Joan declared, striding up to the desk. "Ian always had *her* join us." She nodded sharply at the desk and Cally understood she was referring to Bethany. "Though I don't know why. I keep telling him it isn't proper to get that chummy with staff."

"I would be happy to go and get dinner in town," Cally said, trying to keep her voice steady as she held Joan's gaze and slipped the envelope slowly beneath a stack of electricity bills.

"You can do that tomorrow night," Joan said. "We'll need you at this one. We all need to talk about how to get ready for this TV investigation!" Her expression made it clear the discussion was over.

Cally cocked an eye at her. "Whatever you say. I'll be there, boss."

"Don't get sarcastic with me. It doesn't look good on you." Joan turned toward the dining room, shouting "Maria! We need dinner, chop-chop!"

When the sound of Joan's clomping heels had faded into the back hall, Cally removed the envelope from under the bills and tucked it into the bottom filing cabinet drawer. She noticed her hands were shaking as she did so (probably, she guessed, in frustration at being held back from fastening themselves around Joan's throat.) She stuffed some still-unsorted receipts into a random folder and placed that on top of the envelope. She would ask Ian later, when she had a chance to talk with him alone, what he would like her to do with the will.

16 - All Hands Meeting

Cally had begun to feel confident everything was sorted and filed more or less properly, when Katarina came into the Hall, drying her hands on her apron. "It's quitting time!" she said. "You go freshen up for dinner. I'll put the phones into night mode!"

"There have only been a few calls anyway," Cally told her, "and they were all from people in town, asking how Bethany is doing. Though they all seem to know more about it than I do." Under other circumstances, she might have found this kind of stereotypical small town behavior amusing, but she sighed as she went up the stairs.

She hesitated at the door of the Rose Room. It was unlikely Bethany had had a chance, before everything had gone crazy in the Hall, to tell the staff to stop moving her things around. Steeling herself, she opened the door and looked inside, and then sighed with relief. Nothing seemed to have been touched. Even the purse she had thrown on the bed in her haste to speak with Bethany still lay slumped against a rose-shaped throw pillow.

Then she went in, and swore loudly when she saw George standing next to the desk. His hand rested lightly on the plastic crate of CDs she had left there.

He turned and looked at her, but did not appear the least bit alarmed or sheepish. "You like some very interesting music," he said.

"Yes. Yes, I do," Cally stammered. "But I'd really prefer it if you didn't mess with my things!"

He smiled angelically. With the window at his back, he almost seemed aglow himself with beatific light. "I didn't mean to upset you," he said. "I'm always very careful not to frighten you. I apologize for my curiosity but, you see, I have never heard of

Jonathan Coulton before." He turned his palm up, gesturing toward the titles on the spines of the CDs.

Cally balled up her fists in frustration and opened her mouth to speak. Then she let her breath out as a sudden thought came to her. The last thing Bethany had said to her had been something along the lines of "Georgie isn't really all there." He must have some kind of mental disability, she realized. That would explain his naïve and socially awkward behavior.

She unclenched her fists and said evenly, "I would be happy to let you borrow some of my music. But please. Listen, George. I really would prefer it if nobody comes into my room. It's not that I'm afraid anyone here would take anything." This wasn't strictly true, but she didn't want to make enemies here in the household as long as she was meaning to stay. "How will I be able to find my stuff if people are always moving things around?" She tried to appeal to what she imagined must be his very simple nature.

"Oh, Miss!" His face was earnest. "I could never do that. Maybe it was the White Lady?"

Cally sighed, silently counting to ten. How nice it must be, she thought, to have a resident ghost on whom to blame everything. She walked to the desk and began flipping through the CDs in the crate. Pulling out one of the Jonathan Coulton albums, she said, "If you bring this back to me when you're done, I'll lend you anoth..."

She looked up to hand the CD to him, but he was already gone. She sighed and put the CD back in the crate.

She didn't really have much time, before Joan's mandatory dinner meeting, but she took some time anyway. She put the crate of CDs on the floor of the closet, then took her notebooks and pens out of her purse, piling them on the desk next to her computer. The purse itself she hung on the closet doorknob and nodded firmly at it, defying it to dare move again. Then she locked the door behind her and went downstairs to the dining room.

Most of the household was already seated at the table; Joan had made sure to claim the seat at Ian's right hand before Cally arrived. Ian was walking around the room opening all the windows, while Katarina placed a large bowl of pasta in the center of the table. "This is Ignacio's famous sauce recipe," she said proudly.

Joan snorted. "I bet it tastes like taco sauce."

Cally opened her mouth, but couldn't find adequate words to express her incredulity at the woman's ignorance.

"You may as well come sit down, too, Jose," Joan said to Ignacio, who stood in the doorway wearing an apron. "This concerns you as well."

"No, thank you," he said. "I ... er, tasted, a lot while I cooked." He smiled mischievously.

Joan scowled at him silently until he relented, took off his apron, and took a seat next to Katarina at the far end of the table. Ian took his own seat at the head of the table and Nell began passing the bread basket.

"Anyone want a little brandy?" the Captain offered from his preferred seat near the sideboard.

Joan shifted her scowl to him. "I think we should all try to remain sober for this meeting," she said. "It's important!"

Cally told the Captain she would like a glass of sherry if he didn't mind. He grinned and lifted his glass toward her in an unspoken toast, and Joan looked away, rapping the table beside her plate with a spoon.

"Listen up!" she said. "Here's a chance for you all to earn your keep for once! I have just booked the most wonderful opportunity for Vale House. The Greater Asheboro Area Scientific Paranormal Society..." she spoke slowly to make sure she got it right, "has agreed to come and do an investigation of this property. They will be making video recordings, and if they get enough good footage, they say they will make it into an episode of Ghost Investigations!" She paused and looked around, as if allowing space for applause. Nell was the only one who clapped her hands, though, until Foster gave her a look. He seemed very agitated and kept pushing his glasses up, so vigorously Cally wondered how he didn't bruise his forehead.

Joan continued. "I don't have to tell you all what this could mean for business." She placed a hand over Ian's, and he smiled gently at her. "And if you all contribute exceptionally, it could mean job security for you all.

"Needless to say, with Ms. Chase having had her little 'accident,' you will all have to double up, to take up her slack." She shook her head, as if she felt Bethany had fallen and hurt herself deliberately just to spite her. "This place will need to be spotless. Right now it looks like a pigsty!"

Cally looked quickly at Katarina, expecting her to have some choice words to say about that, but Katarina, who had had years of practice ignoring Joan's remarks, barely even rolled her eyes. Ignacio closed a comforting hand over his wife's hand.

"I think the house and grounds already look immaculate," Cally said. "But I'll be happy to help in any way I can."

"I dunno." Foster spoke around a mouthful of food. "Maybe a few cobwebs would make it look spookier?" His tone was clearly mocking, but Joan's face lit up.

"That's a good idea!" She looked up, her eyes scanning the well-dusted ceiling trim. Not finding a single cobweb in any corner, she said, "Well, never mind. They'll be here Thursday and there's no time for that. I just want to make sure everyone in this room does everything they can to cooperate completely with the investigation crew. Stay out of their way. Help them find things they are looking for. And if they ask for stories about things people have seen here, lay it on thick!"

Nell giggled. " I might get to be on TV!" she said.

"I think you should just focus on the 'stay out of their way' part," her husband told her. Then he said to the table in general, "I don't often agree with Joan's business philosophy, as you all know. But in this case, I think I do, to some degree. Being on national TV will make people aware that Woodley actually exists. Put this place on the map, so to speak. That can only increase everyone's property value. So whatever we can do to give these guys a good show, let's do it right."

Cally found herself growing more and more irritated with the entire discussion. "Maybe Ignacio should tune up the air-conditioner?" she said. "You know. Give these investigators that 'cold chill' they are always on about in those shows."

Nell took the ball and ran with it. "And maybe we can knock things over and run past in the dark so they can jump and yell 'What was that! I felt something!'"

Katarina let out a giggle, and the Captain guffawed silently into his napkin.

"I don't see what's so funny!" Joan pushed her plate away. "This is serious! This ... town... this pathetic little hick village, doesn't attract much business. Getting more visitors to Vale House would boost business for the whole town of Woodley. And it could save all your jobs. Most of you are only here because Ian is just too soft-hearted to turn you out. This isn't a farm anymore. We don't need a full-time handyman and a cook and a receptionist. Not with the little bit of business we get. I'm just trying to get us more business. I don't know why I even try!"

Ian patted her hand. "We all appreciate everything you do," he assured her. "I do have one concern, though..."

Joan was not to be consoled. Her frown zeroed in on Cally. "And you!" she barked. "Of all people! You would think your own living also depends on this sort of thing. You make a living off people believing in ghosts, too!"

Cally felt she was about to lose her temper, but she realized she would be taking out on Joan a years-long frustration with the entire human race, and even Joan didn't deserve that. Instead, she took a sip of sherry and tried to explain as calmly as she could.

"I apologize for being flip about it," she said. "It's just that watching those guys in those shows really bugs me. No, it's true I don't really believe in what they are investigating. But that still doesn't excuse the way these people get paid to behave in ways that go against everything I was ever taught was decent.

"I mean, if ghosts did exist, they would be entitled to the same common courtesy to which anyone else has a right, don't you think? Would you go into the house of a living person and act like that? Would you go into someone's house and demand that they 'say something'? Or challenge them to push you or turn on this little light you're holding? What kind of person feels they have any right to go up to someone who is just minding their own business and demand that they prove themselves? Okay, sure, maybe if they are offering to sell you something, or claiming to love you, but..."

She took a deep breath and ran her hands through her hair, stopping herself just short of pulling at it. She realized she was ranting; everyone had put down their silverware and was looking at her. She let out her breath and tried a different tack.

"Okay. Well. Put yourself in a ghost's place. What if living humans seem just as weird and mysterious to them, as they supposedly seem to us? Imagine you are a ghost, and every time you encounter one of the living they start jumping around and yelling 'Oh, my god, what was that!' How, exactly, is that communication? I'm not sure what these people on these shows are trying to do, but it certainly isn't communication. It's just plain disrespectful."

She unclenched her hands from around her napkin, into which she had squeezed deep creases, possibly permanent. She was thinking *"Geez, what is wrong with me, getting into a tizzy over the feelings of people who are only theoretical at best?"*

Everyone at the table quietly resumed eating. Even Joan didn't seem to be able to think of a snarky comeback but, above her head, from the Gallery, Cally heard applause. She looked up to see George grinning down at her, clapping his hands. She grinned back up at him sheepishly, and wondered why he was not present at this "important all-hands meeting."

"I would call that well-put, Ms. McCarthy," Ian finally said. He took a long sip of his tea, and the ice clinking in the glass seemed to echo in the silent dining room. "Very well put. And you are right. I will request that these investigators conduct themselves respectfully while they are in Vale House.

"But if you all don't mind, I have one other concern."

Cally remembered that Ian had tried to voice a concern before. She listened carefully this time.

"In these shows," he said, "I have noticed the investigators like to set up cameras and recorders in the cellars and service passages under the properties. I suppose those kinds of places look dark and spooky to their viewers. But if it's all the same, I'd rather not have these people going into the cellars of Vale House. The cellars are... old, and the floors are uneven. The stairs are not up to code. It's not safe. I don't want anyone to get hurt."

"Good point," Joan said. "And all those bare wires and things down there. We don't want to show these things to the whole world on national television. It would make the place look like a firetrap!"

Several voices in the room gasped, and Joan snapped her mouth shut. Everyone looked at Ian, except Cally, who looked at everyone else looking at Ian, and wondered why.

"I'll explain later," Katarina whispered to her.

☽

Joan retreated to her office to "make some very important phone calls!" and Ian excused himself from the table, putting two desserts on a plate to take with him. As he started down the hall toward the south wing, Cally called, "Ian, wait, I just remembered something!"

She went into the Hall, gesturing for him to follow her. He set his plate on the desk while she dug in the bottom file drawer and removed the envelope containing his will. This she put into his hands, saying "I think Bethany meant to give this to you earlier, before things got a little crazy around here."

His eyes opened wide when he recognized the envelope. "Thank you very much indeed for taking care of this for me! I wouldn't have wanted it getting into the wrong hands." His eyes said more than his words did as he clasped it to his chest. "Really, Ms. McCarthy, thank you so much for everything. I hope you don't mind me repeating myself: you really don't have to do Bethany's job for us."

"I know," said Cally, smiling at him. "Don't worry, I'm sure it will only be for a couple of days, and I don't mind at all."

"Very well, then." He glanced at Joan's office door before reaching over the desk to put a hand over one of Cally's. "What I really mean to say is, don't let Joan upset you. You are doing us all a great favor, and we all know it. You are not a servant here. Don't let her treat you like one. If you find she is beginning to get on your last nerve, just let me know, and I will speak to her." He smiled and winked, and Cally laughed, relieved that he seemed to understand so much more than he let on.

"She will certainly, at some point," Ian continued, "try to tell you that you are still being charged the full rate for your board even though you are doing work for us. Don't listen to her. I have no intention of charging you at all." He leaned over the desk and spoke more softly. "She's really not so bad, you know. She's had a hard life. Her family was... Well, the word they use nowadays is 'dysfunctional.' And she was abandoned by her husband at a very young age. She's just trying to protect herself from getting hurt anymore."

Cally thought taking random stabs at everyone around one was probably the wrong way to go about avoiding getting hurt, but she smiled up at the old gentleman just as she had seen Bethany doing several times before. "You are a far more generous soul than I am, Ian May," she said. "And I promise I will try to be more like you."

"Well, now," he said, "I have an appointment with this dessert in my rooms. I hope you will have a very good night."

17 - Boo

Cally was gratified, on returning to the Rose Room, to see that nobody had attempted to straighten up the pile of notebooks she had left on the desk. She paused beside the desk chair and considered checking her email. Perhaps she would even send a reply back to her agent, for once. She could mention she had gathered enough notes to possibly start a first chapter. Then she shook her head, and promised herself she would send an email once she actually started writing. Tomorrow, maybe. Possibly.

She left everything where it lay on the desk and took a set of pajamas from the drawer. Passing the bookshelf as she headed toward the bathroom, she grabbed the little plastic bottle of generic rosé wine off the top shelf. She suspected it might only have been put there as a decoration, but she took it into the little bathroom anyway and set it on the edge of the tub next to the rose-scented candle there. While the tub filled, she dumped a generous handful of bath salts "with real rose petals!" into the water and opened the little window over the sink. A night-scented breeze blew in and made all the doilies flutter.

The candle was one of the battery operated types with a "realistic but safe!" flame. She switched it on and sank into the warm water. The old fashioned tub was big enough that she was able to stretch all the way out. Twisting the cap off the wine bottle, she raised it in a toast. "Here's to you, Bethany, and your kind little touches. I hope you are going to be OK."

Presently the warm water, the passable wine, and the shadows dancing in the flickering fake candlelight all contrived to settle the thoughts whirling in her head. Bethany had merely had an unfortunate mishap and would be alright in a short time. The weird summer storm the night before had just been a storm and, despite Joan's little fantasy of Ian's special powers, it had merely passed, as do all summer storms. There had been no figure standing at the crossroads – that had just been a trick of the lightning, rain, and shadows. Ben's eyes were merely blue and he was just a nice guy who worked in a news store and she didn't have enough hormones left anymore to care anyway. She had gathered plenty of notes and stories toward starting a sequel to her book, and she might be able to talk her agent into an advance that would keep her alive long enough to finish it, instead of dying on a park bench somewhere in order to avoid having to go back to technical writing.

She finished the wine, dried off and slipped into her pajamas. Switching off the candle, she returned to the bedroom, taking not one glance at the pile of work awaiting her on the desk. The rose-covered bed had been thoughtfully turned down by she knew not and cared not who; she was confident she would fall asleep the minute her head touched the pillow. The old gray cat was lying in the middle of the bed, purring up at her.

"Oh, you again." She considered trying to shoo it out the window onto the belvedere again, but decided to let it stay. "Doctor Boojums, is it? Or shall I call you Boo? Just you scoot over a few inches, now, and we'll get along fine."

The cat apparently did not want to share the bed. When Cally lifted the coverlet to try to nudge it to one side a little, it yowled and leapt to the floor. "Suit yourself," she said, reaching over to turn off the bedside lamp. "I'm sure you can find your own way out." She slid between the sheets and turned her back on it, settling her head deeply into the pillows.

The cat was not satisfied with this arrangement. It stood at the bedroom door and scratched, yowling every few seconds in a very unpleasant voice.

Cally spat a few unladylike words, slipped out of her warm cocoon and turned the light back on. The cat looked up at her tand yowled again. "What?" she said to it. "*I'm* the one who should be upset!" She sighed a sigh so deep it was almost a growl, and opened the door to let it out. "And don't even think about coming in here again, if that's how you're going to be!" The cat ran out, streaking down the hall toward the stairs.

"You and Doctor Boojums are getting along well!" George was coming up the hall from the direction of the stairs, and the cat dodged between his legs as it passed.

"I wouldn't call it getting along," Cally answered. "But maybe now I can get some sleep," she added pointedly. George was smiling congenially, but Cally didn't feel the least bit congenial, herself, at the moment. She stepped backward and started to close the door, not waiting to see if he had got the hint.

"I am curious," George said at the closing door, as if Cally had said "By all means, please let's chat!"

"What?" Cally opened the door no more than six inches.

"I'm just wondering what color Doctor Boojums appears to be to you?"

"What kind of question... ?" Cally opened the door the rest of the way, holding the throat of her pajama top closed with one hand. "That's... he's gray, of course. Why?"

"I just wondered how things look to you," George said. "He used to be orange."

"Did he?" said Cally. "Well, that's very interesting, but you must excuse me, I was just..."

"I was worried about Miss Bethany," said George. "I said a prayer for her."

Cally gave up. "That's very sweet of you."

"She's going to be fine. They say she's sleeping right now."

"I certainly hope so," said Cally. "At least someone is. Sleeping, that is. But I also hope she's going to be fine, of course. I'm sure she will be."

"I am very attached to her," George said. "It really upsets me that someone would hurt her."

So, Cally thought, the list of people who thought the accident had seemed suspicious continued to grow. "But, why would anyone want to do that?"

"Maybe it wasn't Bethany they were trying to hurt," George suggested.

"That's an odd thought..." Cally considered it nonetheless. As she did so, a loud clatter, as if something had fallen from the butler's desk at the north end of the hall, made her and George both turn their heads to look. The clatter was followed by the sound of labored footsteps, though Cally couldn't see anyone else in the hallway.

George lowered his voice to a whisper. "I have to go," he said urgently.

"Goodnight, then, George." Cally gave him a resolute look, her hand on the door knob. And then, as she watched him standing there with his head cocked toward the footsteps, he vanished.

<h1 style="text-align:center">18 - Further Duties As Assigned</h1>

Tuesday morning dawned sunny and warm. A brisk breeze blew in over the meadow and carried bird song through the window over the desk. Cally stood on the inside of the Rose Room door with her laptop case slung over her shoulder, reaching toward the knob as if it were electrified. It had got to the point, she was thinking, where she didn't like opening that door, not from either side, not at all.

She considered just turning around and putting her computer back on the desk. If she just stayed right there, perhaps taking the opportunity to finally reply to some of her agent's emails, maybe Katarina would miss her at breakfast and come looking for her. She would knock, and Cally could call "Come in, please!" That way she wouldn't have to open the door herself, and that would at least get her past the first awkward hour of this strange new day.

Then she heard the sound of tires crunching on gravel outside. She turned back to the window and looked out to see the red pickup truck pulling into the front yard of Vale House. Katarina appeared from under the porch roof, running across the lawn toward the truck. Even the horses in the meadow drew closer to the fence, tossing their heads excitedly when Ignacio alit from the driver's seat and lifted a wheelchair out of the bed of the truck.

Cally forgot her trepidation and flung open the Rose Room door. She ran down the stairs, pausing in the Hall long enough to drop her computer case on the desk, then hurried out onto the porch. The Captain and Ian were already there, applauding as Ignacio wheeled Bethany up the walkway.

"Oh, stop," Bethany called to them, covering her blushing face with her hands. "This is all too much." When they reached the bottom step, she insisted she could walk, but Ignacio turned the wheelchair around and expertly backed it up the stairs onto the porch. "It's so good to be back," she said, and dropped her head back onto the headrest. She was smiling, but her face was pale.

"It's good to have you back," said the Captain, tipping an imaginary hat to her. Cally held open the screen door so Ignacio could wheel Bethany into the hall.

"If you could just steer me behind the desk, then," she said, but Ignacio wheeled her toward the staircase instead.

"Oh, no you don't," said Katarina. "Ms. McCarthy has kindly offered to fill in for you until the doctor says you can work again. I've got the Daffodil room ready for you." To emphasize the point, Cally stepped behind the desk and began arranging her things.

"Oh." Bethany looked up at the top of the grand staircase. "But how..?"

Ignacio was already bending down to lift her out of the chair. "Just put your arms around my neck," he coached her.

"Mind you don't squeeze my husband too tight!" Katarina giggled. Cally watched the two proceed up the stairs, followed closely by Katarina holding Bethany's little bag of medicine and other things from the hospital.

After they passed out of sight, Cally sat down at the desk, but Ian came and stood before it, smiling down at her. "Your breakfast is still waiting for you," he said. "Katarina made Eggs de Provence, she calls it, this morning. You are still a guest here, and thankful as we are for your help, it's not so important that you can't have a good breakfast." He demonstrated by showing her that he, himself, had acquired a muffin, which he waved happily at her as he headed out of the Hall. "If the phone rings, the voice mail will answer it." He paused in the dining room to grab two boiled eggs from the table before he disappeared into the south wing.

Cally didn't feel like breakfast. What she really would have liked would have been to bury herself in work or, perhaps, to go up and talk to Bethany, but the thought of walking back up to the upstairs hall made her feel queasy. On the other hand, the scent of coffee wafting from the dining room, while it didn't smell quite as good as the coffee at The Bean Garden, was soothing. Finding an outlet under the desk, Cally plugged in her laptop's charger and went in to breakfast.

The Iversons were there, and Foster and Nell, heaping their plates with sausages, fluffy scrambled eggs that smelled of rosemary and thyme, and beautiful brown bread. "Oh, we get to see you one last time!" Celeste Iverson called out, waving at Cally to take the seat next to her.

Cally sat down and wrapped her hands around the warm coffee cup Katarina set before her. "Where are you headed next?" she asked the couple. "Did you see any ghosts while you were here?" She didn't look at them, but focused on filling her plate with food she wasn't sure she was going to eat.

"Sadly, no apparitions this time," said Mr. Iverson, winking at his wife over the brim of his coffee cup. "Though we did hear some footsteps last night."

Celeste nodded excitedly. "It could have been anything, of course, but when we looked out into the hallway, there was nothing to see!"

"How interesting," Cally responded, trying to swallow a mouthful of eggs that stuck in her throat like cardboard.

"We are headed to Charleston next," Celeste Iverson was saying, "where we are booked into another famously haunted inn."

"They say," said Nell, "you can't stick a shovel in the ground in Charleston without hitting someone's grave."

"Well," said Mr. Iverson, "then we promise not to do any digging while we're there." He chuckled good-naturedly, and Nell nodded her approval.

Cally jumped and dropped her toast when she heard knocking from the Gallery above her. Looking up quickly, she was relieved to see Katarina, rapping at the door of the room next to the Rose Room, then opening it and going inside.

Celeste grew serious, then, and said, "Poor Bethany. I hate that we won't be able to say goodbye to her. You'll give her our best wishes, won't you, when you see her?"

"I will," said Cally. "I'm sure I'll need to talk to her quite a bit, as I'll be trying to do her job for a while, and I have no idea what I'm doing."

"You're doing fine so far," Foster assured her.

"We can walk you through the checkout process, anyway," said Mr. Iverson, wiping his mouth and putting his napkin on his plate.

"We've done it at least a dozen times!"

The Iversons got up and went into the Hall, where Ignacio met them with their bags. Cally left her half-eaten breakfast and took only her coffee cup with her to the desk.

Mrs. Iverson handed Cally her room key and pointed to a drawer in the antique desk. This desk held a modern metal key box, and the slots in the bottom of box were labeled with pictures of botanical prints. Cally dropped the Iverson's key into the one with a picture of a wisteria vine in its bottom. "There," Mr. Iverson said. "Now, all you have to do is sign us out in the guest register."

Cally opened the register and wrote in the date and time, then turned the book around so that Mr. Iverson could sign to verify the couple had departed with all their belongings intact. "Well, that was pretty good, for your first time!" he said. "You'll be an old pro at this in no time."

Cally sincerely hoped this would not turn out to be true, but she smiled and thanked them and wished them a safe journey to their next destination.

After they had gone, Foster and Nell went upstairs and Katarina came into the Hall to show Cally how to take the phones off night mode. "Poor Bethany couldn't eat any breakfast," she told Cally, "but I'm going to see if she feels like drinking some tea, anyway."

The Hall grew quiet at last, except for Joan's voice through the closed oak door. Cally opened her laptop on the desk, arranging her notebooks beside it so she could face the sunny doorway as she worked. She created a new word-processor file, naming it "Research." At the top of the page she typed, "Plot." She forced a page break and typed "Characters" at the top of the new page, then scrolled down another page, and typed "Romantic Interests." She folded her arms on the desk and put her head down on them. For a long time, she focused only on trying to keep taking one breath after another.

She could feel someone had approached the desk and was standing patiently in front of it. Cally tried to ignore the intrusion, but it didn't go away. And why should it? she thought. She had been waiting for it all morning. She sighed, took a deep breath, and steeled herself to look up.

George smiled when he saw her looking at him, and took his

hands out of his pockets to hold them straight at his sides.

"What nerve he has, to smile so sweetly at me," she thought, but she did not allow her face to show any expression at all. Her heartbeat sounded like a hammer in her ears.

"I'm sorry," he said.

Cally swallowed. "For what?"

"For frightening you last night."

He was frightening her now, Cally thought, but she refused to show it. *"I am talking to a ghost,"* she heard herself think. *"I am knowingly talking to a ghost, as if that's what one normally does."* The hammering in her ears grew louder.

"You owe me an explanation," she said. She hadn't meant to say it out loud, but it was true.

"I tried very hard to never have to do that," he said. "I had anticipated that the beginning of our relationship would be awkward, but not this awkward. I meant to take it much more slowly. But the White Lady was coming, and I couldn't let her see me."

"You had to hide from another ghost?" Cally's voice came out much sharper than she had intended, and once the ludicrous words were out of her mouth, the noise in her ears began to sound like wind, and she realized she was about to faint.

But George laughed, and that was so puzzling, Cally was able to focus again. "No, no," he explained. "Not all of us are ghosts."

"That doesn't make any sense!" None of it made any sense.

Footsteps at the top of the stairs caused George to turn his head and look up. "Well?" Cally said with a very dry throat. "Don't you have to vanish or something now?"

He shook his head. "No, she can't see me. I'll wait here."

Katarina came down the stairs carrying a tray, and George stepped to the side of the desk so she wouldn't have to walk through him as she came to stand in front of Cally. "She's sound asleep," Katarina was saying, shaking her head. "It's probably the pain medicine."

"I guess sleep is good for her," Cally said. She thought her voice sounded creaky and robotic, and her mind was not at all on the conversation at hand. "It will help her heal, I'm sure."

"You're probably right. You're such a dear. I don't know what

I'd do if you weren't here." She reached across the desk and patted Cally's shoulder as she turned to go into the dining room, and it was all Cally could do not to grab at her hand and cling to it like a drowning person.

"Maybe you and I can pay her a visit around lunch time," Katarina called over her shoulder from the dining room.

"Yes," Cally called back. "I'd like that."

When Katarina's footsteps had disappeared into the back hall, Cally turned her head toward the end of the desk where she'd last seen the ghost.

"You're still there," she said.

"I said I would wait," he answered. He resumed his typical languorous slouch and smiled. His hair was different, today; a mane of short locks stood out all around his head.

"Why can I see you?" It was the first sensible thought she'd had since last night.

"Some people can," he said, shrugging. "You see things all the time that others don't see. No, you do. You always have. It's just the way some people are. It's..." He touched his chest. "Usually it's very hard for me, to talk to people. A lot of work. It's easier with you. Also I can use your battery. It helps." Cally followed his glance to her computer screen, and saw that the "low battery" indicator was lit, even though the computer was plugged in.

"I'm sorry, do you mind?" George asked. "Some get their energy directly from living people, but I don't think it's right to do that. It makes them cold."

"No... no, I don't mind." Cally recalled all the tales she had heard, of people claiming to feel "cold chills" in the presence of alleged ghosts. Now, she was surprised to find her hand reaching for her notebook, as if she wanted to jot this new insight down.

"Do you want to interview me?" George laughed. Before Cally could consider her answer, he said, "I would enjoy that. Maybe someday when we have more time. I just wanted to apologize for frightening you last night, and ask you to please not go away."

"I'm not going anywhere," Cally said without even thinking about it. It was the only thing she could feel certain of, at the moment.

He smiled and nodded, as visibly relieved as a ghost could be.

"Little Nellie will come soon," he added, glancing toward the top of the stairs. "When she does, I must go. I mustn't let her see me. I apologize in advance if I ... leave suddenly."

"Nell can see you?"

"Nellie sees many things that others can't see," he said. "But they frighten her, because everyone tells her they aren't there."

Cally nodded, and tried looking at his shoulder to see if she could see through it to the wall behind him. He jerked his hand up as if something had hurt him. "Please don't," he said.

"I'm sorry. I didn't realize..."

He laughed again. "Aren't we a sorry pair!" Then he leaned in conspiratorially, trying to explain. "It's what I've learned. To... what would you call it? The ghost-hunters, they say 'manifest.' It's what I can do: appear to the living eye. Well, for some. When I first found myself here..." He made a wide gesture with both hands that seemed to encompass everywhere. "It's what I worked to learn. It took a long time, but I got good at it. My appearance has always been very important to me." He grinned. "Others learn other things: how to touch things in this world, how to move things. Whatever comes naturally to them. I'll learn those things, too, someday, I suppose. Maybe. It's a lot of work. But I like to learn."

Cally's hands wanted more than ever to take up her notebook and pen, but she stopped them. "But why are you here?" she asked, and she made the same gesture he had just made, indicating everywhere.

"That is a story that will take a long time to tell," he said. "I promise, I will tell it to you someday. If you will only stay. But Nellie is coming out of her room. I must go and tell the others you are staying. We'll talk again soon, I promise."

"Others?"

Cally heard footsteps on the stairs, and George's pointed look told her she should turn her head away if she didn't want to see him vanish. She did so, and saw Nell coming down the stairs with a small bag in her hand.

"I'm going to take a little walk down to the pond," she said cheerfully. "I'll be back soon. Please don't tell Foster where I've gone!"

"I promise," Cally said, thinking she was certainly making a lot of promises, and keeping a lot of secrets, all of a sudden.

19 - Lunch With Bethany

Cally spent the rest of the morning typing her handwritten notes into her word processor application, and felt pleased with herself for having finally got some real work done. She felt so much better by lunch time, she went ahead and created a blank file titled "Chapter 1," and typed the first sentence into it.

"Why do questions you ask a ghost always begin with 'Why'?"

She chewed her lip, rereading it. The phrasing seemed a bit awkward, but it was a start. She decided she deserved some lunch, and was delighted to realize she actually had an appetite again.

While she perused the sticky note on which Katarina had written instructions for forwarding the phones to voice mail, the phone rang, and the incoming number appeared to have an out-of-town area code. Cally decided she ought to go ahead and answer that. "Vale House – how may I help you?" Her mind went back to when she had first heard Bethany say that to her, on the other end of the line. It seemed now like it had been years ago.

The caller was a man wanting to make reservations for two on Friday night. Cally fumbled open the register and saw Friday was still completely open. It was the day after the paranormal investigators were slated to arrive, but she was sure they would not be staying more than one night, so she went ahead and scheduled the couple.

"Do you allow pets?" he asked. "We have a small dog."

"I don't see why not," Cally said, hoping she wasn't breaking one of Joan's rules, and then decided not to care whether she was or not. "After all, we have cats." She looked through the screen door at Cyndi Lauper and Doctor Boojums sunning on the porch railing. "As long as it stays on a leash," she thought to add.

She concluded the call and forwarded the line to voice mail before it could ring again. She had promised Katarina she would join her for lunch, hopefully with Bethany, but Cally couldn't see any sign of her from where she sat. She stood and stretched, and went through the dining room to the narrow hallway leading into north wing and, presumably, the kitchen.

The hallway ended in a T, and she stopped there, looking left and right. Never having been to the kitchen, she chose right and proceeded hesitantly toward an open door near the end of the hallway. As she drew near it, though, she heard a television playing and saw the knee of a man seated in an upholstered chair near the door. "Oops," she said softly. "That must be the Captain's room."

She tiptoed away and tried the other direction, toward the back of the house, and knew she must be right when she came to a pair of swinging doors with small square windows and brass push-panels. She pushed one side open to find herself in a wide, brightly lit industrial kitchen, complete with massive built-in refrigerators and wide cooktops. Nobody was present, at the moment, but the remains of the loaf of bread from breakfast lay on the butcher-block work table in the center of the room. Cally headed for this.

Ignacio came dashing in through a door that led outside to the back garden. In his arms he cradled a colander overflowing with fresh lettuce, radishes, and scallions. "Looking for lunch?" he asked.

"I thought Kat might be here," she said. "But if she's busy I can just make myself a sandwich. Maybe I could use some leftover sausage from breakfast?"

Ignacio left the bowl on the work table and dug in one of the refrigerators, pulling out an armload of cold cuts, cheeses, and pickles.

"No, really, I only need a little something," Cally insisted, but he ignored her and began cutting off slabs of bread and assembling a platter of thick sandwiches.

"Katarina is upstairs," he said as he slathered the bread with mayonnaise. "We can all join Bethany for lunch. If we can get her to eat something, it might help her feel better. Here." He handed Cally a pitcher of iced tea and a stack of tumblers.

Cally thought the mountain of food might intimidate Bethany rather than pique her appetite, but she followed him as he carried the tray out through the swinging doors into the hall. She headed toward the dining room, but Ignacio opened a doorway just short of it. This opened onto a narrow stairwell.

"Be careful," he said, going up ahead of her. "This is what is called the backstairs. We're not supposed to use it. Insurance and all. There's no railing," he pointed out, "and no room to build one. But it's the shortest way from the kitchen, so we use it all the time anyway." He balanced the tray on one hand and opened the door at the top of the stairs with the other. "Kat thinks it's haunted."

He grinned and stood aside so Cally could step past him. She found herself in the upstairs hallway, diagonally across from the Rose Room. "And now you know all the secrets of Vale House," Ignacio said, grinning.

The hallway was filled with sunlight because the doors of the Hydrangea Room and the Wisteria Room had been propped open. Katarina was inside the Wisteria Room, stripping the bed and piling the sheets in a basket. As Cally looked in, she thought she had figured out one of the sources of "mysterious footsteps" in Vale House, anyway: the Wisteria Room shared a wall with the back stairwell. Just a short time ago, that would have been all the explanation she required.

"Is Miss Bethany awake?" Ignacio asked Katarina.

"She is!" Katarina left her work to join them. They crossed the hall and Ignacio knocked softly at the door of the Daffodil Room, which stood partially open. Ian May was inside, seated in the yellow-chintz upholstered chair beside the bed, and Bethany was sitting propped against a pile of yellow and green throw pillows, smiling up at something he had said.

"We've brought lunch!" Katarina announced. She cleared several daffodil-themed knickknacks to one side of the dresser so Ignacio could set down the tray.

"Oh, I don't think I could eat," said Bethany. "But the tea looks good. My mouth is so dry."

"It's probably the pain medicine doing that," Katarina guessed.

"I don't know," said Bethany. "It's not doing very much for the pain! Foster thinks the dose needs to be adjusted. He's called Doc for me and says he'll be bringing me a new prescription in a little while."

Katarina patted Bethany's hand as Cally set a glass of tea on the night stand doily next to the nearly full pill bottle. The doily was bright yellow with green trim. Ignacio took a small, daffodil-patterned tray from the top dresser drawer and piled one of his heroic sandwiches on it. This he placed proudly on Bethany's lap. She looked at it the same way she had looked up the stairs from the wheelchair that morning.

Ian stood up. "Well," he said, smiling gently at Bethany and patting her hand, "Foster should be back from the pharmacist soon. I hope the new medicine works better." He glanced at Ignacio. "Let's let the ladies talk," he advised.

Ignacio wrapped two sandwiches in napkins and followed him out the door. When they had gone from view, Bethany allowed her cheerful smile to collapse. "Oh, my!" she said. "What a mess this all is!" She regarded the sandwich through slit eyes and said again, "Oh, my!"

"Maybe I can get you some soup instead," Katarina offered. Then she grinned mischievously. "Or maybe just some tacos!" Bethany started to laugh, but then cried out in pain. "Oh, don't make me laugh!"

"Oh, dear," Cally said. "It's your ribs. I broke one on a swing, once, when I was a child, and laughing was the worst. I'm so sorry you have to go through this."

"It's not so bad," Bethany said. "I just hate having to put you both to so much work." She flipped the top slice of bread off the sandwich and eyed the lettuce. "Joan must be treating you both awfully now. And probably complaining about using a guest room for me, too!"

"Don't worry," said Katarina. "I'm sure she'll instruct you to send an itemized bill to yourself as soon as you're able to work again." Bethany started to laugh, but remembered and stopped herself in time.

"Oh, but, Bethany, guess what?" Cally said. "I booked a guest for Friday night, all by myself!"

"Congratulations!" said Bethany. "I'm so glad you're here. You're a godsend."

"Well, I don't know if I did it right," she confessed. "I'll get Kat to check my work later."

"Doc says I should be allowed to get up and walk around in a couple of days," Bethany said. "I'll be more use then."

"Doc can say what he likes," Katarina snorted. "*We* won't let you do any work until you are feeling completely better!"

Cally nodded her agreement. "Don't worry about us, we're fine. And what can we get for you now? How about something to read?"

"Maybe Ignacio can bring the small TV from the Azalea room for you," suggested Katarina.

"No, thank you. You're both too kind..." Bethany picked the lettuce off the sandwich and ate it. Then she nibbled at some of the cheese. "I think that medicine is starting to kick in now," she said. "My ribs still hurt, but I'm feeling really sleepy."

Katarina said, "Good, you sleep. Sleep is the best medicine." She headed for the door. "I have to get back to work, but you be good! Doc specifically said not to try standing up on your own. The medicine will make you dizzy, and you don't want to fall again! Call me if you need to get to the bathroom; I'll come and help." For emphasis, she moved the yellow phone on the nightstand closer to Bethany.

Bethany nodded her promise, but pushed the remains of the sandwich away. "I think that's enough for now. Thank Ignacio for me." She lay back and closed her eyes.

"And stay hydrated!" Katarina called from the hallway. "Doctors' orders!"

Cally demonstrated her agreement with Katarina by refilling the iced tea glass on the night stand.

"Well at least now I'll have time to give you that interview I promised you," Bethany said.

Cally sat in the chair beside the bed and put her hand on Bethany's arm. "There's no hurry about that," she said. "But, Bethany, I was wondering... Do you remember anything? About when you fell? Do you know how it happened?"

"I honestly don't," she said. "I remember getting home with the envelope for Ian. I sat down to put it into the filing cabinet, and I do remember noticing Ian still had not signed any of the papers I had put out for him to sign off on before I left." She smiled at this. "Then the next thing I remember, I was lying in a big mess on the floor and everyone was making a fuss all around me and calling an ambulance."

Cally smiled and shook her head. "I think I must have filed all the things you left out for Ian to sign. They were all over the floor. I'll try to dig them out again. If you could just tell me..."

But Bethany's eyes were fluttering open and shut, and she was not really listening. Cally stood and brushed Bethany's silvery curls back from her forehead, careful not to get any hair into the ointment covering the stitches over her temple. "Never mind, I'll figure it out. You just rest. Kat is right: sleep is the best medicine."

"Oh!" Bethany's eyes flew open and she tried to sit up, forgetting that this was painful for her to do. Between gritted teeth and gasps of pain, she said, "And there was also. Very important. Ian has to sign it and get it back to the lawyer..."

Cally thought she knew what Bethany was talking about. "If you mean Ian's will, don't worry, I found it and gave it to Ian. It's safe and sound in his study."

She laid back, though her face was still twisted with pain, and let out a deep breath. "Good. Maybe Ignacio can take it... back into town. When it's all signed."

"I'll remind Ian to sign it," Cally assured her, but she hesitated to promise to put it into Ignacio's hands, after what Foster had said to her the day before. "I'll make sure it's all taken care of."

"You're an angel."

As Bethany drifted off to sleep, the cats came in and leaped onto the bed. Cyndi Lauper took up a station near Bethany's feet and Doctor Boojums lay down beside her knees. They both regarded Cally as if to say "Don't worry, we'll handle it from here."

20 - How Sofie Died

Cally put her cell phone on the desk and connected her earbuds to it, intending to transcribe the conversation with the Captain she had recorded the day before. This proved more difficult than she had expected, because the phone had picked up some kind of interference or background noise during the recording. It sounded like a classroom full of unruly children who wouldn't stop chattering while the teacher was trying to talk, and Cally had a hard time, at points, picking the Captain's words out from the noise.

She was relieved to have an excuse to look up when a shadow fell across the front door. Ben Dawes from the News Store was peering in through the screen, holding a basket in his arms, smiling at her and saying something that was probably "May I come in?"

"Come in!" Cally said, plucking out the earbuds and pausing the recording. "What can I do for you?"

He came to the desk and smiled down at her. The basket he carried was fragrant with mixed blossoms that spilled over its brim.

"I'm surprised to see you here, Ms. McCarthy," he said, and then, "I mean, here at the desk. They've put you to work?"

"Please call me Cally," she said, and then "I've volunteered. To help Bethany until she gets better."

"This is for Bethany," he said, nodding down at the basket in his arms. "Bree put it together for her, from her herb garden. Wildflowers and healing herbs, she says."

"That was sweet of her," Cally said, still amused at how fast news traveled in this small town. Looking past the basket to his face, she wondered again at the extremely unusual shade of blue in his eyes. "Kind of like blue moonstone," she thought to herself.

He bent over the desk and set the basket down. "There's

chocolate in here for her, too, and some magazines from the store. Some of them are even current!" He chuckled at his own joke. More striking than the blue of his eyes, Cally thought, was the way so many tiny lines radiated out from the corners of them, like rays of sunshine. "I hope everything is going well for you, here. Cally."

"Everything is fine." She barely heard herself speak. Her heart was beating far too quickly, she noticed, and her body was doing things it had not done in years. She tried to remind it that it was far too old for that sort of thing, and besides, blue was only a color. Lots of people had blue eyes. "Bethany's asleep right now, I'm afraid," she said. "The pain medicine knocks her out. But you can leave this with me and I'll see that she gets it. Thank you so much, and thank Bree, too."

Ben stepped back from the desk. "I hope you have a wonderful afternoon, Cally," he said, casting a final smile over his shoulder before pushing the screen door open. Cally sat back and let out her breath. She felt as if she had run a mile.

"Why did you do that?" It was Katarina, calling down from the top of the stairs.

"Do what?" Cally pretended to read over the transcribed text on her computer screen as Katarina ran down to the Hall.

"Just sent him packing like that!"

"What? I told him thank-you!"

"You could have offered to walk with him to take it up to her. Or something like that." Katarina was grinning hugely. "Something to keep him around longer!"

"Why would I do that?" Cally said into the computer screen.

"Callaghan McCarthy, he's *hot*!"

Cally sat up and fixed Katarina with a level look. "I suppose he's fairly decent-looking, for a middle-aged man with graying hair and a pot-belly."

"And nice and skinny at the hip," Katarina added, extending her thumbs and forefingers in a circle to approximate the circumference of a man's hips.

"Kat!"

"Don't tell me you haven't noticed."

"Well, yes. I have. But does Ignacio know *you* have noticed?"

Katarina giggled. "It's not too late! He's still in the shade garden, beside the house. You could go out and invite him to dinner! Tell him it's my invitation, if you're too shy..."

"I am not shy. I'm just over that sort of thing. Never again. Anyway I'm too old now for that sort of silliness."

Katarina snorted, causing her black bangs to fly up from her face. "You are never too old. With Ignacio and me, it just keeps getting better and ..."

Cally put up a hand to make Katarina stop. "Too much information!" she said. Then she grinned. "I am very happy for you and Ignacio. It's nice to see a couple who are really in love, in this world, for a change."

"Well, speaking of this nice little couple, Ignacio and I would like to invite you to dinner at our house tonight. No, we insist! I promise it won't be tacos."

"Kat, I like tacos."

"We'll make you some another time, then. But tonight we are having a nice pozole that Ignacio put in the crock pot this morning. Not too spicy, because we intended to invite you."

Cally smiled and sighed. "Very well, then, but only if you promise not to say anything else to me about Ben Dawes."

Katarina crossed herself, but the look in her eye was still mischievous. "I promise."

Cally put the phones into night mode as Katrina had showed her, and took Bree's gift basket up to Bethany. Bethany was sound asleep, but Cyndi Lauper stood up and sniffed the air when Cally came into the room. "Oh, I hope none of these 'healing herbs' are catnip," she thought, moving things around on the night stand to make room for the basket there. She saw that Foster had, indeed, brought the new prescription for Bethany, but now there were two pill bottles standing side-by-side on the night stand, and though she scrutinized them closely, Cally couldn't tell the difference between them. The name of the drug typed on the labels was the same, and both had the same date. The only difference was that the tiny print stated different strengths per tablet. Cally made a mental note to ask Foster later if Bethany still needed both bottles, or if one of them should be taken back to the pharmacy. In the meantime, she moved them both out of Bethany's reach so she wouldn't wake up in a medicinal fog and accidentally take more than she should.

She made a quick trip to the Rose Room to put her computer on the desk. Locking the door behind her as she came back out of the room, she saw George standing at the end of the hall near the Butler's desk. He looked like he wanted to say something to her, but Cally didn't want to keep Katarina waiting. "I'll be back in a little while," she promised him, waving as she turned away, and she was surprised to find herself actually looking forward to talking with him again.

Katarina had served dessert for Ian and his family, as well as the Captain and Joan, in the dining room by the time Cally met her in the kitchen. Cally cocked her head back toward the dining room. "Where does Joan live, then?" she asked. "She makes so much of all these moochers and freeloaders she believes are taking advantage of Ian's good nature, but I never see her leave here, herself."

Katarina took off her apron and shouldered her purse. "She has a house of her own, down in Charlotte," she said, "but you're right, she hardly ever leaves here. I think she sleeps on the sofa in her office most nights. Though if you asked her, she would probably say that's just because she's up working on 'all this paperwork' all night long!" She laughed. Cally did not.

They went out through the kitchen door into the neat formal garden behind Vale House. Dusk deepened as they walked over the grass to the west end of the property where the little stone cottage stood. "Foster tells me this used to be the kitchen for Vale House," Cally said.

"Yes, it was! In those days, kitchens were always separate buildings. To keep the house from catching fire if the kitchen caught fire, you see!"

"It doesn't seem to have helped keep Vale House from catching fire a few times in its history, though," Cally remarked.

"I'm just glad Vale House has a modern kitchen now," she said. "I can't imagine having to carry food from here to the dining room and expect it to still be warm when I get there!" They rounded the gazebo and from there Cally could see a small, fenced vegetable garden. Ignacio was just closing the door of a tool shed that was apparently also the chicken coop. He reached over the fence to pluck some cilantro and a few tomatoes from the vegetable garden as he joined them.

The little stone building that had once been Vale House's kitchen was nearly swallowed up in overgrown shrubbery and wild grape vines, but its glowing windows peeped cheerfully out over a wide, cracked stone porch. A rich, spicy aroma billowed out in a cloud when Katarina opened the door and ushered Cally inside.

The kitchen was still the biggest part of the cottage, though the rear had been walled off. Cally assumed the back half of the building was now the couple's sleeping space. Ignacio pulled a chair out from the small wooden table for Cally. "Welcome," he said, bowing deeply, "to our little home."

Kat ladled stew from the crock pot on the counter into deep bowls for all of them. It was rich with hominy and vegetables and tender chicken, but if Ignacio had tried to make it "not too spicy" for Cally's sake, he had overestimated her tolerance for spice. She struggled to swallow the first bite, and Katarina blustered with apologies. "No, it's fine, it's delicious," Cally gasped. She was telling the truth. "I'm just getting used to it..."

"Drink this." Ignacio poured her a creamy drink which, when she sipped it, mellowed the spice on her tongue. "I can taste cinnamon," she said of the beverage, and then, braving the stew again, "and lime and oregano. A very good combination. See, I can learn!" she said, still gasping a little.

Cally was glad she had accepted their invitation. Dining with the couple in their humble kitchen was a refreshing contrast to the often tense and pretentious atmosphere in the Vale House dining room, and the way Katarina and Ignacio joked with her and with each other put Cally's heart at ease. She almost forgot Foster's warning to her that Ignacio might not be the gentleman he seemed to be, and she had to make a special effort to keep half an eye open for anything incongruous in his behavior.

After the stew disappeared from the bowls, Katarina whisked them away to the sink just a few feet away, and Ignacio replaced them with tiny cups of strong coffee and plates of mango that he peeled and chopped while Katarina covered the pieces with chili powder and squeezed a lime over them. Cally smiled at how the couple worked together so easily, pausing whenever they passed to offer a loving touch or a word of endearment. She would never have this in her life, she knew; that ship had sailed. But it was still nice to think that other people really could have it. She sat back in contentment, picking at her desert, as the window over the kitchen sink grew dark and night noises began drifting in on the soft breeze.

"Now." Katarina pushed her plate back purposefully and Ignacio jumped up to get the coffee pot to refill their cups. "You remember, Cally, that I was going to tell you something, last night after dinner. But I didn't want to talk about it in front of Mr. May or the rest of the family."

"Yes, I do remember, and I have been wondering what it was."

"It's the story of how Mrs. May died," said Ignacio.

"Oh! No, I'm sorry," Cally said, sitting up. "You don't need to tell me that. It's really not my business."

"It's alright," said Katarina. "Everyone knows it. Well, everyone but you. And you should know."

"By how everyone reacted to what Joan said, I'm guessing it was a fire."

"Well, yes," Katarina said. "But there was much more to it than that. You see, Mrs. May, she... well, she wasn't well. You know how our Nellie is?"

"Oh, yes, I see. Some kind of mental illness."

"Something like that." Katarina's face was uncharacteristically sober as she curled her hands around her cup. "Nobody knows... well, nobody knew then, what it was. Sofia was – they say – kind of like Nell is. I never met her, but that's what they say."

"She was," Ignacio affirmed. "A very sweet woman, but also very odd. Harmless, but easily harmed. Does that make sense?"

Cally nodded, thinking that would also be an apt description of Nell.

"Well," Katarina continued, "She had a good man. Ian protected her and they had a good life. They had little Nell. Ignacio met them when he came here on a guest-worker contract. Ignacio and I were just teenagers then. Mr. May was younger then, too, and he grew strawberries and tomatoes for market, here. He did a lot of the work himself. Ignacio would come every summer to help with the planting and harvest, and every winter when he came home he would tell me about how Mrs. May just got worse every year. The doctors tried giving her medicine..."

"They didn't know what they were doing, back then," Ignacio said sadly.

"The right medication does help some people with mental illnesses lead a more normal life," Cally pointed out.

"Well in those days," said Ignacio, "the medicine only made her worse. Or maybe she was just getting worse anyway. They decided she had to be put away. Ian didn't like it but they told him it was for her own safety." He shook his head.

"It was a nice place, though where they sent her to live," said Katarina. "But it was all the way in Raleigh."

"I guess it was nice enough," said Ignacio. "I visited her sometimes with Ian, back then. Everyone was nice to her there. But it was so far away, and Sofie wasn't happy. She wanted to be home with Ian, and Ian wanted her home, too." He sat back and shrugged. "Ian made up his mind to sneak down there one night and bring her home. He and some of his friends, guys he had grown up with, they were all in on it. The Captain – we just called him Doug, back then – he had been Ian's best man at their wedding, and some other guys who had been their friends for a long time.

"I wasn't really in on the whole scheme, but they didn't try to hide it from me, either. They talked about it on the porch, on the boat, every time they got together. They had it all planned out: they were going to sneak in and make it look like she escaped, then bring her home here, and if someone came looking for her they meant to show the doctors how much happier and better off Sofia was at home. But..." He looked down at his lap and shook his head.

"The building burned down." Katarina concluded for him. "Before they even got there. Something about bad wiring. Ian and the guys got there in time to help, so it's good they had this scheme of theirs, anyway. They helped get everyone out safely, except Sofia. Some say she ran back inside because she knew Ian was coming, and she didn't want to miss his visit. They never found her body. There is a grave for Sofia over there in the family cemetery by the pond, but there is nobody in it." Both Katarina and Ignacio crossed themselves, and Cally felt awkward because she had never been religious and didn't know how to acknowledge the gesture.

"So, Ian was never the same, after that," Katarina concluded. "I came to work here soon after all this, mostly to help with Nell, who was only a young girl then. Ignacio and I both got work visas, and a couple years ago Ignacio became a citizen." She looked up at him when she said this, her eyes glowing with pride. "Mr. May has always treated us like family. But I think really he feels completely alone."

Cally bit her lip. "I'm so sorry," she said. She was thinking she hoped Nell wouldn't suffer the same fate, even if it didn't include the burning part.

"So now Mr. May spends most of his time in his rooms alone," Katarina said. "And we're all very thankful young Nellie has Foster to look after her. Ian's biggest fear was that Nellie would be taken away, too. But Foster seems very devoted to her and makes sure she gets all the proper doctors and medication."

"He's a very successful businessman, back in Raleigh where they live now," Ignacio said. "Nellie will always be well cared for, and that's a big load off Ian's mind."

21 - An Argument With Emerald

Ignacio offered to walk Cally back to the main house, but she assured him nothing could happen to her in such a short distance, on such a beautiful night. Katarina took a key off her key ring and handed it to Cally. "This opens the side door, the one with the cardinal window, facing the shade garden and the street," she said.

"My own key to Vale House," Cally said. "I guess I really am staff now!"

Katarina laughed. "For now, you are! But do me a favor, would you? Please check, before you go upstairs, and make sure the Captain has not fallen asleep on the front porch. Usually Bethany does this before she goes home for the night. We don't want him to spend all night out there in the damp air."

Cally promised she would, and exchanged hugs with the couple on their doorstep. Then she slipped quietly into the dark, quiet space between the house and Main Street. Happy frogs and crickets in the branches overhead filled the night air with a deafening cacophony, and the scent of jasmine on the cooling breeze was almost overpowering. She passed by the little side porch, the stained glass window in its door glowing soft yellow and red, and turned the corner round the side of the house. She could hear snoring from here, and laughed quietly to herself as she headed for the front porch steps.

A waxing gibbous moon hung in a clear sky over the meadow. Only one of the horses was visible at the moment, the white one, standing like such a perfect picture in the moonlight that Cally found herself wishing her talents had run to painting rather than writing. The painted version of the scene would be more perfect because it would not include the cars parked between the house and the fence.

A shadowy figure was walking between the cars. For a moment

it made Cally think of the figure she had seen near the gate during the storm, but this figure was short and hunched over a cane. Cally realized it was only Rum, Ian's neighbor passing through on his way to his "other job." Cally waved at him and he waved his cane over his head at her, walking with perfect ease without it until he passed out of sight down Gardens Road.

The Captain was sitting, sound asleep, in his favorite wicker chair on the porch. Cally touched his shoulder gently and he woke with a start. It took him a moment to orient himself and recognize her. "Oh, hello!" he said then, grinning cheerfully as if he hadn't just been roused from sleep. He raised his flask toward the moon above the meadow and said "Peaceful night." It sounded like a benediction as much as an observation.

"Quite different from the other night," she agreed. She stood with him awhile, declining his offer of a sip from his flask. Then he let her help him to his feet and open the front door for him. Switching off the porch light, Cally locked the front door behind her as the Captain made his way toward the back hall. She felt very much indeed like official Vale House staff.

Lights were still on in the parlor, and Cally looked in to see Nell sitting hunched forward on one of the sofas with a remote control in her hand, deeply absorbed in something she was watching on the old console television. This reminded Cally of the preacher she had last seen sitting in this room, and she wondered what had ever become of him. She slipped past quietly and headed up the stairs.

When she reached the Gallery she heard voices rising from the dining room below and peered over the railing. Ian and Foster were seated at the dining table. The lamp from the desk in the Hall had been placed in the center of the table, amid a sea of papers spread between the two men. Foster was saying, "If you will only look at this, Ian, you'll see that it completely makes sense."

Ian noticed Cally's presence, looking up to wave to her, but Foster was on a roll and clearly wanted Ian's full attention. He tapped a paper in front of him. "Here," he said. "You could double your net worth in only three years, don't you see?"

"I don't think..." Ian began, and Cally didn't think that was the kind of conversation she should be privy to, so she withdrew from the railing and put her head inside door of the Daffodil room instead.

Bethany was snoring softly, as was Cyndi Lauper on her knee.

She returned to the hallway, disappointed she did not see George near the butler's desk or at the gallery railing. Unlocking the Rose Room door, she went inside to find her bed had been made properly, with all the throw pillows back in place. She sighed and rolled her eyes. She couldn't even imagine who might have done that, now. Bethany could not have, Kat knew not to, and Joan certainly would never do anything resembling housework. Maybe it had been Ignacio? "Or maybe one of Georgie's other ghost friends, one who is good at moving things," she said, meaning it to be sarcasm, but not really sure it was.

Still, she was surprised to find it didn't bother her as much anymore. As long as they left her underwear drawer alone, anyway. She went to the dresser to peek into the drawers; that was when she saw it. Someone had opened her laptop on the desk and turned it on. The chat program was running.

"Damn it!" She flung open the door and looked up and down the hall, seeing no one to chastise, human or ghostly, which was fortunate for them, she thought.

Muttering many unladylike words, she sat down at the desk and reviewed the text scrolling by in the chat program. It was a series of inquiries from Emerald, all of them along the lines of "Are you there?" "Is everything alright?" and, "Are you OK?" Cally typed in a quick response to reassure her friend.

Cally>> I'm fine! I was just out.

Emerald<< Thank goodness! I was worried. You opened the chat but never said anything.

Cally>> It wasn't me. I don't know who it was. But when I find out, they are dead meat.

Emerald<< You're right to be upset. Nobody should be messing with your computer.

Cally>> I have a feeling you can tell me who it might have been.

Emerald<< What? How would I know?

Cally>> Emerald. Why didn't you tell me?

Emerald<< Tell you what? I really don't know who did it.

Cally>> Why didn't you tell me George is a ghost?

Emerald<< Oh that.

Cally>> Yes. That.

Emerald<< I'm sorry.

Cally>> That's what he said.

Emerald<< I guess things went faster than I expected.

Cally>> What things? What were you expecting? What the hell, Emerald, have you set me up for something here and not told me? Why would you do that to me!

Instead of feeling calmer, as she usually did when she chatted with Emerald, Cally felt herself growing more and more agitated. In the back of her mind she had been expecting Emerald to be the one who could explain everything to her in her usual, perfectly reasonable manner. Now she began to realize the only explanation she was going to get was not going to be anything resembling reasonable. She felt betrayed, but then, it wouldn't be the first time she had discovered someone she trusted was not as reliable as they seemed to be.

Emerald<< I can explain. This will take a while. How tired are you?

Cally>> Damn it! You know what I hate most about this?

Emerald<< What?

Cally>> My daughter was right! I was crazy to run out into the night following the advice of someone I don't even know!

Emerald<< Cally you do know me. And I know you. That's why I thought this would be perfect for you!

Cally>> How can this be perfect? I don't even know what's going on here! How is that perfect?

Emerald<< I figured it would all become clear in its own good time. And Georgie promised to help. But something is apparently going on that they didn't intend.

Cally>> Who is "they"?

Emerald<< Georgie and his friends. And a few others.

Cally>> How many ghosts are there here? Or do I have to figure that out for myself, too?

Emerald<< They aren't all ghosts.

Cally>> Yes, so George tells me.

Cally pulled her hands off the keyboard. She felt dizzier than she had when she'd realized George was a ghost, when she'd had her first conversation with him. Emerald had been such a good friend for such a long time. She had confided everything in her. They had laughed and cried together about so many things over so many years. Under normal circumstances, she would be telling Emerald right now all about her extremely bizarre past couple of days, but circumstances were no longer normal. Now text was scrolling by on the screen saying "Cally please listen to me!" and Cally just wanted to slam the computer shut. Maybe her daughter was also right that she should just give up on the idea of writing and go live in the guest bedroom and help pay the bills with a series of copy editing gigs.

Emerald<< Cally I am so sorry. I never meant to hurt you!

Cally>> Where have I heard that before?

Emerald<< :(

Cally>> Oh, hell, Emerald. Whoever you are. It's not your fault. I'm the one who's stupid enough to get myself into these kinds of situations.

Emerald<< You're not stupid. I am on your side. But what was I supposed to say? "Oh, just go and meet my dear old friend who is the ghost of a gay pirate. And by the way, you might be chosen to be the guardian of the gateway - it'll be fun!"?

Cally>> Gateway? And pirates! Who is a pirate?

Emerald<< Georgie

Cally>> He's just a perfectly ordinary teenager.

Emerald<< A four hundred year old teenager

Cally>> And what about you? Emerald with no last name or hometown? Of whom I have never seen a real photograph. And never asked for one because I trusted you. Are you a ghost, too?

Emerald<< Not exactly

Cally>> JUST WHAT THE HELL IS THAT SUPPOSED TO MEAN?

Emerald<< It's a long story.

Cally>> I seem to be owed a lot of long stories these days!

Emerald<< You're right. And I will tell mine to you. You can even write a book about it, if you want. Though that makes me nervous. Will you let me type it all out for you and send it to you in the morning? My story, that is.

Cally>> Fine

Emerald<< Suffice it to say, for now, that I exist in the wires.

Cally>> You're a bot, then?

Emerald<< LOL. Oh, please, I hope it hasn't come to that. That would be a fate much worse than being a ghost!

Cally>> Ok, Emerald, listen. I am going to try to get some sleep. You write me a story, and I promise I'll read it.

Emerald<< Thank you. Cally, be careful.

Cally>> Too late.

Emerald<< No, I mean. There's still the question of who opened your computer. Nobody I know of would do that. Something is going on, and I'm worried about you. Please be careful.

Cally>> Apparently caution is not my strong suit.

Emerald<< Oh, and Cally?

Cally>> What

Emerald<< Sarcasm does not become you.

Cally>> Thank you for that insight. Goodnight, Emerald.

Emerald<< Sweet dreams, my friend.

Cally closed the laptop gently, because she knew if she slammed it as hard as she wanted to, she would no longer have even the means of trying to make a living, and would definitely have to go and live with someone more practical than she was. She crawled into the bed, throwing the little rose shaped pillows into the corner of the room. Switching off the light, she drew the covers over her head and cried herself to sleep for the first time in years.

At some point during the night, she thought she felt someone standing by her bedside, and heard them muttering "There, there, dear." She felt her hair being brushed back from her brow by cool, smooth fingers, and the covers being arranged around her chin. She was too tired to wake up enough to determine whether it was a dream, or a ghost, or what.

22 - Nell's Childhood Friends

"George, are you here?" Cally stood outside the Rose Room door, looking left and right at the butler's desks at either end of the hall, but did not see anyone, and did not receive a reply. She closed the door behind her, then went and knocked on the partly open door of the Daffodil Room, again receiving no reply.

She put her head inside the door. Bethany lay fast asleep, and Cally didn't like her color. She seemed very pale, and her skin seemed waxy in the sunlight. Doctor Boojums sat upright on the bed and did not look pleased, either. He watched Cally closely as she leaned over to look at Bethany's face. Her breathing seemed shallow and just a little too rapid.

Both pill bottles were still on the night stand. Cally knew when Bethany did wake up, it would be well past time for her next dose. "We need to sort out which one or ones she is supposed to be taking," Cally said. "I think I'll try to contact the doctor this morning.

"The human doctor, not you," she added with a glance at Doctor Boojums. He seemed to be satisfied with this, and lay back down with his forefeet tucked under his chest.

When Cally went down to breakfast, Nell was the only person seated in the dining room, and the expression on her face was sad. "Foster is talking to Dad in his rooms," she said as Cally sat down across from her. "He and I have to go back to our own house in Raleigh on Saturday." She stirred her oatmeal absently, making no attempt to eat it.

"Well, I'm glad I got a chance to meet you," Cally said. "You must enjoy visiting your dad."

Nell nodded, her customary shy smile returning. "And everyone else. Kat and Ignacio and Bethany and everyone. I grew up here," she said. "But Foster says a girl has to leave the nest sometime."

"I suppose he's right," Cally assured her. "Though someday this house will be yours, and maybe then you can live here again."

Nell smiled, but glanced over Cally's shoulder toward the Hall before saying, very quietly, "No, Foster says dad will have to sell the house before that ever happens. He says Dad is *not getting any younger you know!*" Her voice was a very good imitation of Foster's. "And Joan, well, she humors dad, but she's really on Foster's side. What she really hopes for most is for Dad to be sensible and marry her and go live with her in one of those retirement villages in Charlotte."

"I don't think Ian May will ever sell this house," Cally said quite honestly. She couldn't picture him without picturing Vale House as well; the day he left it would be the day he died. She didn't say this out loud to Nell. She did say, "I honestly don't think he will ever be interested in marrying Joan, either." She kept an eye on Nell's face to make sure Joan wasn't walking up behind her.

"Foster says Dad is too easily manipulated. He thinks Dad might even end up leaving a lot of money to Joan in his will."

"That's none of Foster's business," Cally snorted. "And in any case I'm sure your dad will always see that you are well taken care of."

"Foster takes care of me now." Nell sounded like she was repeating what others often said to her. Then she brightened. "And anyway distance never separates true friends, you know! I still have all my friends I grew up with. Who were you talking to?"

"What?"

"Upstairs, in the hallway, a little while ago. I thought I heard you talking to Georgie."

"Georgie?" Cally remembered Emerald had always used the affectionate diminutive when referring to George, but was surprised to hear Nell speaking of him the same way.

"Georgie the Friendly Ghost!" Nell laughed nervously. "No, there is no Georgie. That was just a silly book I read as a child. I have to grow up sometime. I'm going down to the pond this morning. Do you want to come?"

"I really should get some work done," said Cally.

"Okay. Don't tell Foster where I'm going." She left her breakfast unfinished and went out into the sunny morning.

☽

"Well." Joan surveyed the desk, spying Cally's laptop there. "Now, don't get so caught up in your own work you end up neglecting your duties here! There's lots of work to be done!"

Cally braced herself to ignore, per Ian's advice, the impending talking-to about how Joan would not reduce her room rate just because she was helping out. But Joan seemed preoccupied with other concerns that morning. She dangled her empty mug from one hand and gazed up the stairs.

"That woman," she said. She turned to Cally and looked down at her. "I don't know what she's thinking, but whatever it is, it won't work."

Cally could only give her a puzzled look. Did she think Bethany had got hurt on purpose, in order to get out of work?

When Cally didn't reply, Joan went on. "She's been after Ian for years. Decades! What could she possibly be thinking? She looks so old!" She drew herself up. "Would you believe, she's actually two years younger than I am? But she does nothing to keep herself up. She doesn't even bother to do anything with her hair." She ran a hand over her own brass toned coif, bracelets rattling as she did so. "And those silly, old-fashioned flowered dresses she wears! How could she possibly imagine she could ever compete? I work at my appearance. He'll never choose her." She glared at Cally, as if daring her to disagree.

"I had no idea he was planning to make a choice," Cally replied at length.

"It's not the money!" Joan said sharply. "Everyone thinks I'm after his money. He doesn't even have that much left, anymore, I don't think. But he's a sweet man." Her voice softened at this last.

"He is," Cally agreed. "And very good looking, for his age. I'd hit that, if I were a little older."

"A little old..." Joan's mouth dropped open, then snapped shut again as she turned on her heel and clomped out of the Hall toward the kitchen.

When she was gone, Cally covered her face with both hands. "Callaghan McCarthy, your mouth is going to get you into real trouble someday," she muttered. Then she added, "But it might be worth it."

A choking noise from the direction of the parlor doorway made her look up, and she saw Katarina emerge with her arms wrapped around her middle as she struggled to keep herself from laughing. "*I'd hit that if I were a little older*, oh Dios mío!" she spluttered. "I can't believe you said that! Oh, I can't breathe!" She finally doubled over laughing out loud; Cally was afraid she would fall on the floor right there in the Hall.

"I can't believe I said it, either," Cally said. "I mean, I would. Hit that. Only, if I were younger and more foolhardy, like I used to be. But she makes me so mad. The way she talks about you and Bethany. And everyone. How do you put up with it?"

Katarina wiped tears from the corners of her eyes, trying to master her mirth. "No, we just ignore her." She gasped and caught her breath. "We are here for Mr. May, not for her. Ignacio says: her attitude is not a reflection on us, it's a reflection on her."

"He's a wise man," said Cally.

Doctor Tanahey was reluctant to speak to Cally about Bethany's medication, due to patient confidentiality, but Ian came to the rescue when he passed through the hall and overheard her trying desperately to explain the situation over the phone.

"Daniel and I are old friends," he explained, gently taking the phone from Cally's hand. "And I am the closest thing to family Ms. Chase has, nowadays." He put the phone to his ear and explained the confusion about the medication. "Yes," he said, and "No. Well, no..."

Cally couldn't make much sense of the only side of the conversation she could hear, and waited patiently until Ian lowered the phone and said, "He says she should be taking just the ones labeled twenty milligrams. He says he'll come and collect the other ones. And he wants to know if you remember when was the last time she had any, and which dose she took?"

Cally shook her head. "Katarina says she doesn't even think Bethany has been awake to take any, since yesterday afternoon."

Ian passed this information to the doctor on the other end of the phone, and then smiled and gave Cally a thumbs-up to indicate this was fine. Finally he said "Alright, Doc, we'll see you tomorrow then." He handed the phone back to Cally and said "If you could bring the bottle with the lower dose downstairs and lock it in the drawer here, he will come and take it away in the morning."

"Lower dose?" Cally asked. It seemed to her the lower dose was the one Bethany should be taking, since she was sleeping so much. But maybe now that they knew the proper instructions, Bethany would start to show signs of recovery.

She went upstairs to get the superfluous pill bottle, and paused at Bethany's bedside to straighten her covers and smooth back her hair. Doctor Boojums and Cyndi Lauper were both sitting on the coverlet vigorously grooming themselves, but Bethany was quite deeply asleep in spite of this. It didn't strike Cally as a peaceful sleep. Bethany seemed to be struggling to breathe, a symptom, Cally guessed, of her injured ribs.

She turned to the night stand to pick up the pill bottles so that she could compare the labels, now that she knew what to look for, but was alarmed to find there was now only one bottle on the night stand. Squinting at the tiny print on the label, she saw it was the one with the lower dosage: fifteen milligrams – not the one the doctor had said Bethany should be taking. She shook her head and put the bottle down sharply, looking around the room. The other bottle did not appear to be anywhere in sight. Maybe Katarina had made a guess and taken the other one away?

In her haste to dash downstairs and ask Katarina about the matter, Cally almost ran right into Foster, who was just coming into the room. After they both spluttered and made mutual apologies, he said, "I've just come to check on Ms. Chase. How is she today?"

"Sleeping too much!" Cally said, nodding toward the bed. Cyndi Lauper hissed and leapt off the coverlet when Foster approached the bedside, running out of the room in a streak of orange and black, but Doctor Boojums remained where he was, eyeing the man closely.

Foster picked up the pill bottle on the night stand and looked quickly at the label. "This seems too high a dose for her," he said, explaining "I have a lot of experience with pharmaceuticals, what with having to monitor all the medication Nell has to take."

"Too high? No, Doctor Tanahey said that is the lower dose. Or maybe she's just taken too many, in her confusion," Cally suggested. "Maybe we should have Katarina keep the medicine and just bring it to her on the proper schedule?"

"I don't think that would be a good idea," Foster said quickly. "And not just because Katarina is not trained as a nurse. You see, it could make her, and Ian as well, liable if anything should go wrong. And you know what I fear might be going wrong." He put a hand on Cally's shoulder and bent close to her ear. "Listen, I have to go into Blackthorn in a few minutes. I can stop in at Doc's office on my way out of town, and ask him what to do about this medicine situation. Meanwhile, I hope I can count on you to keep watch over who comes and goes in this room. Have you seen Nell?"

"She..." Cally remembered Nell had asked her not to tell Foster she had gone down to the pond. "I think she said she was going for a walk."

"Damnit!" Foster frowned deeply. "You shouldn't have let her leave the house alone!" The way he looked at Cally, his grip tightening on her shoulder, made her step back in alarm.

"I'm sorry," she said. "I didn't realize." She refrained from finishing the sentence: "*I didn't realize it was my responsibility to look after a grown woman.*" She wasn't sure whether she was defending herself, or Nell.

Turning away, he set the pill bottle back down and clenched and unclenched his fists, taking several deep breaths. "No, I'm sorry," he said. "It's not your fault. You see her as a grown woman. She seems very intelligent, and she is, but she has... issues. It's really not safe for her to wander around outside alone." His face melted into a smile as he turned back and stepped closer to Cally. "I love her dearly, but sometimes it wears me down. Taking care of her can be exhausting."

Cally stepped back instinctively but she said, "I understand. I'm glad she has you. She's so sweet and unique."

"Oh, she's unique, alright," said Foster. His face grew sad. "Sometimes it's..." He stepped toward Cally again and laid his hands on her shoulders. "Sometimes it gets very lonely, you know?

She can be like a child in so many ways, if you know what I mean, and, well, I have needs, too, and she doesn't understand. I'm sure you know what it's like, being all alone, yourself, and..."

Cally wanted to step back again, to get his hands off her shoulders, but the idea of having to take another step back from a man got her back up. She took a step closer to him instead and spoke directly into his face. "I am quite happy with my life as it is," she said. "I decided that a long time ago. And shouldn't we be looking for Nell, if she's in so much danger on her own?" She turned without waiting for his reply, and walked out of the room.

"Yes, of course," Foster called after her, but she was already halfway down the stairs.

☽

Cally did intend to look for Nell, but only in order to warn her that Foster was looking for her. She followed the back hall to the kitchen and went through it, exiting the house through the garden door. From there, she imagined she should be able to round the corner of the house and go down the hill to the pond, and it turned out she was right.

She didn't see Nell anywhere, though, once the pond came into view. Ian and Ignacio were standing together on the wooden walkway leading to the Pirate Ship. A large, lumpy tool bag lay at Ignacio's feet, and the two men were engaged deeply in conversation. "We haven't seen her," Ignacio said, when Cally ran to them and asked about Nell. "But she likes to walk all the way around." He waved an arm to indicate the path that followed the banks of the pond in either direction. Then he cupped his hands around his mouth and took a deep breath to call Nell's name.

"No!" said Cally, putting a hand on his arm. "I'll go look for her. It looks like a lovely walk anyway. If you see her, please tell her Foster is... getting worried about her." She gave him a meaningful look, and Ignacio nodded his understanding.

She started at the end of the path on her left, through the willows and birches that cradled the stern of the Pirate Ship. It turned out she didn't have to go far. Just as she was rounding the bend, where the path dipped down to cross bare mud next to the shore, she saw a pale arm waving at her from the underbrush. Nell's face smiled out from within the birches, looking like a forest elf or some fey creature. Cally tried to find her way through the slender trunks and undergrowth, but branches caught in her hair and snapped at her face, so Nell had to come and help her. Taking her hand, the young woman led her to a narrow path which twisted its way down to a wide, flat rock jutting from the muddy bank into the water. Here Nell sat down and patted the rock next to her. There was just enough room for both of them.

"Foster is worried about you," Cally said, sitting down and trying to get comfortable on the hard, uneven surface. "You should get back to the house now."

"I wanted to show you my secret place," Nell said. "I'm glad you came!" Nell hugged her knees and smiled, looking out toward the water. "You can see everything from here!"

Cally agreed. Swiveling her head around, she could easily see out through the leaves and slender branches to the pond, the old boat, the hill on which Vale House stood and even, on the far side of the pond across the fields, a few distant houses next to the edge of the forest. "You certainly can," she said. "And yet nobody can see you, here."

Nell grinned. "Not if we're very still," she said.

Cally looked up toward the house, expecting to see Foster running down the hill calling Nell's name, but he did not appear, for all his concern, to have left the house at all yet. She turned back to Nell and tried another approach to convince her to go back to the house. "Don't you ever worry about falling in the water?"

"You mean the mud?" Nell laughed, but quietly. "No, I never worry, here. I always feel safe here. My mother's grave is right over there." She nodded toward the field just where it began to run uphill toward Vale House, and Cally saw a short hedge with a white-painted gate in it. "That's our family cemetery. Of course my mother isn't actually buried there, but that's where her headstone is, and Dad and I will be there someday, too."

"How... nice." Cally couldn't quite think how to reply to a statement like that.

"Let me introduce you to some of my friends," Nell said, completely changing the subject. "It's OK, I think they like you..."

She held out a hand, palm upward, toward the pond as if she were inviting a dragonfly to land on it. After the things Cally had seen lately, though, she more than half expected a water spirit or talking frog to rise up out of the cattails instead.

"It's just that Foster really is a bit frantic, looking for you," she pressed. As if to emphasize her words, they at last heard Foster's voice calling Nell's name.

Nell frowned. "People always call me Nell. Or Nellie."

"What would you rather be called?" Cally asked.

"My real name is Helen. That's what my mother named me."

"It's a beautiful name." Cally smiled at her. "But..." She looked again toward the sound of Foster's voice, booming from the direction of the house in increasingly strident tones.

"He wants to get away from here and go back to the city. To Blackthorn, today, but he always misses the city," Nell said. She threw back her thin shoulders and frowned, looking longingly toward the pond.

"You should let him know you're alright, anyway," Cally urged, "Before he calls the sheriff to drag the pond looking for you."

"Oh!" Nell stood up in alarm and looked toward the house. "I can't let that happen. That would be bad!" She reached a hand down to Cally. "Let's go this way. So he won't see where we came from."

She led them, crouching under the overhanging branches, in the direction away from the boat until they emerged in the fields at the north end of the pond. The little family cemetery basked peacefully in the sunshine here, but Vale House could not be seen at all beyond the willow-oaks at the top of the hill. Nell waved her arm toward the distant forest and the cottages at the far edge of the fields. "This all used to be part of The Vale; it all belonged to Vale House, a long time ago, until Great-Granddad sold off some of the land for people to build houses," she said.

"Helen, you remind me of your father when you talk like that."

Nell beamed at her, then led on. They passed around the lower curve of the bank and on into the birches crowding the eastern bank of the pond. Here the path turned uphill once more, and finally emerged into the lawn below Vale House. Nell waved to her father, who was now sitting on the deck of the Pirate Ship with a fishing pole in his hands. Ignacio and his tool bag had gone.

"Nell!" Foster came running down the hill from the house. His face was angry, but when he drew near he got control of himself and embraced his wife. "I was worried about you!" he said. He did not look at Cally.

Ian stood up and ambled slowly over to join them. Foster took Nell's hand and turned to him. "We would love to stay for dinner," he said. "But I've just got a call from the bank manager in Blackthorn, so we're going there tonight. You are coming with me," he said to Nell before she could protest. "I can't let you out of my sight." He explained to Ian, "I'm going to buy the bank manager a nice dinner. Nellie will enjoy a fancy night out. And if I play my cards right, that idea we talked about could become reality! " He pulled Nell by the hand up the hill. "Don't wait up for us."

23 - Moochers and Freeloaders

Cally resumed her work at the desk in the hall. Joan came out of her office and crossed through the Hall several times, on her way to and from the kitchen to refill her tea mug, but she had nothing to say to Cally and did not look at her. Cally began to feel a little sorry about the snarky remark she'd made earlier – but not too sorry.

She dug through the papers she had filed the day before, and found the ones Bethany had told her about – bills with payment checks attached that had not yet been signed, and the notes saying "Ian please sign here." She piled them on the corner of the desk, returning the ones that had been marked "paid" and initialed "I. M." to their proper folders in the drawer.

After Nell and Foster had left for Blackthorn, Katarina came into the Hall to offer Cally lunch. Cally took the opportunity to ask her if she knew what had happened to the second pill bottle. "Only it was the one with the correct dose in it, the doctor said this morning."

"Oh, no." Kat shook her head. "No, I didn't do anything with either bottle. Maybe it fell off the night stand? I'll look for it when I try to get Bethany to eat some lunch. If she's awake and interested in company I'll call down to you, and you can join us!"

"That would be nice," she said, and then thought to suggest, "Maybe you can ask Ignacio if he's seen the medicine?"

Katarina promised to do so, and Cally settled in to try and work on her book for a while, but she had hit a block after the first page of her new Chapter 1. Maybe it was Joan's voice droning through the office doorway, complaining about various matters to unfortunate souls on the other end of the line, that was disturbing her. She turned on her MP3 player and put in her earbuds, combing through her research notes, looking for inspiration. Maybe she could interview Bethany tomorrow, if she was feeling better then.

And maybe she really would interview George, too. She looked up from time to time, half expecting – or hoping? – to see him slouching there smiling at her, but he did not put in an appearance that afternoon.

Over the course of the afternoon, Cally took several phone calls from people wanting to book reservations. Most of them were people who wanted to stay at Vale House during October, due to the house's reputation for being haunted. But when Cally looked at the October section of the register, she found it already booked almost solid. "Maybe Joan has something there, after all," she thought, noting with a smile that the Iversons had booked the Wisteria Room for October 31.

She was, however, perplexed to see the entire page for October 25 blocked out with a large, double X in dark blue marker. In the end, she was only able to find room for one party of four, early in the month of October, and had to express her regrets to the rest of the callers.

Joan emerged from her office with her purse over her shoulder, during one of these calls, and scowled at Cally until she hung up. "Why are you turning down business?" she asked sharply.

"It's for October," Cally said. "You're almost booked up for the whole month already."

Joan grunted, "If Ian would throw out some of these freeloaders and hangers-on," she said, "We'd have room for more paying guests!"

"And then there's this..." Cally turned the register around and showed Joan the page for the 25th of October. "For some reason you are closed for a whole day right in the middle of the busiest season?" She tapped the big, blue X with a finger.

"Nobody stays in this house on October twenty fifth," Joan stated flatly. "Nobody. Even the Captain has to go find somewhere else to mooch, that night."

"But why?"

Joan glared at her. "It doesn't do any good to ask," she said. "It's a rule. It's been that way since Ian's grandfather's day," She glanced up at the portraits above the fireplace behind Cally, then put her tea mug down on the desk. "Take that to the kitchen," she said, pulling her keys out of her purse. "I'm going in to Blackthorn to get my hair and nails done for our big day tomorrow. The paranormal investigators will be here by three o'clock. I hope you also intend to make yourself presentable by then. Good luck with that, since there aren't any beauty parlors in this pathetic little town."

Cally shut the book sharply and put it back in the drawer. "I'm sure I'll manage to make myself presentable, somehow," she said.

As soon as Joan's little white car had left the parking lot, Cally closed her laptop and opened the key drawer. Removing one of the few keys that did not have a flower fob on it, she walked across the hall to Joan's office door and let herself in. A faint twinge of guilt stopped her for only a second as she paused in the doorway and looked backward into the empty Hall, then she shut and locked the door behind her.

The room was dim, lit only by a lamp on the modern office desk and the light of a television on the book case. The television was muted, silently showing a program that seemed to be about renovating old houses for re-sale. The desk was covered with papers, but none of them appeared to pertain to the running of a business. Most of them were junk mail and mail-order catalogs. Heavy, dark drapes on the large windows were drawn shut, and it took Cally's eyes awhile to adjust enough to see the rest of the room.

In structure, the room was almost a mirror-image of the large parlor across the hall, and was even furnished with comfortable sofas and chairs in addition to Joan's desk, though most of this furniture had sheets drawn over it. "This would be a lovely room if someone would clean it up a bit," Cally thought. "And open the drapes and let the sun in." She had a perverse idea she should open the drapes and leave them open when she left the room. Joan could blame the ghosts. Cally grinned, but left the drapes alone.

The room did differ from the main parlor in that it did not extend all the way back to the back hall, but ended instead in a wide closet. Beside this closet, in an alcove, Cally spotted what appeared to be the foot of a dark staircase. "What would you call that, then?" she wondered. "The front backstairs?" She stuck her head into the alcove and looked up. The stairs were very narrow, and after only three steps rounded a corner and continued into the dark. Cally wished she had a flashlight, but she went up the first three steps anyway. The staircase appeared to continue up, winding around every three steps, until Cally could see light at the top. "This is really a bad idea," she told herself, but she couldn't stop now. She went the rest of the way up.

The stairs emerged into a room very similar to all the upstairs guest rooms, but this one had not been decorated in any botanical theme. The walls were plain white and the carpet was beige. Plain white curtains framed windows that looked out on the same view as the one visible from the Rose Room. An unmade bed faced the dresser on which stood a large television set (currently playing a program about a psychologist who was encouraging a young woman to sob out the details of her childhood trauma for the benefit of a studio audience.) More magazines covered the night stand and the upholstered chair by the bed.

"So Joan *does* live at Vale House!" Cally exclaimed. "So much for booting out all the freeloaders and hangers-on to make room for paying guests!" Joan was right about one thing: Ian really was too kindhearted for his own good.

Cally decided it would probably be wisest to leave through the door that led out to the upstairs hall, rather than risk going back down through Joan's office. She did so, nearly tripping on a pair of shoes on her way, and emerged into the south end of the upstairs hall. This door did not face the open Gallery railing, but instead faced across the hall to a narrow closet door marked "Staff Only."

Cally turned to close the door behind her and gasped. There was no knob on this side of the door. In fact, the door on this side was not a door at all, but was instead covered with wallpaper and wainscoting to exactly match the wall. Cally pushed it carefully shut and ran her hand over it. If she had not just come out through it, she would not have been able to tell there was a door there at all.

She ducked her head into the Daffodil room to check on Bethany (who was still sound asleep, with Doctor Boojums snoozing next to her elbow) she slipped back down the stairs to the front desk. She replaced the key in the drawer and checked the voicemail.

24 - Not A Date

"About time to call it a day, I'd say," said Katarina, coming into the Hall with an armload of folded towels.

"Kat, let me help you with that," said Cally, but the woman shook her head. "I'm about to go home, myself. I've made fried chicken for Mr. May and the Captain. They'll be eating in the kitchen, and I am sure they would both be very happy if you would join them."

"No, I can't keep mooching and freeloading," Cally said, grinning. *"This is a Bed and Breakfast, not a Bed and Three Meals a Day!"*

"Oh, your Joan imitation needs work," said Katarina, shaking her head. "Or you could join Ignacio and me again. We enjoyed your company last time. Maybe you can convince Ignacio to make tacos!"

Cally laughed, but insisted on having dinner on her own for once. "I still haven't given young Luke's pizza place any business," she pointed out.

"Tell him I said I hope the Force will be with him!" Katarina chuckled at her own joke. "And maybe while you're in town, you can stop in at the news store."

"Sure, what do you need me to pick up for you?" Cally said, standing up and gathering her laptop and notebooks.

Katarina smirked at her but did not press the issue. "I will check on Bethany one more time before I go home for the evening. You just have a nice time, okay? If you get home late and the Captain has already gone in, you can just use that key I gave you to the side door."

"I'm sure I won't be late," Cally said. She took her things

upstairs to drop them off in the Rose Room, and was pleased to see nobody had disturbed her belongings or even come in to make her bed all day long. She left her laptop and notebooks in a pile on the desk. As she passed by the Daffodil Room she saw that Cyndi Lauper had arrived to relieve Doctor Boojums of guard duty. The little calico was sitting with one leg stuck up in the air, giving her furry belly a wash. "Take good care of our friend," Cally told the cat as she left.

She went out to the parking area to pay her car a brief visit, though she intended to walk into town rather than drive. "I promise I haven't forgotten you," she told all the boxes in the back seat, and patted the car's fender as she left. She saw Ian May and the Captain making their leisurely way up the hill from the Pirate Ship. They both sounded very merry indeed, and waved to Cally. "Ms. McCarthy!" Ian called as they drew near. "You should bring your boxes and things inside. I'm sure Ignacio could find someplace to store them for you as long as you're here."

Cally assured him that though this was a kind offer, she was sure her things would be fine in the car. The two old gentlemen continued companionably toward the house. Halfway up the walk, the Captain's cane hit a tussock of grass between the pavers and he stumbled. Ian caught him under the arm and nearly fell, himself, but they recovered themselves before Cally could run to them, gasping. "We'll be fine!" the Captain called cheerfully to her, waving. She watched them from the corner of her eye until she saw they had got safely through the front door.

As she emerged from the residential oaks into the warm evening light of Main street, Cally saw Merv Arkwright sitting on his loading dock, tuning up an acoustic guitar. She waved to him before he could wave to her first, and made a meaningless remark about the weather, pleased with herself for having, she thought, mastered the art of being a proper small-town denizen. Across the street, Dawes News had its lights on inside, but Cally deliberately averted her eyes and did not look to see if Ben and his skinny hips were there.

She waited until she had passed the news store before crossing the street, then headed down the southern end of Railroad Street. From there she had only to follow her nose past the law offices of Reid and Johnston to where Motherboard Pizza stood out like a glowing jewel in red and yellow between its drab neighbors (Doctor Tanahey's office, she noted with interest, on one side, and the post office on the other.) Delicious aromas emanated from the pizza shop's open door, and computer-printed signs in the windows advertised bargain computer repair rates and hand-tossed artisanal pizza with fresh, local ingredients, including "Champagne Truffle Brie and Artichoke Heart Focaccia." Cally stood just outside the open door, studying the posters carefully with a dubious expression.

"It's actually pretty good pizza," said a voice behind her.

She jumped, and turned to see Ben Dawes. Looking at his blue eyes to keep herself from verifying Katarina's estimate of his hips, she said "It's just that I'm not really in the mood for pizza. Not even gourmet pizza." She gestured at Luke's clever signs. "What this town really needs is a burger joint!"

"Among other things," Ben agreed. "You'd be surprised to hear it, but this town was once a really happening place."

"I haven't heard that expression in a long time," said Cally.

"Guess I'm showing my age," Ben grinned, shrugging and looking away.

"Well, I knew what you meant, so that shows mine, too."

Ben gazed past her to the south end of Railroad Street, where the porch lights were starting to come on in the fronts of the houses on the hill rising there. "Hey," he said. "Do you want to get out of here for a while? There actually *is* a very good burger place in Blackthorn."

Certain parts of Cally did indeed very much want to "get out of there" with Ben, but that made her other parts of her – mainly her brain – want to decline the offer.

"I don't mean it like a date or anything," Ben said quickly, as if he had sensed her discomfort. "Just that you made me think of burgers."

Cally laughed. "I don't know if I should take that as a compliment or not!" Ben stammered, fumbling for a way to respond, and Cally decided to cut him some slack. He was just being a nice guy, after all. She said, "Yes, thank you, I would love to try this amazing burger place. I'll give Luke's Motherboard Pizza a try some other time."

Ben's warm blue-eyed smile returned, and he bowed slightly,

gesturing toward the end of the street. "This way, then." He led her past the pizza shop and around the far side of the post office. From here, Cally could see the backs of the shops along Main Street. Their windowless rear doors faced a gravel parking lot containing, at present, only three cars. Ben led her to one of these as he dug in his pocket for the keys. Near the steel back door of what Cally figured must be the news store, she saw a small gray coupe that looked to her as if it were a very old style, but if it was old, it was in good condition, and gleamed softly in the fading light. "This is amazing!" she said, gingerly tracing a finger along the smooth curve of the hood.

"It's a post-war Daimler. C-class, 1947, or something close to it," said Ben, coming around to unlock the passenger door for her before going back to open his own side. "It's actually Bree's. Our father left it for her. It's pretty much the only thing he left us."

"Oh," said Cally, hesitating. "Won't she be upset if we take it? I don't want to get her mad at me!"

"She doesn't drive," Ben assured her. "I'm the only person who ever lets the poor Daimler stretch its legs."

Cally got in. The car smelled of brand-new leather inside. "You've taken very good care of it," she said as Ben got in and started the engine. It ran so smoothly she could hardly tell it was running. "Your father should have left it to you instead," then, "Oh, sorry, I hope that wasn't too personal."

He smiled at her as he turned to look out the rear window, backing the car around to leave the parking lot. "No, it's okay," he said. "Our father knew Bree would need more taking care of than I would. She does, too!" He grinned. "Even if she won't admit it."

So Bree must be his sister, Cally realized, and not his mother as she had originally assumed. She refrained from asking for the story behind their apparent wide age difference.

"He meant for her to sell it and buy a better house or something," Ben was continuing. "But she wouldn't. She's too sentimental."

While Cally tried to fit the word "sentimental" into her mental image of Bree Dawes, Ben drove onto Railroad Street but instead of turning left on Main Street, as she had expected him to do to so that they could follow the interstate on down into Blackthorn, he turned right, toward the residential end of town. They passed the feed store and could hear Merv Arkwright and two other men trying to cover an old Eagles song. Their guitar playing was adequate, but they were definitely struggling with the harmonies.

When they reached the residential end of Main Street, Cally sank back into the seat as far as she could. She didn't want to have to deal with what would happen should Katarina catch a glimpse of her in a car with Ben when they passed Vale House.

At the meadow gate, he turned right again, passing all the stately old homes facing the meadow along Gardens Road. The big Yellow House the Captain had grown up in looked dark and unoccupied. Only a handful of houses lined the west side of Gardens Road here, and once past these, the road dipped down to cross a small stream by way of a one-lane bridge, and then curved away between the meadow and a completely dark forest on the right.

"It's remarkable," Cally said. "When you reach the town limits in this part of the country, you really know you've left town!"

Ben nodded, winding down his window and letting in a meadow-scented evening breeze. "The sprawl has not reached us here yet," he agreed. "Some of us are very glad about that."

Cally thought she might be glad about that, too. "It is nice," she agreed, watching the thin ribbon of road unwind in the headlights in front of the car. The Daimler ran so quietly she could hear the frogs and crickets in the trees.

The road plunged down a hill and crossed another bridge, where Ben took a wide right turn into the heart of the forest, and the darkness became absolutely black except for what lay in the headlights just ahead. Moths occasionally flew out of the darkness, trapped in the headlight beams, and splattered on the windshield. Cally began to wonder if she had really made the right decision, going off into the night with a person she barely knew, despite Katarina's esteem for him, but then she saw lights ahead. They passed a gas station, under a single street light, that looked like something out of an old movie.

Presently, more street lights appeared ahead, illuminating a street Cally thought at first looked a lot like Woodley's main street. This street, however, was a much more "happening place." Most of the storefronts were brightly lit, and cars – even if they seemed a little dated – were parked thickly along both sides of the street. As

Ben slowed down to look for a parking spot, Cally could hear music coming from an open doorway.

"They play pretty good music here," Ben noted. They managed to park a few doors away from The Fountain, where people inside and outside the door sat talking and eating in chatty groups. Three young musicians inside were playing 1980s hair-band covers. Cally thought she recognized Errin's friend Zenbe among them. Ben and Cally wove between the crowded tables and managed to find an empty booth near the back of the room. Cally's mouth had begun to water at the smell of sizzling beef.

Accepting two large plastic-coated menus from a server, Ben told Cally "I understand they have a fair wine selection here."

Cally shook her head. "With a good burger, nothing is better than a cold beer." Ben seemed relieved to hear her say this, and she relaxed, thinking he reminded her a little of a younger version of Ian May. "Thank you for suggesting this," she said. The little band launched into a decent cover of a Van Halen song, and several people in the room whooped their approval. She realized she was actually having a nice time.

The burgers were perfect: black on the outside and pink on the inside, nestled in thick, soft rolls. The local ale Ben suggested to go with them was frosty and crisp. As Cally reached the point where she was picking at the last few fries on her plate, considering discarding the rest of her roll so that she could at least finish the patty, Ben leaned toward her, wiping foam from his mustache. "You want to hear some *really* good music?"

They paid for their food and returned to the Daimler, and Ben whisked them out of the far end of the little big town. The road almost immediately returned to fields and forests and bridges. Cally relaxed (maybe it was the beer) and Ben told stories about the Woodley residents he knew – and he knew them all. Cally learned how Merv Arkwright had come to own the feed store, how the two "Wyrd Systers" thought they could save Woodley by opening their weird bookstore there, that Jud Thornton, the hardware store proprietor, wanted to just bulldoze the whole town and build a mall and almost owned enough of the town to be able to do it, and how Joan had been trying for years to get Ian May to marry her. Cally lost count of all the turns in the road, and the bridges over little rivers.

At last she could see light in the distance again, but this was not streetlights. It was a fire, glimpsed through the trees. She thought of the Captain's story, but as they pulled off the road and parked on the verge, she saw it was just a perfectly normal campfire, surrounded by a ring of stones. People were walking among the trees, or seated on logs and tree stumps, and some of them were dancing, though the music Cally could hear was not by any means the "really good music" Ben had promised. It sounded more like an orchestra of little flutes and hand-held rhythm instruments, played by inexpert dabblers, and somewhere a fiddle tuning up.

Ben led Cally to one of the logs beside the fire, and she could see that, beyond it, a dark river flowed silently, reflecting the firelight and fireflies hovering over the water. In a clearing near the bank, an old man was cooking over a grill made from half an oil drum, his dark face gleaming in the firelight and his long, white beard tucked behind his apron. Cally thought she recognized him as Ian's old neighbor Rum, but he seemed much taller.

"That's Jerome," Ben said, laying his jacket on the log for Cally to sit on. "He makes the best ribs east of the Appalachians."

"West of them, too!" said a woman in a long, flowered skirt. She handed Cally a mason jar half full of clear liquid, then danced away.

"You don't have to drink that," Ben leaned over and whispered in her ear. "In fact, I wouldn't recommend it." His grin flashed in the firelight. Cally sniffed the contents and agreed. She passed the jar to the next person on the log.

The character of the music changed as the fiddle player began to feel satisfied with his tuning. He came closer to the fire and drew out a long note, and the people with their little drums and random instruments organized themselves into an eight-beat rhythm. Finally someone with a flute began to play a piping tune; Cally recognized it as an old Irish folk song she had in her CD collection. The fiddle and the other little instruments joined in, and the music became a good, solid reel. People all around them stood up and began dancing, some by themselves and some forming into couples. Cally decided to concur with Ben's assessment of the music here as "really good." She couldn't help tapping her feet.

He stood and reached both hands down to her. "Come on," he

said.

"Oh, I don't really have any idea how to dance to this stuff..."

"Neither do I!" Ben laughed. "Come on!"

The music was contagious and Cally couldn't just sit there and not do anything, so she stood up to join Ben among the dancers. He had told the truth: he really didn't know how to dance to this stuff, any more than did most of the people there. But he didn't step on her feet, and that counted for something.

The ground was uneven underfoot, though, and whirling couples nearby kept bumping into them, so Ben steered them through the trees to the side of the river where the flat mud was hard and there were fewer people to bump into. Cally found herself enjoying herself very much. The music switched to a waltz, which was much easier to dance to. Then Cally began to think they had got too far from the crowd; the quiet near the water began to feel just a little too intimate to her. She drew awkwardly back from Ben's arms and tried to make casual conversation about the weather. He seemed to understand. He released her from the dance, and instead stood beside her and began explaining where they were.

"This is the Harmony River," he said, gesturing out over the broad, black water rippling with reflected firelight. "It's actually the same river you crossed over when you first came into Woodley, only it was still just Harmony Creek at that point."

"An appropriate name," Cally said, tilting her head toward the music near the fire.

"And that's Seen's Mill," Ben added, gesturing across the river to the lights of about a dozen windows on the far bank.

"Where's that?" Cally asked. "I've haven't heard anyone mention it. We must have come a long way."

Ben had gone silent. He was staring across the river, but not at the lights. At least, not at the lights of Seen's Mill. Cally followed his gaze to the far shore where she could barely make out two dim, red lights close to the ground. As she watched, they winked out and then reappeared a short distance away.

Ben took her arm protectively. "We should go," he said.

Cally thought this was a little silly of him. "Whatever it is, it can't get us," she pointed out. "It's on the other side of the river."

"But you can see it..." He hesitated and gave her a long look.

"Well, if you can see it, that means it can see you."

Cally didn't understand his discomfort, but he seemed adamant about it, so she let him guide her up the bank back to the fireside. He said his goodbyes to Jerome and some others, dropping a few dollar bills into a jar on a stump next to the fiddle player. "We'll make sure we're hungry next time we come!" he promised, waving to Jerome and to everyone in general. The piper began another reel, and Ben and Cally returned to where the Daimler waited, softly reflecting firelight, by the side of the road.

Ben was silent as he turned around and drove back over the little roads and bridges. Cally didn't mind – she found herself dozing off once or twice, lulled by the crickets and the gentle air, and at some point was surprised to wake and see the porch lights of Vale House outside her window. Ben was opening the passenger door to help her out.

Though she insisted it wasn't necessary, he walked with her to the house. Cally dug the key to the side door out of her purse, but she didn't need it; the Captain was still on the porch, asleep in one of the wicker chairs, which meant the front door was still unlocked. "I promised Kat I'd get him back inside," Cally explained to Ben. "Thank you so much. I really had a nice time." She meant it. "I hope Bree doesn't give you any grief for pinching her car."

He smiled. "Don't worry," he said. "It's just her way of showing she cares."

Cally watched him go back to the car, then bent over the Captain and shook him awake. She supported him by the arm until he was safely through the door, and watched him go into the dining room and turn toward the back hall where his room lay. When he was out of sight, she said hello to George, who was seated at the desk, grinning hugely at her.

"How was your date?" asked George.

Cally locked the front door and switched off the porch light. "It wasn't a date," she said firmly.

George was bobbing his head as if he were listening to music, but Cally couldn't hear anything. "You left your music device on the desk," he explained. "I've been listening. You have many kinds of music. All of it is very good!"

Cally looked over to see her MP3 player on top of the papers Ian still had not signed. It did not appear to be switched on, but George was clearly grooving to something with a backbeat.

"I can do electronic things," he said. "It has always been the easiest for me. It opened up a whole new world for many of us, when radio and television were invented."

Cally looked at him carefully. He was dressed, this time, in what appeared to be a perfectly pressed navy blue oxford shirt. "You weren't ... here... when it was invented, were you?" she asked. " Radio and TV, I mean. When did you... I mean, how long have you been... ?" She felt awkward. Maybe it was a highly personal question.

"Dead?" he asked, and laughed so loudly Cally worried he'd wake someone upstairs, until she remembered most people couldn't hear him.

"Well, what I meant was, how long have you been a ghost?" There. She had said it, and it had almost seemed normal.

"Oh, I've been here a very long time," he said. "I started learning then, and I just kept on learning new things. I love to learn. Unlike most of the others." He shook his head sadly. Then he said, "I love this band, this Rush!" He played a few bars of air-guitar and sang *"Bearing a gift beyond price, almost free!"*

Cally smiled just as she would have smiled at any other young person who was able to appreciate good music from her own youth. "You can borrow my MP3 player any time you want," she said. "Just don't lose it."

"I won't lose it," he said. "Because I can't pick it up." He grinned impishly. "There are some things I still haven't learned how to do. It's a matter of priorities, you see."

"Ah, yes, I remember." He had been telling the truth when he'd told her he wasn't the one who had been moving things around in her room. Back when she'd been assuming he was a living human being – it seemed so long ago, now. "I'm sorry," she said. "I'm still not used to this. You make it all seem so ordinary."

He laughed and reached over as if to pat her hand, but stopped himself just short of actually touching her. "It *is* ordinary!" he said. "You'll see!"

"Well." Cally looked at her MP3 player. "I'd love to let you keep listening, but I shouldn't have left my player lying unattended in plain view like that. Will you still be able to use it if I put it in the drawer?"

He nodded, and she stepped around the desk to do so. "Don't worry," he said, "we won't let anyone take it."

"And how can you stop people from taking it, if you can't touch things? And who is this 'we'?" Cally stopped herself. "You know what, I don't want to know right now. I'm tired. I need some rest. I'll talk to you another time. We can have a regular interview. Is that OK?"

The ghost nodded. "Enjoy your sleep. I'm glad you had a nice date."

"It wasn't a date," Cally repeated as she went up the stairs. A last backwards glance showed her a dark-skinned young man sitting in a modern office chair behind an antique desk, silently headbanging to inaudible music.

25 - Doc

It seemed every member of the household was milling around in the front hall when Cally came down the stairs on Thursday morning. Joan, in her fresh, short haircut and new red manicure, was pacing back and forth, clutching her tea mug, barking orders at everyone. Cally knew she wasn't going to get much work done that morning, but she did manage to get Ian's attention and remind him once more to sign the pile of papers on the corner of the desk. Then, ignoring Joan's speech about how nobody was taking any of this seriously enough, she carried her laptop into the dining room. She opened it and checked her email while sipping coffee and nibbling on a Danish.

Amid several perfunctory notes from her agent was a message from Emerald, with a large text file attached, titled "As Promised." Cally sighed and felt sorry about having had a falling out with her friend, but she only read a few of the opening lines of the text file. It did indeed seem to be written in the style of a story, but it spoke of Emerald in the third person. "She has always lived in the Vale," it began, "but the Vale has not always been the place it is now." Cally filed the story away for later.

She carried her things back into the hall and stepped behind the desk in the crowded hall. Even George was present, she noticed, standing quietly and grinning in the shadows beside the stairs.

"Don't sit down yet," Joan barked at her. "I need everyone to move their cars! We need room for the investigators to park when they get here."

"Now, Joan," said Ian gently. "There's plenty of room."

"It looks like a gypsy camp out there!" she complained. "They're going to need room for their equipment truck, as well as their cars. Come on. Everyone! That means you, too, Pedro. Move that god-awful truck."

Everyone piled out the door with car keys in hand. The Captain didn't own a car, but he went out to watch the spectacle as everyone moved their vehicles to park, per Joan's shouted directions, on the grass next to the fence, further away from the house. Ignacio drove the red pickup around to the back of the barn. The three horses in the meadow seemed agitated by all the activity, running along the fence and kicking up their heels. "Be sure to arrange your vehicles by size, color, make and model!" the Captain shouted, toasting them with his coffee cup and ignoring Joan's glare.

Cally was glad her car still started happily, despite having been neglected for the past few days. She parked it approximately where Joan stood vigorously waving, then reached back and dug through some of the boxes to remove a few of her things.

Just as all the cars had been tidied up to Joan's satisfaction, Foster and Nell arrived and parked in one of the spaces they had cleared. "No!" Joan yelled and ran toward Foster as he emerged from the car. "No, no! Move it over there!" Nell got out of the passenger side and ran to Cally.

"I missed you at breakfast," Cally told her. "I thought you two had gone back to Raleigh already."

Nell gave her an enthusiastic hug. "We wouldn't want to miss the investigation show!" she said. "We went to the Bean Garden. Well, I waited in the Bean Garden while Foster went to the lawyer. Here!" She handed Cally a bundle of cloth she had been clutching to her chest.

Cally unfolded it and held it up. It was a lavender t-shirt, hand painted in an intricate pattern of purple and green flowers. Amid the flowers wound vermillion lettering, in flowing script, that read "Ghosts Are People Too."

Cally laughed with delight. "You bought this for me?"

"I made it!" Nell said. "It's been for sale at the Bean Garden, but I thought you should have it, because of what you said at dinner the other night."

"It's perfect." She meant it. "You have a lot of talent. I'll wear it when the investigation crew gets here."

Nell's eyes shone with happiness, and she ran up the porch steps to hug her father and the Captain.

Joan was having a fit. "There won't be room for you to stay here tonight!" she shouted at Foster. "You should clear out and stay at the Motel Nine in Blackthorn tonight or something!" He ignored her resolutely and took a seat in a wicker chair next to Ian, handing him a legal-size folder full of papers. Nell sat on the porch steps and waited quietly. "No walks today!" she promised.

At least the commotion inside the front Hall seemed to have died down, Cally thought as she went back into the house. She resumed her position behind the desk, not sure whether to be glad or dismayed that it was starting to feel familiar. She glanced at George as she checked the voicemail. He was wearing loose white trousers, today, and an embroidered kurta. His hair was combed down straight, and he had several blue and white beads woven into his bangs.

"So. Emerald tells me you were a pirate," she said.

George emerged from the shadows and drew himself up with a deep frown on his face. "My dear lady!" he said. "I assure you, the work my brethren and I did was perfectly legal! We were not pirates. We were privateers, working legitimately under letters of marque in the employ of the King of England himself!"

That gave Cally an approximate answer, anyway, to her question about how long George had been around. "I apologize," she said. "I meant no offense." His smile reemerged, like sunshine from behind a cloud. Cally glanced quickly at the front door. Joan was suggesting to Ian that he remove Bethany from the premises for the day, and Ian was assuring her that would not be necessary. "Here, Georgie," Cally said. "I brought something from my car for you." She extracted an old e-book reader from her pile of notebooks and laid it on the desk. "Do you think you could use this?"

He came around to her side of the desk rather more quickly than her sense of equilibrium liked, and held his hand out over the device. "Oh!" he said, almost in a whisper, and his eyes grew wide. "*The Lord of the Rings* is on here! And *Finnegan's Wake*. And *One Hundred Years of Solitude*!" He turned his gaze on Cally and his eyes looked very real and very close to filling with real tears. "I can read, you know, in several languages. But I can't turn pages, so I've never..." His voice choked. "This is the nicest thing anyone has ever done for me."

Cally got a little choked up, herself. "I can't leave it sitting out here on the desk," she told him. "But I can leave it in my room for you to use anytime you want."

"No." He held up a hand as if warding something off. "I promised you I would not go into your room anymore."

He had a point. "Alright... how about if I leave it in the butler's desk at the end of the hall upstairs?"

"That would be excellent. My *zemi* is there as well." He smiled, and Cally stood and carried the e-reader up the stairs. George followed closely; sensing him on the steps behind her gave Cally shivers down her spine, and she refrained from looking back at him. By the time she had tucked the device into the wide drawer behind the fold-down lid of the desk (covering it with a few sheets of stationery, just to be safe) he was, in fact, no longer visible, but Cally liked to think he was still there, perhaps perusing the electronic table of contents.

She stopped in her room to change into the t-shirt Nell had made, then went to check on Bethany.

"How nice to see you awake!" Cally said when she saw Bethany sitting up against a pile of pillows. Someone had left a cup of tea and a Danish on the night stand beside her. Bethany cried out happily and reached a hand toward Cally.

"I'm not sure I'm really awake," she said, smiling weakly. "I keep drifting off and dreaming. But at least the pain is better."

Cally sat down in the chair beside the bed. "That's good. I feel so terrible leaving you all alone up here so much, even if you are mostly sleeping."

"Not to worry. I have feline company." She smiled and closed her eyes, laying her head back against the pillows.

Cally agreed. Both cats were sitting like sphinxes on either side of the mound made by Bethany's feet. "Cyndi and Doctor Boojums have hardly left your side," she said.

Bethany's eyes fluttered open. "Boo?" she said. "No, he's been dead for ten years." She closed her eyes again. "I think. Ten. Maybe nine. It was..." She fell silent.

Cally looked at the old gray cat, sitting purring with his paws tucked under his chest. "It wouldn't actually surprise me if you were a ghost, too," she said to it under her breath. The cat – or whatever it was – regarded her with a slow blink.

Glancing at Bethany, who had begun to snore softly, Cally stood and reached out a hand toward the cats. She wondered what she would do if she tried to pet Doctor Boojums and her hand went right through. Her stomach did a flip and she petted Cyndi Lauper instead. The little cat's warm, vibrating softness settled her nerves. Doctor Boojums closed his eyes and purred, also. She could feel the rumbling vibration through the mattress. He had to be real.

"The white lady."

Cally turned. Bethany's eyes were open again, but she was looking dazedly at Cally.

"No, it's just me," Cally reassured her.

"She was here," Bethany said. "She was very kind." She mumbled a few more unintelligible words before drifting off to sleep again.

Cally felt Bethany's forehead, though she wasn't sure what that would tell her. "Don't you start seeing ghosts, now," she told the sleeping woman. "You aren't hurt *that* badly. Are you? I'm sure it's just the medication." She would have to mention this, also, to the doctor when he came. She reached to pick up the remaining medicine bottle from the night stand so she could show it to him as soon as he arrived, and swore. Like its missing twin, the medicine bottle was no longer there. She got down on her hands and knees and looked under the bed and the chair, but neither little plastic bottle was anywhere to be seen.

By the time Cally returned to the desk in the Hall, the front porch was empty except for the Captain sitting in his wicker chair in the sunshine. Joan was behind her office door, shouting at someone on the phone. The household had, for the time being, returned to normal.

Hoping Katarina would know what had happened to the medicine, Cally looked through the sticky notes next to the phone for her cell number. She was interrupted by Foster, who practically danced down the stairs into the Hall and ran to the desk.

"Where's Ian?" he asked. "He's not answering the phone in his room. I just got the most amazing phone call!" He leaned toward her, and Cally was glad there was a solid wooden desk between them. "I've been given permission to submit a provisional plan that could make a small fortune. I could turn this pathetic little hick town into an important center of commerce. The business possibilities would be unlimited!"

He bent down and grinned at her. His eyes were wide and his pupils nearly filled them, even though the Hall was bright with sunshine. Cally wanted to ask him if he'd been drinking, but she didn't smell alcohol on his breath.

"Foster, are you alright?" she asked.

"Never better!" he said, looking left and right as if trying to decide through which doorway to dash first.

"Well, I'm not sure where Ian is at the moment," Cally told him. "I managed to avoid most of this morning's All Hands Meeting."

"Ah, yes, Joan probably saw him last. She probably knows where he went." Foster glanced at the office door. "And maybe I should talk to her first anyway. Joan agrees with me that this place just isn't making enough money to survive, the way things are. Maybe between the two of us we can persuade him to do the sensible thing. She's right that he's just too soft-hearted and sentimental for his own good."

Cally thought of many things she could have said in reply to that, but did not bother to waste them on Foster as he continued to stare at the office door like a schoolchild staring at the door of the principal's office. As he did so, his shoulders sagged and his burst of buoyant energy seemed to sift out of his body like sand. "Well," he said at length, "it's worth a shot. If you catch her in the right mood, she's brilliant, but it's a crapshoot: her moods change like the weather. Some people say she's on something, you know." He looked back at Cally, his expression serious now. "Not something she has a prescription for, if you know what I mean." He took a deep breath and headed toward the closed door. "Wish me luck!" he said as he knocked and went in.

When he had gone, Nell appeared in the parlor doorway. She didn't say anything, but Cally could guess what she was thinking. "Don't worry," Cally told her. "Joan might go for his ideas, but your dad never will."

"He never has so far," Nell admitted, but didn't seem very comforted by the thought.

They could hear Foster's voice through the door, talking a little too fast and pitched a little too high. Neither of them were surprised to hear Joan's voice answer sharply. Both Cally and Nell returned to what they had been doing, and pretended not to notice when Foster left the room with his shoulders hunched and head low, carrying Joan's tea mug toward the kitchen.

Joan left her office and stared after him. Shaking her head, she clomped across the Hall to the desk. "You aren't going to wear that silly thing are you?" she said to Cally.

Cally looked down at her *Ghosts Are People Too* t-shirt. "Yes. I am. It's nice."

"You should put on something more dressy for the PI society. You might end up on TV, you know."

"I think they'll like it," Cally insisted. "Anyway, Joan, I haven't got time for that right now. Bethany's medicine has disappeared. I'm going to have to call the doctor again and... I don't even know what I'll say this time!"

"Probably just as well," said Joan. "She was taking too much of that stuff. They say it's highly addicting, you know."

"Joan, the doctor ordered her to take it!" Cally picked up the phone. "I guess we'll have to ask him for a whole new prescription again."

"He's going to start thinking we're all a bunch of addicts around here," Joan said. "Anyway you can ask him in person. Doc's here right now, down at the boat talking to Ian. I swear, this place is Grand Central Station. Why does it have to be today, of all days?"

Cally left her lamenting in the hall and went out onto the porch. She looked down the hill toward the pond and saw Ian and a silver-haired gentleman about the same age coming up the hill toward her. When he saw her, Ian waved cheerfully and said "Doc, I want you to meet our celebrity guest!" Cally went to the bottom of the steps to wait for them.

"This is Ms. Callaghan McCarthy," Ian said when they arrived on the walkway. "She's an author. Ms. McCarthy, this is Doctor Daniel Tanahey, a very old and dear friend of mine."

"I am not so very old," said the doctor, shaking Cally's hand. "And please just call me Doc. Everyone else does."

"Then you must call me Cally," she replied distractedly. "Listen, Doc, I hate to rush you, but..."

"Ah, no problem," he said. "I am just on my way up to see Miss Chase."

Cally sighed with relief, and practically skipped as she led him through the front door to the stairs. She explained, as they went up, about the confusion with the medicine and about its now having gone missing.

Doc set his little bag on the coverlet beside Bethany, who seemed only vaguely aware of his presence. "Wow," said Cally. "I don't think I've ever seen a doctor make a house call in real life. If this room weren't so brightly colored, I would think we were in the middle of an old movie!"

He grinned as he put on his stethoscope. "We live in such a small town," he said, "we all have to have each other's backs. And anyway, Miss Chase and I are old friends. This is really more of a social call, for me."

Bethany stirred groggily as the old doctor checked her vital signs, but she didn't speak. "Well, I agree with you all that she's sleeping too heavily," he said. "But without a blood test, I won't be able to tell if it's because she's taken too much medicine, or if it's just affecting her too strongly." He put his instruments away in his bag. "To be honest with you, at her age, I would say it's the latter. It should wear off in a few hours, either way. And I'll prescribe a new adjustment to the dosage."

Cally felt a little exasperated. "Then there will be three bottles of medicine floating around this house!" she said.

Doc nodded. "It is a concern. Oxycodone is a controlled substance. But I don't think anyone here is likely to try to sell it on the street. When the missing bottles turn up, call me and I'll see that they are safely disposed of. And I'll tell the pharmacy to mark a big, red X on the bottle when they fill the new prescription. That way you'll know for sure which is the right one." He looked down at Bethany's sleeping face. "No, not an X. A large, pink heart." He smiled at Cally. Bethany muttered something incoherent, tried to shift position in her sleep, and winced in pain.

Ian and the Captain met Cally and Doc in the hall when they returned downstairs. "If Merv was here, we'd be able to get the band back together," the Captain said jovially. "We could have us a proper jam session!"

"Joan might not appreciate that today," Ian reminded him. He turned to Doc. "How is Ms. Chase?"

Doc explained everything to them and asked, "Will someone be able to go to the pharmacy in Blackthorn to pick up the new prescription?"

"Again," Cally said.

"I'll send Ignacio..." Ian's voice trailed off as he looked out the front door to where Ignacio was already busy addressing the long list of lawn beautification tasks Joan had assigned to him.

"You know what?" Cally said. "I'll go. I've been to Blackthorn – I was there just last night. I'm sure I can find it again easily."

All three men looked at her so suddenly she wondered if she had said something wrong. "Are you sure?" Doc asked.

"Well, yes... Really. It's no problem." She was thinking she would appreciate the excuse to get away from Joan for a couple of hours.

"Alright then." Doc used the desk phone to call in the prescription, then told her, "You don't have to go right away. She shouldn't have another dose until this afternoon."

"We'll just be in my quarters if you need anything. Talking about old times," Ian explained. He gestured toward the south end of the back hall.

The three old gentlemen began to make their way to Ian's rooms, but Cally took Ian by the elbow and said, "These papers, sir?"

He smiled broadly and accepted the pen she placed in his hand. Cally took a deep, satisfied breath as he finally signed off on the bills and checks that had been waiting so long. She couldn't wait to tell Bethany about it.

As he rejoined his friends making their way to the back hall, Ian turned back to her and said, "When you get ready to leave for Blackthorn, would you please come and let me know? I ... well, I have one other thing I wonder if you'd drop off for me on your way."

He winked, and Cally thought she knew what he was talking about, so she nodded and said "Of course, Ian, I'd be happy to."

She hummed quietly to herself with satisfaction while she sat at the desk placing all the bill payment checks into their respective envelopes, found stamps in the desk drawer, and got everything ready to go out in the mail. Joan came out of her office to look out the door and make sure Ignacio wasn't slacking off.

"Where does the outgoing mail go?" Cally asked her.

"I don't know!" Joan waved an impatient hand. "Ignacio usually takes it in to town, but he's not going anywhere today! Where is Foster with that tea he swore would only take him a minute to bring?" She stomped into the dining room and turned toward the kitchen.

Cally decided she would just drive the mail to the post office herself, and she was no longer willing to wait until afternoon to get away from the house for a while. She put the phones into night mode, then carried the stack of mail with her to the back hall to tell Ian she was leaving.

The south end of the back hall ended at the side door with the stained-glass cardinal on it. A wide doorway on the left opened into the parlor, where Nell was sitting quietly watching television. To Cally's right, a long, dark-paneled hallway led away into the south wing of the house. The door at the end of this hall was open, and Cally was sure this must be Ian's study when she saw bookshelves and a paper-strewn desk through it. As she approached, she could hear the men's voices, but she thought they sounded a little more strident than pleasant conversation between old friends should sound.

It was Doc's voice that was loudest. "But she needs medication!" he was saying, and his voice was not the gentle, patient one he had used upstairs with Bethany.

"Not that," she heard Ian say. "It makes her so miserable. She says it makes her feel dead." His voice was not loud, but it was adamant.

"The new compounds don't have the unpleasant side-effects that the old style drugs did," Doc said earnestly. "Ian, it would help her live a normal life."

"A normal life!" the Captain snorted. "Hah!"

"What kind of normal life can she ever have again?" Ian said.

Cally knew the person they were talking about could not have been Bethany. This was probably about Nell, she supposed, and in any case it was definitely none of her business. She tried to make her footsteps as loud as possible on the hall rug as she drew closer.

"Look, Ian," Doc was saying. "I've kept your secret for what feels like most of my life. If you would just let me help you..."

"*Our* secret," said the Captain.

"Our secret. But I won't..."

The voices fell silent as someone finally heard Cally's footsteps. She stuck her head through the doorway and knocked on the doorframe. "Hello?" she said. "Mr. May? Hello? Are you there? I'm just heading out now."

Ian stood up from one of chairs that were gathered in a circle in front of a small hearth. He looked tired and sad, but he smiled when he saw Cally's face. "Miss McCarthy," he said. "Yes, well. It's just that, I'm afraid something came up, and my little errand for you isn't ready yet." He gestured toward the disorganized papers covering the desk. "Can I impose on you another time?"

"Of course you can. It would be no imposition," Cally said awkwardly. The Captain and Doc fidgeted, glancing sideways at her. "I'll just be gone a little while. I've forwarded the phones to voicemail. I'm dropping off the mail," she said, showing him the stack of envelopes, "and then heading into Blackthorn."

All four men replied in unison. "Be careful!"

Cally shook her head in puzzlement as Ian bowed slightly and closed the door. Heading back, she saw Foster standing at the other end of the hallway, just inside the dining room. "One of their little secret meetings, then?" he asked her.

"I'm sure that's none of my business," she said. "I'm just going in to Blackthorn to run a few errands. Is there anything I can pick up for you or Nell while I'm there?"

He seemed distracted, peering closely at the stack of envelopes in her hand. "What?" he said, looking up. "No. Um, no, nothing I can think of at the moment." He shook his head and pushed up his glasses. "I'll keep watch over Bethany while you're gone. Those foreigners keep going in and out of her room."

"Seriously, Foster, I think if anyone would be inclined to wish Bethany ill, it would be Joan. And even she..."

"That's an interesting thought!" He lowered his voice and

glanced back into the dining room. "I've always suspected she wants Ian to marry her," he said conspiratorially, "so that it will all be hers when she outlives him. And then what would be the odds she'd leave any of it to Nell?"

"*If* she outlives him," Cally said. She appreciated Foster's determination to solve the mystery, but this was just uncharitable gossip and she was glad to have an excuse to get away from listening to any more of it. "I have to get going," she told him, "if I'm going to get back here in time with Bethany's next dose."

26 - Blackthorn

Cally drove into Woodley first so she could drop the mail off at the collection box outside the post office. The gray stone building next to the pizza shop was easily the largest building in town, and seemed far too large for a small-town post office, but she remembered the Captain had told her it used to be the courthouse and the scene of many hangings. She looked up at the dark windows of the upper stories, but didn't see any swaying figures or anyone peering down from the windows. The old church across the parking lot behind it looked far more atmospheric. She thought it might be a good idea to ask someone about both buildings later. Andi at the Bean Garden would probably know some good stories about them.

She didn't head west out of town, the way she'd arrived on that first night. Instead she turned the way Ben had gone, through the residential district back toward Vale House, and then right, as he had done, on Gardens Road. It might or might not have been a shorter way to get there, but what mattered to Cally at the moment was that it would be a more pleasant drive than the interstate. Also, it made her smile to think of the little tour Ben had given her of the area. Driving south down Gardens Road, she paused for a moment in front of the Yellow House that the Captain had said he'd grown up in. It looked sad and empty, its porch steps crumbling, and the big, round attic window full of cobwebs.

Cally wound down her window when she got to the open road outside of town. It felt good to be back behind the wheel again. The sound of boxes rattling in the back seat was still irritating, though. She considered taking Ian up on his offer to find her a place to store them temporarily inside Vale House.

She crossed the little bridge over the creek, and the road swung right, just as she remembered. After that, though, her memory seemed to fail her. Things did not look quite the same, in the daylight. The road entered a wood, as she recalled, but it did not resemble the dense, mature forest she remembered. Instead it seemed to be a rather thin and scrubby wood, probably re-growth over an abandoned cotton or tobacco field. Dilapidated tin buildings could be glimpsed between the trunks. "I guess darkness lends enchantment to the view," she mused.

Then, quite suddenly, it seemed to her, the trees came to an end. A stop sign brought her to a halt at the side of a four-lane highway. She definitely had no memory of that from the night before. She glanced in the rear-view mirror, wondering if she had missed a fork in the road somewhere, but she was sure there had been nothing like that, and she had not yet crossed any of the other little bridges she remembered, either.

She looked up and down the highway before her, watching cars and tractor trailers roaring by every few seconds. The volume of trucks made her certain this must be I-85. She knew Blackthorn lay south of Woodley, just off the interstate; she had turned around on its exit ramps at least three times, that first night. What she didn't understand was how she could have arrived here the way she had come. How could she have become lost on a simple two-lane blacktop road in broad daylight?

The only thing for it, she figured, was to go ahead and follow the highway in to Blackthorn. Shrugging, she crossed the four lanes and turned southward, hoping she was right. Almost immediately, she began to see signs stating the exit to Blackthorn lay just ahead.

Turning off the highway at the Blackthorn exit, she sighed with relief. Then she frowned with dismay. The town itself also seemed quite different in the daylight. Instead of a somewhat busier main street than the one in Woodley, she encountered a busy gridwork of four lane surface streets lined with retail parks and big-box stores. Blackthorn was stark and noisy, with traffic roaring by everywhere. None of the roads appeared to be the charming downtown street where The Fountain had been, or even the kind of road on which a nice little burger joint like that could thrive.

However, the pharmacy to which Doc had called in the prescription did have a large, brightly colored sign, and Cally was able to keep it in sight and steer her way to it without having to stop and consult her phone's GPS.

She went in and gave Bethany's information at the pharmacy desk, and the young lady behind the counter smiled at her. "All ready to go," she said, "including the doctor's orders for a pink heart drawn on the label." She pointed to it and grinned. "Love is the best medicine!"

"We all love Bethany," Cally said, signing the log book to verify her receipt of the drugs. "Can you tell me the best way to get back to Woodley?"

"Just get back on I-85 and go north. It's to the east, on the right side of the highway," she said. "I've never been there, myself, but some girls from there went to my school. They say there's a haunted mansion there. Is it true?"

"It is definitely an interesting town," said Cally, "though a little hard to find." She decided to give her GPS another chance, and typed the address of Vale House into her phone before she got back into her car. The GPS neatly instructed her through all the turns back to the interstate ramp, and Cally relaxed. Then the little metallic voice in the phone announced cheerfully that the GPS signal had been lost.

"Of course it has," she told it. She had, like most people, occasionally had an urge to throw her phone out the window, but it had never been this strong before.

She had at least learned better than to watch for signs to Woodley along this road. Instead she kept one eye on the verge, watching for the appearance of a nondescript little country road heading east. She was sure she would pass it just as she spotted it and would have to turn around, but at least it was a sunny day and she was much less likely to miss it all together. "I wonder what is the opposite of nondescript?" she thought as she passed a couple of descript roads, complete with exit signs and gas stations, which she knew could not be the one for which she was watching.

After five or six miles, she knew she must have missed it. The little nondescript road she was looking for, the one she had so recently used to reach the interstate from Woodley, had only been a little over two miles north of the Blackthorn exit. She was sure she remembered this clearly. Or maybe it had been a more descript road than she'd noticed at the time. She was growing frustrated, and began muttering curses. "And Bethany will need her medicine soon," she realized. She beat the steering wheel with the heel of her hand and began scouting for a place to turn around.

Just ahead, standing in the tall weeds at the side of the road, a slender figure stood waving to her, its long red hair blowing in the wind. With a dizzy sense of déjà vu, Cally slowed down and pulled off the road next to a young woman dressed in a white sundress. The girl put her head inside the passenger window and said "Hi!"

"Errin. What the hell?"

Errin let herself into the car and sat down. "This is the second time I've had to come fetch you," she said, dropping the cell phone into the cup-holder and putting her seat belt on.

Cally couldn't move. "What is going on?" she demanded. "And don't you dare tell me it's a long story!"

"Okay," Errin promised. "Just go that way. I'll show you. Everyone has been telling you Woodley is hard to find."

"I see that now," said Cally. She put the car in gear slowly, though she was not sure she should be driving at all, feeling as she was at the moment.

Letting a line of trucks go past, she re-entered the highway, crossing to the left lane in hope of finding a place to make a U-turn. But Errin said, "No, no," and pointed through the windshield, indicating that Cally should just keep going straight ahead. "Just watch," the girl said, hunching forward and staring through the windshield at the road.

"Are you sure we aren't halfway to Virginia by now?" Cally asked.

"No. Just watch." She pointed. "Watch the side of the road. Watch! Use your eyes."

Cally watched the road's edge as closely as she dared, but all she saw was that if she stared too long, the white line started to look wavy and double. She blinked to make her eyes focus again.

"There! No! Aw, you almost had it!" Errin shook her curls. "You're going to have to learn how to do this yourself," she said. "I won't be able to come help you every time. Now watch." She demonstrated by redoubling her stare at the road's edge.

Cally didn't like the way the white line seemed to double in her vision if she looked at it too long, but Errin encouraged her with praise every time it happened, so she decided to just regard it as an interesting ocular phenomenon. It began to look almost as if another highway lay on top of the original one, about six inches above it and translucent.

"Now you're getting it!" Errin encouraged.

"Sure," Cally muttered. "Just as long as I stay on the right one.

"Exactly!"

Ahead, the illusory road seemed to be veering off to the right. Cally concentrated on staying on the real one.

"No, go with it!" Errin reached over and grabbed the wheel, jerking it to the right.

"Errin!" Cally shouted and jerked the car back into her control. "Don't *ever* do that!"

Errin sat back in her seat and crossed her arms, sullenly silent.

"I'm sorry I yelled at you," said Cally. "But that is a very dangerous thing to do. I am betting you don't have your driver's license yet, do you?"

"No," she said. "But I know how to get places." She let out a snort of breath.

"Okay. I'm sorry," Cally said. "I think I know what you were trying to show me. It just scared me, is all." It still did.

"Okay, then, let's try again!" Her buoyant enthusiasm returned as if it had never been gone. She sat up and resumed staring at the road.

"Don't I have to turn around now though?" Errin did not reply but merely continued to stare out the windshield. Cally resigned herself. She looked at the white line again until it appeared to double. As the two white lines began to separate, the illusory road curved further and further away from the real one.

"Good, good!" said Errin. She pointed toward where the mirage version of I-85 ran parallel to them, gradually curving away to the right, shimmering across the weedy fields. "Follow *that* one!"

Cally did not want to do any such thing, but she braced herself. She just hoped her poor car would survive the jarring it was going to get when she drove off the road. She followed Errin's pointing finger and steered away to the right. The wheels hummed smoothly over the pavement. There was no jarring. In fact, silence fell as the roaring of the trucks on I-85 faded away. She was no longer driving on I-85 or even a mirage of it. This was a quiet, nondescript little two-lane country blacktop, winding away eastward through fields and little clumps of forest. The interstate was not visible any longer in the rear view mirror.

"You did it! You did it!" Errin praised her as if she were a child who had caught a ball for the first time. "Now you don't need me anymore. You can do it yourself next time."

"I don't think I ever want to do that again. Ever!" Cally relaxed into her seat, but her hands were shaking on the wheel. She glanced at the girl in the passenger seat. "Errin, you said you were sent to fetch me. Who sent you?"

"Oh, you know. Emerald. You know her."

"I thought I did," said Cally. She took a deep breath and tried to calm her shaking hands. "Are you a ghost, too, Errin?"

"What is it with you people thinking everything is a ghost?" She reached over and pinched Cally's arm. "I am not a ghost!"

"Ow! Errin! Don't ever grab the steering wheel, and don't ever pinch the driver!"

Errin laughed. The road curved to the left, and Cally recognized the little bridge over the stream ahead. "There you are, see?" Errin said. "Harmony Creek."

"So it is." Cally drove over it and saw the southern edge of Woodley rising ahead. She could make out the houses of Gardens Road and the fence along the meadow. "So what are you, then, Errin, if you're not a ghost?"

Errin's green eyes danced with mischief as Cally followed Gardens Road along the fence. Slowing down when she came to the crossroads, Cally drove across Main Street and between the pineapple-decorated gateposts into the grounds of Vale House. Two of the horses, the black one and the white one, saw them approaching and ran to the fence to greet them. Errin leaned across the seat so close Cally could count the freckles splashed across her nose. "I'm a unicorn," she laughed. "A uuuuuunicooooorrrrn!"

"You sound like Mia Farrow in that movie," Cally told her. She pulled the car into her Joan-approved parking space and got out into the sunshine. She didn't bother turning around to say goodbye to Errin. She knew she was already gone.

27 - Paranormal Investigators

The Greater Asheboro Area Scientific Paranormal Society had arrived at Vale House. A van with an appropriately atmospheric logo painted on the side stood in the lawn beside the porch, and cables had been strung across the grass and up the stairs. Three young men and a woman were setting up sound equipment and a small camera on the porch while the Captain sat in a wicker chair and watched. Cally stepped back and looked at the scene, wishing she had the cheek to take out her phone and snap a picture of the young paranormal researchers working so seriously there that they were completely oblivious of a figure in white gazing down at them from an upstairs window. Well, she thought, there was no way to be sure the white figure would show up in the photo anyway.

As she started to walk up the steps, one of the men and the woman approached the closed front door and knocked, while another man aimed a camera at them. Joan opened the door and emerged, smiling sweetly and adjusting her perfectly coiffed hair.

"Hello, Ma'am," said the young man. "We're from the Greater Asheboro Area Scientific Paranormal Society."

From his wicker chair, the Captain laughed heartily. "G. A. A. S. P. S! I get it! That's a good one!"

The cameraman lowered the camera, and the other young people groaned. Joan burst through the door and glared at the Captain. "You ruined it!" she shouted at him.

"It's alright," the young woman said. "We can do another take. Don't worry, we always do more than one anyway."

The Captain continued to chuckle softy to himself and Cally said, "Before you start, may I go inside first? I have something I need to give to someone inside." Joan glared at her as she stopped beside the Captain's chair and suggested he might also come inside with her.

"Keep him out of the way!" Joan growled as Cally helped the old man through the door.

The hall was empty and tidy and blindingly bright. A pair of box lights on tall tripods had been set up on either side of the door, and their harsh white beams converged on the grand staircase. Cally led the Captain through to the equally tidy and brightly lit dining room. "Where is everyone?" she asked him as he poured himself some brandy.

"I propose a drinking game!" he said. "Every time one of those fellows says 'Oh my god I felt something' you take a drink. When they say, 'What the hell was that!' you have to finish your drink and pour another."

"I don't think that's such a good idea," Cally said. "We'd be dead of alcohol poisoning by dinnertime. Captain, why don't you take your drink and join Ian. Where is he?"

"Joan has stationed him in the parlor. Kat and 'Nacio are banished to the kitchen. Nellie and her husband have been told to stay in the Cala Lily Room because it is not haunted, as far as anyone knows. You are supposed to be seated at the desk, and Joan will have words for you later, I don't doubt, for not being here for the last few hours."

Cally escorted the Captain to the parlor, where Ian was sitting patiently in a wing chair next to the fireplace. He was dressed in a dapper white linen suit, and if he had had a beard, he would have looked like Colonel Sanders. "I'll just run upstairs to give Bethany her medicine," she said, helping the Captain to the matching seat on the opposite side of the fireplace. "You look great, Mr. May," she added as she slipped back out into the hall. The knock at the front door was being repeated, and Cally hurried across the hall and ran up the stairs quickly so as not to ruin Joan's big scene again.

She found the door of the Daffodil room shut with a sticky note on the knob that read in sharp, angular handwriting "Keep this door SHUT at all times!" She opened it, and was delighted to be greeted by a wide-awake Bethany, who was sitting up and smiling. "You look so much better!" Cally told her.

"I feel much better." Bethany's voice was still a little weak, but her smile was genuine. Cally left the door open and sat down in the chair beside the bed. Little Cyndi Lauper took the opportunity to dash out of the room. Doctor Boojums woke up and began washing his paws. Cally tried to ignore him.

"How is the pain?" she asked Bethany.

"It's okay, as long as I don't try to move. Or laugh. Or breathe!" She almost laughed at this, but remembered and stopped herself in time.

"Well I brought you some new medicine that Doc says won't keep you so knocked out all the time. It's just about time for you to take it. Have you eaten at all today?"

Bethany tipped her head toward a plate of buttered toast on the night stand. It had gone dry, with only one bite taken from it. "I tried," she said. "But my stomach is feeling a bit too squiffy."

"Maybe that's a side-effect of the medicine, too," Cally guessed. "This lower dose should be much better for you." She set the bottle on the night stand, making sure Bethany could see the heart drawn on the label. "I think Doc is kind of sweet on you."

Bethany smiled. "He's a good man," she admitted, but even as she said it Cally knew she was thinking of Ian May instead. Then she changed the subject. "I've had the strangest dreams all day long. It makes me wonder if all those ghost stories, white ladies and night noises and visitations by lost loved ones, maybe they're all just caused by pain medicine. Or cold medicine, or something!"

"Maybe," said Cally. "Side effects can be mysterious."

"I'll tell you another one. My mouth is so dry! I tried to drink this tea but it's *horrible*. Joan must have made it!"

"Don't laugh!" Cally warned her.

"I wonder if you would be an angel and bring me a glass of Kat's good iced tea instead."

"It would be my pleasure." Cally stood and picked up the tray with the tea cup and toast. "Would you prefer to have this door open or shut? Only that paranormal team is here and they might disturb you."

"Shut it," Bethany decided. "Don't want them walking in here with their camera, with me in my nightie."

Cally pulled the door shut and turned around to nearly walk straight into George. Struggling to keep from dropping the tray, she whispered "Don't you have some place Joan has ordered you to be?"

"I can't go far from the upstairs hall," he told her seriously, the sarcasm going right over his head as usual. "My *zemi* is in that desk there." He tilted his head toward the butler's desk.

"What is a *zemi*?" Cally asked. "And where on earth did you come up with that outfit?" She could not help but notice he was wearing a long, green cloak and tall boots.

"I stand in admiration of the character Faramir," he explained with a brief bow.

Cally was impressed. "You read fast! But Georgie remember, the point of reading a book is not to merely finish it, but to take the time to experience it."

"Dear lady, in my world, there is nothing but time, and experience." He looked very somber for a moment. Then he laughed, gesturing over the Gallery railing toward the paranormal crew setting up their gear in the dining room below. "I am going to mess with them!" he announced.

"Joan would probably actually like that," Cally supposed. "But how are you going to mess with them if they can't see you?"

"I told you. I can do other things. I'm good at electronics." He bent over the railing and studied their equipment.

"Just don't give anyone a heart-attack." Cally left him there and carried the tea tray down the stairs. She paused in the dining room doorway and waited for an opportunity to make her way through the lights and cables to the back hall.

Joan spotted her. "Oh, and this is our celebrity guest!" she called out. The paranormal crew, and the Captain, who had already returned to the sideboard to refill his glass, all turned to look at her. "We are so fortunate," Joan said grandly, "to have famous author Callaghan McCarthy staying with us this week. She's the one who wrote *Escape the Haunted Heart*, you know, and she's going to write a sequel based on Vale House!"

Cally sighed and put on her television interview expression as the camera operator swiveled around and pointed his lens at her. "I'm pleased to meet you all," she said.

"I wish you had changed out of that ridiculous shirt!" Joan whispered loudly at her.

But the crew seemed to like it. "Ghosts are people, too," the team leader read aloud. "Do you really think so?"

"Absolutely," said Cally.

"So you're a believer, then."

"If you don't mind, I need to take this to the kitchen." Cally squeezed behind a lighting tripod to get to the back hall, glancing up to see George and Doctor Boojums both peering down through the railing. As she headed toward the kitchen, she heard someone say "Don't worry, we'll just edit that out."

In the kitchen she found Katarina and Ignacio, as well as Foster, who had apparently escaped the Cala Lily room, standing around the work table as if in conference. Kat and Ignacio were dressed in their best clothes, trying to keep them clean with fresh white aprons while they prepared dinner for the crew. "You should serve them tacos!" Cally said by way of greeting.

"Oh, I wish I had the nerve to do that!" Katarina laughed. "How is Bethany?"

"She's in very good spirits!" Cally was happy to report. "But she's thirsty. She asked for some of your famous iced tea." Katarina dashed to get a glass out of the cupboard while Cally took the tray to the sink. The tea in the cup did look murky, she had to admit as she held it over the sink to empty it. She paused, tilting the cup. A white sediment swirled in the bottom of the tea. "Who made this?" she asked.

Ignacio came and looked into the cup, and then at Cally. His face grew serious.

"Not I," said Katarina. "Bethany doesn't like hot tea. It's no wonder she didn't drink it."

"Well, she tried to drink it," said Cally. "She said, and I quote, 'it's horrible'."

Ignacio took the cup from her and sniffed the contents. He grimaced, and started to take a sip, but Cally grabbed the cup out of his hand. "Maybe that's not such a good idea." She set it on the drain board and looked at the others in the room. "Maybe it's time to call the sheriff," she said almost in a whisper.

The room filled with silence as its occupants thought things they did not say aloud. Finally Foster said, "I will call him." He took his phone out of his pocket, put it to his ear and shook his head. "I can't get a signal in here. I'll go use the landline in the Hall." He turned to leave the room, but turned back with his hand on the door. "We must all keep a close eye on everyone in this household. Take note and let me know any time someone goes into or comes out of Bethany's room." Cally understood Foster intended this to be a veiled threat directed at Ignacio, but she figured it would also cause everyone to keep watchful eyes on Joan, as well, and Joan was still at the top of her own suspect list.

Cally took the glass of iced tea from Katarina's shaking hand and turned to take it up to Bethany. "Wait," said Ignacio. He took the dry toast from the tray and threw it out the kitchen door into the garden, where several chickens pounced upon it eagerly. "See if she can eat this instead." He took some strawberries from the refrigerator, sliced and arranged them on a little floral plate, and added two curly spring lettuce leaves for garnish.

"Seriously, Ignacio," Cally said. "Is there anything at which you aren't a genius?" But nobody laughed as Cally carried the tray out of the room.

Turning toward the dining room, she heard one of the investigators shouting. "My battery just went dead. It was fully charged a few minutes ago, and then I just watched the needle go straight down to zero. *What the hell was that?*"

Ian and the Captain were both standing near the sideboard grinning. The Captain was refilling their glasses. Cally turned around and decided to use the back stairs instead.

28 - Other Investigations

Cally did her best to maintain a cheerful expression as she presented Bethany with the plate of strawberries. There was no room to set it on the night stand because Doctor Boojums was sitting there, staring fixedly at Cally. She ignored him and put the plate on the coverlet next to Bethany, handing her the tea. "Oh, this is so good!" Bethany exclaimed, taking several deep gulps. "You are an angel," she added, handing the already half empty glass back to Cally.

"I don't know about that," Cally replied, looking for a place to set down the glass without touching the old gray cat.

"I think I drank it too fast, though. Now I feel all cold."

"No," said Cally. "It *is* cold in here, all of a sudden." She returned Doctor Boojums' stare. He blinked at her, and Cally could swear she saw color rising in his coat, the way color returns to the face of a person who had been feeling ill. George had been right: Boo was an orange tabby. Cally reached, getting up the courage to see what would happen if she tried to touch him, and saw her breath plume in the air before her. Bethany was trying to tug the covers up to her chest.

Doctor Boojums stood up on the night stand. One paw reached, curling, for the pill bottle, while he looked right at Cally as if defying her to try and stop him. Then with a barely perceptible movement, he knocked the bottle off the stand. Satisfied with his work, he jumped to the floor with a heavy thump and streaked out of the room in an orange blur.

"Why you little... !" Cally set the glass down on the now vacant night stand and dropped to her knees to follow the trajectory of the pill bottle as it rolled under the bed.

"What's the matter?" Bethany called down to her.

"Darn it," Cally said, unable to bring herself to swear properly in Bethany's presence. "It has rolled all the way under the dresser. She crawled to the dresser, but she could barely fit her arm under the carved trim that decorated the bottom. She groped around, hoping she would not encounter anything unexpected. Her fingertips brushed something round and sent it rolling, where she heard it bump rattling into something else.

"There's a flashlight in the night stand," Bethany said. "I put one in every room." Then Cally heard her cry out in pain as she tried to get it herself.

"No, don't twist and turn," Cally said, "I'll get it."

She stood to retrieve the little flashlight. Out in the hall she could hear the leader of the paranormal team shouting on the stairs. "Something just brushed past my legs. What the hell was that?" She imagined the Captain and Ian must be opening the special Christmas brandy by now.

Cally switched on the flashlight and knelt beside the dresser. "I wonder why it fell so far?" Bethany said.

"Maybe it was some of that famous ghostly mischief," Cally muttered, causing Bethany to laugh and then yelp. Then she spotted the pill bottle in the flashlight's beam. No, not the pill bottle. Three of them, all lying on their sides together. "What the hell?" she muttered, echoing the paranormal team out in the hall.

She stood to show an equally perplexed Bethany the three bottles. "Well, I think we've figured out where the medicine has been going," she said. "That cat seems to think these are toys to roll around until they get lost under the furniture."

"Dear, silly Cyndi," said Bethany. Cally didn't bother to correct her.

"I'll just put this inside the drawer," Cally said, "so no more adorable feline mischief puts anyone else's health at risk." She placed the bottle with the pink heart in the drawer, but held the other two up at eye level, trying to determine if they were as full as they should have been. "Bethany, I have an errand to run. I'll ask Kat to come dand help you when you're ready for another dose. Please, don't let anybody give you your medicine except Kat or me. Okay?"

Bethany looked at her quizzically. "If you say so," she said. "Maybe that's best. Helps us all to keep track, I guess." She pushed the covers off herself; it was no longer cold in the room.

Cally left the room to find the paranormal crew standing at the Gallery railing, aiming hand-held instruments all around the upstairs hall and commanding any spirits present to light up the little red lights in order to prove their existence. George was standing at the head of the stairs laughing at them. No red lights were lighting, but batteries were dying right and left. Cally pulled the Daffodil Room door shut behind her and said, "Excuse me. There is a person in that room who isn't feeling well. Please, if you could, try not to disturb her."

"Not a problem," said the female member of the crew. "Hey, have a look at this!" She showed Cally the screen on the back of a small digital camera. It showed a freeze frame of the Gallery railing from the dining room below; a wispy white shape could be seen leaning over the railing, looking down at the camera. "Do you think this is the White Lady?"

Cally thought it looked more like George in a dress, but she didn't say so. "I don't know, but if you go into that room right there," she gestured toward the Wisteria Room across the hall, "they say you'll have your best chance of seeing or hearing something." She wondered why Joan wasn't still with them, telling them where to go and what to look at. "If Joan – you know, the marketing manager – asks where I've gone, tell her I'll be back in a little while." She ran past George without disturbing his fun, and went downstairs to the dining room where Ian and the Captain sat chatting at the table. "Have you seen Foster?" she asked them.

"Not recently," said Ian. "Is there something I can help you with?"

Cally decided not to share her half-baked suspicions with them until she knew more. "Just please tell him, if you see him, that I've gone into town to talk to Doc about ... something."

"You're going to miss all the fun!" the captain called after her.

"I certainly hope so," Cally muttered as she went out the front door. The pill bottles were still clutched in her hands – she hadn't even thought to stop and get her purse. Once at the bottom of the porch stairs, she turned into the shade garden along the side of the house and broke into a jog, passing through the rear of the property and out the little white gate onto the street.

She didn't stop running until she reached the business district. Long late afternoon shadows were beginning to stretch into evening, filling the street with cool shade. Crossing Main Street, Cally slowed to a walk as she passed the news store, trying to catch her breath and, yes, she admitted maybe even a glimpse of Ben. But just a glimpse. She didn't really have time to chat with him right now.

The news store was still open and Cally heard voices coming from inside. Bree was speaking very sharply to someone about something. Cally paused between the doorway and the storefront window, hoping the old woman wouldn't catch sight of her passing by.

"Leave her alone!" Bree was shouting. "You have no right!"

"Bree." It was Ben's voice that answered, not loudly, but with a patience that seemed to have been somewhat stretched. "She's lonely and bored. I just wanted to show her a nice time."

"That's not all you want to show her, I'll bet." She laughed, and it was not a pleasant laugh. "Bennet Dawes, you are the last person on earth who should be breaking up her boredom."

"Where's the harm?" Ben asked.

"Shall I make a list?" Cally heard the register drawer and several other things slamming shut. Cally eyed the far side of the storefront, getting ready to sprint for it so she wouldn't be accused of eavesdropping.

"Please, don't worry," Ben was saying. "She didn't see anything."

"You don't think so? She seems to be seeing and doing a lot of things lately that she shouldn't be able to see or do! And what are you going to do if she finds out the truth?"

At this, Cally stopped herself, wondering, "What truth?"

"Maybe that would be a good thing," she heard Ben murmur in a tone that was definitely not his usual calm and cheerful one.

"It's a disaster waiting to happen!"

"A disaster is going to happen one way or another," Ben said. "Maybe it's finally time."

"Oh. Really. You think so? And what is she now? The great star we are all awaiting? The Faerie Queene, maybe? And even if she were, no good would come of it. No good ever comes of any of this!" Her voice finally broke and Cally, looking desperately around her for a way to escape without revealing her presence, could hear her sobbing.

"Hush. Bree. Calm down."

"Don't touch me! Don't you dare patronize me! You can't take care of me forever!"

"I can, and I will." Ben's voice was calm again. Cally pictured him gathering her into his arms. Even though she barely knew him, she knew this was the kind of thing he'd do. "I have told you over and over. I am never going to leave you."

"Yes. You are." Her voice had become very quiet. "They all do. Sooner or later, they all do."

More silence. Cally crouched, thinking perhaps she could duck around the side of the news store into the space between it and the upholstery shop next door. She absolutely did not want to be caught overhearing this exchange.

"Okay. Hush," Ben was saying again. "If it hurts you that much, I won't do it anymore. I won't even show my face when she's around."

A sigh. "Now you're just trying to make me feel guilty."

"You know I'm not."

Cally really didn't want to hear any more, then. Not caring whether they saw her or not, she ran across the front of the open door and slipped around the corner of the building into the parking lot behind it.

The sun was well down behind the tops of the buildings, and the Daimler parked behind the store gleamed softly in the remaining light. Cally closed her eyes and refused to admit tears were trying to slip out between her eyelids. She clutched the two pill bottles in her hand and reminded herself of her mission, remembering she had seen Doc's shingle over the door of the building beside the pizza shop.

When she walked around to the front of the buildings on Railroad Street, she saw the sign in Doctor Tanahey's office door was turned to read "Closed," and she swore with frustration. Of course the doctor in a small town would keep short hours. She felt like throwing the pill bottles into the shrubbery and just getting right out of the "pathetic little hick town," as Joan had called it, for good. There was nothing she could do now, except go back to Vale House and wait for the sheriff to show up. Unless...

She turned the corner back onto Main Street and followed her nose to the Bean Garden. The coffee shop was still open, though it was empty except for Andi polishing the gleaming counter. When she saw Cally in the doorway, Andi smiled and called "Hello, Stranger! Did you bring your laptop this time?"

Cally stepped inside. "I'm afraid not."

Andi put down her polishing cloth. "It's just as well. The WiFi thing is down again. Here." She picked up a white tea cup and held it under the spout of a decanter. "Decaf organic chai. Give it a try."

But the sight of the cup only reminded Cally of her quest. "No, thank you, not right now. I need to find Doc. His office is closed – can you look up his cell number for me? Oh, and call him for me, too, please. I'm afraid I left my purse behind."

"Oh, my! Is everything okay?" Andi put the cup down on the counter.

"I hope so," said Cally. "I just need to ask him some questions." She shifted the two pill bottles in her sweating hands and Andi noticed them. She fixed Cally with a gaze that required an explanation. "I think..." Cally was sure she shouldn't be telling Andi these things, but she felt an overwhelming need for a friend just then. "Some of us up at Vale House are worried that ...someone... might be deliberately trying to hurt Bethany."

"That's a very serious accusation!"

"I know. I know." Cally let Andi take the bottles out of her hands, and stammered on while the other woman squinted at the labels. "I try to tell myself it's nothing, I'm imagining things, or overreacting, but..."

"These are opiates," said Andi. "For what it's worth, there is a rumor going around that someone in this town – I won't name names – is struggling with an addiction to them. Maybe..." She squinted at the bottles and opened one of them. "Well. The labels say oxycodone, but that's not what these are. Look." She tipped a few pills out into the lid of the bottle. They were large tablets, oval-shaped and light blue. "I'm pretty sure these are not oxycodone. I've had that, back when I had a root canal. And my son had them when he fractured his wrist. Those are small and round. Nothing like this." With alarm growing in her face, she opened the other one; it also did not contain oxycodone, but clear capsules with green tips. Andi put the pills back into their respective bottles and handed them to Cally. "Yes, I do think you had better go talk to Doc. And maybe the sheriff, too, while you're at it."

"Foster has already called the sheriff," Cally told her.

"Well, Foster..." She cut herself off and shook her head. "Look, Doc is probably just across the street. At the feed store where the guys like to meet up after work to play their old timey music together." She put her arm around Cally and led her to the door, gesturing up the street to where they could see a car parked in front of the feed store, and three figures just being joined by another on the loading dock. The light was fading, and Cally could hear Merv Arkwright tuning his guitar.

"Thank you." Cally hugged her. "You're a rock."

"Let me know how it goes!"

"Andi, I bet you'll find out before I do."

Andi urged her out the door.

Cally crossed the street and approached the feed store to the sound of a six-string and a harmonica trying to settle into a 1960's folk tune.

"Well, if it isn't our local celebrity!" Merv called as she climbed the concrete steps of the loading dock. "You're just in time." Doc was there, sitting in a lawn chair, as was Jud Thornton from the hardware store and another man she didn't recognize. Luke from the pizza shop was just arriving with a large box in a warming envelope.

"Do you sing soprano?" Doc asked.

"Alto," said Cally. "Hey, I hate to be a wet blanket, Doc, but I have a serious question." She handed him the pill bottles. "What are these?"

"It looks like you've found the missing medication. Good for you!"

"No, I mean, what are *these*?" She opened one of the bottles and showed Doc the contents. His face grew serious. "Foster has already called the sheriff," Cally said quietly to him, "because something had been dissolved in Bethany's tea. But he didn't know about this, at the time."

"He hasn't called me," said the fourth man on the porch. "My pager hasn't gone off." He stood and extended a hand to Cally. "Dunn Mahon," he said by way of introduction.

"I guess Foster decided to wait until after the investigation," Cally said with no attempt to hide her exasperation.

"You should not be conducting an investigation on your own," Sheriff Mahon said sternly.

"No, no, I mean," Cally shook her head. "Vale House is crawling with 'paranormal investigators' right now." She used air-quotes. Everyone nodded their understanding, but nobody was amused.

"Where did you find these?" Doc asked, handing the bottles to the sheriff instead of back to Cally.

"Under the dresser. The cat pushed them off the night stand." She could see that Doc's face was drawn with worry. "I made sure to put the new bottle in the drawer of Bethany's night stand," she told him. "The correct one, with the pink heart on it."

He smiled briefly. "But now I'm worried about someone else at Vale House." To Sheriff Mahon's inquisitive look he added, "Sorry, patient confidentiality."

The sheriff shook his head. "Okay, sorry, fellas. I'm afraid I won't be able to join you after all, tonight." He dug in his pocket for his car keys. "Someone pay the bass player anyway, eh?"

Luke laughed. "I'll put it on your bill." He put the pizza box down on the loading dock and headed back across the street.

The sheriff offered Cally a lift back to Vale House, but she decided to walk. She hoped if she could slip through the back garden and into Vale House through the side door, Joan would not see her and wouldn't suspect she had gone to the authorities. As she walked briskly back up the street toward the residential district, Ben came out of the News Store and waved, calling her name. She did not look at him and she did not answer.

As she ducked into the cool darkness under the oak trees, she heard sirens behind her. A backward glance showed flashing red and blue lights coming up Main Street from the direction of I-85. Cally thought that was a bit extreme – she hadn't expected the sheriff to show up with sirens and blazing lights. But when the vehicle rushed past her, she saw it wasn't the sheriff at all, but an ambulance.

Through the trees, she watched it pass all the way to the end of the street and turn in to the main gate at Vale House.

"Oh, god! Bethany!" Cally broke into a run, praying with her heart in her mouth. When she arrived in the front yard, she saw the ambulance parked on the front lawn at the bottom of the porch steps, it's lights illuminating the house in alternating sickly hues. But the person being carried out the door and down the steps on a stretcher was not Bethany. It was Joan.

29 - Aftermath

"That damn cat!" Joan was shouting. "That damn cat! Ian, when I get home, it had better be gone! Ow, my ankle! Watch it, you idiots!"

On the porch, Nell picked up Cyndi Lauper and clutched her to her breast, casting a pleading look toward Foster, who returned a look of distaste. He and Ian stood beside the stretcher: Ian was patting Joan's hand, saying "Everything will be alright," over and over in his calm, quiet voice.

The G. A. A. S. P. S. team was also walking in and out the door, bumping into the paramedics and adding to the confusion. They were carrying gear out and loading it hastily into their van. Cally guessed they wouldn't be spending the night in the Wisteria Room after all.

"Everything is ruined!" Joan was lamenting. "That damn cat. Ow! Do you really have to do that?" The paramedics were tightening safety belts around her on the stretcher. As they did, they had to tuck a voluminous white garment around her. It took Cally a minute to realize it was not some hospital gown they had put over her, but that she was wearing a rather shabby looking old white ball gown which did not become her at all.

"The White Lady..." Cally murmured.

"Sure," said a voice behind her. It was the leader of the paranormal team. "And we're considering suing that old bat. Maybe this entire hokey establishment. We work hard to get the scientific community to take our work seriously. Charlatans like this, trying to make a fast buck by faking a haunting, just destroy our credibility." He snorted and threw several loops of hastily wound extension cord into the van.

Cally left him and went toward the porch, where Sheriff Mahon was waving for everyone to gather. Nell stopped her at the bottom of the steps and wrapped her in a shaking hug that included an increasingly annoyed little calico cat.

"Please don't let them hurt Cyndi!" she pleaded.

"Helen, I am sure your father would never let anyone hurt Cyndi, no matter what Joan says."

"And anyway," Nell said in a whisper, "it wasn't Cyndi Lauper's fault. It was Boo who tripped Joan."

"And I thought Doctor Boojums died a long time ago."

"Sure. He did. But you know. Um. Cats have nine lives..." She trailed off, glancing around nervously.

"I know." Cally glanced, also, to make sure neither Foster nor Ian were listening. "I know Boo is a ghost. But how could a ghost trip a person?"

Nell shrugged. "He's a cat," she said matter-of-factly. "Cats can do whatever they want."

Somehow, Cally didn't doubt that. As the ambulance moved off across the lawn, followed closely by the G. A. A. S. P. S. van, she encouraged Nell to bring Cyndi Lauper up onto the porch with everyone else.

"She says she tripped over a cat at the bottom of the spiral staircase in her office," Sheriff Mahon was saying. "Did any of you see this happen?"

Ian, the Captain, and Foster took turns trying to describe to Sheriff Mahon how the paranormal crew had spotted the White Lady on the Gallery, looking down at them from above while they ate, and how everyone had run upstairs in pursuit of her only to find her gone. They had checked all unlocked guest rooms and found nothing. Then they had heard Joan screaming in her office. "I had to get the key from the drawer to get in," Katarina explained. "The door was locked." They had burst in to find Joan, tangled in her white gown, at the bottom of the spiral staircase, cursing about the cat.

"It wasn't Cyndi Lauper's fault!" Nell pleaded to the sheriff, clutching the cat as if she expected him to clap handcuffs on its paws right then and there.

"Nobody blames the kitty," Ian assured her. "Why don't you let little Cyndi go, now?"

Nell reluctantly opened her arms and the little calico seized the opportunity to streak down the steps into the shrubbery. She ran, Cally noted, right past an old gray tomcat who sat cleaning his whiskers on the bottom step.

"If only cats could talk," she muttered under her breath, earning a baleful glare from Doctor Boojums. Then she turned back to the sheriff and said "I imagine that oversized skirt contributed to her fall."

"Possibly she was overmedicated as well," Foster put in.

"What? No," said Cally. "She wasn't using it for herself, she was using it to drug Bethany."

"Well, all that is still to be determined," the Sheriff said, putting away his notepad. "Nobody is being accused of anything right now. I am on my way to the hospital to ask Joan some questions, so I'll call you, Ian, as soon as I can and let you know how she's doing." He seemed about to say his goodbyes but Cally put a hand on his arm and said, "May I show you something first?"

He nodded and she led him into the house, then down the back hall into the kitchen. There, she headed for the drain board beside the sink where she had put the cup of suspicious tea, but it was nowhere to be found. "Damn! Kat must have washed it already. Why would she do that?"

"Not I," said Katarina, coming into the kitchen closely followed by Ignacio and Foster. She asked them if they had done anything with the tainted tea cup, but they claimed no knowledge of it. In fact, Ignacio pointed out, the cup was missing altogether, and was not in the cupboard where it would have been returned after being washed.

"We'll find it in Joan's office, I'd be willing to bet," Cally said.

"And why are you so sure Joan is up to no good?" asked the sheriff.

"Oh, she's had it in for Bethany from the very beginning!" Katarina interjected. "She sees her as competition for Ian's affections. As if Mr. May would ever take up with Joan!"

"But to drug her tea? That seems a little extreme."

Even Cally had to admit this was true. "But Bethany did say the White Lady had been in her room, and this was just before I found that cup. Now that I think about it, I saw her – the so-called White Lady – myself a few times." She told them about having seen a white skirt retreating up the stairway when Bethany had her accident. "I thought it really was that stupid ghost, at the time."

"We should avoid jumping to conclusions," said Sheriff Mahon, "until we know more. And I think I should talk to Bethany myself, as well."

"Oh, please don't upset her," Cally said. "I don't want to make her worry about someone being out to get her, while she's helpless in bed."

The sheriff assured her he would be the very model of discretion, and left the kitchen.

"Well," Foster observed, "at least we know Joan won't be able to be a danger to anyone now. Not for quite a while, anyway!" Everyone agreed that there was at least that.

30 - Joan Returns

A soft, gray rain was falling when Joan came home in the morning. Ignacio carried a rain poncho out to the truck for her, but she waved him away angrily and insisted that only Ian could help her out of the truck. Ian stood patiently holding an umbrella in one hand and a pair of shiny new crutches in the other. When Joan tried to use them, they slipped on the wet grass and Joan clutched at Ian to keep from falling. Ignacio managed to keep Ian from falling, but the umbrella landed in a puddle in the lawn.

"Dios mío!" Katarina cried, watching through the front door. "This house is starting to look like a battlefield hospital!"

"Careful," said Cally. "*You* are starting to sound like Joan."

Katarina bit her knuckle. "And this morning Ignacio found three of the chickens dead in the garden. What an awful day!" She turned to get the wheelchair from beside the stairs, and Cally refrained from reminding her about Bethany's discarded toast that Ignacio had thrown out to the chickens the day before. She held the door open for Katarina and the wheelchair, and planned to ask Ignacio if he had thought to set aside the chickens' carcasses for the sheriff to examine.

Out in the lawn, Ian managed to persuade Joan to sit in the wheelchair, while Ignacio covered her cast with the poncho. Cally went back to the desk and watched all this through the screen door. She didn't want to go far from the phone today, because the guests she had booked for that evening might need to call for directions if they ran into trouble finding Woodley. She wondered what she would tell them if they did.

Joan and the dripping wheelchair rolled through the door into the hall. "Good Lord!" Joan was grumbling. "This whole house is starting to look like a hospital!"

"I'll get you a towel," muttered Katarina, running out of the hall.

"Bring me a cup of tea, too!" Joan called after her, and then to Ignacio, "Just get me into my office, José. I don't have time for this nonsense. I have too much work to do!"

When Joan was safely behind her oak door, Nell poked her head out from the parlor. "Have you seen Foster?" she asked Cally.

"I haven't." She noted that Foster's car was not in the parking lot, either.

Nell came the rest of the way into the hall. Apparently she hadn't been hoping to find her husband, but had been hoping not to find him. She gazed out the front door into the rain.

"Probably not the best day for a walk," Cally told her.

"No," Nell agreed. "How about Georgie? Have you seen him today?" She spoke of him as if he were any other member of the household. And really, it occurred to Cally, he had as much claim to that status as any of its living denizens.

"I haven't seen him since the investigators were here. Why?"

"I need to ask him about something. I'll just wait in the parlor. If you see him, please tell me. I have some questions for him."

"So do I," Cally said to herself. In the parlor, she could hear Nell busily flipping through the channels on the television. Cally had not seen George, but she had seen the Preacher, earlier that morning. Just as Bethany had once told her sometimes happened, Cally had smelled smoke, and had glanced behind her at the clean-swept fireplace with its basket of silk flowers on the fender. Turning back, she had seen – instead of the blurry shadow of Bethany's story – the seriously-dressed, sober-faced man she had seen standing in front of the desk when she'd first arrived at Vale House. He was gazing up at the portraits above the fireplace, not speaking, not moving. Cally had got up the courage to ask him if she could help him, but he had not seemed to hear her at all. He had remained there a good twenty minutes and, just as Bethany had learned to do, Cally eventually ignored him and resumed her work. He had faded away, along with the smoky smell, shortly before Joan had returned.

Katarina came through presently with a mug of tea and a large, flowered bath towel for Joan. Cally stopped her. "Do you mind if I take those in to her, while you listen for the phone? I just want to talk to her."

"I don't mind at all!" Katarina said emphatically, plopping herself down in the chair behind the desk. "Good luck with that!"

"Thanks, Kat. If Mr. Delaney calls for directions just... I don't know, tell him whatever you usually tell people." She paused with her hand on the office door knob. "And if you don't mind, I'd like to talk to you about that, myself, sometime soon."

Katarina gave her a deer-in-the-headlights look. "I'll do my best," she promised. "But I'm not sure I'm the best person to ask."

Cally knocked firmly on Joan's door and did not wait for an answer before entering. She found Joan seated on one of the sofas with her injured foot propped up on a coffee table. A pillow had been put under her foot, and the television had been turned to face her. Cally set the mug of tea down on the end table next to a now ubiquitous bottle of pain medication. She handed Joan the towel.

Joan rubbed her bedraggled head with the towel. "My new hairdo is ruined," she moaned. "Everything is ruined! Ian will never get any business at this place now!"

Cally wanted to blurt out, "Well what did you expect, playing at idiotic games like that?" but, in spite of her suspicions about Joan, she couldn't bring herself to kick her while she was down. She took the high ground and approached the conversation in the role of the concerned supporter.

"It was a good plan," she told Joan, swallowing hard to keep her voice calm. "It's a shame it didn't work out. How long have you been the White Lady?"

Joan threw the wadded up towel across the room where it hit the door with a soft thump. "You people act like I'm some kind of criminal! All I was doing was trying to help Ian's business succeed! Ow!" she concluded as the cast slipped off the pillow and rapped sharply on the tabletop.

Cally helped Joan get her foot back onto the pillow, enduring the woman's cries of pain and distress in the process. She tried a different tack. "Have you taken your pain medicine yet?"

This earned her a cold glare. "I don't like pills. And you people can just stop treating me like I'm some kind of addict, too! Honestly, even the sheriff was hounding me about it last night. Questioning me like some kind of criminal while I was lying there in the hospital in agony. What is *wrong* with people?"

"I'm sure he was just doing his job."

"Doing his job! Harassing decent people. Injured people! Look, I don't even want these stupid drugs the doctors are pushing on me. I don't like pills. I never have. Just take them away. Ow!"

"Maybe you really do need them," Cally said quite honestly. Then, "Maybe they'd be easier for you to take if you dissolve them in your tea."

"*Are you out of your mind?*" Joan looked like she was looking around for something else to throw. "Katarina can't make a decent cup of tea to begin with. Putting drugs in it would just make it even more awful!"

Cally decided to stop being coy, and went straight to the heart of the matter. "But that's how you served them to Bethany."

Joan seized a small sofa pillow and squeezed it as if she were strangling it. "I would never serve *that woman* anything! Not even a cup of poison!"

"But she said the White Lady brought her some tea." This wasn't strictly true, Cally acknowledged to herself. Bethany had only said the White Lady had been in her room. Cally simply spliced the two halves of the story together for expedience, hoping to corner Joan into a confession.

Joan snorted. "She was probably hallucinating. I wouldn't set foot in that room she's freeloading in. And anyway I only put that dress on for the first time last night. I bought it at the Goodwill in Blackthorn the other day when I went to get my hair done. All money down the drain now!" She closed her eyes and let her head fall back on the sofa.

Cally didn't believe Joan had only bought the dress so recently. She had seen the so-called Lady in White long before that. Including the time she'd spotted her peering at her from an upstairs window – probably Joan's own bedroom window, she realized now – the very first day she'd arrived at Vale House. She didn't argue with Joan about it; she figured it would be easy enough for the sheriff to find out when the dress really had been purchased.

"Well, I've got to get back to work," she told Joan. "Would you like me to put the TV remote where you can reach it?"

"Yes, and take those pills out of here. I'm no addict! I don't want any drugs."

"I'll leave them in case you reconsider."

☾

"Nobody has called," Katarina said when Cally came back into the hall. Before Cally resumed her seat she asked Katarina if she had a few minutes to talk. "I'm confused and I need some answers."

Katarina repeated that she wasn't sure she had any answers, either, but she did have a few minutes. "Even though now I have to do *all* of Joan's work as well!"

Both women laughed, and Cally felt a little better. "It's just this thing about this town being so hard to find," she said. "And yet people do find it. But they always seem to need help. Nobody seems to be able to just drive to the exit on I-85 and stop in for gas and a pizza. Yet, the mail goes in and out. Sometimes we even get a cell phone signal!" She laughed a little, but not heartily. "Kat, is this place even real? Or are we in the Matrix or something?"

She expected Katarina to laugh at the Matrix reference. Instead, the woman simply looked at her with wide, frank eyes and shrugged. Afterward, Cally would remember that shrug as having been one of the most frightening moments of her life. More frightening than the time she had found the note in her husband's pocket, and almost as frightening as when George had vanished before her eyes.

"I honestly don't know," Katarina admitted. "I just go where Ignacio goes, because I love him."

"Should I ask him, then?"

Katarina shook her head. "Ian knows. I'm pretty sure. Ian and the other men. They sit on the porch and talk, sometimes. It's hard to keep a business going in a town that is ... hidden. They're afraid the town is going to disappear. And I hope it doesn't. I like it here."

"I like it, too," Cally had to admit. "Who are these other men?"

"The friends Ian grew up with. The Captain and Doc, and Merv Arkwright. Sometimes the sheriff, but he's new to their little group. I call them The White Council." She giggled at this.

"Is Ignacio a member of this White Council?"

"Oh, no," said Katarina. "Then it would have to be called the White and Brown Council!" She started to laugh at her own joke but

196

cut herself short when she saw Cally's face. "No, no, I didn't mean *that*! I meant, Ignacio is so much younger than they are. His hair hasn't turned white yet."

Cally smiled. "Well maybe someday they'll make him a Junior Member. And maybe it's time for them to have a Women's Auxiliary, too."

Katarina grinned at this, but shook her head. "I don't know. They have a lot of secrets, it seems. I mean, they're all good men. I don't think their secrets are bad or anything. Ignacio trusts them, so I have never questioned them. But, well, all you can do is ask."

Cally was already starting to think about how she would phrase her question, and to whom, as Katarina headed back to the dining room. She looked around the hall. "George? Are you here?" If he was, he did not answer.

Pushing down a disturbing thought that the incident with the paranormal crew might have scared him away for good, she opened her laptop and located the story Emerald had sent her, the one that was supposed to explain who Emerald was. It really did read a lot like a novel, perhaps a historical romance, about a young woman born in the countryside of a place Cally thought reminded her very much of Scotland. If it was a novel, though, it was a rather rough first draft, and contained a number of continuity gaps. After a few pages, she put it aside for the moment and composed an email to Emerald, asking her to please join her on the chat channel that evening. Then she checked her own incoming email and deleted a message from a Nigerian prince and several messages offering free credit reports. She filed another message from her agent under "Later."

She opened her word processor and created a blank document. "Sometimes the main character of a story can be something other than human," she typed. "Maybe he or she is a ghost. Or an animal. Or even a town." She saved the document with the filename "Maybe.txt" and closed the computer.

The sun came out shortly after noon. The phone rang and Cally answered it on the first ring, even though she was still not sure what she would say if the Delaneys were having trouble finding their way into Woodley. "Vale House; how might I help you?"

It wasn't the Delaneys. A young woman's voice said "This is Danya Barry from the Greater Asheboro Area Scientific Paranormal Society." Cally braced herself for a tirade about how Vale House's shady practices had ruined these young people's entire lives, but instead the young woman asked tremulously, "Can I send you something?"

Cally wasn't quite sure how to reply to that. "I suppose. What do you want to send?"

"It's a photo I took while I was there. Can you stay on the line while I email it to you, so we can look at it together?"

Cally agreed to this strange request, and gave the woman her own email address. She waited in silence, listening to Danya typing it in to her phone, and then opened her computer and watched for new email to appear in her inbox. "Yes, I have it now. Just let me..."

She opened the message and saw it contained the same photo Danya had showed her while the team had been at Vale House, of a figure in white standing at the Gallery railing above the dining room. Cally hadn't paid it much attention because other matters had seemed much more urgent at the moment. "Yes, I see it," she told Danya. "What did you want to discuss about it?"

"Well. It looks real, don't you think?"

It looked real because it was real, Cally thought. It was a rather clear, if translucent, image of George standing in the Gallery above the dining room, wearing a long, white garment. Doctor Boojums was sitting at his feet practically smirking. The outlines of the doors to the upstairs guest rooms could be made out behind them. George was definitely getting to be very "good at electronics."

"It does look very real," Cally replied. "But maybe it's just pareidolia."

Danya sighed loudly in Cally's ear. "Come on. Seriously? I get that all the time. I can't believe you really think that's what it is."

Cally didn't really think that at all, but she also didn't feel comfortable discussing George with a complete stranger.

"It looks like a black man," Danya was going on, "though why he's wearing a robe, I can't imagine. I don't think there would be monks in a house like that. Maybe he's a civil war soldier; maybe the house was used as an infirmary during the war. Do you know anything about that?"

"I'm afraid I don't, but I do know whom to ask. I could call you back and let you know."

"Anyway he's clearly not that crazy woman who was running around pretending to be the White Lady."

"No, definitely not," Cally agreed.

"Well I was just wondering. Because this photo does make me think there's something real going on after all at your bed and breakfast, despite all the shenanigans last night. So, I was wondering if I and a couple of the others might be able to come back and take a second look. Without all the TV equipment this time," she added.

"I don't know," Cally said. The idea of someone hunting George and actually knowing what to look for made her uneasy. "I would have to ask our marketing manager about that."

A snort on the other end of the connection reminded Cally that this woman knew exactly who the "marketing manager" was and wanted nothing further to do with her.

"Alright, well, I appreciate you letting me share the photo with you," Danya said. "Please remember it's copyrighted material and you can't use it without my permission."

"I wouldn't dream of it," said Cally. "I'll delete it right now, if it makes you feel better."

They concluded the call and Cally's hand hovered over the delete button, but she decided to just keep a private copy of the photo for herself anyway. After all, it was of a friend of hers.

"Dear Georgie," she said to the empty Hall, "Your little pranks are going to get you into trouble someday!"

31 - Twilight Arrives

"I like it when you call me Georgie."

He was sitting on the stairs, about halfway up.

"*Georgie* the little ghost," he said, grinning. "Who made the stairs squeak and the doors creak. I used to stand behind Nellie and read over her shoulder, when she was a small child. That was one of her favorites."

"Georgie! I was worried about you!" Cally cried in relief, a little too loudly. She looked quickly around the Hall to make sure she hadn't been overheard.

"Why?"

"Never mind. It's just good to see you. How are you doing today?"

"I never do any differently from one day to another." He shrugged. "Though I have finished reading *The Lord of The Rings* and most of *All Creatures Great And Small*."

Cally realized she was going to have to download more e-books for him soon. "Well, I'm sure you've been watching all that's been going on around here since last night," she told him. "It turns out the White Lady was not really a ghost after all. I should have asked you in the first place."

George laughed and stood up to come closer to the desk. The way he moved from place to place still made Cally's stomach do flips. He didn't seem to bother making sure his forward speed corresponded with the number of steps he took. "No, she was never a ghost," George said. "Though she may be one someday." He sat down on the corner of the desk.

"Do you mind if I ask you about some other things?" Cally said. "Like what happened to Bethany? Did you see what actually happened when she fell and got hurt? Where was Joan at the time? And... Ignacio, for that matter?"

"I don't know the answers to most of those things," he said. "I did see Bethany fall, but I didn't see who unwound the chair and emptied the bottom drawer of the filing cabinet. It must have been someone I don't like, someone I don't hang around much. Anyway I..." He looked around the Hall, out the front door and at the parlor and dining room doorways. "You see, I don't have access to most of this house. I can come into this room, and I can go up and down the stairs and part of the hall up there. But I can't even go into the south end of the upstairs hall. I can't go very far from my *zemi*, you see."

He had mentioned this *zemi* before. "What is that?" Cally asked him. "And why can't you go far from it?"

"I'm not sure. I mean, yes, I am sure what my *zemi* is. My uncle made it for me when I was a little boy. So very long ago. It's a sort of a talisman. A little carving of a god that is supposed to protect me. I always kept it with me, when I was at sea, and now it seems it is keeping me with it. Someone put it into the drawer of the desk, many years ago, and Isbel May, who was a very sweet person, bought the desk, and she had it put upstairs. I have lived here ever since."

Cally could only think spending that many years in the same hallway and stairway must be a true purgatory of tedium, but she didn't say so out loud. "I'm sorry, Georgie," she said. "I really will have to write your story one day. Do you think if I moved your *zemi* around for you, you might be able to go other places? What does it look like?"

He seemed to be considering this, but finally said, "Maybe you shouldn't touch it. I don't know what would happen. We want to keep you safe. You aren't here to save me; you are here to save Vale House." He nodded solemnly, and this made a chill run down her spine.

"I can't even imagine..." She paused as he put a finger to his lips. A car was pulling in to the parking area in front of the house. By the time Cally looked up at the sound, and then back to George, he had already vanished.

Charles and Mary Delaney carried their little white terrier up the porch stairs, while Ignacio followed behind with their luggage.

"Did you have any trouble finding us?" Cally asked as they presented themselves at the desk.

"Well. Twilight started barking just when we were about to pass the exit," said Mr. Delaney, accepting the pen Cally handed him. "Otherwise, we might have gone right past without noticing it. It's unusual, since she hardly ever barks at all," he added, while the little dog strained at the end of its leash, barking at Doctor Boojums in the dining room doorway.

"We are on our way to Wilmington," Mrs. Delaney told Cally, looking around the Hall in awe while her husband signed the register. "And then on to Savannah. Twilight, be quiet!" She reached down and picked the little dog up. "We are fascinated by southern architecture," she explained as the dog continued barking.

"Mr. May would be delighted to talk to you about southern architecture," Cally told them over the sound of the dog's strident voice. She jotted a note to remind herself to ask Ian if he would have time to give them the architectural tour of Vale House later. Something heavy hit the inside of Joan's office door, causing the dog to look around and stop barking for approximately two seconds. "Would you prefer a haunted or non-haunted room?"

This earned her a blank stare, and Cally regretted her flippancy. "It's a popular local legend," she explained. "Some people are very into it. I assure you, all of the rooms are beautifully decorated."

She gave them the key to the Cala Lily room. Ignacio carried their bags upstairs, and Mrs. Delaney carried the little dog Twilight, which did not want to leave the Hall and its ghostly entertainment.

Cally had not had any lunch, and it was almost dinner time. She put the phones into night mode and carried her computer up the stairs. George was not there, but Doctor Boojums was sitting on the butler's desk, washing his paws.

"Are you learning how to read, now, too?"

The old tom gave her a sideways look with his gray tongue still hanging out. Cally tiptoed to the desk, looking around her to make sure George wasn't anywhere nearby. The cat held his ground while she slid the desk drawer open as silently as she could. If George showed up, she thought, she could tell him she was just getting the e-reader to add more books to it. It wouldn't really be a lie – though she wondered if it was even possible to lie to a ghost.

Her e-reader was still there, buried under the stationery with which she had covered it. Above the drawer was a row of pigeonholes, each with its own tiny door, and these she opened one at a time. Most of them were filled with the usual bric-a-brac found in old desks: pencils in need of sharpening (but no pencil sharpener,) handle-less coffee mugs full of foreign coins and bent paper-clips, watches that had not worked in years and broken porcelain figurines eternally awaiting glue.

Cally moved aside a small bundle of yellowed note-cards with kittens on the covers and saw the compartment behind it filled with an assortment of orphaned buttons and brittle rubber bands. Nested amidst these was a small wooden triangle, about four inches from point to point, which had been carved so that each edge of the triangle bore a face. Each face in turn bore a completely different expression, though only one of them looked human. The carving was old and cracked, but worn smooth as if it had once been handled frequently. Cally thought if anything in this house could be called a *zemi*, that would be it. She was careful not to touch it, but replaced the note cards over it and quietly closed the little door.

"Don't rat me out," she told the cat, who had curled up next to the lamp and was regarding her with one eye. "And don't knock the lamp down," she added as she turned away to put her head inside the door of the Daffodil Room.

Her heart rose to her throat when she saw the bed was empty. Turning back to the door, she took a deep breath to shout down over the Gallery railing for help, but before she could form words, she heard the door of the adjoining bathroom open behind her. Bethany emerged, swaying unsteadily but smiling. Cally let out her breath and ran to the woman, hugging her with relief.

"Careful!" Bethany cried out, wincing.

"Bethany, you scared the willies out of me! You're not supposed to get out of bed by yourself."

"It's fine," Bethany assured her, though she did lean heavily on Cally's arm as she was led back to the bed. "I feel a hundred percent better."

"Really? A hundred percent?"

"Well, ninety. Eighty-five, maybe? It did hurt to get up. A lot!" She stopped at the side of the bed. "But I am tolerating the medicine better. I haven't felt nearly so loopy today. And it really is helping with the pain, now. Would you tattle to Doc if I just sit in the chair awhile instead of getting into bed right away?"

Cally realized Bethany was tolerating the medicine better because she was finally taking the right medicine, but she didn't say so out loud. She reluctantly helped Bethany into the chair beside the bed, feeling her flinch with every movement. The older woman sighed with contentment when she was settled. "It just feels so good to have a clean face and combed hair for a change," she said. "Cally, I hadn't brushed my teeth in three days! You know, what I would really love is a nice, hot shower."

"Bethany Chase! Absolutely *do not* attempt to take a shower without Kat or me to help you!"

Bethany remembered not to laugh. "You worry too much. I'm going to have to get back to work sometime, you know," she pointed out. "Poor Kat is run ragged."

"But you are not going to get back to work tonight."

"No, not tonight," Bethany agreed.

Cally made an effort to ease the tense expression from her face. After all, Bethany was unaware of what was really worrying her so much, and Cally thought it best to keep it that way until Bethany was well and truly back on her feet. She moved the iced tea glass, some magazines, and the telephone to the side of the night stand closest to the chair so Bethany could reach them without twisting. "Just next time please call someone to help you. Promise me."

"I promise."

"And no showers!"

"I do solemnly swear I will take no showers without both you and Kat hovering around and taking pictures to put on the interwebs."

"What on earth?" Katarina was just coming in the door with a dinner tray. Cally left Bethany trying awkwardly to explain, without laughing, the conversation of which Katarina had only heard the tail end.

32 - Seven Forks

The confusion in Bethany's room had caused Cally to delay her dinner even longer, and now she was ravenous. She decided to drive into town for her evening meal, instead of walking, and she decided to just take her computer with her rather than going back to lock it up in the Rose Room. Maybe she could stop on the way back and use the Wi-Fi at the coffee shop.

As she and the boxes rattling in the back seat passed out through the pineapple-crowned gateposts, Cally spotted Errin and her blonde friend from the coffee shop; they were just about to walk around the corner from Main Street onto Gardens Road. Errin waved when she saw Cally, and Cally paused, winding down her window to wave back.

"We're on our way to Blackthorn," said Errin. "Zenbe is playing in a band there. Want to come with us?"

"Um. No thank you. That's a long way. Are you sure you want to walk that far?" She stopped just short of offering them a lift, remembering with a stomach-flip the last time she'd had Errin in the car with her.

Errin's friend let out a giggle and Errin grinned. "It's not that long a walk for us," she said. "You sure you don't want to come along? They have a great burger place!"

Cally had no doubt the walk to Blackthorn, for Errin, would be quite different from what she might experience herself, but she did not want to think about the great burger place. "Maybe another time," she said. The two girls giggled to one another and waved as Cally drove away.

She did not so much as glance at the news store when she passed it, but when she reached the intersection with Railroad Street, she stopped in the middle of Main Street with her turn signal blinking. Gazing down Railroad street at the sidewalk in front of the pizza shop, where Ben had found her that evening, she couldn't bring herself to turn. What if she ran into him again? After the things she had overheard him and Bree discussing the night before, she wouldn't know what to say or how to act. After all, she thought, setting her jaw, he'd promised Bree he wouldn't ever speak to her again. She wouldn't want to get him into trouble, would she?

Switching off her turn signal, she stepped on the gas and drove on to the west end of town and into the darkening tunnel of trees. Maybe she would try the Seven Forks diner, out near the interstate, instead. Maybe she would get lost again, and this time Errin would not appear and set her back on the right path. Maybe she would just go straight back out onto the highway and keep on driving until her bank account was empty and her credit card maxed out. After all, most of her worldly belongings were still in the car with her. Well, all except her CDs and most of her clothes. And some people she had come to care about...

She slowed down to cross the little bridge over the creek (Harmony Creek, Ben had told her it was called) and saw the lights of the diner and the gas station beyond the trees. The Seven Forks was well lit from within and looked like a welcoming beacon. Beyond it, through a line of pine trees, she could see the headlights of trucks wending their lonely way along I-85.

Cally parked next to the only other car in the parking lot, tucked her computer case under the passenger seat, and went inside. The interior was furnished with typical diner booths upholstered in red vinyl, and a coffee bar with red-seated chrome stools. The walls were painted in murals depicting oak trees and streams, giving the whole place the impression of a seating area made of magical red mushrooms in the middle of a forest. "Just sit down anywhere!" a woman's voice called from the kitchen beyond the bar.

Cally chose a booth and perused the menu, carefully avoiding looking at the description of the only burger the place offered. She didn't have long to wait. A short, plump older woman appeared beside her with a notepad. "What can I get for you, dear?"

"The Caesar salad looks good," Cally said, closing the menu and handing it to the woman.

"Is everything okay?" the woman asked her, holding the menu in her arms.

"Aren't you supposed to ask me that when my mouth is full of food?" Cally smirked at her own weak attempt at humor.

"It's just that you seem sad." Cally had no reply to this, and the woman apologized. "I'm sorry. I forgot you don't know me yet. I didn't mean to be so familiar."

"It's alright," Cally said. "You're just perceptive. I do feel out of sorts tonight, I guess."

"Do you want to talk about it?"

The woman almost seemed as if she were about to sit down in the booth with her, but Cally was feeling too pensive for company. "I just want to eat a salad," she said, perhaps a little too bluntly.

The woman did not seem offended. She patted Cally's shoulder as she walked back to the kitchen shouting, "Caesar, Rave!"

She returned in moments with a glass of water and a straw. "Would you like a reading?" she asked as she set them down.

"What? No. Thank you." Cally shook her head in puzzlement. That was an odd question to ask a restaurant customer. But then, this whole town was strange, after all. She looked through the window to the street light that stood at the edge of the parking lot. "But maybe you could tell me: If I just drive east on that road there, will I be able to get back to downtown Woodley?" She gave the woman a pointed look.

This earned her a warm smile. "I really do think you ought to let Raven give you a reading," she said, turning to where another older woman, unusually tall with lush, silver hair hanging down to her hips, was carrying a platter toward them.

"I met a girl named Raven," Cally recalled, "who wanted to give me a reading. Just a few days ago." It seemed now like it had been years ago.

"Well, Ravens do tend to bring things to people," the tall woman said, setting the platter of salad in front of Cally. Standing next to her, the other woman looked even shorter and rounder.

The way the two stood there with hands clasped before them, looking at Cally with such sincere concern in their eyes, started to make her feel a little bad for being so short with them. "Maybe I should have listened to the first Raven," she admitted. "Okay, can you give me this reading while I eat?"

Both women broke into delighted grins, and the tall one pulled a bundle wrapped in yellow silk from her apron. Sitting down across from Cally, she unwrapped a deck of cards, but it didn't look like any Tarot deck Cally had ever seen. The cards were perfectly square, for one thing.

"I've learned a lot since I first started doing this," Raven said. "I've become really good at it." She began to turn over cards and arrange them on the table, using so many she had to work around Cally's plate. The images on the cards were also not what Cally had expected to see. Instead of cups and kings, they depicted things like trees, streams, roads, bridges and even a lake Cally could swear looked just like the pond behind Vale House. "This is for you," Raven said, once she had got the cards arranged. She scrutinized them and began turning some of them sideways, and rearranging others so the images on the cards joined up to form a convoluted path. "It's kind of like how a GPS works. You know what I mean?"

Cally had no idea what she meant. She tried to eat without getting salad dressing on the cards. The salad was good and, despite how hungry she had been when she'd arrived, there was a lot more of it than she thought she would be able to finish.

"Well, there you go," Raven said at last. "You will never have trouble finding Woodley again." She nodded with satisfaction, and the other woman applauded softly.

"That's it?" Cally had always thought "a reading" involved much more than that.

"That's the main thing you wanted, wasn't it?"

Cally wasn't sure she actually wanted it at all. She could think, though, of a lot of things she did want, and many other questions she would have liked to have answered, or at least guessed at, by someone who claimed to be able to read things in cards. Most of them were not things she was willing to discuss with these overly-familiar strangers, though. "There is one other thing," she said at length. "Can you see, there, if Bethany is going to be okay?" She also wanted to know what had happened to Bethany in the first place, and who seemed to be continuing to try to hurt her, but if this woman could really answer the first question, maybe that answer would lead to others.

Raven leaned over the cards and cast her gaze along the paths and bridges and streams in them. "All I can really see here is that there's a friend you need to make amends with."

"Which friend would that be?" Cally was pretty sure she knew exactly which friend this referred to, but she wasn't completely certain making up with Emerald was even an option anymore.

The shorter woman cleared her throat and shoved her way in to sit down on the seat beside Cally. "She's really on your side, Cally," she said, patting one of the cards next to the plate.

"How do you know my name?" Cally asked. Of course, everyone in this town knew who she was, but most people tended to refer to her by the name on the cover of her book.

Raven laughed. "Oh, Willow knows a lot of things!"

"Willow?" An odd name for such a short woman, but the oddest thing was that it seemed strongly familiar somehow. A sense of *déjà vu* began to make Cally feel a little dizzy.

Willow stood and picked up the plate, which Cally had managed to empty in spite of herself. "I'll get your check," she said.

Raven was also standing and collecting her cards. "Everything always works out in the end," she assured Cally, "despite all our best efforts to make them do so."

Cally had no trouble finding her way back into Woodley. The main street was deep in dusk, and the only other car on the street was parked in front of the coffee shop. The lights were still on inside the news store, and Cally thought she saw someone leaving it, but looked away quickly and pulled over to park next to the Bean Garden instead.

33 - Old Friends

"Is the Wi-Fi working tonight?"

Andi was sweeping, and most of the chairs had been put up on top of the tables.

"It always works fine when nobody's trying to use it." Andi laughed, leaning the broom against the counter. "What can I get for you?"

Cally opened her laptop on one of the tables that still had its chairs on the floor, and let Andi talk her into trying the decaf vanilla chai. "How is Bethany doing?" Andi asked.

"She's in much better spirits today," Cally said. She explained what had happened to Joan, as well, but Andi – and the whole town – had already heard all about that. "Now Bethany is trying to get up and get back to work. She's awake enough to be bored, since the whole thing with her medicine has been straightened out."

"Sheriff hasn't showed up to arrest Joan yet?" Andi grinned as she brought Cally's chai to her, but she seemed to already know he hadn't, and Cally imagined Andi would probably be the first to find out about it if he did. She smiled and shook her head. "Well, I'll let you get on with that Great American Novel, then." Andi returned behind the counter and began sorting a pile of receipts. "Stay as late as you like! I'll be over here working on my own books, if you need me."

Cally pushed down a wave of guilt as she did not open her word processor but instead opened the chat program. Emerald's avatar showed she was online, as she had always been, every night since Cally had met her. Cally cleared her throat and began typing.

Cally>> I'm sorry I haven't logged in to chat lately. The internet around here has been a little wonky.

It wasn't technically a lie, but Cally knew that Emerald knew this wasn't the real reason she hadn't sought her out in such a long time.

Emerald<< It's alright, How are you?

Cally>> It's been an interesting week. Also I started reading your story.

Emerald<< Oh. What do you think?

Cally>> I haven't got very far yet. Only to the part where you fell in love with that gypsy.

Emerald<< Ah, yes. So much still to be revealed.

Cally>> Yes probably. Look. Emerald, it doesn't matter. I don't need to know. I mean, yes, I'd like to know, and I will read the rest of the story, but what I mean is, I'm sorry. I know you're my friend, and I know you have my back. Inasmuch as you can, anyway, and I'm sorry I flew off the handle. You didn't deserve that.

Cally held her breath waiting for Emerald to finish reading this long entry, though she already knew what the reply would be.

Emerald<< It's alright. I understand.

Cally gazed at the silently winking cursor, trying to think of what to say next. So much had happened since they had last spoken, and Cally's list of questions had grown so much longer than it had been then. She tried to think of where to start, but Emerald was already composing a long message of her own.

> **Emerald<<** I have apologies I should make as well. I'm sorry I never shared any of this with you before. At first I just didn't know you very well so I never said anything about it, and then when I did get to know you, it just felt really good that you treated me like I was just a normal person. It almost made me feel like one. I didn't want to give it up. And anyway I'm sorry.

> **Cally>>** You don't need to be sorry. To be honest, you were probably right and I would have reacted badly. Before, when I didn't know the things I know now.

> **Emerald<<** :) There are no mistakes, only lessons.

Cally sat back and smiled at the screen. That kind of philosophical quote was more like the old Emerald she had met and befriended over the wires so long ago.

> **Cally>>** An old woman who calls herself Raven told me earlier: "Everything works out for the best, despite our efforts to make it do so."

> **Emerald<<** You've met Raven! Did she give you a reading?

> **Cally>>** She did. Apparently, I will never have trouble finding Woodley again.

> **Emerald<<** Excellent

Cally did not understand why this seemed to make perfect sense to Emerald, when it made none at all to her. And this, in turn, only served to remind her that there was still so much she did not understand about what was going on at Vale House and in Woodley and what Ian would call "the entire Vale." She wanted to press Emerald for more information, but she didn't want to reopen the rift between herself and the friend with whom she had only just reconciled.

Emerald<< Can I tell you something else?

Cally>> I was hoping you would.

Emerald<< :) I hear you, my friend. There's a lot I need to tell you. But I hardly know where to begin, now.

Cally>> Neither do I. Here, pick one: What is the deal with Woodley being so hard to find? Or, Who else is here? What are all these other things Georgie says "aren't all ghosts"?

Emerald<< I think understanding one might help you understand the other. As to the people who aren't all ghosts, you've been seeing them, too, right along. You've met Errin, for instance.

Cally>> I have. She says she's a unicorn. But she says a lot of silly things.

Emerald<< LOL. She's very sweet, though she has a chaotic spirit. But yes, she's not a ghost, and she's not human. And she's probably not a unicorn, either.

Cally>> What is she then?

Emerald<< If I were human myself, I'd be shaking my head right now. All I know for sure is that she is Errin. And she's on our side.

Cally>> Why does THAT not give me a lot of comfort?

Emerald<< LOL ok, well, let's try another example. Have you been down to the pond yet?

Cally>> Nell tried to introduce me to some of her "old friends" the other day. Something came up, so she never did but, is that what you mean?

Emerald<< Possibly. Probably. But I think it's best if you don't involve Nell. She's so fragile.

Cally>> I think she's stronger than most people give her credit for. Anyway what are these Old Friends, and should I meet them after all?

Emerald<< They are old earth spirits. I'm almost certain you've already met Rum. There was quite a ripple in the community when he spotted you. He's kind of a big deal.

Cally>> He passes by Vale House often, Ian says. We've nodded, but not spoken. What should I say to him? What should I do?

Emerald<< You really don't have to do anything - - just be open to them. They can show you things, much more than I can over the internet. More than George can, with his limitations. Maybe you should try going over the fence.

Cally had a vivid and wistful recollection of her first morning at Vale House, sitting in the sunlight on the porch steps with Nell and watching the white horse leap in one fluid motion over the fence.

Cally>> Into the meadow?

Emerald<< Yes, I think you'd be safe there. They know about you, now, and they like you, by all accounts.

Cally>> You get accounts from them?

Emerald<< I used to live among them. For a while, long ago - you'll see if you keep reading that story I sent you. Oh, but do keep something on you to give them as a gift. It can be anything, a coin, a button, whatever. Just as long as it's something that is yours to give. You can learn a lot from them, but don't ever go to them without something to leave as a gift.

Cally>> You're making me nervous about even trying it. But you know I'll probably do it, don't you? I've got to understand what's going on around here. Dammit I wish I were as good as I used to be at just rationalizing these things away.

Emerald<< You were never good at that, Cally. If you had been, you'd still be married to that jerk.

Cally>> Bree Dawes seems to think I am meddling in things that are none of my business.

Emerald<< Dear old Bree. How is she?

Cally>> Not so dear, I'm afraid. But apparently in excellent health, if that's what you mean.

Emerald<< And what about Ben?

Cally>> What about him?

Emerald<< I am sure he's in excellent health as well, don't you agree? Very excellent health.

Cally>> He's fine.

Emerald<< Yes, he certainly is. ;)

Cally>> Emerald, if you say one more word about Ben Dawes, I am going to close this chat.

Emerald<< Ben. Ben Dawes. LOL Ben, Ben, Ben!

34 - Over The Fence

Cally didn't close the chat right away, but she did change the subject, filling Emerald in on Bethany's accident and all the suspicions she'd had about it since then. Emerald had no insight to offer about this, other than she didn't believe it was a ghost doing these things, with which theory Cally had to concur.

She logged off and packed up her computer, saying goodnight to Andi who took a break from her balance sheet to come around the counter and give her a hug. "Don't worry," she said, "I'm sure the sheriff will get to the bottom of this whole thing. Meanwhile you be careful, okay?"

Cally was pretty sure the sheriff would only get to the bottom of a very few things worrying her at the moment, but she promised Andi she would be careful, and drove down the completely silent street back to Vale House.

The front porch light was still on, and as Cally got out of her car she waved at the Captain sitting on the porch. He did not wave back, so Cally assumed he was asleep. She decided to let him sleep until she returned. Turning, she walked back out the pineapple gate to the fence where Main Street ended and the dirt road into the meadow began.

The metal gate was still warm from the day, she noticed when she put her elbows up on it and peered out into the dark sea of grass. A gibbous moon was just rising beyond the meadow's horizon, where the dark silhouette of one of the horses could be seen grazing a little way off. The night was warm and windless, and far off to her left she could hear a ringing chorus of crickets and frogs down at the pond.

"Is anyone there?" Cally asked the darkness. Her words sounded ridiculous in her ears, like something right out of one of those ghost investigation shows. "Emerald sent me." In reply, she heard only laughter, loud and clownish, in the oak trees overhead as three owls emerged to fly on broad, silent wings over her head toward the moon. They sounded like rowdy drunks as they dipped and spun around one another until they were out of sight.

That, she thought, at least explained Andi's legend of the laughing trees along Bells Road. Only, she realized, it probably didn't. Not really. Not for her, not anymore. At last she said, "Alright, I'm coming over." The gate was held shut by a loop of chain over the fence post next to it. She lifted the chain off and dragged the heavy gate across the ground enough to make a space she could squeeze through.

The noise of the frogs and crickets down by the pond seemed to grow silent as soon as she stepped into the grass on the other side. It occurred to her it would be foolhardy to set off across that vast, unmarked meadow even in daylight, but she had never been very good at turning back, and she knew she would not be able to convince herself to turn back now. There was, at least, the dirt road to follow, though it faded after just a few yards to little more than two deep ruts in the grass. She followed them across a flat expanse to the foot of the low, round hill just past where the horse stood grazing. It was hard to tell, in the moonlight, whether it was the black horse or the chestnut.

The wheel-ruts soon became shallow and hard to see in the darkness. Cally turned to look around herself, and was comforted by the sight of Vale House's front porch light, and the distant lights, beyond, of Woodley's main street. To her left, Gardens Road glittered in the moonlight, stretching away southward to places she might or might not ever be able to find again on her own. All along the other side of the fence, it seemed to her, the ground looked pale and rutted, as well, almost as if another road ran along it, joining Gardens Road with Bells Road beyond the fields. Cally wondered if there had indeed once been a farm road there, before the grass had grown up and become the parking area in front of Vale House.

Behind her, to the east, the ground rose gently to the round crest of the next hill. She turned to face this, hesitating, but felt fairly secure that once she reached the top of it, she would still be able to turn again and see Vale House. Maybe that would be far enough. She noticed the horse had begun to follow her. It was keeping several steps behind and to her left, dropping its head to graze after every three or four steps, but it was clearly interested in what she was doing, and she found its presence comforting.

The slope was steeper than it had seemed from a distance, and by the time she reached the top, Cally's calves ached. She turned and was reassured to see the lights of Vale House, smaller now and more distant, but still glowing softly like a night light in a dark room. As she watched, a light in an upstairs window came on, and went out as a different one came on.

The horse stopped when Cally stopped, still keeping its distance, and dropped its head to graze. All around her, the meadow rose and fell like a sea of soft swells, the hills growing higher, and the valleys between them deeper, as they rolled into the distance under the moon. The only sounds to be heard out here were the breeze riffling softly through the grass and the high "*peent!*" of night hawks calling to one another from hill to hill, interrupted occasionally by the grinding noise of grass between horse's molars. "This is far enough, I think," Cally said to the horse, sitting down in the grass facing away from Vale House. "At least, I am certainly not going any farther, not tonight."

Although, she mused, during the daytime, a horse would certainly be a nice companion to ride in exploration of a grassy field. Might be nice, she corrected herself, as she really had no idea how to ride one. Maybe someday, she thought, she would offer to teach Errin to drive, in exchange for riding lessons. It was the first time she had thought of herself as staying in Woodley for more than a few weeks.

She wondered what she was supposed to do next. She wished she had brought her phone so she could text Emerald for more instructions, but somehow she felt phones would be completely inappropriate in this place, even if a signal were available. It seemed enough, somehow, to just sit here in the warm night air under the moon and listen to the night hawks and the horse grazing. At least, it seemed enough until her backside began to itch from sitting in the grass, which took the romance out of it all.

"Well, I don't think anyone is coming," she said at last to the horse and to the general vicinity. She stood to leave, but then she remembered Emerald had said something about bringing a gift to offer. She had seemed very adamant about this, yet Cally had forgotten; she had left her purse and everything else behind in her car.

"Alright, then." She reached up and plucked three strands of hair from her head and twisted them around the end of a stalk of tall grass. Two of them were gray ones, she realized with some chagrin as they glittered in the moonlight. "I hope this is okay. Goodnight." She bowed toward the distant hills.

Turning, she started down the hill toward the distant glow of Vale House's front porch, but before she took the first step she saw someone walking slowly up the slope toward her, bent unsteadily over a cane. "Captain?" she called, hurrying toward the figure. "Hello? Are you alright?"

"Ah, it's you," said a voice which, though old and creaky, was not the Captain's. "Hello!" he called, straightening up and waving his cane.

"Hello... Rum?" Cally thought this must be Ian's old neighbor, then, and felt relieved, as Rum was clearly much more fit for this sort of thing than the Captain was. And probably not mortal anyway, she recalled from her chat with Emerald. The old man waved his cane over his head at Cally as he continued up the hill, and on the breeze she caught the distinct smell of smoke and barbeque sauce. "No, wait, Jerome?" She was confused. Maybe it was Jerome from Seen's Mill, as he seemed much taller than she remembered Rum having been, though that still didn't explain what he was doing here at this hour.

"Just on my way home from work," he explained. As he approached, he seemed to grow shorter, until the top of his head came up only as high as Cally's shoulders. He bowed deeply as he arrived to stand with her at the crest of the hill. "I remember you," he said. "You were at the river with the Siennadair."

Cally didn't know what a Siennadair was, but she did remember the river. "So, then, you are Rum during the day," she guessed, "and at night you are Jerome, and your other job is to make the best ribs east and west of the Appalachians."

"Some say, some say!" He laughed. "You're alright, Callaghan

McCarthy. I like you! Now, are you sure you want to leave this lying around? It's very precious." He planted his cane in the ground and dug in the pocket of his overalls. Reaching up, he showed her three strands of her own hair. They glittered like cool flame flowing across his palm in the moonlight.

"I left it as a gift," she said. "And anyway I can't use it anymore. But how did you..." All the breath left her body as she gazed down into his wrinkled face, which looked less human and more like a mossy stump every moment.

"You might not be able to use it anymore," he interrupted, "but others could. I'll tell you what: I'll keep it safe for you. I'll keep you safe." He thrust the hairs inside the bib of his overalls. "You have a bright head and a high heart."

"There are those who might disagree with you," Cally said.

"Well I didn't mean you had a lot going on in the brain department," he chuckled, tapping his own head with a long, crooked finger.

Cally shook herself and took a deep breath to make herself stop staring at him because it seemed the longer she stared, the less clearly she could see him, and besides, it was rude. "Are you one of Emerald's friends, then?" she asked. "She said I should ask you some questions."

"I'm your friend now," he said. "Come on, let me show you." He plucked his cane out of the ground and walked past her, eastward over the crest of the hill and started down the far slope.

"Um..." Cally cast a nervous look at the lights of Woodley. The horse, however, picked up its head and followed the retreating figure with alacrity. "Oh, I hope I'm not going to regret this," Cally said under her breath, hurrying to catch up with them, glancing over her shoulder every few steps. The hill rose behind her and gradually its dark bulk blocked her view of the lights of Woodley.

The moon had cleared the horizon and the grass looked silvery in its light. The horse and Rum cast moon-shadows behind them, pointing back toward Vale House, which Cally noted with hope. They also left a wake in the grass that might have been harder to see in the available light, but which could still provide some kind of bread crumb trail back home. She swallowed her misgivings and quickened her pace to catch up with the horse and the walking stump of a figure it followed.

They had paused at the top of a much taller hill ahead, and the horse's ears were pricked forward. Cally thought she understood why: a sound like distant music was coming from beyond the hill. Rum stood leaning on his cane as he gazed out toward the horizon. By the time Cally reached the top of the hill herself and joined them, she was panting. Below them, a dark stream ran curving across the foot of the hill, glittering in the moonlight as it flowed from north to south, but that was not what they were looking at.

The distant hills beyond were not dark and empty, as Cally had expected. Under the moonlight, glittering cities seemed to crown several crests in the distance. Warm red and yellow lights glowed across the slopes like camp fires, and music hummed from each of the cities in a tuneless harmony that rose and fell on the warm night air. As Cally watched, she was able to see individual buildings more and more clearly. The buildings, though, were oddly shaped, she thought, with rounded walls and curving rooftops. Many of them had bright towers at their corners or spires at their tops. The music emanating from them grew stronger by the moment, and as it did the cities glowed ever brighter, until it seemed even the valleys between the hills were clearly illuminated with warm, dancing light resembling fire. Was it fire, or was it people carrying torches through the valleys – or were they alleys – between the hills?

Cally's first coherent thought was that this must be what the Captain had seen, as a child, from the gable window of the Yellow House. Then suddenly she was seized with a sinking feeling; the solid ground of the hill beneath her feet seemed to heave like a wave. She understood, somehow, even though she tried very hard not to think about it, that if she should turn around, the Yellow House, and Vale House and Woodley would not be visible any longer behind her. It was not just that they were out of sight – she sensed with growing terror that they were actually not there anymore at all. She put a hand up to her mouth to stop herself crying out in panic.

"Don't you think it's beautiful?" Rum asked. She wrapped her arms around herself and nodded, but could not speak. He reached a knobby hand resembling a wooden branch up to her and said "Come, let's go closer."

Cally did not dare take her hand away from her mouth to decline his invitation, because she knew if she did, she would sob out loud.

"Really, it's alright," said Rum. "When did *you* start being afraid to set off into the unknown? Come on, let's go!"

Behind them, the horse snorted. "Alright, alright," Rum relented. He looked up at Cally and laughed. "Maybe another time, then." Taking her by the elbow, he turned her around and led her back down to the bottom of the hill, then on up another one ahead of them until the lights of Woodley came back into view. The sound of music faded behind them, and the horse wandered slowly, grazing as it went, back toward the fence next to the barn.

Rum stopped just before the metal gate. He grabbed Cally's right hand in both of his and pumped it up and down, throwing her off balance. "I meant what I said," he told her. "I'm your friend now. I've miles to go before I sleep, but you just call me, and I'll be right here. Well, you know: around here somewhere." He made a whirling gesture over his head with his cane. Then he ducked between the fence rails. "Sweet dreams!" he called, turning to continue on his way, down the hill toward the pond. He seemed to grow smaller with every step until he was out of sight among the willows.

35 - Nell and Melissa

While manning the reception desk the next morning, Cally heard Nell talking in the parlor, though as far as she knew, there was nobody else in there. She went in hoping to find it was George Nell was speaking to, even though he had told her he could not go beyond the Hall.

But Nell was only staring at a television screen full of static. She grabbed for the remote when Cally came in, looking up with a sheepish expression. "I think the cable is broken," she stammered.

Cally didn't press Nell about why she had been talking aloud to the television. She knew the young woman probably got enough harassment about her quirks. Instead, she just said honestly, "I was hoping George was here."

Nell relaxed and put the remote down, smiling. "No, not George," she said, gesturing toward the television screen. "This is Melissa." Cally looked, but saw only gray snow. Her puzzled expression put Nell on the defensive again. "It's okay, I can put on something else if you want."

Cally heard a car pulling in to the parking area in front of the house. "It's alright," she said, "You can introduce me to Melissa another time." She was certainly in no position to tell anyone there was not really a woman named Melissa in the television set. "Only I think Foster is back."

"Oh!" Nell switched off the television and sat back, quickly opening one of the magazines from the end table.

"Where is Ian?" Foster shouted as he rushed through the front door. He held a thick sheaf of papers under his arm. He caught sight of Cally and explained, "I just found out... well, I have some more news for him."

"I don't think he's come out of his quarters since this morning after breakfast," Cally said.

Foster pushed up his glasses and leaned over her. She noticed his hands were shaking, and was glad for the solid desk between them. "I've been given provisional permission to submit a plan that could make a small fortune!" He glowed with elation, and spoke so quickly it was hard for Cally to keep up. "If they extend Main Street through that empty field there," he said, gesturing through the screen door toward the meadow, "it would eventually connect I-85 right to US1 and make it much faster for people to get to Raleigh, and all the coast destinations, too. They'd have to four-lane the whole thing, of course, but the value of all that wasted land would skyrocket!"

Cally no longer believed it was possible to go directly from any point to any other point through that meadow, but she didn't say so. Instead she said, "I didn't think Ian owned all that land?"

"Oh, he doesn't," Foster said, undaunted. "Well, not all of it, not technically. A lot of it belongs to the Arkwright family, and some to other old families around here. The Thorntons, the Daweses, a few others. But Ian May owns the best access to it, and that affects everyone else who owns it. I need to tell him about this!" He was breathing heavily as he gazed around the Hall.

"I can try to call him on the phone extension in his study, if you want."

"No, never mind, that's alright. I'll just go and see him myself." He waved her away as he ran through to the back hall. Cally heard him rapping sharply on a door and calling Ian's name as she returned to her work.

She spent the better part of an hour trying to concentrate on writing, but she was distracted by many other thoughts, and the silence coming from Joan's closed door distracted her far more than the woman's loud, complaining voice ever had. Cally thought about calling the Sheriff to ask him what he had found out, if anything, about Bethany's drugs that had been tampered with, but she was fairly certain he couldn't legally talk to her about that sort of thing. Even if he could, it would only answer a small handful of the questions whirling in her head.

Maybe, she thought, she should just come right out and ask Ian to explain everything to her, about Woodley and the secrets held by what Katarina called The White Council. She could picture him explaining it all very thoroughly to her in his soft, gentle voice the same way he talked about the history of his home. At the same time, she could also picture him using his impeccable southern manners to gently inform her that none of this was any of her business.

Charles Delaney came in from the porch, carrying his little dog which looked around the Hall in excitement, then in disappointment because there were no feline or human ghosts currently present at which to bark. "Do you think it would be alright if we stay another night?" he asked Cally. "While I was taking Twilight for her walk, I saw this town is just full of beautiful old houses, and my wife and I would love to spend the afternoon strolling around looking at them, if that's okay."

Cally pretended she had to check the register to determine if there was any problem with the Delaneys staying an extra night. "Well, it appears your room is still available," she told Mr. Delaney, reaching up to scratch Twilight's head. "I'll just go ahead and pencil you in."

He set the dog down, then ran after it to fetch it from the parlor where it had immediately run to jump into Nell's lap. On his way back through to the stairs, he turned again to Cally and said, "Hey, you know, I think I've figured out why some of your guests think this house is haunted."

"Oh?" Cally looked up with what she hoped was a non-committal expression.

"Yes! The closet in our room, Twilight discovered last night, contains a communicating door."

"I didn't know that," Cally said honestly. "That's interesting."

"I peeped through it, mainly to get her to stop barking at it last night, and it opens into an adjoining room. This one was decorated in a wisteria theme. You should check it out when you get time. Guest rooms with connecting doors could come in handy if you get guests with children."

"I definitely will check it out," she said sincerely as he continued up the stairs. It occurred to her that such doors should have locks on both sides. She made a note to mention this to Ignacio, and then wondered if he already knew.

☪

When she took a break at lunch time, Cally went first to her own room and pushed aside her dresses to look into the closet. There was indeed a small door set into the back wall. Actually it was not a door so much as a rectangle cut into the gypsum board, about four feet high, with hinges on one edge and a grommet set into it where a door knob would normally be. Cally put a finger through the grommet and pulled the door open toward her. Behind it was the back side of a similar door. Looking through the grommet, Cally could see dim yellow light and guessed she was looking into another closet. She was also pretty sure which room it belonged to, so she did not feel self-conscious as she pushed the door open and went through. She found herself standing in an empty closet with its door partly ajar. Daffodil patterned wallpaper was visible through the opening, and Cally could hear the sound of soft snoring. She poked her head through and smiled at Bethany sleeping peacefully with both cats on the coverlet beside her, then went back to her own room.

The bed was still unmade as she had left it that morning. She ignored it, pausing by the window to gaze out at the view of the meadow in the sunshine of high noon. Little birds flitted from hillock to hillock, disappearing from view whenever they landed in the tall grass. The sky shone clear blue above, except for fine strands of high cirrus clouds streaming in from the south. That was all she could see, for miles across the tops of the green hills, and she was not surprised about this at all.

36 - Gourmet Pizza

As the clouds over the meadow grew thicker, Cally's mood grew darker. She was tired of being a receptionist with not very much to do, and she was tired of staring at her word processor screen and not seeing any words appear on the page. She was tired, also, of trying to speak to the ghost of a preacher who kept appearing and standing in front of her desk and not saying anything or acknowledging her presence at all, making her feel like she was the one who was the ghost.

Mostly, she couldn't stop thinking about the questions she wanted to ask Ian, and she was tired of waiting for Foster to come out of the back hall so she could go and request an audience with Ian, herself. She began seriously considering just approaching "the White Council" herself and flatly demanding an explanation.

The only thing she had the power to actually accomplish, at the moment, was to send Emerald a brief email asking her to please sign on to chat later that night. "I am wondering about this Vale your story speaks of," she wrote, "where you grew up, and what relation it has to what Ian once told me, about how the area around his house used to be called the Vale. I am thinking maybe we are neighbors, now, and that maybe someday soon, somehow, we can finally get together for that cup of coffee we always talked about." Her hand trembled as she clicked the button to send the email, but she sent it anyway, and then resumed watching the minutes tick slowly away.

Katarina passed through the Hall from time to time, bringing Joan a fresh cup of tea, or running up the stairs to check on Bethany. "Her color is much better!" she was happy to report as she returned down the stairs. "The only trouble is, now she thinks she should be able to get up and take a shower and get back to work, and I don't think she's well enough for that yet."

Cally's unchecked internal response was to wish Bethany could get back to work very soon indeed, and then she felt like a heel for thinking that way. "No," she agreed with Katarina, "though it might be good for her if you can help her sit up in the chair for a little while. Let's just hope she won't try to take a shower without one of us there to help. We don't want her to fall again!"

"Maybe I can get Ignacio to help her come downstairs and relax in the parlor for a while." Katarina looked to the parlor doorway through which Nell's voice could be heard. "Nell could keep her company. But I thought she and Foster were leaving to go back to Raleigh today?"

"I thought so too," Cally said, "but Foster found some new information he wants to impress upon Ian."

Katarina had no reply to this, but the way she blew her bangs up out of her face told Cally what she would have liked to have said, and Cally agreed with her.

Afternoon was well over before Foster came back into the Hall. Stopping at the desk he asked Cally, "What are you doing for dinner tonight?" It didn't sound like an invitation so much as a challenge.

Cally sighed. Ian would be surrounded by friends and family at dinner for the next couple of hours, and then he would take his dessert and retreat to his quarters as usual. She would not have a chance to talk to him that night, and she was tired of waiting. She made up her mind to try a different approach to getting the answers she wanted. "I thought I'd go into town and try some of that gourmet pizza," she told Foster. "I don't want to be a moocher or a freeloader." She would try the pizza, she was thinking, but mostly she would try to join Merv Arkwright and his cronies on the loading dock and attempt to pry some answers from them.

"Well," said Foster, pushing up his glasses, "I hope you have a nice time. Nell and I will probably be gone by the time you get back. It's been nice getting to know you." He did not sound sincere, and was in fact not even looking at her as he spoke, but through the parlor doorway toward Nell's voice.

"You're right," said Cally. "I'd better say goodbye to Nell now while I can."

She tidied the desk and slung her computer case over her

shoulder, then went into the parlor. The television was off and Nell was sitting quietly with her hands in her lap while Foster went upstairs to see to their packing. "I just came to wish you a nice trip home," Cally said.

Nell jumped up and ran to give Cally a hug. "I'm going to miss you!" she said. "I can't wait to see you again!"

Cally didn't expect she would still be at Vale House by the time Nell visited again, but she didn't say so out loud. "I'm so glad I got a chance to get to know you," she said sincerely, and then fumbled for how to conclude the conversation. Phrases like "I hope all your dreams come true," and "Thank you for all you've given me," went through her head, but didn't seem like they would make sense if she said them out loud. She returned Nell's hug, and then went up to the Rose Room.

The bed had been made, and the rose-themed knickknacks on the dresser had been lined up neatly according to height. It didn't even bother Cally anymore. She knew for certain now that it could not be Joan, even dressed as the White Lady, doing this, and it wasn't George. She was sure he was telling the truth when he said that touching objects was not in his skill set. Maybe it was Melissa. Or some other entity entirely. "Just leave my computer alone!" she said to the empty room. She dropped the laptop case on the desk chair and locked the door behind her as she left.

The evening was still hanging on to late afternoon when she walked into town, and the clouds thickening overhead tinted the sky a vivid palette of reds and purples which made Cally think of one of Nell's paintings. Merv Arkwright was inside his feed store and had not yet come out onto the dock. Cally walked on past, but was determined to come back later and ask him the questions she had meant to ask Ian. She had even brought her note pad, as a ruse to pretend she was just doing research for her book. The book she was doubting, more and more all the time, she was ever actually going to write.

The entire town seemed particularly quiet that evening. The only cars parked in the street were Andi's in front of her coffee shop and Jud Thornton's in front of his hardware store. There were shadows moving inside the News Store but Cally made a point of not looking closely. She stayed on the other side of the street until she came to the crossing with Railroad Street. Here she turned the corner and made her way to Motherboard Pizza.

"Ms. McCarthy!" Luke greeted her with a large wooden paddle in his hands. "I hope you're hungry. I am experimenting with a new spinach and artichoke sauce. How is Ms. Chase?" He put the paddle down and took off his orange and green stained apron.

"Call me Cally. Bethany is doing much better. And that experimental pizza actually sounds really good. Do you have dining-in facilities here?"

He laughed. "For you, the finest seat in the house." He escorted her to a small table next to the front window. It was the only seat in the house. "And no charge tonight. I've made a large, and won't be able to finish it myself. I'm frankly kind of, well, burned out on pizza, you understand."

Cally nodded and sat down. "I think I can help. I haven't even had lunch."

"I'm afraid all I have to drink is water," he said, setting two plastic bottles in the middle of the checkered tablecloth. "I wish I served wine here, because nothing would go with this pizza so well as a nice pinot noir. Unfortunately I have been having an uphill battle trying to get a license to serve alcohol. It's so hard to get *anything* done in this town," he sighed.

"Bless you for trying," Cally said. "People like you might be able to save this little town." She looked out at the shadows lengthening in the street. "Speaking of that, I was hoping to talk to Merv Arkwright. Do you think the boys will be playing their music tonight?"

"They've ordered their usual large pepperoni and mozzarella," he said, "So I assume so. Excuse me." A timer had gone off and he turned to retrieve the big wooden paddle from the counter.

As he was slicing up the very fragrant pizza with a cutter the size of a dinner plate, Andi appeared in the doorway. She let out a cry of delight to see Cally there and bent to hug her. "I just stopped in for a sandwich to take home with me," she said.

"Not tonight," said Luke. When he set the pizza down, it nearly covered the whole table. "Sit, sit," he insisted, and went to get the kitchen step-stool to use as a third chair for himself.

Cally had to admit, the spinach and artichoke pizza ("with cave-aged gorgonzola" Luke explained) really was very good, and the three ate in silence, except for "mmm" noises and the licking of fingers. Then Luke looked at his watch and got up. "The guys are probably ready for their basic pepperoni," he said, picking up the warming envelope from the counter. "You ladies take your time. If a sudden rush of hungry customers comes in, please take their orders and tell them I'll be right back."

As soon as he was gone, Andi took the opportunity to ask Cally how things were going at Vale House. "Joan's still not in jail?" she laughed.

"I thought of calling and asking the sheriff, today, about that, but I'm pretty sure he wouldn't talk to me about it."

"No, he wouldn't." Andi said. "That wouldn't be ethical. Just be patient. He's a good sheriff, he'll get to the bottom of it. How about you, though? Do you really think she's guilty? Why would she do something like that, anyway? Do you have any ideas?"

Cally picked at a piece of pizza crust. She had lots of ideas, but she wasn't sure she should be talking about them. Someone might start thinking she needed medication, herself. "I thought I knew what was going on," she said carefully. "But when I tried to grill Joan yesterday, well, now I'm not completely sure. Everything I thought I knew has been turned on its head lately." She didn't say so, but she realized this was true about everything that had happened since she'd first packed up her car and headed for Woodley. "Andi, you're Not From Around Here. Tell me: how did you discover Woodley? Was it hard for you to find, for you to get here?"

"I've heard people say this place is harder to find than a daisy in a snowstorm," Andi said, laughing. "But for me it was a no-brainer. I found the listing for a vacant storefront in the paper. I was like you: starting my life over. Again. Anyway, the listing agent for the storefront was Jud Thornton. He gave me a lift here and showed me the place, and I was sold. I've called this town my home ever since, and the locals are even sort of starting to agree." She laughed, then grew serious again and laid a hand on Cally's. "But that doesn't really answer your question, does it? Cally, what are you getting at? What's bothering you?"

Cally shook her head. "I've started to wonder if I'm just losing my mind," she said. "Like my daughter always said I would.

Nothing seems to add up. I..." She stopped suddenly, because a figure was passing by outside the window and she recognized the easy, rolling walk of Ben Dawes as he headed toward Main Street. If he saw her and Andi through the window of the pizza shop, he gave no indication.

"Oh." Andi smiled broadly. "I see. Yes, he's a looker, isn't he?"

"I guess so," said Cally, "but he needs a haircut." Andi wasn't buying it, so Cally stopped trying. "What's his deal, anyway? He's an odd one!"

Andi stopped smiling and shook her head. "I honestly don't know. You're right, he's an odd one. There's this whole town mystery around him, and Bree Dawes, too, that nobody really talks about, even though it's right there in front of their faces."

"What? Are they married to each other or something?" Cally felt a twinge of the old heartsick, betrayed feeling she'd thought she'd left behind her forever, but Andi was shaking her head. "No, no, he's not married, that anyone knows of. Though I understand he does have children who don't live around here. No, Brigit Dawes is his baby sister."

Andi waited silently until Cally's expression showed the words had sunk in.

"His. *Baby* sister?" Cally squinted, trying to make this add up in her head. It didn't. "How is that possible? Does she have that disease that makes people age fast?"

"She's the normal one. Well, normal for her, anyway. No, Ben is the one who doesn't seem to be the right age. I've only lived here a short time, so it isn't obvious to me. But people talk, you know how they do. People who have lived here for a long time, sometimes they let something slip and I hear them make a reference to the way he never seems to get any older."

Cally cocked her head and gave Andi a level look. "What is he? One of those sparkly vampires or something?"

Andi threw back her head and let out a hearty laugh at this. "Oh, God love you, Cally! No! Well, I don't know. I mean, I don't think so. He's a truly nice guy. Everyone loves him. But now you mention it, you hardly ever do see him outside the news store. No." She shook her head. "That's probably not because he's a sparkly vampire. I just figure, if a person mysteriously never seems to age, they would tend to lay low, to keep people from talking.

"But you know what: since you've come along, this is the third time in as many days I've seen him outside the store, walking around town."

"I guess I should be flattered," Cally grumbled, picking a slice of Greek olive off her pizza and eating it as if she meant to hurt it.

"Sarcasm does not become you, Cally." Andi stood and opened the door, craning her head to see around the corner to Main Street. "Look, he's sitting in with the guys on the dock. You should go and talk to him."

"I don't think so!"

Andi sat back down and took both of Cally's hands in hers. "I think he really likes you," she said.

"I wonder where I've heard that song before?"

"I'll go with you."

"Dammit. I'm sorry, Andi. I'm acting like a petulant child, aren't I?"

Cally pressed her palms against the tablecloth and gave herself a firm mental shake. She was here, she reminded herself, for a purpose, and she wasn't going to let Ben's presence deter her. Standing up quickly, she went around the table to hug Andi. "Finish the pizza," she said. "Don't let it go to waste. When the rush comes, take lots of orders for Luke." She stepped out the door into the darkened street, but paused to turn back and say, "And thank you for being a friend."

37 - The White Council

She had heard the expression "shaking in your boots" before, but as she climbed the concrete steps to the loading dock, Cally finally understood what it meant. Everything below her knees trembled uncontrollably while her face smiled and her voice said cheerfully, "Mind if I join you fellas?"

"Not at all!" cried Merv as he, Doc, and Jud Thornton all stood to offer her their lawn chairs. Without looking at him, she accepted the overturned milk crate Ben vacated for her. "So what are we singing?"

"Actually we were just talking," Jud said. "Business, I'm afraid."

"That can wait," Doc told him. "How often do we get an alto to join us?" He turned and smiled to Cally. "You can sing Greg Allman's part!"

"Dammit, Daniel." Jud seemed to have already been on the edge of losing his temper. "This needs to be discussed!"

"Maybe I should join you some other time?" Cally offered perfunctorily, pretending to get up to leave, though she had no intention of actually doing any such thing.

"On the contrary." It was Ben. "Maybe your input would be welcome, and timely." He touched her arm, and then she could not have walked off the loading dock if she'd tried. "You could stand in for Ian May, since he can't make it tonight. His knees are acting up again, apparently." He looked at the other men on the porch as if he were awaiting their replies to this, but the way he urged Cally to sit back down told them the matter was not, as far as he was concerned, actually open for discussion.

Merv said "Hmm. Maybe so. Well, Ms. McCarthy, we were

talking about what would attract more business to Woodley, to keep it from falling right off the map. What do you think?"

Ben stood behind Cally and said, "Ms. McCarthy just recently suggested to me that we could use a burger restaurant here."

Luke, who was standing in the street next to the loading dock, said, "I wouldn't mind the competition. Heck, I'd probably be their first customer!" He shouldered the pizza warmer. "But I have to be getting back now. Can't leave Andi all alone with that huge, hungry mob!" He saluted and went back across the street.

"I don't see what good it would do to open more businesses," Jud complained, "if nobody can even find this place. What are we going to do about that? We need to lift the..."

"Now, there are lots of things we need to consider," Merv interrupted him.

A cold breeze rushed out of the woods west of town, causing leaves and discarded wrappers to tumble up the street. Cally shivered and shrank back toward Ben's warmth, then caught herself at it and sat up again, listening attentively. She was pleased to realize the very questions she had meant to bring up seemed already to be on the table, without her even needing to ask them.

Judd, it seemed to Cally, was insisting that "someone" needed to stop making Woodley so hard to find, as if "someone" were doing so deliberately. The other men seemed to think they didn't want "just anyone" to be able to find their way into the heart of their little town. Jud told them he thought "just anyone's" money was just as good as anyone else's as far as he was concerned. Merv and Doc seemed uncomfortable and kept glancing at Cally sidelong as they argued with Jud.

"We really shouldn't even be discussing this without Ian and Doug," Merv pointed out.

"We might make more progress without them," Jud snorted.

"Now I hardly think..."

Cally felt Ben's breath on her cheek. "They've been dancing around like this for years," he whispered. "They won't talk about it, not really, in Jud's presence. Nor yours, I think. Not yet. Come with me."

All conversation on the dock ceased as the men swiveled their heads around and caught sight of Ben and Cally. Merv grinned hugely and his eyes twinkled. "Ah. I see. Why don't you kids go talk about something more interesting, then, eh?" he suggested.

Cally moved away from Ben. "No, I... it's not..." Doc winked at her. Ben's hand was already under her elbow, urging her to stand. "I'll talk," he whispered in her ear, his breath warm on her cheek.

"Goodnight, you youngsters," Merv called, waving as Ben guided Cally down the steps.

"Don't do anything I wouldn't do!" Doc added. Jud grumbled something in reply to that but Cally and Ben were already too far away to hear what it was.

Cally was shaking again, including everything above her knees, but this time it was with anger, not trepidation. "What was all that about?" she whispered in a hiss. They were headed up Main Street toward the residential district, and she wondered why she was whispering. "That was insulting!" she blurted out as they entered the oaken hall at the end of town. "They just shooed me away as if I were some kind of impudent child!" She yanked her arm out of Ben's grip. "I know I'm not from around here, but why can't the White Council talk in front of me? This is worse than junior high school!"

Ben stopped walking and looked at her. "The White Council?"

"That's what Kat calls them," Cally explained, feeling a little foolish. "All that gray hair."

Ben laughed out loud and Cally looked sidelong at his mostly brown hair with gray temples and beard. "Are you part of them?" she asked.

"It's complicated," he said.

"No doubt!" She turned away and started walking again, having made up her mind to return to Vale House and try again another evening, preferably when Ben was not around.

"Sarcasm does not become you," Ben called after her.

"I'm not trying to be becoming!" she threw back over her shoulder.

He ran to catch up with her. "I said I'd talk," he said. "And I will. If you want."

38 - Ben's Story

They were almost to the end of Main Street – Cally could see the meadow gate and the lamp lights of Vale House's pineapple gate. A cool breeze rattled through the branches above them, sending little clouds scudding past the moon.

"Are you sure you can talk to me?" she asked. "Won't Bree have a fit if you do?"

"Bree can get over herself." He threw a laughing glance back toward the news store, it's glowing front window still just visible beyond the trees. Then he grew serious and looked back at Cally. "No, it's just that, when you've lived as long as I have, you lose the heart to lie." He slipped an arm around her and led her off the sidewalk to the little wooden gate leading into the back garden of Vale House.

The gazebo glowed white on the lawn in the intermittent moonlight overhead. At the end of the property, lights in the windows of Katarina and Ignacio's cottage showed the silhouettes of the couple passing back and forth in their little kitchen; Cally could hear them talking softly to one another. The smell of good food – still not tacos – wafted from the open windows. It was all the perfect picture of an idyllic summer evening, but Cally was seeing everything through new eyes, and only knew enough to know she had no idea what she was really looking at.

Ben stepped up the three wooden steps into the little gazebo and sat on one of the white painted benches, leaving room for Cally to join him. She chose the bench opposite him, instead, and sat down, watching him, waiting for him to make good on his promise to talk.

He sighed and gazed upward at the jasmine vines weaving their way through the latticework, as if he thought they might spell out the words for him to begin. Finally he said, "This is a special place."

She looked around at the tidy garden and grounds. "Yes," she agreed provisionally.

"No, I mean." He gestured toward the house, not at Vale House itself, but up and over it, and to the north and south as well. "Woodley is a gateway, you see. It guards... things. A lot of secrets. Places that are vulnerable. Places and things that the rest of the world needs. And they need protecting, you see. From the outside world. Vale House is the heart of it, and the town is the gateway and if they go..." He spread his hands and shook his head. "I'm trying to find words."

She could see that he was. "I know about the ghosts," she offered.

"They aren't all ghosts."

"So I've been told."

He smiled at her when she said this, and something in the way his eyes crinkled at the corners made her think he might have been content to just sit there and look at her. But he had promised to talk, and he continued to do so. "They aren't all ghosts. They are..." He looked toward the sky, gesturing broadly with one hand. "Oh, all kinds of things. Everything! And." Words failed him again.

Cally looked up at his face until he stopped looking at the sky and looked back at her. When he did, she moved across to sit on the bench beside him, still holding his gaze, and said, "And you, Ben Dawes. What are you? And don't you dare tell me it's complicated."

He looked out into the darkness, into the cool wind coming from the west end of town, and as the moon came out from behind a cloud she could see resolution growing in his expression. "I am human," he said at last. As if to demonstrate, he took her hand and uncurled her fingers, pressing them to his chest so she could feel his heart beating. "I am human," he said again into the darkness, as if he were daring anyone to argue with him about it. She didn't understand why tears seemed to be leaking between her eyelids as he started to tell her his story.

"Our father...Bree's father, and mine...he had a wife. Well, of course he did. That's, well, she... She was *not* human. She was from right over there. In the forest." He tilted his head toward the meadow gate, but as far as Cally knew, one of the things that did not exist in that direction was a forest. "She stayed as long as she could. But it wasn't her world. She couldn't stay."

"She was a fairy." Cally remembered that was how these sorts of stories always went.

"Something like that." He took several deep breaths. "She left when Bree and I were little. Well, I wasn't so little anymore. She wanted to take us with her but my father refused. I remember a huge argument. They had to take it to arbitration. Not by human lawyers, you see, but by the ruling council in her world. A bargain was struck. She could take only one of us, and we would be allowed to stay here until we were old enough to decide for ourselves which one would go. I don't remember most of this very clearly. I just remember she told us she would be back, then she left."

"I'm so sorry," said Cally.

He gave her hand a gentle squeeze and released it. "It was a long time ago," he said, shaking his head. "Anyway that's not all of it. I don't have much time tonight, but I feel like I need to tell you all of it. I'm afraid if I don't tell you now, I might never get another chance."

Cally nodded, and he continued. "Bree took it really hard. I don't remember how I took it. Maybe I don't want to. But Dad took it hardest of all. He had known what she was when he married her, but he thought he could make it work. He thought his love was strong enough to make her stay. But in the end, it turned out to be strong enough to make him go.

"He waited until we were older, and then told me to take care of Bree, and went to find his lost love. I only remember being very angry, but Bree was devastated. And that made me even angrier. I set to work to learn all about this town. This Vale. Did you know Woodley used to be called Ghoston Bhaille? The Home of Spirits...

"One night, once I was sure I had figured out all the secrets and tricks and roads, I took the Daimler and set off to find my father. I'm not sure what I hoped to get out of it. I guess I needed to tell him how I felt. I wanted to make him sorry for what he'd done to Bree. I found him, too. And I also found my mother. She was... terrible. I don't mean bad. I mean great and bright and terrifying and beautiful. She had gone back to being what she had been before, before she had taken this whim to experiment with being human, with having children."

"That night you drove us to Blackthorn," Cally interrupted, as she had suddenly realized something. "It wasn't really Blackthorn, was it? It was..." Now she was the one fumbling for words. "It was another place..."

He stopped looking at the sky and faced her, looking directly into her eyes. "The roads are bent, around here," he said. "Tangled. They go to... many places. Many places. If you learn the trick of them, you can find things most people will never know exist." He looked away through the gate that opened onto Main Street, where leaves tumbled in the wind and made skittering noises along the sidewalk, then he sighed and shook his head, returning his gaze to her. "I only took you around a couple of the turns. Bree is right: it was reckless of me. But you... I've been feeling reckless ever since you arrived. I felt like you were meant to see these things. I still believe that. Everyone who finds the exit, who finds Woodley, is meant to be here, for one reason or another."

Cally laughed under her breath. "Even Joan?"

"Even Joan Cromwell," Ben said, not laughing. "Even Jud Thornton. Not all the reasons are good ones."

He put his hands on her shoulders, and the warmth of them seemed to shield her entire body from the growing chill of the breeze. Then, nodding, he continued to speak gravely. "It can be a perilous world for ordinary people. They have different rules there, in my mother's country. Different values. They don't understand how we see the world, any more than we understand how they see it."

Cally thought about this for a moment. Finally she said, "What I want to know right now is how *you* see it."

He closed his eyes, leaning back with his face turned upward. "It's beautiful," he said. The cooling breeze was turning into strong gusts through the garden and, as Cally shivered, at least part of her mind pointed out to her how much warmer it would be if she should shrink the rest of the way into his arms. She stayed still and watched his face carefully as he repeated, "It's beautiful. I mean, their world is beautiful, yes, but. This world, this world is so much more messy, dusty, and sticky, and clunky, and beautiful. I love *this* world."

Then he did pull her into his arms. He tucked her head under his chin as he continued telling his story, and she found she had no wish to resist.

"My mother told me that since I had seen her world, I was the one who would have to join her there. She reminded me of the bargain she had struck with my father, and I reminded her that no bargain she had struck with any other person had any power over me, as I was my own person, with my own free will. I was a teenager, remember." He chuckled, and to Cally it felt like a deep rumbling in his chest. "I think she was impressed by this. She said I got my attitude from her. And in the end I did prevail in striking my own bargain, or at least an altered version of the original one. I would be allowed to come back here, to take care of Bree. But I would have to spend part of every day in my mother's court until Bree was able to take care of herself, at which time I was to come and join my mother's people permanently. I agreed, having privately made up my mind that day would never come, not as long as Bree lived, anyway."

He smoothed a hand over her hair and sat back so he could look at her again. "So there you are. I came home. I thought I'd been gone only a few days, a week, at most. But in the meantime, Bree had married her high-school sweetheart, endured years of abuse, and dumped him. Some wonder where she dumped him, as he was never seen again. But that's another story. Anyway, years had passed, and it took me a long time to get back into Bree's good graces, insofar as anyone can, now. So I spend my days helping her in the family store, and at night I journey to visit my... other family. But while I am there, no time passes for me."

"And that's why you appear to be only half your age," Cally suddenly understood.

"Only half?" He gave her a wry smile. "Are you trying to flatter me?"

"No, well, I mean..." She squinted and touched the silver streaks along the side of his beard, trying to make calculations in her head, something at which she had never been any good.

He shook himself, as if waking from a dream. Standing, he

looked at what stars were visible, between the flying clouds, the way most people would look at a clock. "I have to go. But I will be back in the morning. Do you believe me?"

"I believe you." Cally stood as well. "And it means the world to me that you would tell me all this. Thank you."

"Don't thank me yet," he said, laughing. "You may yet find yourself agreeing with Bree."

She shrugged and smiled at him, and he embraced her quickly once more before he turned and went down the gazebo steps. Cally shivered as the chill returned, watching him slip through the little white gate back out to the street, turning east toward Gardens Road. Then she wrapped her arms around herself and went through the shade garden back to Vale House.

39 - The White Lady

She used the key Katarina had given her to let herself in through the side door. The house was quiet, except for the sound of static coming from the television in the parlor. Cally went in to shut it off and was surprised to find Nell still there. She had fallen asleep on the sofa, and someone had covered her with a crocheted throw, so Cally left her there and went back out to the Hall. George was standing on the third step from the top of the stairs, wearing a long, gray robe with the hood pulled up over his head.

"Let me guess. Gandalf?"

"No," said George. "Jimmy Page. I have discovered there are videos on your music player device, too!" He played a brutal riff on his air-guitar and sang a few lines from "Ramble On." He had a good voice, Cally thought, but he was no Jimmy Page.

She wished she could hug him. "Okay, but no Stairway!" she teased. George pushed back the hood of his robe, gazing down at the stairs in confusion. "Sorry," Cally said. "I have never put that song on my player, but I'll download it tomorrow, just for you."

"You're in a good mood. Did you have another date with that young prince?"

"It wasn't a date," said Cally. "I am in a good mood because somebody around here finally gave me some straight answers, for a change."

George looked hurt. "I always give you straight answers," he said.

"Where is everyone?" Cally asked him. "All in bed already?"

"I don't know. I only just got here."

"And where do you go when you're not in the halls? I thought you couldn't roam far from the Gallery."

"Just a while ago I was in Ankh Morpork," he said. "And that is a straight answer."

"I'm glad you're enjoying the e-reader." Cally put a hand on the knob of the front door and found it unlocked. "I'm going to do a check around of all the patients," she said to George. "I hope we can talk tomorrow."

"Sweet dreams," he said. He pulled the hood back up over his head and uttered some very credible light-saber noises as he parried an imaginary foe below him on the stairs. At least, Cally hoped it was imaginary.

She put her head outside the door and asked the Captain if he was alright. He waved, gesturing with his flask at the brooding sky, and told her he'd be just a few more minutes.

She shook her head gently and smiled, then turned and knocked on Joan's office door. Hearing no reply, she opened the door and tiptoed inside, nearly tripping over the fragments of a broken tea mug just inside the threshold. She had a pretty good idea she could guess the story behind that. Joan herself was asleep with her head on the arm of the sofa. Her injured foot was hanging down to the floor, and Cally was sure that was against doctor's orders. Praying she would not wake her, Cally carefully lifted the foot in its cast and maneuvered it back onto the cushion while Joan snored softly on. Cally thought Joan almost looked peaceful in her sleep, but then she jerked and muttered something that was probably a complaint before falling silent again.

"I guess she must have decided to take that pain medicine after all," Cally thought. She looked at the pill bottle on the end table. It was definitely not full any longer. "Not an addict, are we?" Cally murmured. She tiptoed across the room and went up the spiral stairs to fetch a blanket and a pillow from Joan's room. With these she tried to make the sleeping woman as comfortable as possible, then picked up the shards of the tea mug and left the room.

George was no longer on the stairs as Cally went up them to check on Bethany. She found the daffodil-printed covers pushed to one side of the empty bed, but she didn't panic this time. Seeing the bathroom door shut, she knocked and called "You'd better not be taking a shower!"

"I'm not!" Bethany called back, laughing. "I'm taking a bath!"

The sound of splashing could be clearly heard through the door.

Cally sighed, but was glad Bethany was feeling better. "OK, just please call me when you're ready to get out, so I can help make sure you don't slip. Knock on the wall. I'll hear you."

Bethany promised to do so, and Cally slipped back out into the Gallery

A light shone under the door of the Cala Lily room and Cally could hear the Delaneys through the door, talking in animated tones about the wonders of the architecture they had observed that day. Their little dog was silent, though Doctor Boojums was sitting a few feet away from the door, looking as if he might be considering stirring up some trouble by scratching at it.

Cally unlocked the Rose Room door, and was dismayed but not surprised to see her laptop on the desk, open and powered on. This, she was determined, she would *not* get used to, not ever, and would get to the bottom of it and put a stop to it.

The chat program was running, and this reminded Cally she had asked Emerald earlier to join her for a chat tonight. She was late for the meeting she herself had arranged. She sat down to type an apology, but the screen was already full of messages from Emerald, and none of them were the usual greetings and niceties. Emerald had apparently been trying to contact her for quite some time, and the entire screen was full of text.

> **Emerald<<** Cally, something is not right. I think you should leave.

> **Emerald<<** Are you there? Is everything OK?

> **Emerald<<** Seriously, I hope you're not there.

> **Emerald<<** Listen to me. If you're there, just get out of the house.

> **Emerald<<** Just get in your car. Text me once you're on the road. I'll send Errin.

> **Emerald::** Cally, are you there? Where are you?

Cally had started to type something reassuring when another message scrolled across the screen.

Emerald<< CALLY GET OUT OF THE HOUSE
RIGHT NOW!!!

"People who use all caps" were the butt of some of the favorite jokes between them, so Cally knew Emerald must be serious. She typed "Why?" but before she could press the Enter key to send the message, she heard a crashing sound in the hallway, and a woman's voice calling "Help me!"

Cally ran into Bethany's room, where the door to the bathroom was still closed. "Bethany, are you OK?" she called through the door with her hand already on the knob.

"I'm still fine!" Bethany called back, laughing. "Almost done! Give me just a few more minutes."

It hadn't been Bethany's voice, anyway, Cally was sure. She went back out into the hallway and ran to the Cala Lily room. She could still hear the Delaneys chatting amicably inside, but the butler's desk outside the door had been completely disarranged. Its little drawers and compartments hung open, and papers and bric-a-brac lay scattered over the carpet.

"Help me!" came the call again; it was coming from the stairs. Cally turned to see an old woman standing on the top step, pale and frail and white haired, dressed in a long white gown.

"The real White Lady!" Cally breathed.

When the woman saw Cally, she ran toward her. Cally had thought she was used to spirits by now, but this truly frightened her and she shrank back, covering her face with both arms. By the time she steeled herself to look up, the woman had run past her and opened the door to the backstairs. Standing in the open doorway. She looked at Cally with huge eyes and called, "You have to help me!"

Cally gathered her courage and approached the doorway as the figure disappeared into it. The only light in the narrow stairwell came from the open door at the bottom, where the fleeing figure had stopped to open the door to the back hall. Apparently, unlike George, this specter could touch things.

It ran out into the back hall, then, while Cally still hesitated. She heard the Delaneys' dog start to bark as Doctor Boojums ran up behind her and dashed between her legs – or did he run right through them? – and down the stairs to the open doorway below. "Fine!" she said, and followed.

The figure in white had paused in the back hall as if waiting for her, but when she had nearly caught up to it, it ran away toward the kitchen. It did not enter the kitchen, however. Instead it opened a narrow door across from the kitchen and disappeared into the darkness inside. Cally followed, and stopped once more as damp, musty air from the dark doorway struck her face. Groping inside for a light switch, she put her foot out into nothing. This was, apparently, the cellar stairway, and with all her heart Cally did not want to go down those stairs.

"Help!" the voice called plaintively from somewhere below. Cally felt with her foot for the top step, still unable to find a light switch. Her groping hands came to rest on a pipe railing, and she used this to feel her way down the first three or four steps until her eyes began to adjust to the darkness. She could just make out the white figure waiting below. As soon as her gaze came to rest on it, it ran again, still calling for her to come and help it.

Cally took a deep breath and felt her way down the rest of the stairs, brushing aside cobwebs, and other things she didn't want to know about, that kept catching in her hair. As she reached the bottom, the room was suddenly filled with light. The white lady had opened a door, and the light from the room that lay beyond it seemed dazzlingly bright compared to the darkness of the cellar.

She followed as it slipped through this door, then stopped, squinting against the brightness.

The room was painted in cheerful pastel colors, though there was no sign of Bethany's floral decorating style. A four-poster bed stood in one corner, and the rest of the room, though small, was crammed with bookshelves and curio cabinets, each overflowing in turn with knickknacks, books, and framed photos. Silk draperies at one side appeared to be merely nailed to a blank wall, and the ceiling above was an open network of rafters and ducts and electrical wiring.

The woman in white was crouched over something on the floor. She shrank back as Cally came closer to see the sprawled figure of a man, lying face down just inside another doorway on the opposite side of the room. It looked as if he had fallen down the flight of wooden stairs which rose beyond the door. The old woman knelt a few inches away, wringing her hands and watching Cally, begging for help. Cally finally began to understand: this woman was not a ghost at all. Her rheumy eyes were brimming with very human tears; her white garment was not an antebellum ball gown but merely a threadbare cotton nightgown printed with faded lavender flowers. Her thin, bony hands plucked at the man's shirt sleeve as she pleaded in the voice of a truly heartbroken, very real woman. "You have to help me," she said again. "Johnny won't wake up!" Cally knelt beside her and with some effort turned the man over just enough to see his face. It was Ian May.

Before Cally could begin to piece this together in her mind, Foster appeared on the stairs beyond the doorway, holding a thick sheaf of papers in one hand and a large flashlight in the other. A whiff of kerosene accompanied him. "What in hell?" he said, looking down at the lady in white. He was clearly just as mystified about her as Cally was. "What is this place? Who is *she*? What is going on here?"

Cally spread her arms, indicating the whole room, and shrugged. "I don't know," she said. "But I think she brought us to help Ian." She loosened Ian's collar and was relieved to find he had a pulse. She assured the old woman about this, putting a comforting hand on her thin, trembling shoulder. The woman flinched, wide eyed, at her touch, but she did not back away. Cally said to Foster, "You should call for Ignacio. I think he's has some paramedic training."

"Yes," Foster said, coming the rest of the way down the stairs and looking around. He put the stack of papers down on the bed. Fishing his phone out of his pocket with one hand, he reached to put the flashlight on the bookshelf. Then he turned and struck Cally over the head with it.

40 - In the Shuffling Madness

Cally passed in and out of consciousness, watching in fleeting glimpses as Foster pulled back the drapes on the wall to find the drapery cord, which he yanked off and used to bind the hands of the old woman, and then her own. When she was finally able to focus through the pain and the fog in her head, she was sitting propped against one of the book cases. The edge of a shelf dug painfully into the back of her neck, and the drapery cord felt like wire cutting into her wrists. Beside her, the white lady wept softly. Ian still lay unconscious on the floor at their feet, and the room reeked of kerosene.

"What the hell!" Foster was repeating as he paced the room. "What the hell! This was just supposed to be a simple... Dammit!" He turned and looked at Cally. "The best laid plans of mice and men, eh?" He snapped his fingers under her nose. "You weren't even supposed to be here. I specifically waited until you were out. I figured, based on the stuff you talk about on your computer with your friend, you'd be off somewhere teasing the hell out of that freak tonight. Why did you have to come back? I have nothing against you. I'm not some kind of monster."

Cally's head was throbbing, and she fought to keep down rising nausea; she didn't bother to debate Foster about whether or not he was a monster. She did ask, "Where is Nell?"

"Nellie is fine." He was busily brushing objects off the bookshelves in a frantic search for something he apparently hoped to find behind them. "I gave her some of Bethany's painkillers so she'd stay asleep. I'll get her out of the house before..."

"Foster, you shouldn't have done that! She's taking other medication. You never know what kind of reaction combining drugs could cause!"

He paused and laughed. "Don't worry. I've done it lots of times before. She's even building up a tolerance to it. She'll be fine by morning. I just want her to sleep through ... all the excitement. She's much easier to handle that way."

"You *are* a monster!" Cally said, slowly beginning to understand what he was doing.

Foster ignored her and continued looking through drawers, opening and shutting curio doors, and swearing. Doctor Boojums sat atop a Queen Anne style curio cabinet, next to a tall brass statue of a winged Greek goddess, hissing down at him.

"If you're looking for Ian's will," Cally guessed, "it won't do you any good, even if you find it. A copy has been filed with his lawyer."

"The will is right here," said Foster. He picked up the papers he'd thrown on the bed and waved them at her before slapping them down again; they were the source of the smell of kerosene pervading the room. "It hasn't been filed yet. I brought it back from the lawyer today so Ian could work on it some more. And believe me, it needed work! I'm just looking for a lighter. Why is there not one single lighter anywhere in this entire house? Doesn't Bethany provide a flower-themed one in every room?" He slammed a drawer shut and squatted in front of Cally.

"It didn't have to be this way," he said earnestly. "Ian May is an old man. He's led a full life, and now he's in his declining years. He wouldn't have lived much longer anyway. But then he had to go and change his will. Do you know, he's leaving a small fortune to those women? To Bethany and Joan, and even to those foreigners! There's hardly anything left for Nell! I tried to stop him, get him sent to a hospital at least, but he's so addled, he never did sit down to sign those damn bills Bethany set out for him."

"Then it was Ian you meant to have the accident, not Bethany?"

"Yes!" he said, throwing his hands up in exasperation. "See? Even you understand. And he only would have ended up in a nursing home. Probably. Maybe. I don't know. I never meant for anyone to get hurt! I've given him plenty of Nell's old tranquilizers," he said, jerking his head toward Ian's unconscious form, "so he wouldn't feel anything. He would have slept right through everything, and gone peacefully. But now we have this interfering old biddy, wherever she came from. And you! It's her fault you're in this situation, not mine." He stood up, paced a few steps, and returned to stand in front of her, staring beyond her into space as he went on. "You should have stayed in town. If you weren't such an ice queen you could be rolling around in the sack with that freak right now, though I'm sure he'd disappoint you." He snorted and pushed up his glasses, focusing on her face again. "Now I'm afraid you're just going to have to go down with the house, and I can't spare enough of the painkillers that are left to drug you both up. I've already wasted too many. I am truly sorry about that. I am." He spread his hands before her; they were shaking.

Cally thought he sounded like a ranting villain in a bad spy movie, but it also seemed to her he was having cold feet about what he was intending to do. She wondered, if she could keep him talking, whether he might come to his senses. "Think about it, Foster," she said. "It's not too late. You can still work out your differences with Ian. But if you let yourself become a criminal, you won't ever be able to come back from that."

"I am not the criminal here!" He resumed pacing the room, punctuating his words with wide gestures of his arms. "What's criminal is how all this land is just sitting here, not making a profit for anyone. This crumbling old house and grounds, taking up space where dozens of houses could be built for people to live in. What's criminal is how this seedy little town could be a hub of commerce if the stupid old farts who hold all the power around here would just bulldoze the whole damn thing and build something useful! From now on, things are going to be done my way. And Nellie will be rich." He crouched down in front of Cally again. "Doesn't that make you feel better?"

"For as long as you keep her around, anyway," Cally thought, but did not say aloud. Her bound hands were beginning to grow cold and numb. In fact, her feet and legs were, too. She glanced at the old woman next to her and noticed her breath pluming from her mouth in thin wisps of vapor. She did not see Ian's breath, and she tried not to think about that. Instead she looked to the top of the Queen Anne cabinet on which Doctor Boojums had now stood up beside the brass statue of the winged goddess. His gray coat was taking on a distinct brassy tint of its own.

"What I don't understand," Foster muttered, "is how someone would set up a nice room for a lady... I assume this is your room," he said to the woman in white. "All the pretty books and figurines and things, but no candles. Females love candles. It would make a perfectly reasonable story, that a scented-candle loving female would knock one over on the duvet while reading *Anne of Green Gables* or some other good kindling like that." He sat down on the bed and stacked the kerosene-soaked papers in a neat pile on the pillow.

"Think, Foster!" Cally tried not to sound desperate. "You wouldn't get away with that. The first thing the fire department does when they investigate a fire is check for accelerants. They'd detect traces of kerosene, easily. They'd know it was started on purpose."

He turned and looked at her, and Cally found his sudden, toothy grin truly disturbing. "Yes," he said. "They will. And they will also find the kerosene can missing from Ignacio's tool shed. And the remains of the fly bait that was on the toast that killed the chickens. Once Ignacio gets hauled off to jail, his wife will be deported. So that takes care of *that* problem!"

Cally tugged at the bonds on her wrists, but her hands had gone numb. "Foster, there are people sleeping upstairs! You are about to kill perfectly innocent strangers who have never done anything to you. I thought you said you weren't a monster!"

"I'm not," he assured her. "I'll pull the fire alarm as I leave. I'm sure Mr. and Mrs. *Paying Guest* will get out in time, and their little dog, too. Even you and Ms. Ghostface here could have got out if you hadn't butted in and seen old Dad like this. As for the house, good riddance to the old heap. It's been rebuilt too many times already. Time to put it out of its misery.

"I bet Ian has a lighter in his quarters," he finally said. "He doesn't smoke, but some of his cronies do, and he is a perfect host, after all." Foster retrieved his flashlight and stepped over Ian's prone form to open the door through which he had entered the room earlier. Through it, from her position propped against the book case, Cally could see up the narrow stairs; at the top of them she recognized the small fireplace and wing chairs of Ian's study. Inside her aching head, another piece of her mental puzzle of Vale House clicked into place.

"I'll be right back. Don't go anywhere," Foster said, smirking to Cally, hefting the flashlight in his hand as he took aim again at her head.

He had begun to swing his arm back when the golden goddess statue fell from the top of the curio cabinet, striking him squarely on the top of his head. He fell to his knees, cursing and gripping his bleeding scalp, but he did not fall over. Cally looked up at the bright orange tom cat who stood, with a smug expression on his face, on the top of the cabinet. She made a mental note to be nicer to him in the future, if she had a future.

The cat leapt from the cabinet to the doorway and disappeared into the rooms above. The old woman beside Cally began to struggle as Foster slowly staggered to his feet. Throwing herself down on her side, Cally stretched her legs across the floor and hooked her foot around one of the curved legs of the curio cabinet. "Close your eyes," she said to the old woman as she gave a hard yank with her leg. The cabinet toppled, spraying her and everything in the room with bits of glass and broken porcelain. Shaking her head to clear debris from her hair and face, Cally looked around behind her to see if she had hit her target.

Foster lay under the bulk of the broken cabinet, but he was still swearing loudly. Twisted wood heaved up as he rose to his knees and brushed debris from his bleeding head. "That," he growled at Cally, "was going a bit too far!" He picked through the rubble and seized the brass goddess. "Now be quiet!"

"Wow!" Nell's voice came from the top of the stairwell. They all looked to see her standing in the doorway above, and Cally saw Doctor Boojums rubbing luxuriously against Nell's ankles. "What is this?" Nell asked. "A secret room! What a mess," she added as she descended the stairs slowly, leaning against the wall with one shoulder to balance herself. She was wearing a lumpy, uncomfortable looking garment and as she arrived in the room, Cally realized with horror that it was a straitjacket.

"Oh, hello, dear," said Foster, letting the statue slip from his fingers. "You should be sleeping. We have a long drive ahead of us tonight." He stepped through the rubble and put a hand on the arm of the canvas jacket. "Just let us all finish cleaning up this mess, and then I'll come get you. Wait in the parlor."

"I can't sleep anymore," she explained, craning her head to try to look around him. "Boo told me someone needs help."

"Cats can't talk," said the old woman.

"Cats can do whatever they..." Nell pushed past Foster and lowered herself carefully to her knees before the old woman. "Mama?" she asked.

The white lady smiled. "My little Helen," she said, and began sobbing again.

41 - Stay Down

Foster grabbed Nell by the arm and threw her at the bed, not bothering to watch whether she landed safely or not. "You just stay there!" he shouted at her. Nell pushed herself with her feet to the far side of the bed and cowered, shaking. Foster paced back and forth in what little clear floor space remained, clutching his head. "Okay, this can still work," he muttered. "According to the last will anyone has a copy of – that would be me – Nell is the sole inheritor. I was still married to her at the time this happened so... well, it has to work. It's the best we've got. Nobody will question. They respect me. I'm a successful businessman!" This last he spat, sneering, at Cally as if daring her to think otherwise.

He squatted in front of the old woman. "So I guess you're Sofie. Hello, I'm your son-in-law." She shrank back as he extended a hand she could not shake, even if she had wanted to. "I'm so glad you and your daughter had this chance to have a nice little reunion. And this certainly explains why Ian was always going 'to bed' early. What a sicko! What an entire family of sickos. I'm doing the world a favor, ending this lunatic genetic line. Here, Nellie, come sit with your mother and be quiet." He stood up, kicking through the rubble. "Where did that pretty statue go?"

Nell did not move, except to shrink further back to the far side of the bed. Foster reached for her angrily, and while his back was turned, Cally rolled onto her back. In this position, she was able to put her wrists against the floor and push herself up into a sitting position, and from there she rolled onto her knees. The exertion made her sore head throb wildly, and she was not sure whether she was going to pass out again or merely throw up.

"Oh, no you don't!" Foster returned his attention to her, his face so contorted with rage that he truly did resemble the monster he claimed not to be.

Fear gave Cally a sudden surge of strength, and she clambered to her feet, avoiding his clutching hands as he stepped on a broken Hummel figurine that rolled under his foot. She kicked her way backwards through the debris to the far side of the room, then turned and ran through the door that opened into the cellar.

It was difficult to keep her balance with her hands bound behind her, especially once she was in the dark cellar with no visual frame of reference other than the faint light from the top of the stairs. She knew if she fell now, she would never be able to get up again. Stumbling repeatedly, she headed for the stairs. Her hope was that Foster would follow her; she could think only that if she could keep his attention on her, he would not have time to hurt anyone in the room behind her. Maybe she could lead him away from them altogether, though she had no clear idea what she would do after that. Just as long as he followed, she hoped, she could buy them some time.

She was all too right: Foster did follow her, and he was fast. She heard something behind her in the cavernous cellar crash to the floor as he collided with it in the dark. His voice muttered continually as his footsteps scuffled closer. "No!" he said over and over. "No! You will not ruin this for me! No, God damn it, you bitch, get back here!"

Feeling with one foot in the dark for the bottom stair, Cally skinned her shin on its rough wooden edge. She held her breath, then, leaning carefully sideways, as Nell had done in her straitjacket, until she felt the pipe railing against her elbow. This she pressed hard against, sliding along it as she ascended one step and then another. She struggled to keep her breathing silent, hoping her footsteps on the stair treads would not betray her location to her pursuer.

By the time she reached the top, the sound of Foster's muttering indicated he was near the bottom of the stairs himself. She heard him swear as he, too, barked his shin on the bottom step. She staggered through the door at the top of the stairs and turned, throwing herself against it to shut it. She knew she wouldn't be able to lock it, but at least this would deprive Foster of even the dim light of the back hall. She took a moment to regain her balance, then took a deep breath and ran through the swinging doors into the kitchen.

Running to the middle of the room, Cally realized she was clearly silhouetted against the light from the coach lamps outside the back door; she ducked down into the shadows beside the work table. Then she heard the cellar door slam open against the wall, and Foster's voice shouting a stream of obscenities into the back hall, but he did not come into the kitchen – his footsteps faded away into the east end of the hall. Cally sat down on the floor and worked her bound hands past her hips and feet until they were in front of her at last. Then she was able to use her teeth to work loose the knot in the drapery cord.

She breathed a sigh of relief, trying to rub the feeling back into her wrists, and dared to allow herself a glimmer of hope when the hall outside the kitchen remained silent. Then she panicked, realizing if Foster stopped pursuing her, he would go back to the white lady's room where the others waited helplessly. She pushed one of the swinging doors open a few inches and listened. Foster had stopped muttering and cursing, but she could hear his breath and his footsteps at the far end of the hall near the door to the Captain's room.

Taking a deep breath, she shouted "Monster!" She let the door swing shut as she made a dash for the back door at the other end of the kitchen, and as she ran through to the outside, she made sure to slam the door loudly behind her.

That worked. Foster had heard her, she knew, because as she ran around the corner of the house, she heard the swinging doors in the kitchen bang open, and then heard Foster resume swearing loudly in the kitchen. Leaning out carefully from behind the shrubbery, she peered around the corner of the house and saw him emerge from the back door to stand in the light of the coach lamps, looking around him into the darkness. She ducked back behind the corner of the house and headed down the hill toward the pond.

A light, misting rain had begun to fall and the grass was slippery, so that Cally's feet slipped with each step and she seemed almost to be running in place. It reminded her of dreams she had had as a child, in which she would be running from a pursuer but her legs would simply not move fast enough. "Fine, then," she muttered, and threw herself down feet-first in the wet grass. She slid much faster than she could run, bumping over the slick lawn, down the hill until she fetched up against the trunks of the little birches at the pond's edge.

She knew on some level that she had badly torn the skin of her elbows, but she didn't feel the pain. Flipping over onto her stomach, she looked up toward the house. She could see Foster standing in the circle of lamp light just outside the kitchen door, arms spread wide as he turned one way and another, pushing up his glasses, trying to figure out which way she might have gone. Cally struggled to hold her breath, even though she knew he almost certainly could not hear her panting at that distance.

"Where the hell are you!" His sudden shout made her skin jump and almost succeeded in making her let out a yelp. She pressed a hand over her mouth and kept it there, urging herself to think. If Foster started to go back inside, she knew she would have to shout, after all, to draw him to her again.

Beyond him, beyond the gazebo in the garden, she saw a light go on in the window of Katarina and Ignacio's cottage. Cally entertained a flicker of hope; she had no doubt Ignacio would be as good at subduing murderous maniacs as he was at everything else he did. She looked around her as a curtain of rain blew over her and across the lawn, wondering if there was enough cover of trees and shrubbery for her to be able to run back up the hill to the cottage before Foster could see and stop her. She realized she had made a serious mistake not running to the cottage in the first place. There had been no room in her mind for any thought other than getting Foster away from Ian and the others, and she wished now she could go back in time and do it differently.

Foster turned in the lamp light as if he were considering heading through the little side gate that opened onto Main Street. Then he hesitated, made a rude gesture, and growled a stream of what Cally was sure was profanity as he turned back toward the kitchen door.

Cally realized he meant to go back and resume his original plan of setting fire to the kerosene soaked papers on the bed. She dug her fingers into the wet earth and took a deep breath. With every ounce of air in her lungs she shouted "Help!" She hoped it had been loud enough to attract Ignacio's attention, because it had certainly been loud enough to attract Foster's. He turned toward the sound of her voice, and her only choice now was to flee even further from the house.

As Foster slipped and swore down the hill toward her, Cally ducked her head and crawled through the birches. She did her best to head in the general direction of the rock at the edge of the water. Her memory of it as Nell's safe and comforting hiding place drew her like a beacon. "Please let me through!" she whispered, imploring the branches and roots impeding her.

The sound of Foster's running feet hit the pier, away to her right in the darkness, and Cally realized he must have assumed she'd shouted from the Pirate Ship. She could hear objects falling and breaking inside the old boat, while Foster's voice promised repeatedly that he would find her and that she would not die quickly once he did. She dragged herself the rest of the way through the mud and leaves to the rock by the water's edge and curled up on it, sobbing silently.

The sounds of crashing and swearing inside the boat ceased. Cally swallowed her tears and listened as his footsteps returned along the pier and then fell silent. She strained to see through the branches to determine whether he had headed back up toward the house or had turned onto the path around the pond's edge. The moonlight was only intermittently available, however, and patches of rainfall swept over more and more frequently, the drops becoming bigger and colder.

"You called?" said a voice behind Cally, and she let out a short, sharp scream. But the person standing behind her was not Foster – it was Rum, or Jerome, or whoever he was at the moment. She turned to him in exasperation as she heard Foster's footsteps break into a run along the path toward them. "Someone needed help?" Rum asked.

"I don't think you can help," Cally whispered harshly. "Unless you think you can take *that* on?" She jerked her head toward the dark shape moving along the shore toward them, crouched over and looking for all the world like the silhouette of a stalking bear.

"No, I can't interfere with any mortal's free will," Rum explained with infuriating patience. "But I can go and fetch someone who can. And you, what you need, my dear, is one more minute. Maybe two. That should be enough. I'll see what we can do. You stay down." He turned and began walking away through the birches, not even crouching or putting out a hand to brush them aside. Cally stood to follow him, but he turned sharply, hissing "I said *stay down*!" He extended his hands toward her and made a pressing motion with both palms. "Right where you are."

Unladylike words went through Cally's mind but she did not speak them aloud. After all, if anyone could make it to Ignacio's cottage quickly in the dark and wet, she reasoned, an old earth spirit could. She watched him vanish into the shadows and, struggling to still her breathing, lowered herself down to lie flat on the rock. She didn't know if Ignacio would come out of his cottage before Foster found her but, she hoped, he would at least find Nell and the others in time to help them before Foster returned to the house.

The footsteps on the path grew closer and Cally could see by Foster's silhouette against the pond's shimmering surface that he seemed to be carrying something clutched tightly in his hand – a knife, perhaps, or some other tool he had found on the boat. She closed her eyes as he drew abreast of her on the path. Her terrified mind retreated into the childhood logic that if she could not see him, he could not see her. She trembled so violently, though, she felt that alone must be as good as a beacon in the dark. She groped with one hand for a rock big enough to use as a last-stand weapon.

A heavy presence closed over her and her heart jumped in terror, but the rest of her body grew inexplicably still. Her trembling ceased. Her hand dropped the rock as her breath grew silent. She felt herself enveloped in warmth and she felt for all the world as she had as a child, hiding from monsters under the covers in the dark. Beside her, on the path, she heard Foster run by, muttering "Where are you, witch?"

Cally didn't understand what was happening. She looked up and saw Foster clearly against the water as lightning sheeted overhead and a cold, wet breeze blew across the pond's surface. He turned around and passed by her again on the bank, not five feet away, but he did not see her. She felt utterly warm and safe and invisible. Somewhere across the field, a dog began to bark, and then another.

Foster stopped and straightened up, shaking his head. "There's nothing else for it, then," he said, and turned and began to make his way back up the hill toward the house. He didn't head for the kitchen door this time, but went around the front of the house and up the porch steps. Cally, still unable to move, heard the screen door bang shut. The sound of another dog barking, this one a higher pitch than the others, joined the cacophony as distant thunder rumbled overhead.

The strange, warm calm that had held Cally in stillness began to dissolve, exposing her wet skin to the cold breeze, and she stood up. The sound of barking was drawing close to her. She looked up the hill through the rain and saw something silver streaking down the hill from the house toward her. It was the Delaneys' little dog Twilight.

42 - Riding the Storm Out

Cally was torn between following Foster or running to the back of the house and down to Ian, Nell and Sofie. Her brain was not communicating with her legs in either case; she still felt the heavy sense of stillness around her, but it lifted slowly until she felt it only as if it were a person standing behind her. When she turned, though, she saw only a deeper darkness in the rainy night, lifting up off the rock and drifting over the pond toward the meadow. She only understood it to be real when the little dog dropped something it had been carrying in its mouth and sat up to watch it go.

"Great, Lassie, have you come to save the day or something?" She looked down at the object that lay between the dog's paws, gleaming wetly in the moonlight, and recognized the carved wooden triangle from the butler's desk, the one she had suspected might be George's *zemi*. She picked it up; now it had a couple of extra carvings in it, made by dog teeth. "Shame on you," she said to the dog. It replied with several happy yaps. "Couldn't you have brought a gun or at least a sharp letter opener or something?" Then it occurred to her that if this really was George's *zemi*, he might be nearby, something that would at the very least be incredibly comforting at the moment. She called his name, but there was no reply.

Clutching the carving in one hand, she started up the hill. She would go into the house through the front door, she decided, and find Foster and, she didn't know what, then. Maybe jump him from behind and keep him busy until Ignacio arrived. Or maybe use the desk phone to call 911. She wasn't sure which she should do first, but she'd worry about that when she got there. She knew it was all hopeless anyway because Foster had probably already returned to

Ian's study and lit the kerosene soaked papers on the bed, but she wasn't going to give up yet. Who knew – maybe Rum really could find her an extra minute or two, as he had promised. She had already seen stranger things happen in the past week, in just the past hour. An extra minute or two was all she really needed...

"You stay!" she said to the little dog as she reached the walkway. The dog ran ahead of her and up the porch steps, barking joyfully through the screen door into the Hall to announce her arrival. "Damn!" Cally spat, and ran after it. A dark figure rose suddenly before her. She tried to stop, but skidded on the wet flagstones. She stumbled right into the figure, and then through it as she realized who it was. "Oh, god, I'm sorry!" She tumbled and rolled in the lawn, jumping back to her feet and turning around. "George, I'm so sorry!"

He didn't appear to have noticed. His face was turned toward the meadow, and he was saying "You were supposed to stay down."

"I can't, George. I have to do something. Foster is going to set the house on fire!"

He turned his face to her and his cheeks were luminous with rain or tears – she couldn't be sure which. "Vale House is already burning," he said. "You are going to have to go over the fence, now."

"What? No! I'm not going to just run away!" She turned toward the house. "I have to do something!" She thought she could smell smoke. Was that really smoke, or had George merely put the idea into her head? Her feet reached the porch steps, but like in her nightmares, each step seemed to take forever.

"Please, Cally," George was calling from behind her. "You have to go over the fence. It's the only way, now."

Something shoved her from behind and she fell on the steps, rolling over instinctively and striking out at her attacker with the only weapon she had: the carved wooden triangle in her hand. Then she stopped in confusion. It was the white horse, standing over her; it was shaking its head up and down like a hammer, and its front hooves stood on the bottom step. "We don't have time for this shit," it said in a distinctly feminine voice.

Cally shrank backwards on the step. She thought she must have hit her head, when she fell, and was hallucinating. But George knelt beside her and said quietly "You aren't going to be able to hurt anyone with a *zemi*." His gentle smile brought her back to herself. If she was hallucinating, she reasoned, she had already been doing it for several days now.

The horse was still there. It was snorting and stamping its feet. "Look, are you coming or not?" It turned sideways to Cally, clearly indicating that she was meant to get on its back.

"I don't know how..." she began to protest. The horse released a long string of profanity in its musical voice, while George explained patiently to Cally once again that the only thing that would help would be for her to go over the fence and find help there. "Ian isn't able to help right now, you see..." he said as lightning arched overhead and thunder censored the horse's comments. "... so you have to do it. Nobody else can. This is Mima. You've met her before. She's on our side."

"But..." Cally stood up and looked back toward the house. She could definitely smell smoke now, and a red glow could be seen reflecting from the leaves and branches that were visible above the peak of the roof. No fire engine would be able to make it in time, now, Cally knew. "I hope you know what you're talking about, George," she said. "Maybe there's somebody out there who knows how to make it rain harder." She reached out to hand his *zemi* to him. He smiled until she remembered, and she bent to set it gently on the bottom step. "Don't chew it!" she told the dog, then turned toward the horse, which seemed impossibly tall to her, even though she stood on the third step above it.

"I don't want to hear it," the horse said. "You wouldn't be in this situation if you had stayed down like you were told to."

Cally grasped two fistfuls of the horse's silvery mane. "I have never been very good at staying down when I'm told to," she said, pulling herself over onto its broad back, which was warm and dry despite the rain.

"Well, I hope you're better at staying on," said the horse. It left her no time to say goodbye to George, but swung away down the walk, heading straight for the fence. Cally crouched down over its neck and poured all her concentration into keeping her grip on its mane and her body centered above it as it gathered itself under her and sailed into the air.

She watched the fence pass beneath them, and almost slipped

from the horse's back when it landed hard on the other side, but staying on was easier after that. The horse's gait opened out into a level run through the grass. The rain had stopped all together as soon as they had cleared the fence, and the only sound to be heard was the horse's breathing and the sound of grass parting around its running hooves. Cally dared a glance over her shoulder but could no longer see George, or Vale House, or anything but meadow, stretching for miles around them in every direction, and a little dog, running joyfully in their wake with a *zemi* in its mouth.

With a jolt that almost made Cally lose her grip, the horse lunged into the air again and cleared a broad, dark stream. A hill rose before them and the horse slowed to a lope as it climbed this. Cally could see light beyond the crest, and a drift of music blew past on the breeze. The horse paused at the crest of the hill and Cally peered over to see a massive tree standing at the top of the next hill. Just like the one in the Captain's story, its branches and leaves glowed with golden light, but Cally thought the light danced in a way that reminded her not so much of fire as of masses of writhing, burning snakes. People were moving in the circle of light cast by the tree, and Cally wondered if they were glowing, also, or if their golden clothing was merely reflecting the light of the tree.

"It's best if we do not attract their attention," the horse advised, speaking in a soft voice for a change. It turned its head to gaze southward, and Cally thought she could see a star glowing on its forehead, just above its eyes, which were blue and huge.

"Mima," Cally said. "I do remember you..."

She decided the people beneath the tree were indeed glowing with a light of their own – it resembled moonlight under their red and gold clothing. They walked as if dancing, or sat on log seats around the tree, passing golden cups to one another. Only one of them did not shine with this sliver light, and because of this he stood out from among them like a beacon. Cally watched as one of the luminous beings, a woman of grace and poise so profound it made Cally feel clumsy and inferior even at this distance, offered him a golden cup. He took the cup from her hand, but did not drink from it. Instead he passed the cup to the figure nearest him as all the luminous people began to dance slowly at the base of the tree.

"You probably recognize that one, don't you?" said the horse.

Cally could only nod, trying to swallow past a lump in her throat.

"We are going that way." The horse turned away and began to canter in a counter-clockwise circle around the base of the hill on which the flaming tree stood, leaving the golden dancers behind. The little dog ran ahead of them as if it knew where they were going, letting out an occasional excited, if muffled, yap around the object in its mouth. Cally lost sight of the luminous people, while the tree seemed to grow ever larger and brighter.

It seemed to her they must have gone all the way around the hill, but she did not see the dancers come into view again. Mima stopped and faced the tree. "Okay," she said. "Here is what you have to do." She stamped a forefoot to punctuate each instruction she gave. "Shut up. Stay on. And Shut Up. Do you think you can do that?"

"I don't see how this is helping," Cally said. "I want to go back. People I love are in danger. They're probably already..."

The horse uttered a particularly unpleasant word and ran straight at the glimmering golden tree, barely giving Cally time to squeeze her eyes shut and brace for the impact. The impact did not come. The horse kept running, and the sound of its hoofbeats changed; they were no longer the dull thump of hooves running over grass, but had become a loud, hollow clatter as they galloped over a harder surface. Cally dared to open one eye and looked down to see the glowing trunk of the tree beneath them, flashing past in glimpses of gold between the horse's white legs. They were running steeply upward along a wide road of golden bark, dodging the occasional protruding branch. Cally opened her mouth and the horse said "Shut up."

Mima's neck dipped as they crested a rise in the golden trunk road and emerged into a level place between the enormous branches. Here a green field stretched out before them amid the massive crown of the tree. As the horse slowed to a walk, the horizon fell back until Cally could not see branches at all anymore, but only a wide, dark meadow ringing with the calls of night hawks under the moonlight. The hair on Cally's arms stood up as she recognized where she was. They were fast approaching a bump in the horizon that resolved, as they neared it, into oak and willow trees, and houses beyond a long fence with a single gate in it. The front porch light of Vale House glowed before them, just beyond the fence.

As they neared the fence, they passed under the thick cover of storm clouds and rain fell on them again in heavy, cold sheets. Cally shuddered. She felt the lightning sizzling in the air around them before she saw it, arching directly over their heads to reach Vale House before they did. It struck the porch roof with a deafening explosion. The lights of the house went out, and wet bits of splintered wood blew back to strike Cally's face and arms. She cried out and begged the horse to stop and let her get down.

"The lightning is only metaphorical, you know," Mima said, but stopped just before the metal gate at the end of Main Street. Cally threw her leg over the horse's back and hung from its mane until her feet nearly touched the ground, then let go and ran to the gate. The little dog ran ahead of her, jumping through the bars of the gate. The lights of all the houses on the street were out, and every dog in the neighborhood was barking.

"What are we doing back here?" Cally muttered, more to the world in general than to the horse or anyone else. "We haven't done anything except waste time." She ducked to squeeze her way between the rails.

"You aren't going to be able to get past..." the horse began, but thunder drowned out the rest as Cally straightened up and ran into the darkened street. She was brought to a sharp halt by the presence of a tall, hooded figure standing between her and Vale House. It loomed larger – or did she shrink before it? – as it turned to her and raised what appeared to be a dark, shuttered lantern in its hand.

The little dog Twilight ran to its feet and put the zemi down on the wet ground before it, yapping excitedly and adding to the cacophony of the other neighborhood dogs in the night. Cally moved to step around the figure and run to the porch, but her legs absolutely would not move. She became furious at her body for not obeying her, and for trembling so hard, but she was even more furious at the figure in front of her. "Let me by!" she shouted at it.

"You have to offer a gift," said the horse behind her.

Cally knew she didn't have anything in her pockets, and Rum had already made it clear body parts were a bad idea. She was frankly fed up with the entire concept. She raised her fists and let out a cry of sheer frustration; she would have struck the figure it if she could have moved, even if it would be the last thing she ever did.

The figure bent its hooded head over the *zemi* lying on the ground where Twilight had dropped it, and Cally shouted "No! That isn't mine to give." To her horror, the figure bent to pick it up anyway. "I said no!" It didn't appear to have heard her, and Cally watched the *zemi* disappear into its dark robes as it turned away, heading slowly down Main Street. The wind stopped, and the rain grew softer, soft enough that the figure was able to open the lamp it held. Two soft circles of light bobbed along the wet sidewalk beside it as it headed toward town.

"Look," Cally called after it, and found her legs had regained their mobility. She ran after the figure. "My car is right there, in the parking lot. See? The red one. You can have anything in it. Hell, you can have the whole car. Only don't take George's *zemi*. It belongs to him!"

The figure continued to walk down the street, and Cally followed. With the rain fading away, and in the light of the lamp it carried, it didn't look so intimidating anymore. Its robes were a soft bluish gray, and it might even have seemed beautiful if Cally had not been so upset. It paused beside the little white gate at the end of the Vale House grounds. Holding the lamp over its head, it took a key from its belt and unlocked the gate, which puzzled Cally because she had never noticed that the gate even had a lock. As the gate swung open, the figure vanished.

43 - Two and a Half Minutes

She rushed through into the back garden, steeling herself for the sight of the damage she would see and praying she would not find herself searching for bodies amid charred rubble. To her consternation, though, nothing appeared to have been damaged. She could not smell smoke or charred wood, but only the fragrance of rain-washed grass under moonlight. The house was completely dark, but it was clear it had not burned. "Thank god," she whispered, wondering just which god she might be thanking.

She ran to the kitchen door and peered through the little window. She couldn't see anything but long patches of moonlight on the floor inside, but she did catch a whiff of kerosene. Apparently, the papers in the room below had not yet been ignited, so maybe she wasn't too late, after all. She tried the door, but found it locked, and wished the mysterious figure with keys on its belt had stayed a few moments longer.

As she looked around for something with which to smash the window, she saw movement inside the kitchen. A figure ran into the center of the room and stopped beside the work table, looking around before crouching down quickly into the darkness. Cally tried to peer into the moonlit dimness, but the figure's face was turned away from her. She could not make out who it was, and she had a sudden sick, dizzy feeling she did not want to know who it was. Beyond the kitchen, she heard the cellar door bang open and saw Foster's face appear in the windows of the swinging doors. She watched it withdraw, and heard his muffled voice shouting "Where the hell are you?" The person beside the work table rose to their feet, putting its wrists to its mouth. Cally instinctively averted her eyes, then, and crouched backward into the shrubbery next to the kitchen door, because now she understood who it was, standing there in the dark kitchen, and she knew what was going to happen next.

She squeezed her eyes shut as someone burst out from the kitchen door, slamming it loudly as they went, and she heard them turn the corner of the house to run down the hill to the pond. She shrank further back into the shrubbery when Foster emerged from the kitchen shortly after. She watched him stand peering into the darkness, turning his head from side to side and muttering profanity. When he made up his mind and turned back toward the house, Cally wrapped her arms around herself to keep from sobbing out loud. She knew she would soon hear herself scream for help from the direction of the pond, and then Foster would run away from there, down the hill himself. The shout came, and Foster headed off into the darkness muttering "When I get my hands on your skinny little neck…"

Then she tried to stand up, but she could only crouch there against the wall behind the rhododendrons, sobbing softly until a pair of bare brown feet entered her field of vision. She followed denim-clad legs up to a gnarled black face with eyes glittering above a white cloud of beard. "Come now," said Rum. "It's not that bad. You're doing fine. Even though you don't follow instructions very well." He reached down and put a knobby hand on her arm, gently urging her to stand.

Cally rose to her feet, and Rum reached up and brushed mulch off her clothes with his long, brown fingers. "You've got your two extra minutes, now. Use them wisely, while I go and get the cavalry, 'kay?" She could only nod down at him, but she did stop crying. "Come on," he said, "You've got this!" Then he shambled off toward Katarina and Ignacio's cottage. The light was not on, this time, in their cottage window; the electricity being out was the only thing that was different this time. That and the other thing Cally did not want to think about.

"I so do not have this," she said to Rum's retreating form, but she stepped out from behind the shrubbery and went into the kitchen anyway, making sure to leave the door open behind her. "That should save Ignacio an extra half minute or so, too," she thought, daring to hope maybe she was clever enough, after all, to know what to do now.

The back hall was pitch dark, but this time Cally knew the way.

She felt along the wall until she found the open cellar doorway, and groped for the thin railing on the right. She knew Foster would still be rummaging around in the Pirate Ship, at this point, so she did not hurry as she felt her way carefully to the bottom in the dark. By the time she reached the bottom, her eyes had adjusted to the darkness enough that she could see a thin line of light coming from under the door to Sofie's room.

The room reeked of kerosene when Cally pushed open the door, where someone inside was holding a flashlight. The light flickered weakly as someone sobbed softly. Cally called out, "It's okay, Nell, it's me. I'm coming!"

44 - Our Nell

When she entered the room, she could see Nell sitting on the edge of the bed. She held Foster's huge flashlight between her knees, and Cally could not imagine how it had come to be switched on. Nell grinned broadly in the wobbly light. "I knew you'd be back," she said. It had not been she who had been sobbing, but Sofie, who had made her way to Ian's side again and was crouched next to him. "Everything is going to be okay now," Nell told the old woman matter-of-factly.

"We're not out of the woods yet," Cally said. "But, Helen, that jacket does not become you." She sat down on the bed beside her and began undoing the buckles.

"Foster is coming back," Nell said, shrugging her way out of the sleeves and rubbing her elbows.

"Yes," Cally agreed. "I still haven't figured out what the plan is when he gets back." She honestly wasn't even sure she would still be present when he did. She found herself struggling with the strangest feeling she wasn't actually there at all, herself, or if she was, she was just some two-dimensional projection of herself while her real self crouched on a rock next to the pond. Would she simply vanish when that self got up and started walking around? "It doesn't matter," she said, shaking her head. She crouched down next to Ian's still form. "How is he?" she asked the old woman. "Sofie? I'm here to help. I need you to calm down please."

"She's right, Mama," said Nell. Cally knelt beside the old woman and unbound her hands, then helped her to her feet. Nell put her arm around Sofie and made her sit down on the bed next to her, while Cally turned her attention to Ian . He still had a pulse, she noted, though it was shallow and rapid, but his skin was warm. She held the flashlight above him and pushed back one of his eyelids, smiling with relief to see his pupil contract in the light. Then she looked around the room, trying to think how she and Nell together could carry him from the room. It would be difficult, under the best of circumstances, to get him up either stairway. The easiest course would be to take the shorter flight of stairs up to Ian's quarters, she thought at first. Maybe they could get him out of the house by way of the side door into the shade garden. The problem, she remembered, was that Foster would come back into the house through the front door. He would probably be returning to this room through Ian's quarters. There was a much higher chance of encountering him that way, so maybe it would be better to try and get Ian out through the cellar.

A crashing sound from above let them know Foster had already entered the house. "Okay, then, let's go to Plan C," said Cally. She stood and grabbed the large flashlight. "I'll distract him," she said. "Nell, you take your mother and get out through the cellar, okay?"

"She won't leave Dad," Nell stated with certainty. "You should be the one to go."

"Fine, then, you just get out, yourself. Ignacio is coming, I think. You go and help him find us, okay?"

"Cally, I don't think..." was all Nell could say before a door crashed open above them. The sounds of banging and slamming accompanied Foster's swearing as he bumped into something in Ian's quarters above, and then more crashing as he went through the various drawers in the room. He apparently found a flashlight in one of them, as Cally could see a beam of light begin to flicker wildly as his footsteps thundered along the floor above them.

Cally moved to the side of the door and held the flashlight above her head. She jerked her head toward the other door to try to urge Nell to run for the cellar, but Nell had already crouched down in the shadows at the foot of the bed. Cally sighed and switched off the flashlight.

With an angry shout, Foster shoved the door and the broken furniture in front of it back far enough to let himself squeeze through into the room, and then he tripped over Ian's leg, just missing Cally's attempted strike at his head with her flashlight. Cursing and kicking fallen books aside, he stood and waved his own flashlight wildly around himself. He was panting heavily and trembling. He stopped when he saw Cally, clearly confused. "How the hell did you get back in here already?" He turned the flashlight beam on Nell, who stood up beside the bed and gazed sadly at him. "And you? Why can't you ever do as you're told?" He swung a fist at her and she shrank down into the shadows again. "Oh, it doesn't even matter anymore. Just stay there, I don't care!"

Cally took a step toward him, holding the flashlight out at her side as if it were a sword. "Foster, just turn around and leave this room," she said. "It's not too late. You are about to make a horrible mistake. Come on, this is nuts!"

"No, it is too late," he said, more to himself than to her. The flashlight beam wavered in his shaking hands. "I have got to salvage this situation, and fire is the only thing that can save me now." He switched his flashlight to his other hand and fumbled in his pocket until he withdrew the yellow plastic lighter Ian had used to open beer bottles on his boat. Backing toward the bed, he began flicking the wheel of the little lighter, producing only dim, red sparks. Cally knew she wouldn't get another chance. She leaped across the debris on the floor and brought her flashlight down on Fosters arm as hard as she could. She felt the flashlight break in her hands as the lighter fell from Foster's grip. His glasses fell off as he swore loudly and threw his own flashlight at her.

Foster's flashlight went out when it hit the wall behind Cally, plunging the room into total darkness. Cally heard him scrabbling under the bed for the lighter. She lunged for him and locked both hands in his hair. He twisted in her grip, closing his hands around her throat, but she didn't care – she still had the strangest feeling she was about to disappear anyway at any moment. She hung on and thought, because she couldn't speak, "OK, Nell, now would be a good time for you to get out of here."

She didn't disappear, but the room definitely seemed to be growing silent around her as the strength left her hands. Foster broke free of her grip and she heard him resume his search under the bed, then she saw him stand up in the light of a tiny yellow flame. He reached out and held it under the edge of the kerosene soaked papers on the bed.

They ignited instantly. Sheets of yellow flame filled the room suddenly with bright, white light as they swept softly across the wall to the drapes. Foster was panting heavily as he stood over Cally, looking around the debris on the floor. "Now," he said, "Where did that nice, heavy brass statue go?"

"It's right here," Nell said cheerfully as she stood up behind him and brought it down on his head. He went down, and this time he stayed down.

Cally sat on the third step of the grand staircase, rubbing at the bruises on her throat. Nell was gliding like a nymph through the hubbub of all the people gathered in the Hall, talking to the sheriff's deputies and encouraging Sofie to sit in the desk chair and drink a cup of tea. The paramedics were trying to persuade Ian to let them put him on a stretcher, but he insisted he would be fine and did not need to go to the hospital. Nell poked him in the chest and said "You just do what the doctors tell you to do!"

"I have to be here to take care of your mother," he told her gently.

"I'll take care of her now."

Sofie wanted to go back to her room, but the smoke and water damage there would take a long time to repair. Nell put a crocheted throw from the parlor around the old woman's shoulders and shooed away anyone who attempted to question her. "She's scared and upset," she told them sternly. "Just let her be!"

"Who even *is* that young woman?" Cally asked. "I don't think I recognize her!"

Bethany, seated next to her, rubbed at her hands which had had to be bandaged after she'd injured them pounding on the inside of her locked bathroom door. "That's our little Nell," she said to Cally.

"No." Cally shook her head. "I believe that is Miss Helen May."

On Cally's other side, George sat two steps up and continued to apologize to Cally for not having been able to do anything to help, promising her he was going to learn how to range farther from his *zemi*, or at least how to unlock bathroom doors. Or maybe how to use a phone to call 911. He was certain if he only had access to his own cell phone, he could pick this up quickly. "Or maybe if I had a computer with a connection to the internet," he said. "Could you get me one?" Cally shuddered at this idea, though she wasn't sure why. She knew a long conversation with him was coming later.

A paramedic came and shone a small flashlight into Cally's eyes, telling her to look into the beam as he switched from one eye to the other several times until he was satisfied. He told her she was going to be fine, but suggested she might ask the doctor for a prescription for pain medication.

"No!"

Cally, Bethany, and Joan all shouted at once. The paramedic backed away slowly and went to find out who else needed attention.

"I think we've all had about enough of *that* stuff!" Joan exclaimed, wobbling unsteadily on her crutches as she tried to lean against the stair railing.

"I don't think I will ever want a bath again, either!" Bethany joined in.

"And I will never be able to stomach tea again," said Joan. She wrinkled her face and made hacking noises, still trying to get the taste out of her mouth. "He put six of those things in my tea. Six!" She wrinkled her nose in disgust. "No wonder just tasting it knocked me out." She gave up with the crutches and sat down on the stairs next to Bethany. "And here he was going around trying to make me out to be the addict, when he's the one who's been horfing all the drugs he could lay his hands on for years."

Cally hated to admit Joan was right for once, but two sheriff's deputies were busily going through one of Foster's suitcases on the desk, bagging and tagging a growing pile of pharmaceuticals they were finding tucked within the folds. The stash contained, so far, the remnants of every expired sedative, antidepressant, and mood stabilizer that had ever been prescribed to Nell over the course of her illness, as well as unmarked bottles concealing pain medication he'd lifted from many friends and acquaintances, and plastic bags full of pills whose sources had yet to be identified. Doc was shaking his head, saying, "I should have seen it all along. The symptoms were right there in front of my face but I just didn't question..."

Nell had made her way across the Hall to see if the three women on the stairs needed anything, and she took the opportunity to explain patiently to Joan, "People don't become addicted to medicine on purpose."

"But once they do," Bethany pointed out, "they will stoop to any level to cover it up. Including finding ways to blame others for their own behavior."

"And to get more money to support their problem," Cally noted.

"I just wish I had hit him with that mug!" Joan spat.

Nell smiled generously at her. "Then you would have been the hero!"

"Instead, you are the hero," Cally told her.

Nell shook her head. "Ignacio's the hero!" she corrected. "He's the one who came running with the fire extinguisher."

"Who knew he was an expert firefighter, on top of everything else?" said Bethany.

"He would have been too late for some of us, though," said Cally, "if it hadn't been for your quick thinking. Helen, I apologize for having underestimated you. You are one tough woman."

Nell shook her head until all her curls fell into her face, and then shook them out again. "Well a girl's got to leave the nest sometime," she said with a sly look in her eye. She sat down on the stair next to Cally, being careful not to sit on George's feet. "I always knew he didn't really love me," she said in softer tones. "But everyone said I should be thankful he was taking such good care of me."

"Oh, he took care of you, alright!" Joan shook her head and pulled herself up on the railing, slinging her crutches under her arms again. Ian had successfully talked the paramedics out of making him lie on the stretcher, but they held onto his arms, one on either side of him, as they led him toward the front door. Joan did not stop to speak to him as she went back into her office.

Nell nodded. "That's what it was all about, after all," she said. "Dad just wanted someone to be here to take care of me and of Mama after he was gone. He figured out Foster wasn't going to do that. Foster was going to have us both put away so he could build a city here. That's why Dad was trying to change his will. Well, I'll take care of everything now."

Cally stood to join the crowd that was following Ian out the door. Fire engines, police cruisers, and ambulances filled the front yard of Vale House, lighting up the night once again with their red and blue flashing lights. Sheriff Mahon was standing beside the squad car where Foster sat slumped in the back seat with a bandaged head.

Ian paused as he was being led to a waiting ambulance. He managed a wry grin as he nodded toward the sheriff's clipboard thick with case files. "I see you've incurred a considerable amount of paperwork, there, Dunn," he said.

"I hope you're feeling well in the morning," the sheriff replied without smiling back. "I won't hassle you tonight about it, Ian, but we will need to talk soon about this whole harboring of a fugitive thing."

"She's not a fugitive," Ian insisted. "Please don't make her go back into a hospital. It would kill her."

"They don't do things that way anymore," the sheriff assured him. "Frankly, Ian, I'm just a little bit ticked off that you've never told me. And by 'a little bit ticked off' I mean, it feels like a goddamned slap in the face."

"I am sorry. I am." Ian sighed and looked up at the sky, from which a fine mist of rain sifted down. "We just figured, the fewer the people who knew, the safer it would be."

"Yes, and I was the newcomer, after all." The sheriff shook Ian's hand. "Well, maybe things are changing. One thing is certain: the emergency crews sure do know how to find Woodley now."

Ian was able, with assistance, to climb into the ambulance himself as rain began to fall in earnest. Away to the south, Cally heard thunder rolling, but it sounded halfhearted, as if there was no point in putting on a good show if Ian May wasn't going to be there to watch it. Katarina did not even bother to count.

Everyone stood on the porch and watched all the emergency vehicles file out the gate. As Cally started to turn to go back into the house, she heard a voice beside her saying "It's been a long night." It was Ben. Her heart fluttered in her chest when he put an arm around her and drew her to his side.

"I thought you weren't going to be back until morning," she said.

"It is morning." He nodded toward the sky over the meadow. It was shining silver through the rain. A flash of lightning parted the rain curtain for a moment, revealing a shadowy figure standing at the crossroads. Cally nudged Ben. "Do you see that?"

He didn't answer, because he had turned his head to where Katarina was saying, "Oh, the poor Captain! He's slept through all the excitement. Let's get him inside before he catches pneumonia!"

The Captain was slouched in his favorite wicker chair, smiling dreamily, with his flask about to fall from his hand. Ignacio bent over and touched his shoulder, shaking him gently. Then he looked up and regarded everyone thoughtfully in the growing light. "He isn't asleep," he said.

45 - Somebody's Calling

They buried Corporal Douglas "Captain" Arkwright in the May family cemetery, just a few steps away from Sofie's empty grave. All of Woodley turned out to see him off, and quite a lot of people managed to find their way from all over the country, as well. After the formalities, in true Scottish tradition, Ian May invited everyone into the house for a drink. Fortunately, many people also brought food, so Katarina and Bethany were only run ragged trying to find plates and glasses and little tables on which to set everything. Cally did her best to find lodgings within Vale House for the out-of-town mourners, but some people who knew each other very well had to double up. This even though Bethany felt well enough by then to vacate the Daffodil room and resume commuting from her cottage on Bells Road. There was No Vacancy at Vale House that day. Even the Preacher's ghost put in a brief appearance in the Hall, but all the coming and going through the house seemed to discourage him, and he faded away after a short time.

"Well, that is how I want to go."

It was the most common topic of conversation in the parlor. This time it was being raised by Ian May, seated next to the fireplace with a glass of brandy in his hand. "Quietly, in my sleep, in my favorite chair with a drink in my hand."

"By the looks of it, Ian," someone said, "I'd say there's a very good chance that is exactly how you'll go!" Everyone laughed and Ian raised his glass and proposed yet another toast to the Captain.

Joan hobbled quietly up beside Cally and cleared her throat. A taxi driver stood behind her, laden with bags and luggage. "Well," she said, "I just wanted to say thank you and slip off quietly now." She raised her chin and made her way over to Ian with as much dignity as she could muster on crutches, and he stood at her approach. "It's been a pleasure working for you," she told him. Balancing on one crutch, she put out a hand, but he did not shake it.

"You really don't have to go," he said.

"No, I think it's better this way." She glanced to where the taxi driver waited, struggling with bags that kept slipping from under his arms. "I never was any good at this Country Living thing anyway. I'll be much better off back in Charlotte."

"Well, then." Ian kissed her on the cheek. "Thank you for everything you have done for us. Drop a line, now and then."

She did not promise to do so, but turned and followed the driver out of Vale House. Cally felt genuinely bad for her.

"She held out hope for so long." It was Nell who said this quietly at Cally's side. "Well at least she'll have a pleasant surprise one day when she finds out how much money Dad is leaving to her!"

Cally asked, "How is your mom doing now?"

"She's staying in her room. I mean, you know, Dad's room. It's their room, now. She's enjoying tidying everything up and making the bed and lining up the pens on the desk. It makes her feel calmer. All these people make her nervous."

All these people didn't seem to make Nell nervous. Cally marveled at the change in her. She wondered if it was due to the absence of Foster in her life, or just due to him not meddling with her medication anymore.

"Cally, you should come work for us!" Apparently this new Nell had adopted the entire bed-and-breakfast business as her concern. "You know, now that Joan is gone."

"No, I think Kat and Bethany can more than handle everything around here. Once things calm down after today, anyway. You know your dad never really needed Joan's help. He was just being nice to her."

The atmosphere in the parlor was growing more and more jovial as more toasts were conducted, and scandalized expressions were appearing on the faces of everyone present who was not of Celtic descent. Cally looked around and smiled. "The Captain would have loved this. I wish he could be here to see it." Then it occurred to her to wonder if maybe he might actually be there, at that. She would have to ask George about this later.

Ian had returned to his seat by the fire, and he beckoned with his glass for Cally to come and join him. As she sat in the chair opposite him, he picked up a glass of wine from a nearby side table and pressed it into her hand. "Nell is right, you now," he said. "You should come and work for us. Will you consider it?"

His expression was so earnest, fresh tears started to spring into Cally's eyes. She shook her head. "But you don't really need me," she said. "And I don't need charity." *Not yet, anyway,* she added silently to herself.

"It's not charity," he said. "We really do need you. Now, I know you do not want to be fated to be a receptionist for the rest of your life. I am talking about the other skills you have. Ones I don't have, and that someone around here really should have."

Cally tried to take a nonchalant sip from her wine glass and ended up gulping it a little too quickly. "Which skills are those?" she asked, not looking at him.

He grinned at her until she met his eyes. "You know exactly what I mean," he said. "You can see them. All of them. And you can talk to them. I can't. I know about them, and I am charged with protecting them. But it's only because I inherited this house. I am usually at sea when it comes to knowing exactly how to discharge my responsibilities. Nell is a little help. She can tell me what's going on, sometimes. I realize she is doing very well lately, but she... well, she lives in her own little world. She doesn't really understand what's at stake here."

"I don't understand what's at stake here, either," Cally pointed out.

"This is a very special place," Ian said.

"So I've been told." Cally glanced up to where Ben Dawes stood behind his sister's chair, sharing stories about the Captain's life with Luke and Sheriff Mahon.

"And I'm not going to live forever," Ian said, drawing her attention back to him.

"Ian, is everything okay?" She reached over and took his hands.

"Everything is fine." He laughed and placed her hands together palm to palm between his own. "But I need to retire soon, and when I do, Nell will become the Armadeur. You can be... her assistant. How does that sound? We'll think of a good title for you."

Cally didn't know what an Armadeur was, but the prospect of a steady income was tempting. She took a deep breath and said, "I don't know what to say, Ian. I gave up writing for a 'real job' once before, and I lived to regret it."

"You don't have to give up writing," he said, releasing her hands and patting her knee. "And you don't have to decide right away. Just please tell me you will think about it."

"I promise I will think about it."

Bethany approached them, her arms laden with dirty plates. "More guests arriving in the Hall!" she said, out of breath. "I don't recognize them from the funeral. Their car has out-of-state plates."

Cally stood. "I'll handle it, Bethany." She ran to the Hall, hoping whoever it was didn't need overnight accommodations. "We need a No Vacancy sign!" she said, a little too loudly as she ran behind the desk. She remained standing, because George was sitting in the chair.

"Oh, Mom, we didn't come to stay overnight." It was her daughter, waiting in front of the desk. "We just came to check on you and make sure you're alright."

"Kelleigh!" Cally ran around the desk and hugged her daughter, then her son in law, and then her daughter again. "As you can see, I'm fine." She was thankful Kelleigh hadn't shown up three days ago.

"Well you never answer your phone. Or your email."

Cally did not argue, but quietly smiled at the younger, prettier, much more sensible version of herself. "It's just a little crazy around here right now," she explained.

"So I see." Kelleigh turned her head at a sudden cheer going up in the parlor. Someone had toasted the Captain again. "Not at all what I pictured when you described this Quiet Country Life."

"She's cute!" It was George. "Is she the one who put Jonathan Coulton on your MP3 player?" Cally ignored him.

Gordon shifted uncomfortably. "Well, also, we um... we thought maybe if you want to come back with us, we could caravan, and stop at Cracker Barrel on the way. You always enjoy Cracker Barrel.

"And our regional manager has an opening for a production editor," he continued as Kelleigh nudged him in the ribs. "We showed her your rant... your essay, about Linguistic Drift, and she says she thinks you'd be perfect for the job."

Cally smiled and shook her head. "Thank you for the vote of confidence, but I don't feel quite ready to... It's just that I don't want to..." She had tried many times to explain all this to them. She didn't have the heart to try again. There was also the fact that she wouldn't have been able to leave with them that day anyway, even if she had wanted to. Her car keys had gone missing the night Foster had been arrested, and nobody had been able to find them since; she had a strong feeling this was directly connected to the fact that George's zemi had mysteriously reappeared in its proper place in the butler's desk.

As she groped for words, Brigit and Ben Dawes emerged from the parlor. "I'm just going to give Bree a ride home," Ben called across the Hall to her. "I promise I'll be back in a little while."

"I know you will," said Cally, smiling as he turned away.

"Ohhhh..." Kelleigh turned and looked at Ben as he helped his sister out the door. "I get it . Now I see why you don't want to leave this place!" She winked at her mother, and Gordon nodded, grinning.

"No! That's not it!" Cally blustered. "He's not... He's just..."

But Kelleigh was having none of it. "Seriously, I could literally see little hearts floating around your heads when you looked at each other."

"Figuratively," Cally corrected.

"My mama didn't raise no fool," Kelleigh countered.

Cally took a deep breath. "No. Honestly. It's just that I have already accepted a position, here at Vale House." She couldn't believe the words coming out of her mouth, but as she said them, she knew them to be true.

She heard a whoop behind her and turned to see Katarina applauding. George was jumping around the Hall, high-fiving someone Cally couldn't see. "You can take over Joan's old office!" Bethany said excitedly. "I can decorate it in a dogwood theme!"

"Oh, thank you, Bethany but I don't think..." Bethany had run up to hug her, even though doing so made her wince. "You know what?" Cally said. "Dogwood would be lovely."

☽

Much later that evening, Cally sat at the desk in the Rose Room and typed "Sometimes, at the end of the story, the character you started with is not the same one you end with." She paused, pondering different ways to make the sentence flow more smoothly by switching the phrasing around. Doctor Boojums lounged on the desk, directly atop a sheaf of notes she was trying to use. Cyndi Lauper sat a few inches away from him, slowly pushing paper clips off the desk one by one. Cally started a blank file and typed, "It's funny how ghost cats are essentially exactly the same as living cats. What's even funnier is how living cats are essentially exactly the same as ghost cats." She liked it, but she had no idea yet what she wanted to do with it, so she saved it under "cats.txt."

A knock came at her door, so soft she barely heard it. She called for whoever it was to come in, but they only knocked again. Standing with a sigh, she wove her way around all the boxes Ignacio had helped her move from her car to the Rose Room (Ignacio was, of course, also an expert at getting into locked cars) and opened the door.

"Georgie!" she exclaimed in sincere surprise.

"I'm sorry. I didn't mean to alarm you."

"No, it's just that... You knocked!"

"I did." He smiled with false modesty, very pleased she had noticed.

"I thought you couldn't touch things?"

"I've been practicing." He made a knocking motion where the door would have been, had it been shut. Again, Cally heard the soft knocking sound. It was a little unnerving to hear it coming from empty air, and she said "You should keep practicing."

He thrust his hands deep into the pockets of tattered gray trousers. His shirt was, if possible, even more threadbare than the trousers. "Who are you supposed to be dressed as now?" Cally asked him.

"I am dressed as myself," he said. "I came to tell you my story. I want you to make it into an e-book, so I can read it. If you have time," he added thoughtfully.

"Georgie." She smiled. "I have nothing but time." Standing back from the door, she said, "Come on in."

"Are you sure?"

"Only when I invite you," she clarified. "And I am inviting you now."

She shut the door behind him and he sat on the bed as she went to the desk to get her notepad. "I was born in a place far, far from here," he began, "in a land we called The Mother of All Lands, but after I left there I heard it was called Hispaniola by others, out in the world." Cally scribbled quickly to keep up with him. "I was named after an ancestor of mine, a famous prophet, a great prophet, some said, whose name was Guacanagarix. But after I left there, my boss could not pronounce my name, so he just called me George. And George I have been ever since."

Cally held up her pen. "Wait a second," she said. "Can you spell that for me, please? Gwaka... what was it?"

He grinned patiently. "Cally, I wanted to tell you one other thing, too."

"And what is that, George?"

"Welcome home," he said.

Questions

Brisk autumn breezes out of the north rattled the yellowing oaks and made the horses kick up their heels in the meadow. Cally had taken her laptop out onto the porch, because her office was being "renovated." Ian May had given Bethany carte blanche again.

Emerald<< There are still some things I don't understand.

Cally>> Good, that's what I wanted you to tell me.

Emerald<< For instance, you still never said what all the other things are that "aren't all ghosts"

Cally>> I can't very well answer that until I figure it out, myself, can I?

Emerald<< Your readers are not going to be satisfied with that answer. You will have to write more to explain it all.

Cally>> I promise to, as soon as I know what to say.

Emerald<< I mean, I don't even know what I am, at this point, and I am me!

Cally>> That isn't why I asked you to read my rough draft. I was looking for continuity issues, grammatical errors and awkward phrasing.

> **Emerald<<** Well it's awkward not knowing what's going to happen with you and Ben.

> **Cally>>** Not for me, it isn't. I kind of like it. And so does he. So you and everyone else can just stop playing matchmaker. :)

Nell was sitting in the wicker chair on Cally's right, with her own printed copy of the rough draft in her lap. She peered over Cally's shoulder, watching this exchange. "I agree," she said, nodding at the monitor. "There are more questions, at the end, than we started out with. For instance, I want to know what's going to happen to my character!"

Cally smiled at her. "I'm afraid you're just going to have to find that out for yourself, Helen."

> **Emerald<<** And we still never found out what George is doing here, so far from any Pirate Ships. Real ones, I mean.

> **Cally>>** That's a whole different story.

> **Emerald<<** Then you have to write it!

> **Cally>>** Can we just stick with one book at a time, please?

> **Emerald<<** It's not like we have all the time in the world, you know. Time is running out.

> **Cally>>** Until what?

> **Emerald<<** Until, you know, when everything we've been preparing for happens... when all the things Woodley is protecting have to face their fate.

> **Cally>>** You lecture me about not answering all the questions, yet you're the one being vague.

> **Emerald<<** I'm telling you all I know. Your job is to figure out how to fit all the pieces together. Isn't that what authors do?

Cally>> No pressure, right?

Emerald<< No, no pressure. :)

"No pressure," Nell added.
In the wicker chair at Cally's left, the Captain's ghost snored on.

Playlist

George has selected the following songs from Cally's MP3 player and suggests that, played on shuffle, they would create a suitable ambience to this story, if you happen to have access to a music device such as Cally's and if you like – as humans often do – to read with earbuds in.

A Talk With George - Jonathan Coulton
Already Gone - Eagles
An American Girl - Tom Petty and the Heartbreakers
And She Was - Talking Heads
Are Ye Sleeping, Maggie? - Alasdair Fraser
Blackbird - The Beatles
Dream On - Aerosmith
Fisherman's Blues - The Waterboys
Fly By Night - Rush
Green Grass and High Tides - The Outlaws
Heel Turn 2 - The Mountain Goats
Here I Go Again - Whitesnake
Homeless - Ladysmith Black Mambazo
Hungry Heart - Bruce Springsteen
Landslide - Stevie Nicks
Lawyers, Guns and Money - Warren Zevon
Livin' on a Prayer - Bon Jovi
Locomotive Breath - Jethro Tull
Love Walks In - Van Halen
Not Dead Yet - Styx
Old Man - Neil Young
One Headlight - The Wallflowers
Paperback Writer - The Beatles
Peaceful Easy Feeling - Eagles
Ramble On - Aerosmith
Ridin' The Storm Out - REO Speedwagon
Seven Bridges Road - Eagles
Seven Turns - The Allman Brothers Band
Should I Stay or Should I Go - The Clash
Spirit of Radio - Rush

Strathgarry - Simon Wynberg
The Long and Winding Road - The Beatles
The Weight - The Band
Tonight Tonight - The Smashing Pumpkins
Uncle John's Band - The Grateful Dead

O Mistress mine, where are you roaming?
O stay and hear! your true-love's coming
That can sing both high and low;
Trip no further, pretty sweeting,
Journeys end in lovers' meeting —
Every wise man's son doth know.
                    --William Shakespeare

ABOUT THE AUTHOR

Kim Beall lives and writes in a small NC town that may or may not remind you of Woodley, USA. She has never yet met a ghost in person, though her cats do frequently manage to walk through closed doors. When not writing she gardens, hunts mushrooms, and raises chickens.

She sincerely believes every adult still yearns, not so deep inside, to find real magic in everyday life.

Other Books by Kim Beall

Moonlight and Moss – May 2019
Ghost of a Chance – May 2020
A Midnight Clear – November 2020

www.kimbeall.com
www.kimbeall.com/blog
amazon.com/author/kimbeall
goodreads.com/author/show/18012965.Kim_Beall
facebook.com/kimbeallauthor
@KimBeallsGhost